THE VENUS
DEAL

THE VENUS DEAL

♩ ♩ ♩

KEN KUHLKEN

For Iris, a person
as delightful as her
name. Ken Kuhlken
5-8-98

ST. MARTIN'S PRESS   NEW YORK

Production Editor: David Stanford Burr

Library of Congress Cataloging-in-Publication Data

Kuhlken, Ken.
    The Venus deal / Ken Kuhlken.
        p. cm.
    "A Thomas Dunne book."
    ISBN 0-312-08918-X
    I. Title.
PS3561.U36V45   1993
813'.54—dc20   92-40374
                                                        CIP

First Edition: April 1993

10 9 8 7 6 5 4 3 2 1

For my half sister, Marilou, wherever you are,
in memory of our father, Tom Hickey's best pal

Many thanks to Larry Clinger; Sylvia Curtis; Evangeline
Garfield; Jojo Field; Corinne Hunt; Woody and Bob Halley;
Dennis Lynds and Gayle Stone, whom I failed to thank in
The Loud Adios; Ivy Rivard; Denver police technician Mike
Shonk; and Vera and Ralph Steinhoff, not only for facts and
ideas but for the love you've given my kids and me.

THE VENUS
DEAL

ONE

♪ ♪ ♪

TEN DAYS AGO, BEFORE CYNTHIA MOON HAD RUN OFF ON HER mysterious errand, Clyde McGraw's orchestra blew like crusading angels. Now they sounded like they'd spent the weekend playing at a funeral and they were battling just to stay alive for the next one. The four-man horn section might've had lung disease; the two violins, string bass, electric guitar, and drummer looked arthritic. Clyde could barely lift his baton. The only one who appeared alive was the singer, Billy Martino. Dressed in a burgundy dinner jacket, slippers to match, black pin-striped trousers, his shiny hair poofed up high except for the spit curl that adorned his forehead, he crooned "White Christmas" as passionately as a French legionnaire condemned to an outpost in Tunisia.

Tom Hickey sat on a stool, leaning on the bar at the opposite end of the nightclub, across the dance floor under its flickering chandelier and beyond the dining room furnished with oak tables and leather-upholstered booths. Hickey was a big man, shoulders so broad he didn't use padding in his suit coats, or else he'd

1

appear monstrous. He had a ruddy complexion and thin, scraggly hair beginning to gray. His nose was long, his chin cleft, his eyes steady and quick, azure blue. He gazed around at the clientele.

In the half-empty dining room were a few couples, two small gangs of secretaries, a family with whiny kids. They ate and drank heartily, disregarding Martino. The only couple on the dance floor had stopped to gab. One fellow at the bar sat with his hands over his ears.

All through November, until ten days ago, every night the place had been jammed. At midnight the line outside used to run a short block down Fourth Street toward Broadway. Over the weeks since Clyde discovered Cynthia Moon, word had reached L.A. Carloads of men trekked a hundred miles to gawk at her.

By now the military brass, flyboys, enlisted fellows who'd been saving all month or won big at poker—the crowd that until last week made Rudy's Hacienda the hottest club in town—had found better action than Martino.

As "White Christmas" faded, Hickey admired the rich baritone, no matter if he made Billy for a vain weasel who wouldn't know an honest emotion if it tried to strangle him. He faked the passion as well as most crooners. But he wasn't fooling this crowd. They must've been saving their goodwill for Christmas, eleven days off.

Christmas and New Year's Eve were already booked full. If Cynthia didn't show by then, Hickey might pack up his wife and daughter, flee up to Lake Arrowhead, and leave his business partner to make the apologies. Castillo deserved the aggravation.

When the singer bowed, a few paws clapped dutifully. A kind secretary whistled. A man at the bar, three seats from Hickey, hollered, "Send the pansy back to Mars."

Hickey sighed, rose, and stepped in front of the loudmouth, a tipsy banker with jowls that quivered and a bow tie. Hickey'd seen him around, usually in the Playroom in the basement of the U. S. Grant Hotel. "Be nice," Hickey said. The banker held his smirk about a second, then gulped and wilted.

Returning to his stool, Hickey wondered if a host who owned

the place ought to let himself act like the bouncer. His partner would've sent the doorman over. Castillo wouldn't risk getting his pointy nose busted—if the Cuban was going to fight a guy, he'd sneak behind him first.

On nights like this one, and the whole past week, when the best they could hope was to break even, Hickey wondered why he'd gone into business with a shark like Paul, as if he didn't find enough trouble in his day job, junior partner in Hickey and Weiss, Investigations.

The musicians got livelier as they hopped off the stage, lighting cigarettes and heading outside for air or to a booth to charm a secretary and take her for a stroll around the block.

Clyde McGraw dragged his patent-leather shoes across the dance floor, his head down, mumbling like a priest. Without looking up, he shuffled around the tables and booths, nudged the stool next to Hickey out of his way, and leaned both elbows on the bar, chin in his hands. "Double manhattan."

Clyde had skin like milk chocolate, mahogany brown hair parted in the middle, a gray-flecked pinstripe mustache. He wore a beige cotton suit, his lime green silk shirt buttoned at the collar, jeweled rings on six of his long pianist's fingers. Finally he raised his head and turned his bloodshot eyes on Hickey. "Mister Castillo comes back in the kitchen while I'm taking supper, says if the girl don't show by the weekend, we gonna be blowing on the corner with the Salvation quartet. Merry Christmas, no? I tell him, 'We got a contract till Valentine's Day, if you recall.' The cat winks, that's all. I jump on the phone, gripe to Arlo down at the union. He's got to check with somebody. When he rings me back, here's what I get. 'Somebody mess with Paul Castillo, somebody be hurting.' Looks like you got a mob behind you, Tom. That a fact?"

"Naw," Hickey said, and meant it, but a grain of doubt made him shiver. He'd checked as far as he could on Paul Castillo, and the man came up clean. But that was a half year ago, and a dozen times since, Castillo had miraculously got what or whoever he wanted in spite of the wartime rationing. Creamery butter, lob-

3

sters still shivering from the waters off Maine, a quintet of Stan Kenton's musicians away from their booking at the Pacific Ballroom.

"You let him break the contract, Tom?"

"It's a tough business," Hickey said. "Guys'll pay a cover to see the girl. All you got now's Martino. Maybe we have to drop the cover charge, we don't make enough to pay a whole union orchestra, we got to find a three-, four-man combo instead."

"Girl wasn't specified in the contract, Tom."

"Maybe she was implied."

"Ah, you gonna step on me too."

"Not if I can help it," Hickey said. "You go find the girl, or get another one like her."

"Like her, yeah." Clyde turned to his drink, ate the cherry. "Where I'm gonna find one like her? No such thing. She's a crackerjack, Tom. I'm losing my wits, ringing up her landlady, fretting, you'd think I was her pop."

Hickey snatched his pipe and tobacco pouch out of a coat pocket, filled the pipe, tamped, and fired it up. "Where's she live?"

McGraw's eyebrows lifted, his chin jiggled. "There we go, you find her. That's your game."

"Yeah," Hickey said. "For twenty a day, plus."

TWO

♪ ♪ ♪

McGRAW WASN'T THE ONLY FELLOW WORRIED ABOUT CYNTHIA Moon. An admiral, pilots enough to make a squadron, ensigns, corporals, attorneys, stockbrokers, a San Diego Padres shortstop who'd led the Pacific Coast League in stolen bases—men pestered Hickey about her every night. The orchestra, in mourning for the crowds that used to jump and shimmy with the music when they had Cynthia, now could turn "Goody, Goody!" into a lament.

Each evening since she'd failed to show after the week off Clyde gave her, Hickey'd met the band as their cars pulled up, hoping Cynthia would climb out of one. Whenever he called his answering service, the message he most hoped for was about the girl.

A tremendous loss, Cynthia Moon. A slender, high-cheeked face, milky skin, emerald green eyes, all of which set off her wavy red hair, a mix of burnt orange and auburn. Smallish mouth, lips full and restless. She moved regally, self-conscious but poised as if it were natural law that whatever she did would be admired and imitated. In heels she stood over six feet, eye to eye with Hickey.

Most of her was legs. Modest breasts and hips, a small waist, broad, square shoulders, a long, graceful neck usually trimmed with pearls.

Her voice was sultry, smooth, and aloof when she spoke to the men who sent her flowers, offered her drinks, invited her for weekends at swank resorts up the coast or in Palm Springs. She kept the flowers, turned down the drinks, fielded and tossed off the seductions without blinking.

Onstage, it seemed her insides caught fire, as if she were in love or pregnant. When she sang old standards, you heard passions in them that had slipped past you before. Listening to Cynthia Moon, you could believe she'd been everywhere, done everything, yet magically kept her innocence. Nobody would've guessed she was only seventeen.

The age was a secret. McGraw had confessed it to Hickey and Paul Castillo after the audition, before they wrote the contract for three months, six nights a week. Hickey's first impulse was to send Clyde packing, but Castillo outtalked him. The girl was a star on the rise. Boys her age were screaming at God in the Tunisian desert, on the beaches of New Guinea and Guadalcanal, and the cops had bigger chores than running kids out of nightclubs. Besides, Castillo said, if she got them in a jam, he'd talk to a pal of his.

For three weeks Hickey watched her sing and gabbed with her between the last set and closing time, after Castillo disappeared, the way he always did about midnight. Hickey drank scotch while the girl sipped ginger ale. He would've given her a cocktail or two if she'd wanted, but she never did. He guessed she feared losing her head. From the talking and because they both had music inside them, he'd gotten to know her at least as well as anyone seemed to. Slight gestures—cocking her head at the wrong instant, a tiny grimace where there should've been a smile, a word out of place—told him she was hardly the unflappable, worldly character she played. She was a girl. Only something, maybe the war, made her grow up too soon.

Hickey wheeled his '41 Chevy coupe, a frisky little number

with a radio and camel hair upholstery, out of his reserved spot in the public parking behind Rudy's, tossing a quarter to Skeeter, a buck-toothed kid wearing a Yankees cap, who kept an eye on the cars. Hickey turned up Fourth Street, driving slowly until his eyes dilated. Like all the West Coast cities, San Diego was running on dim so the Japs would have to squint to bomb it. Neon signs, streetlights, theater marquees—all dark. The only lights seeped from behind shaded windows and from the bottom half of head-lamps painted brown or black across the top.

At Broadway—the intersection between his office, above the Owl Drugstore, and the U. S. Grant Hotel—he cut right, toward the docks. The view ahead looked as if mobs of looters had invaded a ghost city. Not a single Christmas light sparkled. Two years ago, before Pearl Harbor, you would've seen moms out gift shopping, tugging the kids by the hands so they wouldn't stagger into traffic while gawking above at the giant red stars and strings of pastel lights that hung across Broadway four stories up, or at the lighted trees on every corner from the harbor to a mile inland. Dads would've been carrying armloads of glittery packages out of Marston's. Carols would've echoed up side streets from blocks away.

Christmas season 1942, if you went out after dark, more likely it was to drink or pray than to shop. All that stayed open after dusk were nightclubs, movies, coffee shops, the burlesque and peep-show arcades, tattoo parlors, the bus station. The chiropractor who moonlighted in abortions, across the hall from Hickey's office.

The sidewalks, dark except when moonlight sneaked through a break in the foggy clouds or where the glow spilled out of a doorway, were jammed with soldiers and sailors, country girls who'd moved to the city to type and wear scarlet lipstick, burly stevedores, Swedes, Mexican hustlers, salesclerks wrapped in shawls and mittens. Most every kind of adult human except bigshots milled around the Horton Plaza movie houses, smoking, storytelling, flirting, nipping from flasks while they waited sometimes three hours to watch a two-hour-long movie at the Cabrillo or Plaza Theater.

On a corner on the north side of Fifth and Broadway, a gospel quintet of Negroes in top hats and capes sang, "O Holy Night."

Hickey paused too long at the stop sign, listening. From behind him a horn trumpeted. He jumped an inch and snarled. One of the fastest ways to earn Hickey's wrath was to blast him with a horn. Even a toot sparked his temper these days, since he'd bought into Rudy's, begun working eighteen-hour shifts, and watched Madeline turn from his darling to a nag, as though she'd finally lost hope and started hunting for reasons to forsake him.

He knocked the shift lever into neutral, pulled on the hand brake, bounded out, and strode toward the Buick behind him. The horn blower resembled a tortoise. Wide, flat mouth, head sinking fast between his shoulder blades. He reached out and slapped down the locks on both doors. Hickey walked up close, grinned at the fellow, turned back, and strolled to the front of his Chevy. He leaned on the fender and watched the carolers.

"A thrill of hope,
the weary world rejoiceth,
for yonder breaks
a new and glorious . . ."

The Buick shot around him, the tortoise-man yelling, "I got your number, hot stuff, and I'm calling a cop."

Hickey ambled into his car and continued down Broadway. By the Greyhound station beneath the Pickwick Hotel on the corner of Second, he got stalled by about a hundred marines parading across the street to join the line outside the Spreckels Theater. Six blocks farther, at the far end of Union Station, bells clanged, red lights flashed, and the arm dropped in front of the railroad tracks. The Santa Fe crept past, slowing to deliver its load to the docks at the foot of Market Street. Hickey counted forty-six bin cars full of oranges, carrots, lettuce, and onions.

He cut north on Harbor Drive, past the docks where tuna

fishers sprayed down their nets, and workers like gangs of ants plodded with their crates and skids stacked with boxes up and down the gangway of a merchant ship flying the Union Jack. Ships usually anchored in midharbor until after dark when they got tugged in to load, as if the Japs had no spies or maps and couldn't judge except in daylight where the docks and warehouses might be. Hickey figured the Port District ought to build docks in the south bay, as far down as you could take the ships without them running aground, and spread the action instead of clustering it all within a mile of downtown where a single raid of half the bombs they used on Pearl would ravage the tuna fleet, flatten the heart of the city, sink a dozen ships, and knock out aircraft factories, three military bases, and Lindbergh Field.

No one consulted Hickey on military strategy. Except when Admiral Van Vleet asked him whether to order the filet or New York cut, and Colonel Creaser sought his opinion about what kind of flowers Cynthia Moon would like best, the military had passed on its opportunity to benefit from Hickey's wisdom. Last year, along with the millions of other patriots who'd swarmed the recruiting offices in the weeks following Pearl Harbor, Hickey had volunteered for the navy. They ran him through a physical and determined that thirty-five was too old, at least for a borderline diabetic.

The same week they'd turned him down, a chilly evening in March just before dark, he'd been fishing off his pier on Mission Bay when Madeline called him inside. To introduce a fellow she'd brought home from the Del Mar Club in La Jolla. He was new in town, had plans, needed a partner. A couple hours and tumblers of scotch later, Hickey decided that if Uncle Sam didn't want him, he ought to go ahead and make a killing off the war, like any bigshot would.

Four thousand dollars and a couple months of labor—carpentry he'd learned on weekends and on vacation from high school when he was trying to save the money to study at USC—he'd sunk into Rudy's. They got the place ready about the time half the poor sailors and GIs who remained stateside landed in San Diego.

During 1942 the population had doubled. After six months, Hickey's share of the club was worth ten times what he'd invested. It added a decimal to his income. At Rudy's he could make two, three hundred dollars on a good night, just for gabbing with folks, mediating a squabble between the chef and a waiter, watching Cynthia Moon. If he could find her.

Beneath a cargo plane that sounded doomed to explode before it dropped the last few hundred feet to Lindbergh Field, Hickey swung onto Pacific Coast Highway. Just as he'd hit cruising speed, he had to slow for a wailing fire truck that crossed Harbor Drive in front of him and turned in to the main gate of Consolidated Air, a quarter mile long of factory surrounded by a cement wall *and* a chain fence, all of it draped in camouflage netting, even the walking bridge over the highway. Through the open gate, Hickey caught glimpses of welders' torches sparking. He drove under the bridge through the echoing whack and clang of machines.

He turned on Bay Street, rattled across the tracks and a couple blocks east, cut north again on India Street, and rolled over the hill into Old Town, where the houses were mostly Victorian, the landscaping desert—hillsides of aloe and agave, palm trees, stunted yuccas that barely survived the fog.

Four-sixty-three Jones Street was a shabby Victorian a block and a half up Presidio Hill, high enough to overlook the harbor, the naval training center and beyond, the private marinas of Shelter Island, and Moorish villas on the inland slope of Point Loma. The paint had faded to appear like whitewash tinting the redwood slats. The green trim was chipped, spotted with white primer. Each window had a different style and shade of curtain, most of them frilly. The balconies were strung with clotheslines, one adorned with ladies' slips, pearl-colored in the mist, hanging all in a row like a chorus line.

Hickey climbed the steps, crossed the rickety porch, and tapped the knocker on the door. Heels clicked inside. The door flew open and a doll face gazed at him. A button nose. Eyes

10

glittering like polished china. Cherry gumdrop lips. The girl wore a green dress with hat and gloves to match.

"It's about time. Oh. . . ." She recoiled as though Hickey held an ax raised.

He stepped into the foyer. After he introduced himself and got the girl's name, Loraine, he apologized for being the wrong guy and asked for Mrs. Ganguish, the name Clyde had given him.

Loraine sauntered down the hallway, knocked on the second door. In the minute or two Hickey waited, three young women appeared—two at the top of the stairs, one peeking out of the first door in the downstairs hallway. Each of them eyed him closely and brightened for a second before she disappeared. Since the war had carried most of the young men overseas, those left behind, even if they weren't so young, got attended to. Hickey was no pretty-boy, but his face was strong, clothes fit him well, his manners were smooth.

The place, Hickey decided, was either a storybook whorehouse or one of the dormitories spinsters or widows ran for young ladies on their own, shelter from the cruel world full of devious men. Loraine had gone into the parlor, probably to watch the clock. It was 9:30. If the dame who ran this home was as strict as some Hickey'd known, Loraine's boyfriend could show now and only get a half hour to give her candy, beg her forgiveness, and smooch on the porch before her curfew.

A woman stepped out of the second doorway in the hall. Mexican or Spanish, small, tough. Her arms swung stiffly. She had eyes of pure white and obsidian black, breasts like the mother of twenty, long black hair pulled back sternly.

Hickey gave his name, offered his hand, said he was looking for Cynthia Moon.

The woman squeezed his fingers hard. "Call me Dolores. You run that bar?"

"Rudy's is a supper club."

"You serve booze?"

"Sure."

"It's a bar."

11

"You got me. Cynthia around?"

The woman shook her head wearily, turned, walked into the parlor, and collapsed into a faded love seat. She motioned to the sofa where Loraine knelt on the cushion, leaning on the backrest and staring through the front porch window. Hickey took a seat beside her.

"All the time I'm worrying about my girls," Mrs. Ganguish said. "If they don't come home two hours after they supposed to, I don't get no sleep. You think they care? Not much, they don't. Cynthia, she promises to come home last Friday. Maybe somebody kills her, I don't know. Say, how many of you guys I gotta tell this to?"

"Somebody else's been asking?"

"Sure, this crazy man calls me over and over. Every time I forget to worry, a couple minutes later, he calls. Now you?"

"Crazy man?"

"His name's Clyde."

"McGraw. Why do you say he's crazy?"

Dolores's hand sliced the air in front of her face. She wagged her head as if remembering some knowledge too hard or complex to explain. "Musicians, I know about them."

"Uh-huh. How about a boyfriend? She got one?"

"No, sir."

"Girlfriends, family?"

Hearing the shuffle of bare feet and skirts rustling, Hickey glanced through the parlor door. Beyond the foyer, atop the stairs, two young women leaned on the rail. One looked dwarfish, not so short but as if she'd once been taller and gotten squished. The other had a crop of golden curls bouncy as springs. When Hickey spotted them looking, they turned to each other, bent into a huddle, and whispered. A second later Loraine slapped the back of the couch. "The hell with him!" She jumped up and rushed out of the room, up the stairs.

"*Ay, Dios,*" Mrs. Ganguish whispered.

"Cynthia got friends or family?"

"She been here two months, mister. Nobody calls her except

this Clyde. I think she don't give nobody her number. Family, I don't know. First thing, when this Clyde brings her here, I ask, I want to know what kind of family my girls are from. She says they all are dead. No aunties or cousins, no nothing. I don't believe her. Everybody has somebody. I almost don't take her because maybe she lies too much. But I think I give her a week or so, watch what kind of girl she is."

"She's behaved herself?"

"You bet. She's working two jobs, you know? One with a lawyer. Six days a week, she's leaving at twenty to nine o'clock, to run for the bus. Maybe you never seen her in the morning. She don't wear perfume, smells like Palmolive, no kind of makeup except a dab of lip rouge."

From upstairs came a giggle. Dolores heaved herself out of the love seat, marched to the parlor door, and yelped, "Scat, you vixens!" She leaned against the door frame and sighed. "Every day she wears a nice plain dress and flat heels so she don't look like no giant. By six o'clock she's home just long enough to dress fancy and speed off in the taxicab. I don't know what she's eating."

"Usually a T-bone, swordfish on Fridays, and a salad. At Rudy's. How about the other girls? They her friends?"

"No, sir. They don't like her because she don't want no friends. When she got time for friends? On Sunday she goes to church or shopping for a new fancy dress or shoes."

"What church?"

"Catholic. I don't know which one she's going to."

For a while Mrs. Ganguish had seemed to warm to his questions. Now her voice was getting brusque, and when Hickey asked to have a look in Cynthia's room, she woodened her lips and squinted at him as though he'd asked to borrow her underwear. When he argued that the girl, who'd always acted responsibly, must be in a jam, Dolores suggested they call in a cop. He told her he used to be one and gave her a Hickey and Weiss business card. Finally, dubiously, she led him toward the stairs.

The two girls who'd eyed him and a new one, a frizzy brunette in a white robe stretched and belted so tight the resulting bulges above and beneath made Hickey's eyes water, glided out of the first upstairs room to meet him on the landing. Stiffly, as though on a dare, the dwarfish girl stepped forward.

"You're Moony's boss, huh?"

"Yep."

"Lucky her."

The brunette squirmed forward. "Take us out for a drink, cutie, we'll tell you what you need to know."

"Wash your mouth, Brenda," Mrs. Ganguish snapped. She tugged Hickey's arm, hustled him down the hallway to the third door. She kept a tight grip on his arm while her other hand fumbled in several pockets of her housecoat until she found the passkey. Like a burglar on her virgin outing, she needed both of her hands, one steadying the other, to turn the key in the lock and shove open the door.

The room was as small as those in old hotels. A single bed required half the floor. On the faded once-rose-colored wall above the bed hung the portrait of a handsome man about forty with dark hair and worried eyes bright blue as Cynthia's were green. The portrait was so expert that Hickey looked for the signature. Joshua Bair. Better known for the landscapes Hickey'd seen when his daughter Elizabeth dragged him to the art museum.

The bed was piled with a half dozen large pillows, each with a differently flowered pillowcase. The bedspread was solid black. The small window had no curtain, only a lowered manila-colored shade. Beside it sat a small mahogany desk with a vanity mirror on top and drawers left open, same as they were on the oak dresser against the opposite wall, next to the door. The dresser top was littered with stacks of clothes, a towel, and a flatiron. To the side of the dresser was a hat rack on the wall, every post occupied, ladies' hats with lace or flowers, beside the cowboy sombrero, sailor's cap, marine campaign hat, fedora, and panama, which she'd worn as costumes at Rudy's. In place of a closet, a clothes rack stood in the corner. A dozen or so dresses and a few coats hung there.

Hickey reached for a pull chain, flicked on the overhead light. He stepped around Mrs. Ganguish and into the narrow space between the bed and the desk. On the left side of the desk, leaning against the wall, were three stuffed dolls—a ragged teddy bear, a dusty white elephant, and the remains of what must've been a raccoon. The right half of the desk was crowded with jars of perfume and makeup, half of them open. Between the makeup and the animals he found the stuff that chilled his brain and fingers. A drawing in what looked like pencil and crayon, and an open tin of bullets.

Dolores wedged in beside him. "What you got there?"

The bullets were .22 caliber. The tin looked about half empty. A few of the bullets had spilled out onto the picture.

"She have a gun?"

"No sir, I don't allow no guns. I only got ladies here. They are good girls, except Brenda, who only gets to stay because she's my cousin's daughter. By marriage," she added, as if that explained Brenda's libertine behavior.

Hickey swept the bullets off the picture and picked it up. He dug into a coat pocket for his glasses and put them on.

The sketch was on legal-size white paper, above a note a few sentences long written in a stylized hand at the bottom. The drawing was no Joshua Bair, but its message seemed clear. On the dirt floor of a room with cracked brown walls, a female lay. From the awkward angle of her arms, out to her sides and turned upward at the elbows, and from the way her face fell sideways, cheek against the floor, she looked dead.

A thin person stood over her. A smallish long-haired man or shapeless female, leaning down, hands pressed on the inside of the fallen woman's knees as if to push her half-spread legs farther apart.

Both faces were turned away. The fallen person had dark hair with flecks of yellow and red crayon. She had broad shoulders, a long waist, legs so long they looked to have been stretched. Wide, flat breasts with dark nipples. Behind the hipbone, where the flesh of buttocks started, it looked like the woman had a tattoo.

15

Eleven tiny circles in three upright rows, five circles in the middle one. Each was connected to the closest on every side by a branch. The lowest circle on the right was colored green.

The standing person was less defined. Even the lines were blurred, as if the artist had intentionally smeared them, implying that this might not be a person at all but an apparition, a spook or vision out of a half-lost dream.

Mrs. Ganguish, who'd been gazing over his arm, reached tentatively for the picture. Hickey nudged her hand away and read the note on the bottom.

"Beloved, you saw through him from the start. He truly is a fiend. You must rescue us, before your wife and daughter are lost. Otherwise, I have been deluded these many years, and loved a cowardly, pitiful man. Every day the Fiend grows bolder. Soon I may die."

Hickey checked the back. A blank page, no signature or date. "Whew. What the hell?" He passed the picture to Mrs. Ganguish.

She read the note first, her lips buzzing as they moved, and sat back onto the bed as she studied the picture. The fingers of her free hand lifted to her eyes as if to pluck them out.

"Make any sense?" Hickey asked.

Dolores wagged her head fast like a tremor, and Hickey started rifling through the desk drawers, looking for an envelope with an address, or something. He found more bottles of makeup, a stack of sheet music, receipts from Marston's. A drawer half full of crucifixes and rosary beads. Another full of tags that came off flowers and gifts, greeting cards from her admirers. Most of the names Hickey knew from Rudy's. Captain Mitchell. Barney Pottinger, the stockbroker. Both of the Schwartz brothers.

Hickey gathered the cards and tags to sort through later, crammed them into a coat pocket.

"You gonna steal them, mister?"

"Borrow," Hickey said, and plucked the picture from her hand. He folded it carefully along previous folds and stuck it into a separate pocket inside his coat. He stood up, squeezed past

16

Dolores, and went around the bed to the dresser by the door. Three drawers, the top one open. He slid it farther out.

"Get out of there," Dolores snapped.

Hickey lifted the scarves and shawls, found nothing. The second drawer had leather purses, small ones in a half dozen colors, and all the sweaters Hickey'd seen her wear. The bloodred angora was his favorite, the way it tucked snugly around the waist and the short sleeves form-fitted her graceful white arms. "Looks like she didn't take much with her, except a couple dozen bullets." He lifted a hot-water bottle and a heating pad. Nothing.

Mrs. Ganguish whacked him from behind with her elbow. "I tell you stay out of there, mister. You already got a dirty picture, what else you need?"

The bottom drawer was stuffed with bras, stockings, garter belts, and panties, cut low and with lacy designs, mail-order stuff, Hollywood- or Paris-style. Dolores grabbed his bicep and tugged. "That's far enough. You're no police. Out of here, now, you don't got to paw her dainties."

With his free hand, Hickey scooped underthings while the landlady grabbed the hat off him and slapped him on the crown with it. Still he kept rooting in the drawer until he found the red ledger.

By the time he got it out and shut the drawers, his head stung and his hat was limp and shapeless as a hobo's. He snatched it from the landlady, mashed it onto his head. Mrs. Ganguish tried to grab the book. He had to keep nudging her back while he leafed through it. A journal or diary.

"You give me her stuff, mister," Dolores shouted furiously, her brown face turning a color like redwood, her eyes bulged and sparking. "Maybe Cynthia walks in here tonight. What do I tell her, I let a man go stealing her secrets? Give me!"

She grabbed for the book. He pressed it to his chest and made for the door. He had to use his shoulder to move her out of the way. When he got past her, she socked him in the kidneys.

The dwarf, Brenda, and Goldilocks, all in pajamas, suddenly blocked his way. Instinct told him to bend his knees, lower his head, and run that gauntlet like when he played fullback for Hollywood High, yet he tried to slither gently between them. For thanks he got his cheek clawed and coat sleeve ripped. He raced down the stairs, outside, and away. He yelled from the car, "Simmer down. Jesus. Blame it on me. Tell her I picked the lock."

Goldilocks heaved a flowerpot that crashed on the sidewalk as he pulled away.

THREE

♪ ♪ ♪

A MILE NORTH OF OLD TOWN ON THE COAST HIGHWAY, HICKEY crossed the bridge over the dry river and pulled into an all-night truck stop, Milly's Texaco Beanery. He wanted a jolt of coffee, a moment of peace to recover from being turned against by those females, and a quiet place to read Cynthia's book.

With Milly's windows shaded, the neon sign out, her place looked like a deserted roadside fruit stand. A marine truck convoy had commandeered most of the gravel parking lot. Three old rust-spotted cars with Kentucky plates waited in line at the single gas pump. A gathering of hillbillies milled around them. Inside at the register, a balding, weather-beaten fellow in overalls was giving Milly hell. Arms stiff at his sides, voice quavering, he seemed about to crack from the strain.

Milly looked stocky as a wrestler, with oranging peroxide hair and makeup applied liberally. Because her voice could squawk and bellow at the same time, which alone might've sent the hillbilly running, Hickey thought she could be the offspring of a buccaneer and an Amazon parrot. Leaning patiently on the cash register, she let the hick unload on her. Hickey gave her a salute.

In the one long booth, a gang of marine drivers hooted over some gag. A sergeant, albino blond, reached under the table and grabbed a fifth of brown liquor from the next guy, shot it into his coffee, then spotted Hickey noticing. The marine crimped his bushy eyebrows and steeled his eyes to duel with Hickey's. After a few seconds, he gave a sheepish wince and turned to his coffee.

Hickey took the corner booth closest to the lamp, laid his hat and the book on the table, reached for his glasses and fitted them on, and opened the book. Red, leather-bound, with ledger pages. From Woolworth's. The first six pages, numbered in the top right corner, beginning with "83," were filled with medium large feminine handwriting.

The Bitch was trying to murder us. She hates cooking, but she was happy, and Daddy thought it was swell to watch her in the kitchen, chopping the fish and vegetables with the biggest knife. She had brought her radio she got from a pawnbroker in trade for the one she stole from me, because Daddy had got it for my birthday. He had to search all over to find the Motorola that could tune in the "Dreamland" show from L.A., the only one that gives us Kenton live and all the great Negro bands. The Bitch hummed along with the radio, pretending to feel the music, which she never could, since she has no heart or soul.

For dinner she changed into the green skirt and cashmere sweater she got from the Mormon Tramp in trade for my Pendleton suit she stole that I bought for church. I know because last Tuesday I saw the Tramp going into the Grant wearing my suit.

She set the table with Daddy and Venus's Haviland china and Miss V's needlepoint tablecloth and the silver candlesticks. She waited until after dark, and she had brought candles to use so in the dim light we wouldn't notice her only nibbling salad, not touching the chowder. She kept smiling the hateful way Daddy couldn't see the hate in because he loved her in spite of everything, and she cleared the table fast, hoping we wouldn't notice that all she ate were the salad and Mexican crackers, and she kissed Daddy and ran off before the poison hit us.

It was about a half hour before Daddy groaned just after my stomach began to cramp. I had to lie on the floor and try to stretch and he lay beside me, writhing, both of us feverish. Daddy's face poured sweat and tears. I tried to get up, I was going to drive us to the hospital, but my head spun so, I could hardly see to find the door. Daddy wouldn't let me call anybody. He tried to convince me it was just bad fish and we would be sick awhile and throw up, then feel okay, but truly he was afraid the doctor would report to the police that the Bitch tried to kill us. He still loved her, even then, Daddy is so forgiving. I prayed to Saint Ophelia and finally slept on the couch at Daddy's feet.

Milly showed with a mug of coffee. She set it in front of the ledger, between Hickey's arms and under his nose. He hardly noticed. When Hickey got engaged in reading, Japs could've raided the city by land and air without his catching on.

On June 5 she killed him. God forgive me. I was gone, because that day, Saturday, Bobby Wisdom's combo held auditions. I didn't tell Daddy, so he wouldn't worry. He knows horn players make me wild, so he would never trust musicians with me, even though I promised to stay a virgin until Saint Ophelia brings me the Man.

The Bitch came to kill me. The first thing she asked for was me. When he said I was gone and she stomped into my room, and he asked her not to take anything, she went berserk. First she threw a saucer. Then the Haviland teapot and the painting by Mr. Bair of the Indian rock and eucalyptus. So she killed him. She picked up the Remington typewriter. The cover was off because he had been writing a brief when she came. Strong as the devil, she lifted the big Remington over her shoulder and heaved it at him. He didn't want it to break because Venus bought it for him, so

21

he tried to catch it in his arms, and it hurled him back over the credenza.

The doctors say broken ribs don't give anybody TB. They lie because they're afraid of the Bitch. Daddy still forgives her. Even after she killed him, he won't help me destroy her. Father, here is why evil survives—because good people don't have the heart to kill evil ones. So the evil ones keep killing the good.

The story ended there, on page 89. Hickey sat brooding on the last few lines while Milly showed, topped off his coffee, stood over him. Finally she set the coffee pot on the table and kneaded Hickey's shoulders while he eased out of his trance.

"Tom, how you fixed for gas stamps?"

"I got a few."

"That's all, huh?" Milly leaned on the table and bent close enough to nibble Hickey's ear. "Story is, you got pals on the ration board, is what's making Rudy's the hot spot—you holding all the prime beef in town."

Hickey turned on her. "That's a lousy story, babe," he growled. "Don't bother telling it to anybody else."

She jerked upright and grabbed her hips. "We're pals, Tom. Only reason I asked was, you seen the fella up front. Family's been working their way from Kentucky, doing what they had to for little bits of gas. They got three dry tanks. Claims there's a job of dock work in San Pedro his cousin's saved for him, but only to tomorrow morning."

Hickey already had his wallet out. He peeled off fifteen gallons—a month's worth—of ration stamps. Milly took them, leaned close again, and gave him a kiss on the bald spot. "What I like best about you, Tom, is you take off your hat when you step inside. You got manners. You oughta get the hat blocked, though. Losing its shape. I'm gonna bring you a hunk of banana cream pie."

"Naw. Had one earlier."

"Coffee's on the house, then."

Hickey nodded and turned to his coffee, to shut her up before he lost his fix on the ledger.

Besides the general stuff he'd learned about Cynthia, such as she was several times wackier than he'd guessed, he'd collected a few details. She had a father who might be dead or alive, and she doted on the guy. If he was alive, he probably had tuberculosis. She believed in God, in some guardian saint, and maybe in the devil. Also, it seemed she didn't want to call anybody by name. Instead she entitled them. The Mormon Tramp, Miss V. And the Bitch who wanted her dead.

The Bitch, Hickey mused. A relative, neighbor, longtime friend, maybe her daddy's lover or ex. He could check the pawnshops, see if anybody'd given up a Motorola radio in the past year. There wouldn't be many. You could sell one on the street for ten times what you gave for it a couple years ago, now with all the new ones going straight to the forces overseas. He could ask around the U. S. Grant Hotel for a Mormon hustler.

The only real names besides Stan Kenton's were of local personalities. Bobby Wisdom, a pianist, regular entertainer at the Del Mar Club, Madeline's hangout, and Mr. Bair, whose paintings, one of which the Bitch had slung at Daddy, sold for plenty. The same guy that painted the portrait over Cynthia's bed. Hickey would've bet Cynthia didn't know either of them personally or she would've dropped their names in conversation. Maybe the only way she acted like a seventeen-year-old was in idolizing even the marginally famous.

The best odds seemed in hunting for Daddy. He'd been typing a brief. Could be a lawyer. Tomorrow Hickey'd call the county bar association, ask for an attorney named Moon. He wasn't in the phone book. Clyde McGraw had called all the Moons who were.

Daddy might be dead or down with TB. Maybe in Greenwood, the mortuary where most Catholics got planted. Or Mercy Hospital. Dolores Ganguish claimed Cynthia attended a Catholic church, and the girl's desk had held a couple pounds of crosses and rosary beads. Needing somewhere to start, Hickey'd try the

Catholic angle. Cynthia hadn't mentioned being a Catholic—God hadn't figured into their chats. She always steered the talk to music, gossip about jazz people and bigshots around town, and the war. In the *Tribune* and the *L.A. Times,* she followed every move as though she had a loved one in each battle. Her night off, she'd stand in line at the Spreckels, not so much for the movie as for the newsreels.

Outside Milly's, a little Kentucky girl squatted beside the rear fender of a '32 Ford coupe, making a pool on the gravel. As soon as she hopped into the backseat, the three old cars pulled out onto Pacific Coast Highway. Hickey got stuck behind the caravan. Cruising speed about ten mph. One car's dragging muffler shot up sparks, the brightest spots on the highway. In the dark, with dimmed headlamps on some cars, lights out on the rest, you didn't want to cross the center line to pass. If he used the shoulder, passed them on the right, he risked bowling over a gang of Mexican hoboes. Yet if he kept driving ten mph, impatience would detonate his brain. He flipped his headlights on and off a couple dozen times until the hillbillies got the message. One by one they edged over. Hickey whizzed by at twenty-three mph.

He turned left onto Grand Avenue, headed west on Pacific Beach Drive, and cut left on Fanuel, which dead-ended on the bay. He pulled up by the posts at the dead end because his carport was already being used. A blue '39 Caddy. Paul Castillo's.

Hickey locked the car and stood awhile, Cynthia's book tucked under his arm, breathing the salt air and fragrances of his neighbors' orange trees and their trellised wall of bougainvillea. He listened to the ripples from a motorboat lap against his pier, to the squawk of a parrot, somebody's pet that had gotten loose and haunted the neighborhood, perching atop the eucalyptus, pepper, and palm trees. Finally he started toward the house, restrained himself from kicking a dent in Castillo's chariot. He wondered why the sight of it riled him so deeply. Maybe it was just that the guy had swiped his parking spot again. Typical, for Castillo to act like every morsel belonged to him. Or Milly's remark about the rationing could've piqued Hickey's conscience, which he'd been struggling to ignore. He didn't know what kind of strings Castillo was pulling on the ration board. Logic told him not to question, to stash the money away without looking to see if it was dirty. That was the problem with money—you wouldn't find much both clean and numbered higher than twenty.

So Hickey'd concentrated on his tasks. He'd decorated Rudy's, and now he was hosting, motivating, and pacifying the employees. While Castillo procured supplies, created the menu, kept the books. Sure, he wasn't Hickey's first choice for a business partner. Madeline had brought Castillo to him. But in some things she knew best, like which guy had the Midas touch.

She and Castillo stood in the kitchen holding glasses, Madeline wearing a nightgown Hickey hadn't glimpsed since last summer. It showed a square yard of pale shoulders, back, and chest. She was immune to the sun. Though she'd lie out and swim every summer day, her skin never darkened past the shade of milk with a dash of nutmeg. Her hair was down, wavy, tawny brown with golden highlights, the bangs flipped over her right eye. Her cheeks were flushed and her mouth, even poutier than usual, had fresh cherry lipstick. She put the glass to her mouth, chewed on the rim, finally took a sip.

"Find your songbird?" Her voice was lusciously dark and cool. When she used to sing, tough fellows would dance gaily and smooth characters trying to charm her stuttered like Boy Scouts.

Hickey touched her hair, kissed her cheek. "Not yet. Who said I was looking?"

"Clyde phoned. Said call him as soon as you've got a clue. She's a precious little thing."

Turning to Castillo, Hickey tried to summon a cordial voice. "What brings you over, Paul?"

The Cuban set his drink on the counter, folded his hands, turned them backwards and stretched them out in front of him. The knuckles cracked. With his thick ebony hair, pomaded flat, always hatless, Castillo looked a few years younger than Hickey, though he wasn't. Their birthdays were only weeks apart. His face was mountain-shaped, his nose a jutting peak. A little taller than

25

Hickey, a few inches over six feet, he was thin, erect as a manne-quin. The black linen suit with burgundy pinstripes hung per-fectly on him. His voice was what people called liquid. Like vinegar, Hickey thought.

"Visiting, it's all. I been watching the talent at the Mission Beach Ballroom. I hope tomorrow, Tom, you will go there and listen to Charley Wayne's Orchestra. If we having to break the contract with McGraw, they can open for us in one week, day after Christmas, that is if you don't find the girl."

"Snoop out any clues?" Madeline drawled.

"I got a few ideas."

The Cuban bowed shortly to Madeline, reached for Hickey's hand, and shook. Castillo's hand, too lean and hot, always felt like it belonged to a different species. Maybe a spider monkey. "I will leave you to your pleasures."

As the Cuban disappeared, Madeline lit a Pall Mall. Watching her husband as if he were a coiled snake, she let the match flame until it reached her fingertips, then flipped it into the sink. "Why the frown, Tom?"

"Tired, a little gloomy. Lots on my mind."

"Such as?"

"How come you're wearing that outfit?"

Her eyes flashed then darkened, as though she were plugged in and lightning had struck a power line. "When Clyde called, I figured you might stop by the songbird's place and still get home early."

"You and Paul have a nice chat?"

"Better than sitting out watching the fish jump. Reading the latest potboiler. It's got so the high spot of my day is walking with Lizzie to the drugstore, looking for a new shade of rouge. You working days and nights, you don't even make messes for me to clean anymore."

"Lunches at the club. Tennis lessons."

"I'm bored, Tom, get it?"

Hickey laid the book on the sinkboard beside the fruit bowl, dug into a coat pocket for his briar and Walter Raleigh. "How about you, and Elizabeth if you want, meet me at Rudy's a couple nights a week, for dinner and a drink or two? Matter of fact, anytime you want to host the place, I'll stick around here with Elizabeth." He detected a caustic note in his voice and caught Madeline's fleeting sneer. "How about, give me a day or two to find the girl, I'll take off, make Paul run the joint all weekend? We jump on the Santa Fe about noon Saturday, get a couple drinks in the club car, have a room waiting at the Beverly Wilshire. I'll find out where Basie or Harry James are playing. We rent a car, some fancy British number, and do the town."

Madeline's shoulders, neck, and arms went rubbery. She leaned on the sinkboard, ran the tap, and drowned her cigarette. "Sure, Tom, I'd love that." She gave him a cautious smile. "What's that thing?" she asked, motioning to where the book lay.

"I dug it out of the girl's room. Not exactly a diary, more like part of a story she's telling."

Madeline slid along the counter and fingered the book as if it were mink. "You going to let me read it?"

"Naw."

"Tom, she's not your client. You got no more right snooping through her things than I do."

"Nice try, darling."

"The hell!" She grabbed a banana from the fruit bowl and flung it, smacking him in the lower abdomen. "There's stuff in there about what a handsome brute you are? Maybe how good you kiss?"

Rather than fuel her temper, Hickey shook his head mildly. He picked the banana off the floor and set it back into the bowl. Finally he picked up the book. As he turned and started into the living room, he heard Madeline stomp down the hallway. He crossed the living room to the back porch, a screened-in place with wood-slat floors and shelves full of driftwood and shells. He'd built it for sleeping cool in summers. He stared at the black-glass surface of the bay, at the pool of moonlight around the first buoy, trying to find a piece of oblivion. When the rooms behind him darkened, he went back there and looked in on Elizabeth.

Her little room held a single four-poster bed with a canopy he'd bought for her fourteenth birthday last May, a small white mirrored dresser, and two chests that used to hold toys. Now they were stuffed with photos of singers and movie stars, letters from friends who'd moved away, school papers she'd gotten As on, and her drawings, mostly of tall women in elegant gowns she'd designed. The walls were each a different bright color—yellow, green, orange, and blue—muraled with jungle flowers, a tiger, a couple of monkeys, a giraffe whose head turned onto the ceiling. She'd worked most evenings for a month last year. The window above her head was open. Misty breeze fluttered the curtain that touched her golden hair, the color Hickey's used to be. She had the quilt tucked around her neck, tight as a noose. She hardly breathed. Hickey swept back a curl and kissed her forehead.

" 'Night, Daddy," she murmured.

He walked out to the sleeping porch, flopped into the hammock, listened closely. All sounds were muffled by the water. He tuned to the creaking dock, a distant motorboat, sea gulls. A splash as somebody belly flopped into the water, and one of his drunken neighbors howling. He drifted, picturing girls, women. Madeline, Elizabeth, Cynthia Moon.

FOUR

♪ ♪ ♪

EVA THE POTTER LIVED ABOUT A MILE SOUTHEAST AROUND THE bay. Her husband, Captain Dick, USN retired, had taught Hickey sailing before he fled to Guadalajara, where liquor was cheaper. Eva dressed like a fisherman. Every morning she and six or eight of her cocker spaniels circled the bay, under the piers, across the mud flats and channels. When Hickey slept on the porch in summer, the yapping woke him at dawn. He usually ran out and threatened to hang her mutts by the ears, for which Eva loosed her cockers to snarl around his feet. Hickey and Eva would glare at each other until one of them laughed, and they'd sit on the pier and gossip awhile. Eva knew everybody around the bay. She was like the daily news.

This morning she stood a minute gazing at his window, the signal that she'd brought a scoop for him. But Hickey had plenty more on his mind than neighborhood gossip. After she moved along, he got up, pulled on the slacks he'd left hanging across the chair beside the hammock. He slipped into his shoes, shirt, hat and coat, picked up Cynthia's book, then tiptoed through the parlor and kitchen, out the carport door.

He didn't want to hear any of Madeline's sighs or complaints. Months ago, about when Rudy's opened, she'd taken up griping, like a hobby. Not that she wanted him to give up the nightclub. Rudy's was going to make them rich. Madeline wanted him to shove the detective work onto his partner Leo. No matter if investigating was the business that had paid for their bayside cottage, the new Chevy every few years, the private Episcopal school in La Jolla for Elizabeth, which Madeline insisted on, where Elizabeth could meet classy friends. Madeline wouldn't consider that next month the fickle public might empty its wallets in some other dive besides Rudy's. Before Christmas, the guys who shoveled out their bucks at Rudy's might be on the bridges of minesweepers, flying missions against Bora Bora, digging fox-holes somewhere in Europe. By the New Year, Japs might bomb Rudy's into bite-size chunks, along with the harbor, shipyards, Consolidated Air, and the rest of San Diego. If none of the above, then the strings Castillo was pulling might snap. Without the eight hundred pounds a week of Grade A prime T-bone and New York cut they sneaked between the cracks in the rationing laws, and without Cynthia Moon, Rudy's was just another overpriced hash house. But Madeline didn't worry about any of that. She was hardly one of your security-minded dames. Her favorite bets were long shots.

Besides, if Hickey hadn't bolted out of the house this morning, she'd likely have tried to convince him to let Cynthia disappear, tell Clyde McGraw to go fiddle elsewhere. To grab this Charley Wayne's Orchestra from the Mission Beach Ballroom. Madeline could've put Castillo up to going over there and scouting last night. She might've invited Castillo over and worn that nightgown as persuasion, to get rid of Cynthia Moon. Though you wouldn't catch her admitting it, Madeline was crazy jealous of the girl.

Madeline was a lifetime's worth of puzzle. A cross between hellcat and cherub. A fiery lover who could frost over the instant you rubbed her wrong. A bright, elegant, gracious companion. A shrew jealous as Lucifer, on account of her unquenchable vanity, like all but a few rare beauties.

The motor had warmed. Hickey sped to get downtown before the traffic jammed. At 6:15, beside Harbor Drive, cargo planes taxied across Lindbergh Field. Three merchant frigates and a Norwegian-flagged passenger liner had anchored in the harbor since yesterday. Around them, tugs, daysailors, barges, fishing skiffs, houseboats bobbed on the swells. The harbor was mottled with shadows of the barrage balloons that were supposed to confuse and snag Japanese aircraft. People called them flying silver fish. A line of them floated over the tuna clippers, fat and sturdy as whaling boats. Dozens more shadowed the half mile of piers lined with warehouses. Cranes, forklifts that weaved and dodged like mosquitoes, and gangs of stevedores filled holds and piled decks with sides of beef, bins of lettuce, crates of mortars and rockets.

Hickey turned up Market Street, swerved around double-parked trucks, had to jam his brakes and skid to a stop a foot from smashing a wino who stumbled, leading with his head, off the curb beside the Salvation Army Mission. Hickey turned down Fifth. Outside the Hollywood Burlesque Theater, a line of flashy hustlers leaned against the wall. Posing. Smoking. Gaping at their images in compact mirrors. For an instant he thought the redhead could be Cynthia Moon, but she was somebody else he knew. Melinda. She waved. He tossed her a salute.

A cab pulled out, giving Hickey a parking spot. He locked the car, walked a block up to Fourth and Broadway, entered a four-story brick building. He climbed three flights of stairs, passed the credit dentist and chiropractor's offices to a door lettered HICKEY AND WEISS, INVESTIGATIONS.

The office had a single desk, a wardrobe closet, a stuffed chair and sofa, photographs tacked to the wall. Leo Weiss with his wife and two daughters, back when Leo still featured hair and Vi was slender. Before their oldest girl, Una, got her face battered by a Nazi gang while she was studying music in Vienna. Hickey and family on the beach, arms around each other. A photo of Madeline singing at the old Agua Caliente casino in Tijuana. Elizabeth at five years old, drifting in a rowboat on Lake Arrowhead. Hickey receiving an award from the La Jolla Women's Club for tracking Mrs. Fox's daughter and arranging her escape from the Okie Communist guitar player with whom she'd eloped. Beside the memories hung a collage of Elizabeth's drawings—a brown trout she'd caught on vacation, a flattering portrait of her dad, a line of Parisian cancan dancers.

From the wardrobe Hickey got a clean shirt, underwear, socks, and a green-and-blue tie with a sailboat painted on it. He dug a razor and toothbrush out of the desk and walked down the hall to a rest room. In ten minutes he was back, looking sharp, smelling like spice, dialing his partner's number. Leo grumbled hello and kept chewing the last crumbs of breakfast.

"Leopold, you got a couple hours for me today?"

"Hold it while I count. Last I heard, there were about twenty-four every day. Between us, not including your tours at Rudy's, we got about twenty-seven committed, of which you been covering maybe six a day. That leaves twenty-one for me. Three left over. What you need?"

"I'm trying to locate Cynthia Moon. There's a diary, kind of, in a ledger book. I'm gonna leave it here for you to browse. You're apt to think she's a little peculiar."

"A doll like her's allowed to be."

"Read it over. Maybe you'll zero on something I missed. Call Bobby Wisdom, the pianist. Number's with the musician's union. Then try Joshua Bair, the painter. Somebody at the Frenchman's Gallery could tell you how to reach him."

Leo grumbled. Hickey said thanks, hung up, locked the office. He walked back to Market Street and down to the Pier Five Diner, a couple blocks from the tracks, an old railroad car backed by a small Quonset. At the end of a counter lined with uniforms, sailors, and two cops, Hickey ate Bobo's delectable thin, grainy hotcakes, drowned in syrup to make up for the lack of butter. No place in town save Rudy's could get butter these days.

He stayed long enough for an extra cup of coffee and a smoke, then hustled to his car and drove north on Fifth, up the hill winding between the eucalyptus groves and canyons of Balboa Park where a thousand or so mangled boys arrived every day. The museums, the recital halls—the whole showplace erected for the Expositions of 1915 and 1935 had gotten commandeered by the navy and makeshifted into hospital wards. A gang of bandaged fellows in pajamas and several pretty nurses sat smoking on a roadside lawn. A great shriek jolted Hickey before he recognized it as the bellow of an elephant from the zoo. Birds screeched angrily as if cussing the elephant for waking them.

At 8:35 Hickey wheeled into the parking lot of Mercy Hospital. He found a corner spot where at least one side of his Chevy could be safe from getting whacked.

There were padded wing chairs in the hospital lobby. The Catholics didn't buy junk, Hickey mused. The faint scent of lavender mixed with acrid and putrefying smells. While nuns in white pushed gurneys and escorted visitors, whispering their news and consolations, Hickey told the records clerk his occupation, the day job, briefed her on his mission, and asked if there'd been a TB patient named Moon within the past year.

The clerk was a portly, ageless Mexican woman with eyes so white and animated that Hickey would've loaned her money, listened to her troubles; if he weren't a true husband, she could've easily led him astray. She scanned a book. Nobody named Moon. So he asked for a list of the past year's TB cases. Cheerfully, she offered to type a list for which he could wait or come back in an hour. She held out a box of Christmas candies and he took one, a chocolate crème bell with a bow on it. He ate it on the way across the lobby to the pay phone, from which he called the county bar association. They claimed no member attorney named Moon.

A half mile east, at County General Hospital, Hickey argued with a straw-haired female who spoke like a mynah bird in the throes of asphyxiation. She couldn't help him. Such information was confidential. She waved him away, and when he wouldn't budge, she whisked herself into a back office. After ten minutes she returned with a large-headed fellow in doctor's garb, who heard Hickey out and commanded the straw-haired person to accommodate him. It took her thirty-five minutes to inform him they'd not had a patient named Moon and to add that she could possibly type the list he'd requested, of the year's TB cases, by next week.

"Swell," Hickey said. "In return, I'll write Santa Claus, tell him to bring you a wig."

Angel Eyes at Mercy Hospital gave him a list and another chocolate. In trade, he wrote an IOU on the back of his business card, dinner and drinks for two at Rudy's Hacienda.

He sat in the Chevy, propped the list on the steering wheel, and studied it. Of sixty TB cases, thirty-four had been discharged to home—none to a daughter named Cynthia. The rest had gotten sent to various nursing homes. Fourteen of those had gone to the Saint Ambrose Home, out east in La Mesa.

He took University all the way, racing the streetcar to the end of the line. The shops turned to houses, the houses got smaller and farther apart, the Victory gardens more frequent and lush, with flower beds surrounding the winter tomatoes, lettuce, pole beans, cabbage. He passed a chicken ranch, citrus and avocado orchards, a desert stretch with prickly pear cactus, sagebrush, granite outcrops at the base of a hill beneath a stand of oak trees. La Mesa was a single main street winding between foothills, and outlying neighborhoods that ran up the several hillsides. On the east end of the main street, the Saint Ambrose Home looked like a monastery. Three stories, stucco with Spanish tile, topped with three arches housing eight large bronze bells in graduated sizes. Across the front of the place were dozens of small windows, not much bigger than portholes. The walkway, bordered with beds of pansies, led past a carved redwood sign:

SEE GOD IN ALL.
SERVE GOD IN ALL.
LOVE GOD IN ALL.

The double entrance doors were solid carved wood that opened into an oak floored lobby graced by two love seats and several wing chairs more plush than the hospital's. The ceilings were two stories high. On each side, a tunnel-shaped hallway led off into gray darkness where it appeared ghosts could dwell, like caves Hickey remembered from dreams. Wheelchairs crept in and out of sight, near the entrance to each hallway.

A nun materialized, standing an arm's length straight in front of Hickey, who didn't care for nuns. At a distance they looked harmless, but up close they aroused in him a mix of awe and fury. Too often, their suspicious, unpampered faces made him think about his mother.

The nun called herself Sister Johanna. Her mouth looked hard as a beak. She had dark freckles set off by pale skin, pale blue eyes, and eyebrows like white fuzz. The way her nose twitched, and her watery eyes, made Hickey imagine a rabbit with allergies. Her voice was loud but mild until Hickey showed her a photo of Cynthia Moon.

A publicity shot. Hair cascaded over her right shoulder. A noose of pearls glittered around her neck. Gypsy earrings dangled and flashed. Her parted lips were brightly rouged, her eyelids darkened. Her knee and a half yard of thigh angled out from the slit of a floor-length sequined evening gown, teal blue, the bodice slashed low, like an arrow pointed at the danger zone.

With a first glance at the drawing, Sister Johanna gave a muted shriek. "Oh dear," she muttered.

"Know her?"

"Why, I believe it could be Henry Tucker's girl. Sir, I speak to her every day, until . . . ?"

Hickey allowed her a moment, then urged, "Until what?"

"Oh, the last two weeks, she hasn't come."

"Name's Cynthia?"

"Yes, it is. She's a modest girl. I've never seen her with a speck of powder or paint." The nun looked behind her for one of the wing chairs, picked the nearest, and guided herself into it. She

35

motioned Hickey down close where she could whisper. "Is she a harlot?"

"Naw. Jazz singer."

"Oh dear. Perhaps her father learned? And that could be why . . . ?" She looked up plaintively. "He's dying, sir."

Hickey returned the photo to its manila envelope, tubed the envelope, and stuck it into his coat pocket. He scooted a chair close to the sister's, perched on the edge of it while he explained why Cynthia was his business, and the nun related how the girl would arrive every morning on the 9:15 bus, dressed simply, to sit with her father all day, walk him on the grounds, or take him to sun in the patio. Between July, when Henry Tucker was admitted, and two weeks ago, she'd only missed a few days. She'd nursed him so well that he'd been recovering miraculously, his lungs almost clear, his spirits high.

"Toward the end," Sister Johanna said, "commonly he became effusive. I overheard him telling Cynthia stories about his past and their mother and . . ."

"Whoa," Hickey said. "Toward the end of what?"

The nun bowed her head. "Of his life, I fear? Two weeks ago, nearly. Monday, after she'd missed two or three days, Mister Tucker had a relapse. I found him gasping for air? As soon as the doctor arrived and they'd secured him with oxygen, I tried to phone Cynthia and discovered we don't have an address or number for her. Do you think, sir, there could be a connection between his relapse and her disappearance? Couldn't it be she saw him failing and ran away, to escape the pain."

Hickey nodded. "How about her mother? She alive?"

"I believe so. Perhaps Father Berry can tell you her whereabouts. He'll surely want to speak to you. He's quite fond of Mr. Tucker, and Cynthia?"

The way this nun asked statements and stated questions, Hickey thought she must've learned punctuation on April Fool's Day. "Anybody else visit Mr. Tucker?"

"Last summer there was a lady. . . . Emma . . . Vidal? Quite attractive. Splendid black hair. One day, at my request, she let it

36

down. Sir, it reached below her knees? In my opinion, she loved Mr. Tucker deeply. But, in September, it was, her visits stopped. I asked Cynthia if Miss Vidal would return. She wouldn't talk about Miss Vidal. In fact, she grew angry and hissed at me, sir?"

Two nuns passed, driving a herd of old people across the lobby to the French doors that led to the patio. A woman in a head wrap and blue dress that looked new and expensive used two canes and still had to concentrate fiercely to hobble in front of the nun who steadied her shoulders. The woman's false teeth had gotten loose from her gums and slipped sideways, molars out front.

"Cynthia have any brothers or sisters?" Hickey asked.

"Yes. A sister, Laurel. I've tried to call her since the relapse but the phone was disconnected. I sent her a letter. Shall I give you the address?"

"Before I leave. How about you show me to Mr. Tucker now?"

Sister Johanna frowned, rose, and started toward the glass doors. "He may not speak. He rarely does anymore, except to the angels when he asks them to carry him away."

The patio was sunny and bright with marigolds, a tall jacaranda, a rose garden in the middle, and more roses climbing a stucco wall. Hickey thought the place smelled too sweet, like gumdrops. He was gazing around when the old woman in blue lunged off the bench and landed on her knees in front of him. The head wrap had unraveled. Her wiry hair was gathered into three bows. Her long, sharp chin trembled, and loose teeth clacked as she shrilled, "Are you the devil?"

A chill shot up his neck and spread across his skull. It felt like his hair catching fire. Before he could answer, a nun was lifting the old woman and Sister Johanna was leading Hickey around her. "Don't be startled, sir? Donia commonly asks men if they are Satan. She was a Russian countess who personally knew the wicked Rasputin. He made quite an impression."

The sister led him up the path beside tall birds of paradise and into the rear wing. The heavy doors opened to another hall like those off the lobby, only the smells of decay were fouler here, mixed with incense and dramatized by ghostly sounds. As soon as one groan or cry faded, another would rise. In the first room, the skeleton of a woman no bigger than a doll lay curled, knees up, on top of her sheets. A cadaverous man with purplish skin sat in the next room. Bare legs dangling off his bed, he was naked except for one maroon sock and a sailor's cap so large it almost covered his eyes. He shook his fist at Hickey and the nun. The third doorway on the right led to Henry Tucker.

Cynthia's daddy might've already been in his coffin, the way he lay prone with arms rammed against his sides. He wore red pajamas. His black hair was thick and tawny, his flesh chalk white under and around the brown stubble. Hickey recognized him from the portrait above the bed in Cynthia's room. The way he looked now, all the worries that Mr. Bair had captured in his expression must've come true. His eyes were closed, the lashes long and thick. At his side was a mask hooked by a tube to a large tank beside the bed. Sister Johanna closed the valve on the tank.

"He pulls it off the minute we leave him alone."

Taller than the bed was long, Tucker's bony feet stuck through the rails. His arms and hands were long and gangly, the shoulders wide but skeletal. Like a powerful man in his final defeat. His broad chest had caved in. He breathed in shallow gasps and puffed out like spitting. When the nun touched his arm, he quivered and jerked. His eyes opened halfway, enough to show their color. Like sky blue, only with its light snuffed out.

"Go away," he rasped.

Sister Johanna picked up his hand, cradled it. "Please talk to the man, Henry? He's trying to find Cynthia."

"Why?"

"I'm a friend. Your daughter works for me." Hickey avoided mentioning the nightclub, suspecting her daddy wouldn't approve. "She took a week off, said there were family problems, didn't show up when she was due."

All that changed in Tucker's expression was that it kept tightening, as if some force or gadget slowly stretched his skin. He gasped and spit air like a worn and rusted machine. There was a rare gentleness about his eyes.

Aching for the man, Hickey asked softly, "Any idea where she went?"

"No."

"You figure her mother knows?"

Tucker wrenched his hand free from Sister Johanna and pushed on the middle of his chest as though trying to hold his heart in. Sister Johanna gripped Hickey's arm tightly, tugged and led him out to the hallway, where she released her hold on him and stood wagging her head. "We've troubled him enough, sir."

"Let me talk to him alone for one minute. I've got something might change his attitude, shock him into action."

"Or kill him," she whispered.

Hickey led her farther down the hall. "You said he was dying anyway." The nun's face puckered and flushed as if she'd never heard a line so cruel. "I'm guessing the girl's in trouble, see. Don't you think Tucker'd want to risk his life for her?"

"It's not for us to say."

Hickey pulled from his coat pocket the tubed manila envelope, slipped out the drawing of two naked people with the plea for help beneath and handed it to her. She squinted at it until her eyes wetted and closed. She plucked a handkerchief out of a crease in her robe.

"I found it in her room," Hickey said. "Next to a tin of bullets. A couple dozen of them were missing. You get the idea."

Head down as though in a procession, the nun led him back to the room where Tucker lay facing away from them. The nun pulled a cord and flicked on the overhead light. Using only one hand, she propped two pillows against the head rails, then lifted and coaxed the man to a sitting posture as easily as if he'd been sewn of canvas and filled with straw. His only reaction was to lift a hand to shade his eyes. Under the light, Hickey saw how handsome his face must've been with the graceful high cheekbones, delicate lips, and deep blue eyes. He looked like the ruin of a prince. When Sister Johanna held the picture in front of his face, he stared diffidently, his eyes scanning from top to bottom, side to side.

"Can you read it?" Hickey asked.

"I read."

"What's it mean?"

"Nothing."

"Tell me who sent it, or who they sent it to? Tell me anything."

Tucker rolled onto his side and suffered through a rattling cough. When it finished he lay still, breathing mechanically as before. The man was dead already, Hickey saw. There might still be a heart inside him, and part of a brain, but the spirit was gone. The coughing subsided and Tucker lay still with his back to Hickey.

Hickey took the drawing from Sister Johanna, stuck it into the envelope, rolled the envelope into his pocket. "Say, who's the Bitch?"

Henry Tucker shuddered for a couple seconds, no more. Sister Johanna pulled up the blankets, smoothed them, and led Hickey out, looking grim as though she'd begged forgiveness and was waiting for the answer, terrified that it would be no. She led him across the patio. Beneath the jacaranda was a path leading to an arched door. She opened the door and showed him into a parlor furnished in cherry wood: cushioned straight-backed chairs, a coffee table, a bureau, and a china cabinet. There was a bell on a platform beside an interior door. The sister rang it.

The footsteps were hypnotically slow and measured. The door opened on a barrel-shaped man in black with a priest's collar. "McCullough," he declared, grabbed Hickey's hand, and pumped it like a well handle. His face was ruddy, eyes blue and zesty, his hair strawberry blond, shaggy down the back of his compacted neck that barely allowed room for his collar.

Sister Johanna introduced Hickey, said he was here about the Tuckers, and rushed off as if the priest spooked her. He motioned Hickey into his office. The cherry wood desk was so big and slick they could've tipped it to forty-five degrees and skied down. The two small windows looked out upon lemon trees. The cherry wood shelves held photographs, diplomas, a dozen or so football trophies. Hickey motioned that way. "You play ball?"

The priest beamed. "Notre Dame. Guard. I'd take you for a . . . fullback."

"Hollywood High, and one year at SC."

"An injury?"

"Yeah. I ran out of dough."

Hickey sat on a love seat, the priest behind his desk. He lay his elbows on the desk, folded his hands, rested his chin on them. "I hope you've brought news about Cynthia Tucker."

"Questions. She's missing."

The priest sighed dourly. He reached into a drawer and produced a fifth of Irish whiskey, reached twice more for tumblers. "I welcome company." His eyes enlarged, his face flushed and he grinned. "You see, I won't drink alone, barring my nightcap and the sip to whet my appetite for supper, and it's certain you won't catch me drinking with a nun. Imagine living with nuns, Tom. Twenty-two celibate wives." He gave a wink and loaded the tumblers, delivered one to Hickey and returned to his seat. "The glass has been washed."

Hickey downed a healthy swallow, glad for the jolt. Consorting with a nun, a priest, and the living dead hadn't rose-tinted his day. He asked the priest if he could smoke then, before he filled his pipe and torched it, he got up and lay the manila envelope on the desk. "Look at what's in there. Tell me what you make of it."

The priest looked first at the photo of Cynthia. He smiled, caught his breath, and gulped what was left in his tumbler. Lying the photo facedown, he picked up the drawing, held it first at arm's length but kept inching it closer until it masked his face. When he dropped it onto the desk, he rubbed his eyes and turned his chair to face the window and lemon tree.

"What's it mean?" Hickey asked.

The priest wagged his head silently. After a minute he turned, gazing distractedly around the room, reached to fill his tumbler halfway, and neatly placed the photo and drawing into the manila envelope.

"What's the matter?" Hickey asked. "You recognize somebody?"

"The symbol. The tattoo on the girl's behind."

"Yeah?"

"It's a kabbalistic version of the Tree of Life. You may remember the Tree of Life from Genesis? The circles are called *Sefirot*. Each represents a spiritual or occult power. The lines are paths a seeker, or magician, will use to climb the tree."

"Yeah. Go on."

"You noticed the one circle in green?"

"You bet."

"It's the color of Venus—not Venus Tucker, Cynthia's mother. Venus, the goddess of all things feminine—and that *Sefirah* is the abode of Venus. It's called *Nezah*, which I remember because it happens to be the name of the faith Venus Tucker preaches. A brand of Theosophy. You know of the Theosophists?"

"A little."

"That Venus and Henry were longtime Theosophists?"

"Okay." Hickey rolled his hand.

"It's a society of maverick Hindus, who also glean what serves them from other doctrines."

"Swell," Hickey said. "Now tell me why that tree thing spooked you."

"Last month a parcel arrived for Henry Tucker. I delivered it myself and opened it for him. It was a ring that looked handmade by an amateur, a band with a small golden circle attached, that may have been a coin before the markings were rubbed away and the symbol etched on it. A tiny green gem had been set into the Venus *Sefirah*. Henry begged me to save it until he died, then place it on his hand, on the wedding finger."

Hickey relit his pipe, held out his glass for another jolt. "The parcel have a note or anything, a return address?"

"It was postmarked Redding, California. Venus lives up there, near Mount Shasta."

"Cynthia get along with her mother?"

"Not well. Laurel is her mother's child, Cynthia the father's. Now, with Henry dying, what's she to do?"

"Maybe shoot somebody," Hickey muttered.

The priest wheeled his chair to face Hickey straight on, grabbed the rim of his desk. "What?"

"I found bullets in her room."

Father McCullough wiped his brow with a sleeve and kneaded his forehead. "If I were a beauty of seventeen who's allowed to sing in a nightclub, leered at by servicemen, rakes, and mobsters, I too might carry a gun in my purse."

Hickey raised his tumbler, downed the last of his whiskey. "Here's hoping."

The priest drank up. Hickey sat, smoked, waited for the father to quit feeding him the Tuckers' story by the teaspoon and come clean. But the priest wasn't offering.

"Okay. Two more things. How about you give me the sister's, Laurel's, address and tell me how you know about the night-club?"

"Cynthia takes me into her confidence."

"Ah. Then you'd know about her friends. Uncles, cousins. What church she goes to. Who she hates."

The priest shifted his eyes away, fished into a drawer for an address book, a notepad and pen. He scribbled an address and held it out. "You might find Laurel here. It was their home before Henry got stricken with tuberculosis."

Hickey stood, accepted the address. "Yeah, about Henry getting stricken, Cynthia tell you about somebody she calls the Bitch, who clobbered her daddy with a typewriter?"

The priest's jaw clenched and shoulders thickened as though he were preparing to rampage across the scrimmage line. "Sorry," he murmured.

"It could mean I find her."

"I don't tell tales, Mister Hickey. That's why people trust me."

Hickey crammed the sister's address into the manila envelope, told the priest thanks and good-bye. Father McCullough walked him across the patio where old folks crowded every bench and chair, wearing sun hats or holding newspapers over their heads as if the midday sun would rain on them. Those who could hear listened to the bells start clanging "Silent Night." On the roof of

43

the front building, behind the facade and beneath the bells, a Mexican fellow stood pulling ropes. Each note chimed clear and rich, and hung a long while in the air. Hickey listened eagerly, trying to figure how the man got two full octaves, including sharps and flats, with only eight bells.

FIVE

♪ ♪ ♪

WHILE THE BELLS PLAYED SONGS ABOUT CHRIST, HICKEY SAT OUT
front in his Chevy, sorting through what he'd learned, trying to
give it some order, maybe draw a hypothesis or two.

Every day for months Cynthia Tucker Moon had ridden the
bus out here to visit her father, dressed in the business suits
Dolores Ganguish thought she wore to a job with an attorney.
Hickey wondered about the lies, why Cynthia had told nobody at
Rudy's or the Ganguish house about her family. She could be a
pathological liar; she might want mystery to become part of her
image; or there were family matters she didn't care to reveal.
Because the priest wouldn't spill all he knew, Hickey would bet
on the last choice. Dark secrets.

It seemed her mother and father, who used to be Theosophists,
had split apart and the mother gone to live up north. The older
daughter, Laurel, who might be living at Tucker's home in North
Park, was probably on Venus's side, while Cynthia doted on the
father. An attractive woman named Emma Vidal—the Miss V in

Cynthia's book?—had visited Henry Tucker through the summer, then stopped. About a month ago Henry Tucker received in the mail a ring, maybe from Venus—or Emma Vidal?—which Tucker petitioned Father McCullough to hide from Cynthia and to place on his wedding-ring finger when they laid him away. A couple weeks later he suffered a relapse. On account of the ring? Because Cynthia disappeared? Or told him something before she left?

Or Cynthia might've run off because of his relapse, fled to the mother for solace or to bring the mother back in a desperate attempt to resurrect Henry Tucker's spirit. If Venus didn't want to come back, if Cynthia loved her daddy as much as it appeared, with only a little strain Hickey could imagine her cornering whichever woman Henry Tucker needed—Cynthia might be wild enough with passion and fear for Daddy, deranged enough to persuade the woman with a gun.

Aggravated because his theory was nothing but guesswork that might lead him nowhere but astray, he drove off in the middle of "O Little Town of Bethlehem," to look for Laurel Tucker.

He passed the college, rows of cafés, hardware stores, crowded motels, a half dozen tracts where carpenters pounded together cheap bungalows. Farther west along El Cajon Boulevard, about every fourth retail space—a car lot, appliance outlet, furniture shop—was boarded up or makeshifted into a recruiting office or a thrift store. The factories were thriving on war production. Nobody made cars, vacuum cleaners, or sofas anymore.

The Tucker house was on Wisteria Court, a cul-de-sac that dead-ended overlooking a canyon out of which spiked giant eucalyptus, their shadows waving over the small homes on cramped lots, identical except in color. The Tucker house was faded Mexican turquoise, stucco with a tile roof and several dead prickly pear cactus in pots along the half wall that enclosed the front porch. Hickey wondered how many months of neglect it took to murder a cactus.

On the porch, about a dozen newspapers lay in a heap. Hickey rapped on the door and waited. He noticed two old women staring from across the street, one on each side of a rose garden that separated their yards. The older of the two, hardly over four feet tall, gripped a trickling hose. She turned it away from the roses, pointed it in Hickey's direction like a rifle in position for a hip shot. He knocked again, waited a few seconds, then squatted beside the newspapers and shuffled through them. The oldest, on the bottom, headlined STALINGRAD OFFENSIVE KILLS 169,000 GERMANS. 74,500 PRISONERS, was dated December 10. The day after Cynthia's last night at Rudy's.

A heavy blue curtain was drawn over the porch window. Peering along the side, Hickey saw envelopes and handbills lying on the entryway floor where they'd been dropped through the front-door mail slot. He wanted a look at that mail. Maybe there'd be a card from Cynthia or Venus.

The old dames still gaped at him, and a man came limping to join them. He used a cane and wore a cowboy hat folded up rakishly on one side. As soon as Hickey started jimmying the lock or snooping around back for a window to crawl through, one of those vigilantes would hobble to her phone, the others would memorize his license plate number.

He crossed the street, pulling out his billfold and unfolding the photostat of his investigator's license. He greeted them cheerily, gave his name, passed the license to the first outreached hand, which belonged to the dame with the hose. The others squinted over her shoulder.

"I'm looking for Laurel Tucker, or Cynthia."

The one with the hose asked, "They in a mess?" Her voice sounded filtered through a whistle.

"Could be. Cynthia's missing."

The taller, younger woman with dyed black hair and scarlet rouge made a humming noise. The older one laid down her hose at the base of a rosebush, adjusted her spectacles.

"Cindy ain't been around since June," the man croaked.

"Cindy," Hickey muttered. "How about Laurel? When'd you see her last?"

47

"Week or so. Zoomed off in that DeSoto, missed an inch from squashing the butcher's dog. Red tick hound."

"Tell me about Laurel?"

"A looker," the man said, and reached a few inches over his head. "This tall."

"Gadabout," the black-haired lady added. "She comes to home maybe half the time. Goes on long trips. She had men in to stay the night, a couple of sailors."

The man waved his hands to cancel her statement. "One sailor, and a marine. Can't you tell a marine?"

"Laurel got a job?" Hickey asked.

"You bet. Thinks she's the queen of real estate. Got one of them signs on the side of Henry's DeSoto. Somebody and Associates."

"Murphy," the small lady whistled.

"And Associates."

Hickey dealt them each a business card, asked for a phone call if either of the sisters showed, and drove off. At Fortieth and University, he stopped in the Piggly Wiggly market for gum, a sack of peanuts and to use the phone booth. No Emma Vidal was listed by the directory or information line. The only Vidal was Joaquin, and he didn't answer his phone. Murphy and Associates was listed, with an address less than a mile away, on the 3600 block of Adams Avenue.

Dark clouds were massing over the coast like the shield of a devilish army. Airplanes swarmed in and out of them. The atmosphere and traffic got Hickey distracted. He passed Murphy and Associates, parked down the street, and walked back. The office window was papered with photos of houses, estates, farms, hotels, bank buildings, each priced about triple what they might've asked last year. Most of them bought and sold by investors, Hickey knew. It wasn't a time for working people to buy a piece of earth and settle down. Everybody had gotten upturned by the war. Some fought. Many worked two jobs, volunteered with the Red Cross or YMCA giving comfort to the GIs and sailors. Others, plenty of them—hookers, realtors, and opportunists like Tom Hickey—found their angle and raked in loot.

A few of the properties, the ones priced shockingly low, were located up north, from Redding to the coast and north into Oregon. Seaside or pine forest lots with log or stone cabins, trout streams or salmon fishing nearby, five hundred dollars or so. Summers before the war, Hickey and family used to drive north, rent a cabin, fish, hike, and ride horses until their spirits got refueled and they could tackle another year. If he had to chase Cynthia in that direction, he could keep a lookout, maybe buy a couple acres, now that he possessed Ben Franklins enough to toss one in the air if he felt like checking the wind.

As he stepped into the office, a bell attached to the door clanged, yet the receptionist didn't look up from her dime romance until Hickey'd gazed around at the gray walls blighted with diplomas and plaques, and at the four steel desks cluttered as if a bomb scare had chased everybody else away, and drummed his fingers on the counter for a minute.

Like somebody too busy carousing to sleep except daytimes on weekends, she creaked out of the chair, stretched her puffy eyes open. Her legs were short, hips sprawling as though molded to fit the chair. On the way to the counter she smeared on lipstick, smooched it around, and gave a smile she might've learned at gunpoint.

"You're an investor, I bet."

"Yep," Hickey said. "You're a broker?"

"Naw, Mr. Murphy's the broker. I like your tie."

"Be nice, I'll buy you one like it for Christmas. Murphy in?" He gave her a business card from Rudy's.

"I'll go see." She swished between the desks to a rear office, poked her head in, and delivered the card, then stepped out and beckoned Hickey with a finger. As she blockaded half the doorway, he had to brush her arm and skirt to get by. The door shut and left Hickey facing a blond man aged thirty or less, whose bulky shoulders, in a tan woolen suit coat, slumped as if they each carried a bag of cement. He was behind an oak desk, sitting in a wheelchair.

Hickey reached across the desk. The man either grimaced or smiled. Everything about him looked woeful. His firm handshake seemed to require mighty effort. "Chet Murphy." He plucked off his tortoiseshell glasses and set them atop a stack of legal papers. "This morning's been a rush. We've taken on several new properties." He didn't talk with the brash prattle of most salesmen. His pitch seemed to imply: buy something, see if you can make me less miserable. "We have some exquisite harbor view lots in the South Bay and Coronado."

Hickey decided to play along, see if it got him more than the truth had gleaned from the Catholics. "I'm looking farther north. A lake, a river, mountains. Tahoe. Maybe Shasta."

"I can help you there."

"Tell you what. I got a referral to Laurel Tucker."

Murphy's eyes narrowed and his hands rose stiffly from his lap to splay out flat on the desk. "Laurel," he snapped, "is bright, competent. Unfortunately, she's out of town, on business."

Hickey would've bet his share of Rudy's against an ice-cream pushcart that this fellow's grudge against Laurel cut far deeper than professional jealousy. "She up north?"

Murphy's hands folded around a pencil, as though to squeeze the lead out. "You're looking for a resort? Residence? Development property?"

"I'm a skeptic," Hickey said. "I figure, when you're in the market for something like stocks or land and you aren't that familiar with the territory, you gotta trust your agent. You know Laurel Tucker long?"

"Yes."

"Ah, you're family?"

"We were both raised at Otherworld. Mr. Hickey, I could show you our listings. When Laurel returns, if you'd rather be in her hands, fine."

"Otherworld. You a Theosophist?"

50

"Not any longer. Excuse me, I'll call Mary to bring us the upstate listings."

"Whoa," Hickey said. "I'm not in a hurry. Let me ask—where I got the referral to Laurel was from her sister, Cynthia. She sings at my nightclub. I guess you know her, too."

Only his paralysis kept Murphy in the chair. It looked like he'd suddenly bound over the desk and bash walls or people to splinters. Even his ears were crimson, and he spoke with an accent on every word. "I know the whole family, but I'm not going to talk about them, Mr. Hickey, except to assure you that Laurel is a good agent. You can trust her with your money. Personally . . . to speak of Laurel, her family, or Otherworld revives memories I'm in no mood for. Especially not now. A dear friend has died."

"Sorry," Hickey mumbled, honestly grieved to be pestering the man.

"You didn't know better." Murphy loosed his hands and wiped them on opposite sleeves, watching Hickey rise.

"Sorry anyway. One question, though. I might find Laurel around Mount Shasta?"

"Dunsmuir."

"With her mother?"

"Yes."

As Hickey weaved between the desks past the receptionist, lost in her novel, he brooded on the apparent coincidence that today he'd found, in the vicinity of Cynthia and the Tuckers, two strong men who'd both lived at Otherworld, both been Theosophists, and both gotten broken so cruelly it'd take an age full of miracles to fix them.

He followed Adams Avenue through Hillcrest and down off the mesa. Harbor mist and smoke from the Consolidated Aircraft factory blended into a haze that turned the sun cherry red and shot rosy streaks at the new moon. He turned off the Coast Highway into Pacific Beach hoping to get home and find a message waiting, from Clyde or Leo, about the girl turning up. Other-

51

wise, he'd be driving all night. Which seemed painless compared to telling Madeline he had to leave.

He turned in to the alley and parked in the carport, noting that he should feel lucky the carport wasn't inhabited by Castillo's El Dorado or the sports coupe of some rich kid Elizabeth had met. He wasn't keen on Madeline's allowing boys to hang around. Though Elizabeth looked and acted older, she was only fourteen, until January. Going beyond your age could get dangerous, like it might've for Cynthia Tucker Moon. The couple times he and Madeline had argued about Elizabeth's boyfriends, she'd patronized him, left him feeling like a doting wretch afraid to let his precious fly out of the nest.

He walked in through the kitchen door. A half dozen chicken drumsticks wrapped in butcher paper lay on the sinkboard. The shower was spraying, not loud enough to cover Madeline's song. A number she used to sing with the orchestra Hickey led, years ago, about a guy who says he's busy, but she thinks he's out making whoopee.

He lay the manila envelope on the counter beside the drumsticks and stepped into the living room. The phone was on the coffee table. He sat and called Leo at home, where you could always reach him around suppertime.

"Weiss here."

"Leonardo. What'd you learn?"

"That Bobby Wisdom's a hophead, for one thing. You ever go to that flophouse of his, wear your gas mask."

"Anything about Cynthia?"

"All he knows about her is what he saw one night at Rudy's. Why'd you let the bum through the door? Only issue he'd address is which part of her he'd nibble first, given the opportunity. The other guy, the old painter, he's never heard of anybody named Moon."

"The girl's real name's Tucker," Hickey said. "I found her daddy in a rest home. He's not talking, but I got an idea where she went. I'll be gone a day or two. A couple things you could do for me. See if you can locate an Emma Vidal."

"Spell."

"V-I-D-A-L. She's not listed. And call Thrapp or somebody, tell him we got a missing person. File a report, then wheedle him into getting a warrant and escorting you into the Tucker house. Three-sixty-six Wisteria Court. Got it?"

"Yep."

"Snoop around in there. Look for stuff on the mother, Venus. She might go by Tucker or a different name. She lives in Dunsmuir, near Mount Shasta. I'm on my way up there." Madeline padded in, barefoot, tying her red silk bathrobe. "I'll call you tomorrow at breakfasttime. Bye."

He hung up and kissed his wife on the forehead and dry lips. Her hair smelled like a jungle in the rain. He glanced into her wide brown eyes and smiled, thinking how animated they always looked, as if besides being part of somebody, they had lives all their own. She backed off a step, folded her arms.

"Mount Shasta?"

"Yeah. I'm going for a drive. I got a feeling."

"Oh. What feeling's that?"

"Like the girl's too screwy to be running around the state with a loaded gun."

Madeline's cheeks puffed out slowly as if they were filling with words she could spit at him. "Day after tomorrow, wasn't it, we were taking the train to L.A.? The Beverly Wilshire, you remember?"

"Maybe I'll get back in time. If not, we can go next Saturday, or during the week."

"Fine." With a bitter smile, she turned and padded into the kitchen. "You want me to be a good little wife, pack you a bag of sandwiches for the trip?"

As long as you don't lace them with rat poison, he wanted to say. But she'd make a comeback. He'd retaliate and finally leave her with some crack he'd regret. It was the damnedest thing, how words always were riskiest with the people you loved.

He followed her into the kitchen, where she'd picked the photo of Cynthia and the drawing out of their manila envelope. He

53

stepped closer to intercept her if she started tearing them into confetti.

Elizabeth threw open the back door from the sun deck, ran through the sleeping porch and living room. She'd been out in the boat; you could tell by the way her hair kinked and glistened with mist, by her parched lips and rosy cheeks.

At fourteen she looked like a woman—a starlet, the way her mom used to. A couple inches taller than Madeline, otherwise the same figure. High, modest breasts. A waist made tiny by the swell of her hips. Long, thin legs and long, narrow feet. Walking like a dancer, she tiptoed up to Hickey and kissed him on the nose.

"Daddy, my friends are going to the Cove Theater tomorrow night. Could you drop me there and pick me up at Gwen's house on your way home? I don't care if it's late. Gwen's folks will let us stay up. Please. Mom won't let me ride with the kids after dark."

"I won't be here, babe. I'm going up north on business."

"Oh." She sighed, then an idea twinkled her eyes. "San Francisco?"

"Nope. To Mount Shasta, up past Sacramento."

"There's snow, huh? Daddy, can I go? We could take the toboggan and . . ."

"Forget it, Lizzie," Madeline snapped.

Hickey petted his daughter's hair. "It wouldn't be much fun, kiddo. Mostly driving; I'm not staying long."

"Jesus, Tom, you don't need to talk her out of it. She's just not going anyplace where you or anybody is carrying a gun."

With a sneer at her mother, Elizabeth rushed off to her bedroom. Something heavy smacked the ground. "Got your temper," Madeline said.

"Why don't you pack a few things, go along for the ride?" Hickey offered. "There's a ski resort at Mount Lassen. I could drop you two there. If things work out, on the way home we swing over to the coast, finish the weekend in San Francisco."

"Aw, Tom, listen to yourself. 'If things work out.' When did they ever?" She turned to the sinkboard, where the pictures she'd

54

taken out of the manila envelope lay, picked Cynthia Moon's publicity photo, and held it out in front of him. "You think Lizzie and I want to hold your hand while you're chasing this slut all over the state?"

"Slut? You think that's what she is?"

"You bet she is." Madeline laid down the photo, picked up the drawing, and displayed it before Hickey's eyes. "Exhibit number two."

"It's not her, Madeline. Look at the dark hair."

"Oh, she drew it of somebody else?"

"I don't know, babe," Hickey sighed. "I'm going to find out."

"It's Cynthia. Look, she's as big as the man."

"What if it is? You think I oughta only work for somebody if they're a virgin?"

"Who's paying you to work for her?"

"Every man that walks into Rudy's."

Madeline wheeled, grabbed the water faucet and cranked it on full, snatched up a drumstick and scrubbed it viciously. Hickey went to their bedroom and bath, packed a few things and stepped into Elizabeth's room to say good-bye. She lay on her bed, propped against the headboard, her lips in a pout, shoulders hunched. There was a pencil in her hand and a drawing pad on her lap. In a few minutes she'd already sketched pine trees and the outline of a horse pulling a sleigh.

"You're tops," Hickey said. He got out his billfold and handed her a ten. "Your mom'll probably let you go meet your friends in a taxi."

"Thanks, Daddy." It took a minute for her to fashion a smile. "Be careful," she said, urgently as if he were shipping off to war.

SIX

♪ ♪ ♪

THE SKY ABOVE PACIFIC COAST HIGHWAY WAS BLUE-BLACK WITH
patches of gray where the fog thinned enough to let traces of
moonlight through. On the bluff north of La Jolla, Hickey pulled
in to a clearing beside a stand of wind-bent pines, got out, and
used a pocketknife to scrape the brown paint off the top of his
headlamps.

Relieved of having to peel his eyes at every inch of road, he
flipped on the radio, tuned in "Dreamland," the L.A. show that
was Cynthia's favorite. There were few vehicles on the two-lane
highway. Now and then some bigshot in a V-12 sedan would blast
by, highballing down from L.A. Hickey whooshed along about
seventy mph, wondering if he could stay awake the whole fifteen-
or-so-hour drive. Every few miles he'd catch up with a military
convoy, a quarter mile of trucks, and have to lie behind until they
got to a mile-long straightaway. On empty stretches, he yanked
the hand throttle and whizzed along the sea cliffs, his elbow out
the window, listening to a run of Basie and Duke Ellington tunes,

56

and to Justine Brell, a new singer with Charley Wayne's Orchestra, who sounded eerily like Madeline used to.

Les Butterfield had discovered Madeline, not long after Hickey had joined Butterfield's band on alto sax. They played the L.A. ballrooms, weekend and summer resorts on the coast and in the mountains around Lake Arrowhead and Big Bear. When Butterfield gave up music to concentrate on liquor and Hickey took over as bandleader, he booked them jobs from San Francisco to Agua Caliente across the border. With Madeline singing, they got all the work they could use. Her phrasing, gestures, and the passion in her eyes, as though she were on a quest, muddled Hickey's brain, moistened his eyes, made him want to comfort her, protect her, give her the universe. She married him in Reno, June of 1926.

For a couple years Tom Hickey felt like king of the mountain. He'd risen from shoe-shine kid and street punk to bandleader and won the girl. Everybody's darling. Like Cynthia Moon was now.

That was the thorn pricking Madeline's jealousy. She didn't worry about Hickey's faithfulness. Sixteen years she'd been his only lover. But she hated Cynthia, for getting what they both wanted most—to sing and be adored.

When she'd given up singing, she'd only meant to be gone long enough to get her shape back and nurse Elizabeth. A year or so. But the stock market crashed, and there came to be plenty more work for cops than for musicians. All but a few of the nightclubs closed, the resorts that didn't fold only booked cheap local bands. The Dorseys, Glenn Miller, Benny Goodman—guys like that kept their orchestras working. Hickey wasn't one of them.

Highway 101 carried him past miles of orange groves and strawberry fields, through Whittier, across the dry San Gabriel River, past the municipal golf course and into East L.A. where even after 9:00 P.M. trucks rumbled out of warehouses, and machines whacked and clanged, barely muffled by the factory walls. Whittier Boulevard took him past City Hall and dozens of bars and movie houses where servicemen and working girls huddled outside the doorways in lines or bunches. Then Highway 101 cut left on Sunset Boulevard, ran alongside the parks—Elysian,

Silver Lake, Griffith, and swung left again onto Hollywood Boulevard.

The farmer's market, the theaters, the aroma of eucalyptus, tainted by soot, drifting on the sea breeze—every sight and scent aroused Hickey's memory. Thirty years he'd spent around L.A. First on a cattle ranch near Long Beach, before his dad ran off and his mother got religion—Hickey couldn't remember which happened before, and might've caused, the other. The ranch got sold, the money vanished. With his mother and younger sister, Florence, he moved to a cottage at the foot of the Hollywood hills, a mile from the intersection where he sat this moment. When the light changed, he gunned the motor, accidentally screeched rubber trying to leave behind the smell of Hollywood: the sea air blending with dust from the hills and canyons, burning gasoline and the scents of imported trees like cedar and redwood, dry and brittle. He stared at people in cars, ones who paced sidewalks and remembered how they were. A few bigshots, the rest scavengers, prowling to be the first to spot and grab a dollar when it fell. Hickey's family were scavengers. His mother, named Harriet, became a seamstress. All she could do—besides torment her son, curse his father, praise God and the prophet Mary Baker Eddy—was sew, cook, and clean. Hickey shined shoes and stole things until he got his saxophone. A year later he was blowing with combos at parties and school functions. The saxophone and football would've gotten him through USC, except that his sister caught rheumatic fever. In 1925, aged nineteen, he signed on with the LAPD, the first time.

The memories that made him damned glad when he'd dropped into the valley, passed the Hollywood Bowl, and was speeding toward the mountains beyond San Fernando as if he'd escaped from jail were the same ones that plagued most everybody who spent longer than a weekend in Hollywood. Failures. Dreams that proved greater than you were. Superficial memories that kept him distracted from the real nightmares. He was almost to the Grapevine before he dwelt for more than a second on his mother. The saint. This moment she'd be sitting on a hard chair with her nose in the Bible or *Science and Health,* looking for something she hadn't gleaned in the first thousand readings, anything that would make her feel more hallowed. She lived in the mansion Florence's husband built, a mile up the hill from their old cottage. Hickey wondered who she was fondling these days. The reason Florence gave for remaining childless was that a baby would irritate Mom. Florence was subtle, diplomatic. Hickey knew what she really meant.

On the grade, Hickey ate tuna sandwiches, smoked his pipe, and watched the scattering clouds, the clusters of stars, and the big slice of moon. He crossed the Grapevine an hour before midnight, coasting fast down the zigzag highway toward the San Joaquin Valley. He loved driving, ranked it directly behind his family, his work—the day job—and music. He didn't long for a swanky house or wardrobe, a yacht or trips to Rio, like Madeline. The bayside cottage, a half closet of tailored coats, slacks, shirts, and a dozen hand-painted ties, a good hat and a rowboat, plus the dream of one day buying a sloop or ketch, suited him fine. But every few years he got a new car. Not a monster or showboat. Something responsive, tight without rattles, so you trust it'll turn like you mean it to, and if you goose the throttle, it goes zoom. So every twitch it gave was under his control. And a good radio.

He'd lost "Dreamland" when he'd crossed the divide. There wouldn't be much radio in the middle of the night through this valley. He settled in for the long run, four hundred flat, weary miles. He tried to contemplate and solve some problems, like how to please Madeline; the whereabouts of Cynthia Tucker; whether Phil the maître d', whom Hickey'd put in charge of Rudy's, could pacify LeDuc the chef without a fistfight; whether LeDuc would keep his fingers off the cigarette girls' behinds. But as the night got heavier, those subjects taxed his mind, so his mind refused them and chose a trancelike stupor. He sailed through patches of fog, past vineyards, almond groves, musky ranches, stockyards, endless farms. Even at 2:00 A.M. there were tractors plowing and bin trucks at the silos loading. Grub for the war. In Fresno, beside a bin truck loaded with fertilizer and a couple stakebeds hauling wetbacks and Okies, Hickey gassed up and bought a thermos of coffee.

A hundred miles vanished. Sacramento flashed by. Everything lightened. A band of dawn appeared above the Sierra Nevada and spilled over like a flood of syrup. Rivers of mauve and fern green ran down the snowy mountainsides. The best part of driving all night was dawn, Hickey mused. The clouds made angel patterns. Piles of fallen leaves sparkled in the orchards like heaps of gold and jewels. Out of a checkerboard of rice fields, white cranes and snow geese flew up and away.

Hickey made Redding before 8:00 A.M. At a truck stop alongside the Sacramento River, he filled his tank and thermos, bought a half pound of coffee cake and bribed the cashier—who either had a sixteen-year-old figure and the face of a crone, or Hickey was demented with fatigue—to let him use the phone. He reached Leo, who hadn't found the girl or got into the Tucker house yet.

A few miles up the road, the valley dead-ended into a mountain range. The road narrowed, got icy, weaved beside the arroyos of churning streams, beneath cutaway red dirt hillsides, across bridges and around the bays of Shasta Lake, into dense pine forests. A sign proclaimed CHAINS REQUIRED. Hickey didn't have any. He tightened his grip on the wheel and skidded for a long spell without much chance to admire the landscape until, at the crest of the Trinity Alps, Mount Shasta appeared.

Like unsuspectingly opening a door and colliding with a giant—suddenly the mountain was the whole panorama, a great white pyramid that stood alone without foothills leading to it, as if it had dropped in one piece out of the sky. Hickey marveled at the sight while he skidded down the grade and into Dunsmuir.

A strangely dark town, crouching in the shadow of the Trinity Alps as though it had reasons to hide from the sun. The one main street led off the highway. A mix of gravel and slush. Along it, in the mile before it disappeared into forest, there were ten or so buildings, half of them built of stone, chunks of dark granite wedged together and mortared. The rest were made of stacked logs. There was a Texaco station and garage, a hardware-grocery, a café that doubled as bus depot and post office. The Outpost. One of the log buildings. A few old pickups sat out front. Hickey pulled in beside them. He slid out of his Chevy, stretched, whiffed the pines. When he started shivering, he walked inside.

Left of the counter was a wall of postal boxes. Hickey stepped over there for a look. They were tagged by name. No Tucker. Right of the counter, in a cramped, dimly lit area, were three tables with checked tablecloths and flowered napkins. At the first one sat two young farmers. Three of the town's old watchdogs, none under seventy, had the farthest table. They'd probably finished breakfast an hour ago, would digest for another hour, then wander outside, take a seat in the sun, and rest until nap time. They'd know Venus and everybody else in town.

Hickey took the middle table, sat watching the cook and waitress. The cook had a lion and an eagle tattooed on one arm and the tattooed face of a woman peeking out from his collar. The waitress was a little plump, a lot buxom. She had a schoolgirl face, blanched complexion, dimples, frizzy blond hair. SUE LYNN stitched onto her blouse. After a couple minutes she turned from gabbing with the cook and smiled at Hickey.

Her voice was a quavery drawl. She took Hickey's order, a country omelet, corned-beef hash, milk. Her hips swished free and easy, going to the counter and back with his milk and water. Hickey asked about a motel.

"Well, you're gonna have to stay at the Castle Crag, 'cause it's all there is. I hear it's elegant. Where you from? Don't tell me. Las Angeleez."

"San Dago."

"Watcha doin' way up here? Running from a gal?"

"Hunting for one."

"I'll be." She nibbled her bottom lip. "Got a particular type in mind?"

"Yep. Name's Cynthia Tucker."

"Uh-huh." Sue Lynn gazed coolly around, nodded to one of the watchdogs who flagged her. "Pardon." She swished off and made a turn around the room with the coffee pot, then fetched Hickey's order and brought it over. "Bone apeteet."

"Yeah," Hickey said. "Listen. You know somebody named Venus that lives around here?"

The farmers, the watchdogs, the cook, and Sue Lynn dropped their other occupations and stared at him. Not with glee. Finally Sue Lynn nodded. "Sure, everybody knows Venus. She's one of them Netsocks that're buying up the town."

Hickey set down his fork, his eyes widening. The waitress eased into the rickety chair across from him. "Netsocks call theirselves a society, but they ain't no society, a church is what they are. Everybody knows that. Well, they ain't exactly a church either, in a Christian sense. What they are, according to Pastor, is a gang of loonies. Know what he says? They believe there's a tribe of goblins-like that're living inside the mountain, right smack in the middle of Mount Shasta." She broke off for a hearty giggle. "They're all the time up there, searching for some tunnel where they can sneak inside. You going up there?"

"Where's that?"

"Their place. You go to the end of the road then keep going until you see this big sign, says Black Forest Lodge. You go up there, promise you come back and tell me about 'em?"

Hickey nodded. "What'd you mean, buying up the town?"

"Just like it sounds. This past year or so, most every parcel that's offered, she's plucked it up. But they ain't selling to her no more. Least if anybody does, they're gonna get whooped. How'd you like your town getting took over by a gang of loonies?"

Hickey smiled. "My town already has."

"That so?"

He picked up his fork and started nibbling, let Sue Lynn get back to her work. The omelet was too cheesy, the hash like military surplus. It cost almost a dollar. He gave Sue Lynn a four-dollar tip, enough to make her chirp when she saw it.

Outside, two of the watchdogs leaned against the bed of a pickup, admiring Hickey's Chevy. A stone-bald fellow, who looked too frail to stand as straight as he did, pointed at the car. "She a fast one?"

"Yep," Hickey said. "Six cylinders is plenty, car this small. Want to give her a spin?"

The old guy cackled. "Hell no. Maybe I'd wreck her and you'd skin my ass."

Hickey shrugged. "I bet you know Venus."

"I seen her around. One of them Nuthawks. Maybe not just *one* of 'em either. I hear she's the top dog."

"Hell she is," the other fellow growled. He was short, box-shaped, hidden in a bundle of clothes, a jacket and overcoat, hat pulled down to his eyes. "Top bitch maybe. Top dog's that nigra."

"Who's that?"

"The swami. Sissy boy. You ain't looking to join up with 'em."

"Naw. I'm looking for Venus's daughter, Cynthia."

"Big pretty gal, brunette?"

"Redhead, last I saw."

"Sure, I seen a redhead get off the bus," the bald man said. "Week or so back. Lady with hair enough to keep her butt warm, she'd drove down in a Ford, thirty-one or -two, picked up the redhead. The two of 'em stood there, squeezing the other and bawling like President Roosevelt died."

Emma Vidal, Hickey thought. He said thanks, fired up his Chevy, and drove the half mile to the end of the road and the Castle Crag Motor Hotel, a fifty-yard-long stone building with arched windows and shingle roof.

The woman who checked him in wore a wedding ring big as a cupcake. About forty, tall and lithe, with shoulder-length dark hair, opal earrings, keen hazel eyes, impeccable makeup and hairdo, like a city girl who'd just returned from the beauty salon.

Hickey paid, filled out a card, and was set to ask about Venus when the phone rang and the woman—Fay Giles, according to the nameplate on the desk—began talking heatedly with some-body about water rights on a certain ranch. Hickey found his own way to the room. It was spacious enough and furnished with the best of the Sears catalog. Even an alarm clock. He set it for 2:00 P.M., which would give him a couple hours of sleep and leave a couple more of daylight, and collapsed.

After whacking the alarm clock, he shaved, slapped on cologne, changed his underwear and shirt, and walked to the office. Fay Giles was sitting on the desk, manicuring her toenails. When he and a blast of cold wind teamed to sling open the door, she spun to sit correctly and primped her legs together, blushing as though he'd caught her trying on naughty underwear.

"I should've rung the bell?"

"Please. Do you need something?" She had a husky, smoker's voice.

"Sure. Whatever advice you can give me about the *Nezah* Society."

She paled and crinkled her roundish, delicate face. "Are you in real estate?"

"Why, you selling?"

"Look, mister, if you're fronting for the Tucker women, if you're planning to buy up more of Dunsmuir or the Shasta Highlands tract, I call my attorney, he calls the sheriff, and the sheriff calls you a fraud. Ever seen Alcatraz?"

"I hear you," Hickey said. "Tell me, if I were fronting for the Tuckers, why would I ask you about the *Nezahs?*"

"Maybe you're a sharp one."

"You said Tucker women. Meaning Venus and who?"

"What's it to you?"

"I'm looking for Cynthia Tucker, Venus's younger daughter. You know her?"

"Venus and I don't go to the same tea parties, mister. All I've got to say about their society is, the closer you get, the more it stinks. What I see is a land-grab operation and a breeding farm."

"Breeding farm? What're they breeding?"

"Go look for yourself."

"Yeah. Thanks." He walked out, thinking that every little town must have its Fay Giles, who'd moved there to escape some person or city she'd watched go wrong. Usually she'd be the town's staunchest defender, while the natives sat on the fences and observed, not so sure the place was worth defending.

At the end of the gravel road, a dirt trail ran to the left, beginning a spiral climb up the mountainside. It looked cleared and plowed since the last snow, but it got slicker and darker as it tunneled through overhanging trees before opening into a glen. A meadow of snow, patches of dead grass, pools of iced, swampy water, surrounded by fir and aspen trees. The light was gray and shimmery. Hickey imagined giant bats and witches. The trail ended at a stone wall with an iron gate and a carved wood sign. BLACK FOREST LODGE.

Hickey parked in the middle of the trail. On either side he would've gotten stuck in snow or slush. He stood a moment at the gate, surveying the place. It looked like a motor court designed by a pre-Renaissance German. Surrounded by the stone wall were eight buildings, each the size of a single garage, built from mortared slabs of granite. The slabs were so large you wondered who could've lifted them. A labor only giants could've performed. Like Stonehenge or Egypt's pyramids. Each building was a miniature castle, with a turret and several tiny windows about head-high to the center on a basketball team. The meadow lay in a wedge of the mountain that rose steeply on three sides. You had to crook your neck to see the only visible strip of sky, which the sun wouldn't take more than three hours to cross, allowing the place about as much honest daylight as winter solstice gave Alaska. The lodge was entirely in shadow, though the sky was steel blue, not a cloud except the one that haloed Mount Shasta, all of which you could see from where Hickey stood. Commanding the whole northern view, Shasta looked like a glacier creeping south to flatten California.

The gate was unchained. Hickey pushed it open, got into his car, and drove through. An elderly man in khakis and a black woolen coat, and two children barely old enough to walk, stood beside the first building eyeing him. As he approached, the man took both kids by their hands and towed them across the compound toward a glass building, apparently a hothouse. Through the steamy glass he made out the shadows of seven people besides the ones who'd just entered. Hickey parked next to the only car, a grimy ten-year-old Ford. He glanced in the window in case the registration was visible. It might belong to Emma Vidal.

A woman stepped out of the second building across the compound. Tall and erect. Wearing a man's work shirt over a gingham dress almost to the ground. She took large, graceful strides that made her appear light-footed even in the hiking boots. She had a mane of glossy black hair, peach-colored skin, and a smile that kept growing as she neared Hickey. From ten feet away she looked warm and serene. It wasn't until she got close enough to shake his hand that he read a kind of mournful skittishness in her eyes and noticed her protruding belly.

"Hi," she said cheerfully. "I'm Katherine."

"Tom Hickey. A friend of Cynthia Tucker."

The smile froze in place. For an instant her jaw quivered, before she recovered and said, "Pleased to meet you."

"My pleasure. Cynthia around?"

"I'm afraid she left yesterday."

"Hmmm. Venus here?"

"No, she and the master left yesterday also."

"A regular exodus," Hickey said. "Emma Vidal leave, too?"

The smile withered. She stared at her boots as if they'd suddenly pinched her. "Would you like a cup of cider?"

Hickey nodded and followed her across the compound to the second building. Inside was steamy hot and dim. Fire crackled in a wood stove in one corner. There were three pallet beds, a long plank table and benches, handmade of pine, a bookcase of stacked bricks and boards, dozens of books. Hickey noticed the *Tao Te Ching* of Lao-Tzu. A collection of Coleridge's essays. Madame Blavatsky's *Secret Doctrine* and *Isis Unveiled*. From an icebox, Katherine pulled a gallon jug. She poured cider into a pan that had hung alongside others from the wall above the icebox, set it on the stove.

She sat on the bench across the table from Hickey. "As I said,

Cynthia left yesterday, with her sister. Did you drive up from San Diego?"

"Yep."

"They might've passed you on the road. Too bad."

"Venus, the master, Miss Vidal—you expect any of them back soon?"

Katherine's head jerked as if an invisible hand had slapped her. "The master and Venus will be gone several weeks on a speaking tour." She folded her hands and whispered, "Emma has gone to the Almighty."

For all Hickey knew, to these folks the Almighty could be a guy with a turban who told fortunes in Reno. "Dead?"

She nodded. "In an avalanche, on the Holy Mountain. Last Saturday, the day of Cynthia's communion. The master and Emma had shown her to the temple at the center of the world, where she would seek audience with the Ancient Masters. Our master and our Emma got swept into a culvert when a snowpack broke free. Our master barely escaped."

Hickey conjured an image that fitted what he'd learned of Emma Vidal. Long-haired, attractive, generous. He leaned back, watched flecks of soot rise toward the ceiling, and grieved for a minute, while a scheme of answers came to him. Suppose the relapse of Henry Tucker had stirred in Cynthia the need to make peace with her mother, for whom she decided to join the *Nezahs*. She would've returned to San Diego in a week like she'd promised Clyde, except for the avalanche. In grief, she could've failed to call McGraw or Rudy's. The picture and note—suppose she'd drawn and written them herself. Maybe they were scenes from a nightmare of hers. She might've brought the gun, a small one that could be concealed, because she worried they'd leave her alone on the mountain, and she wanted the gun to scare off wolves. All that could be, Hickey thought but didn't believe.

"Cynthia and Emma Vidal, they were close?"

"Like mother and daughter."

Hickey nodded. "Venus mind that?"

"Oh, I think not. Venus is much more than just a mother. Do you know her?"

"Nope."

"You'd love her. She's everything female. Patience, endurance, charity, serenity."

"Cynthia take it hard? The avalanche?"

Katherine's lips parted, then shut several times, and her eyes flicked around while, Hickey figured, she sorted through the truth, deciding which parts to tell. "We held the burial on Monday. Cynthia became hysterical. She had to be restrained and finally . . . sedated. After a few days, though, by yesterday morning, she seemed to have accepted the loss."

"Drugged, you say?"

"Sedated."

"There's a doctor here, or did you call one in?"

Katherine's eyes furled as if he'd made her a rude proposal.

"I'd like to have a word with the doctor," Hickey said. "About Cynthia."

"The master is our doctor. He practiced medicine in India. If you wish to try and reach him by phone, I can give you their itinerary."

"Yeah," Hickey said. "Please."

She went to the bookshelves, thumbed through a stack of papers, then noticed the cider boiling. She poured them each a cup, delivered them to the table, got paper, pencil, and notepad from the bookcase, and sat next to Hickey.

He stirred, sipped, and watched while she copied the itinerary and handed it to him. "The master, would he be the guy a fellow in town called the nigra?"

The cherry but haggard smile she'd worn at first reappeared. "Yes. They wouldn't know the difference. The master is half Indian, half British."

"He's got a name?"

"Pravinshandra Chapman. What else did the townies have to say about us?"

"That you're a bunch of loons."

"Did you believe them?"

"I took their opinion under advisement."

"Would you like to know about our beliefs?"

"Make it quick," Hickey said. "A long time ago I got weaned off religion. A kind of Theosophist, is that what you are?"

"Do you know the teachings of Madame Blavatsky?"

"As much as I care to. No offense. I like you, so far, and you can believe the universe is a grapefruit, it's all the same to me. I've got a phobia, is all, like some people can't abide spiders. One thing, though. The townies say you folk believe there are goblins in the mountain. That right?"

She grinned, finished her cider, put the mug down, and clapped her hands. "Goblins, they said? Oh my. No, you see, we believe there are spirits everywhere. The ether is composed of spirit beings. We can go no place, imagine no place, where we wouldn't be surrounded, and inhabited, by spirit beings. I'm sure there are spirits inside the mountain. That there are creatures of the flesh, immortals, inside the mountain, is Indian lore."

As she concluded, another young woman entered, a stringy-haired blonde in men's overalls and a logger's jacket, looking flushed and sweaty as if she'd just escaped from a Turkish bath, wearing gardener's gloves. Hickey didn't notice her belly until she leaned her arm on Katherine's shoulder and he saw her in profile. Katherine introduced her as Rosemary.

"Come summer," Hickey said, "you ladies are gonna need a big pile of diapers."

Rosemary chuckled. "Yes sir. Four of us are due this winter or spring."

"Coincidence?"

"Well, each of us came here soon after they sent our husbands overseas, if that's what you mean. It's a safe place to raise our babies for the duration, isn't it?" She wiped her brow, pardoned herself, and trudged to a mattress, flopped onto her back and lay cradling her belly. Katherine gave Hickey a weary smile of dismissal.

As she walked him to his car, he looked around, spotted the

69

outlines of two people in the hothouse. Out of eight residents, at least, only two had been curious enough to approach him. Reclusive or afraid? he wondered. He scanned the place one time, looking for insights. All he noticed were three smoking chimneys and a little boy who dashed across the compound and fell smack on his face in the snow.

Hickey skidded his Chevy down the mountain, asking himself whether to leave for home that evening or do what his nature advised: stick around, snoop a little more into the death of Emma Vidal, maybe uncover some dirt about these *Nezahs*. If this master or Venus were, say, usurping the bank accounts of their followers and using the money to buy up Dunsmuir, or taking in unwed pregnant gals and peddling the babies—in Hickey's eyes, a religious charlatan might pull any wicked ruse—he could pass the evidence to Fay Giles, who'd use it to hang them.

But Cynthia'd returned to San Diego. Where Hickey had a daughter with the blues, a restless wife, a business to run. If he left the Cuban on his own too long, Rudy's kitchen might be sporting craps tables and roulette wheels, like the Havana casino where Castillo'd learned his trade.

A phone call would tell him if the girl had returned safely. Once that got settled, it was best to presume what he'd supposed earlier—Cynthia had come up here to make peace with her mama, get religion, shoot wolves.

Otherwise, he might ask himself, if somebody who doesn't normally pack a gun buys one, loads it, then goes on a sudden trip—if at her destination, somebody dies, might one and one equal a murder?

SEVEN

♪ ♪ ♪

ONCE HE GOT AWAY FROM THE BLACK FOREST LODGE AND MADE up his mind to go home, when he put aside the puzzles—about the Tuckers, the Bitch, the death of Emma Vidal, why Venus and the *Nezahs* would scheme to buy up Dunsmuir—he realized the more and quicker miles he crammed between Tom Hickey and a gang of believers, the better. Leaving the Black Forest, he felt as if he'd scurried out of a hole in which he'd got infested by parasites.

The curious part of him wanted to gab with Fay Giles, ask if she'd heard about the avalanche, get her a little riled about the *Nezahs,* buy her a drink or two, and see what spilled out of her delicate mouth. The remainder of him, weary and apprehensive, was relieved to find her gone, the office locked. He slipped a ten into the key drop, packed his things, and left the motel.

Sue Lynn and the tattooed cook still worked The Outpost. Friday night, the place was jammed with females, kids, and men old enough to escape the military, a few boys probably exempted as farm workers. Everybody except Sue Lynn wore a hat. Hickey took his off.

While he was waiting for a spot at the counter, he bartered with the cook, finally gave him three dollars to use the phone. Violet Weiss answered, chatted a minute, then got Leo out of his bath.

"Catch any wild geese, Tom?"

"Meaning she's back in town."

"Yep. Now, what was the cause of you sending me to Laurel Tucker? Some lousy joke?"

"Why's that?"

"The dame's a hellhound. The captain and me, we walk up to her door figuring to use the warrant, bust in, and snoop around. But there she is, glaring like a banshee. I tell her we're looking for Cynthia. The lingo she used to say 'get lost' polluted my ears. Now, Thrapp, being a cop, takes offense and waves the warrant around. She attacks us, breathing fire, swinging with both claws. Thrapp and I scamper out of there. He's ready to call in reinforcements, but I convince him we consult you first."

Hickey sent his partner back to the tub, chuckled with relief as he walked to the stool that had opened at the counter. He sat down and lit his pipe. When Sue Lynn appeared, he ordered chicken fried steak and a glass of their hardest liquor. She gave him a Schlitz and a water glass half full of bourbon whose label he didn't want to see.

After Sue Lynn plopped ice cream onto three slabs of apple pie and delivered them to a bearded fellow who was picking his teeth, she returned to Hickey, leaned close, face in her hands, elbows on the counter, and let him tell her what he'd seen at the Black Forest Lodge. All he admitted seeing up close was two pregnant women, nice enough, who believed in a screwy religion that imagined spirits—not goblins—lived inside Mount Shasta, and who claimed they both had husbands gone to war.

"Shoo, everybody gets pregnant says that."

She whisked up his glass and went to fetch him more bourbon. Hickey took a swallow, sighed gratefully. "Say, the ladies told me about an avalanche on Mount Shasta, last Saturday."

Sue Lynn pursed her lips and frowned. "I ain't heard about no avalanche this winter."

"Hmmm."

"They tell you what Netsock means?"

"It's one of the *Sefirot* on the Tree of Life."

"I'll be darned. What kind of tree's that?"

"Looks something like a mulberry."

The cook whistled, she served Hickey's dinner, then a couple tables emptied and refilled. Still busy when Hickey walked out, Sue Lynn blew him a kiss and stood forlornly watching him leave.

A sheriff's car was parked in front of a log building across the street, a hundred yards up the hill. Hickey would've gone there, asked the sheriff about the avalanche, except he didn't care to arouse any suspicions that might lead to incriminating Cynthia Moon. Not yet.

As he drove into the Trinity Alps, he wished he'd remembered to buy chains. The sky was black and jagged as a field of lava stones. Each time he rounded a turn he got shaken by wind or a snow flurry. He gripped the wheel tight and kept reviewing lines he remembered from Cynthia's book, wondering if Miss V and the Bitch could be the same person, Emma Vidal—if she'd clobbered Henry Tucker with a Remington typewriter, maybe delivered the final insult when she returned his ring, and in payment got a bullet in the head.

His nerves began to thaw and his mind to light on more pleasant topics as soon as he'd crossed the summit, out of the shadow of the Holy Mountain.

Near Stockton, he found a hot bath and a lumpy bed in a highway motor court. Thick fog poured through the window Hickey'd left open because he couldn't sleep in a stuffy room. The wall heater switch didn't work. He curled up under three blankets and his overcoat.

Feeling small and endangered, he remembered long ago. When he lay curled like this on a four-poster bed. A door clicked open and a shadow entered, wearing a black dress and veil. Its arms

were out, feeling its way. Hickey shivered, rolled over, pressed his
face and belly into the mattress.

"Tom?"

He squeezed his arms tighter to his sides and pinched his
mouth and eyes closed. The creature knelt and lifted the covers
off him. Its cold bony hands started kneading his shoulders. One,
then the other tracked down his spine and veered out to his waist.
Fingers, splayed like the legs of a spider, crawled over his hips,
down his thighs to his feet, then crossed over and started up his
legs on the inside. Hickey's guts boiled. He socked the bed and
cussed, rolled and tossed until the room began spinning and
whirlpooled him down into sleep.

Almost noon, the room air was still icy. Another hot bath sounded
fine, but it was either that or breakfast, or risk not making San
Diego in time to catch Cynthia at Rudy's that night. He dressed
and shaved, crossed the parking lot to the Blue Ribbon truck stop,
a converted barn. He got steak and cornflakes and filled his
thermos.

Highway 99 was slow, forty-five mph tops, and he had to stay
alert to go that fast, with cars backed up at traffic signals appearing like spooks out of the fog and northbound produce trucks
squeezing the white line, littering the highway with Imperial Valley tomatoes, lettuce, alfalfa. He'd crossed the Merced River
before the fog lifted, freeing him to drive on instinct and ponder
things, to confront monsters the nightmare had loosed, ones he
should've killed twenty-five years ago.

He saw his mother in a chair stitching him a pair of trousers.
All day she'd perch there, straight and prim in a flowery dress, her
knees together, both feet on the floor. She worked as a seamstress
for the actress Mary Pickford. Every pattern she cut and sewed
by hand.

When Hickey came home from school, sandlot baseball or
shining shoes on Hollywood Boulevard, a cookie or bowl of
strawberries from her garden would be waiting. First, though, he
was required to kiss her forehead or suffer through her lecture

about ingratitude being abhorrent to God. Then she made him sit beside her while she stroked his hair with her bony fingers and read to him. "There is no life, truth, intelligence, nor substance in matter. All is infinite Mind and its infinite manifestation, for God is All-in-All."

Maybe he'd could've understood, even believed, if she'd gotten her wretched hand off him and if she hadn't worn a look that enraged him, the one declaring that he was a dunce, while she knew everything.

By his ninth year, at nights he'd lie dreaming of the north, of forests where she couldn't find him, where he could fish, carve a bow and arrow, or wash dishes or shine boots in a logging camp. Every week he saved a couple dollars, buried them in a can under a rock up the hill from their cottage on Gramercy Place. He bought a heavy woolen coat for three dollars from a rich kid, two flannel blankets from a rummage sale. He carved the knots off a long manzanita branch for a walking stick, bindle staff, and club to whack robbers.

A couple months before his tenth birthday, the date he'd settled upon to run away, he started worrying about Florence. She was three years younger. He couldn't leave her alone with the saint. He pictured Florence and himself huddled over campfires beside wild-eyed hoboes with hooks where their hands used to be. He heard Florence whimpering. What if she starved or got mauled by a bear? Finally he decided not to run. In that moment, his fear of their mother was transformed into hatred—once he understood she'd backed him into a corner. It was fight, or get chewed up and swallowed.

The next year, when he started growing hair all over, when his voice began to squawk and girls suddenly appeared more precious than exasperating, he bought a hasp and padlock for the bathroom door, borrowed tools from a neighbor. When she got home and found him locked in there, she rattled the door and yelled. He told her to scram. Faintheartedly, she called him a devil, as he lay there cupping his groin in both hands, smiling. Never again would she bathe him or stand watching him on the toilet, waiting to scrub him raw, to make him clean as God demanded.

For seven hours through the San Joaquin Valley, the litanies of Christian Science pulsed through his brain like the lyrics to inane, catchy songs.

> *Spirit is immortal Truth;*
> *matter is mortal error.*
> *Spirit is the real and eternal;*
> *matter is the unreal and temporal.*
> *Spirit is God,*
> *and man is His image and likeness.*
> *Therefore man is not material;*
> *he is spiritual.*

At times he went goosefleshed and tasted bile, from remembering Mom's hands as they bathed, massaged, or petted him. Once he socked the dashboard and gashed a knuckle, recalling how many times she'd caught him with an erection and pinched it to death with her fingernails.

He hadn't seen the saint since 1933 when he quit the LAPD and moved to San Diego. In ten years they'd only spoken a few stiff minutes on the phone around Christmas. The last two summers, Florence had invited him to send Elizabeth to stay a week with her and their mother and Florence's husband Bob, a gentle man who owned a factory that made airplane propellers. Florence offered to take Elizabeth shopping at Bullock's in Long Beach, buy her a new wardrobe in the latest Hollywood styles, which the old woman could tailor to fit perfectly.

"Yeah," Hickey said, "she can smooth the material over Elizabeth's breasts and hips, down her legs, cooing about how lovely she is, like she used to do with Mary Pickford."

"Tom, she's seventy-four. She's not the same."

"Hey, Flo, you put Mother in the nuthouse where she belongs, then I'll send Elizabeth."

The last few miles before Griffith Park, he thought about

76

taking Glendale to Hollywood Boulevard, going west, then right on Highland up to Florence's place, seeing for himself if the saint had truly gotten as frail and mild as his sister claimed. If he could forgive her, it would please Elizabeth, and Florence. Even Madeline would be proud of him.

The trouble was, the old woman would never understand what she'd done to him. She'd still believe she'd raised him to holiness. No question she blamed only him, his father, and the devil for his being a spiteful, negligent son. Nobody that pure, who conversed with God daily, a practitioner and healer who lived for good works and righteousness, had to blame herself for anything.

Unless she begged his forgiveness, which she'd never do, there was only one way to settle the account. And Hickey preferred not to kill his mother.

EIGHT

EVEN AFTER DARK HICKEY MADE GOOD TIME UNTIL HE GOT STUCK behind a navy convoy. It was nearly eleven when he caught a side street he knew through Anaheim, sneaked around the convoy and back onto 101, and yanked the throttle, still hoping to make Rudy's in time to catch the girl's last set.

There were big guns blasting in the dark hills of Camp Pendleton, a trio of ships, two destroyers and a carrier, heading south about a mile off the coast at Cardiff-by-the-Sea. Tanks prowled the sea cliffs of Camp Callan, north of La Jolla, and the rattle and pop of machine gun and rifle fire carried toward him on an onshore breeze.

The palms along Harbor Drive rustled and swayed. The flying silver fish fluttered and bounced like party balloons. Hickey turned up Broadway. Saturday night, 12:35, around the arcades, tattoo parlors, Greyhound depot, and YMCA, soldiers and marines lounged and strolled beside sailors from England, Russia, Brazil. A visitor from an earlier century might've thought every enlisted man in creation had showed up tonight on lower Broadway. Most of them whistled and catcalled at the few young women who strutted by, risking whatever virtue they had left. Across from the Pickwick Hotel and Greyhound depot, a drunken ensign steadied himself with his right arm wrapped around a lamp post, while his left hand cupped the bottom of every female who passed.

Hickey made a left on Fourth Street, coasted past three stop signs, wheeled into the lot behind Rudy's. He dug into his briefcase for the drawing he'd found in Cynthia's room, rolled and stuck it into his pocket, then got out and passed Skeeter the keys to his car.

"It's swell we got Miss Moon back, boss," the lot boy said. "Guys sure tip big after they watch her. When Martini's singing, folks stiff me, like they're blaming me he's a bum."

As Hickey stepped into the kitchen, LeDuc the chef and a waiter named Jaime rushed him, chattering complaints. Hickey raised his hands for peace and slipped around them. It had been twelve days since he'd heard Cynthia, and he didn't want to miss a song.

He stood just outside the kitchen door and watched. Cynthia gripped the microphone with one bare hand, the other wearing a glove that matched her red silky gown, low cut, hemmed at the calves, slit on her right side to six inches up from the knee. The skin of her upper chest and arms looked whiter than ever. Her hair was down, curled into medium waves and flipped toward her left side so it covered part of that eye and cheek. On the right ear, she wore a dangling piece of turquoise. Above the ear, she had an orchid pinned into her hair. In red pump heels, she towered above Clyde, who stood close by, holding his baton still, watching the girl, her head cocked back a little, making her neck appear especially long and vulnerable, as if she were offering it to be kissed or chopped off, whatever you pleased. She sang, "I'll Never Smile Again," or laugh again, and hopelessly asked what good it would do. Her foot didn't tap, her leg didn't bounce or shimmy, both arms, as she let her hands fall away from the microphone,

79

hung still at her sides. Her lips hardly moved. She glanced around the room with eyes dull and dry as sandstone. So mournful that the audience looked stunned, as if the girl had announced her decision to slit her throat. A waiter had stopped in passage holding a tray. He drew a sleeve across his eyes so tears wouldn't plop into the soup. Hickey wondered if she were singing to the ghost of Emma Vidal. She bowed slightly as the drum rolled and clarinet riffed a fade.

After the hush, a few people sighed, others whistled, yelped. Most of them bashed their hands together as though trying to knock them off.

Phil the maître d' materialized beside Hickey. A tall, sleek, blond young fellow who'd lost both kneecaps when he crashed a race car. The maroon dinner jacket looked as comfortable as if invented for him. "Good trip, boss?"

Hickey nodded. "How'd things go?"

"A few complaints, you know, cold soup, a suspicious particle in the salad. Only thing I oughta bother you with—Louie orders up a bloody rare prime rib, so LeDuc's gotta hack into a new roast when he's still working on the old one. He's chopping and griping away, slices his finger. 'Bastard wants bloody rare,' he says, 'I'll give him bloody rare.' Wipes his damn finger on the meat and sends it out."

Hickey scowled, patted Phil on the shoulder, made a mental note to fire the savage as soon as he found a better chef, meanwhile to threaten the guy. He pardoned his way through a crowd of folks waiting for tables. Just inside the door, Paul Castillo leaned against the hatcheck counter whispering something to the cigarette girl. When he saw Hickey, the hint of a smirk crooked his lips. He lay his arm across Hickey's shoulders. "Glad you can make it back, pal. It's a killer of a drive for nothing."

Castillo never missed a shot at proving himself smarter than you. One of those guys whose nerves flutter and spook him into action anytime he's less than top dog.

Though Hickey would've preferred to pâté the man's nose, he only nodded, trying his damnedest to keep the peace between them, knowing that once they began to spar, Castillo wouldn't stop for the bell, he'd go for the knockout. Because that was his style, and out of jealousy that Hickey had Madeline. If they got to quarreling, Hickey'd use impolite adjectives—greedy, crooked, phony—and probably a few unfriendly nouns. Castillo would escalate the language, find himself on the floor. Maybe jump up waving a gun. No matter how the skirmish got resolved, the golden goose would remain stewed. Hickey and family would be eating meat loaf once again, and to Madeline he'd once again be a loser.

"Good house," Hickey said. "I gotta get some bread and water."

Instead of taking his dinner in the office as usual, he grabbed the only unspoken-for stool, carried it to the end of the bar, cleared himself a spot between the martini olives and the cherries. He told Hwang, the bartender, to rustle him up a T-bone, potatoes, carrots, and a splash of Dewar's.

Cynthia had transformed. Loose and vivacious, she invited everybody to Niagara, Saint Paul, Bermuda, any good place to get away from it all.

Hickey's scotch arrived. He gulped half of it, started on the next gulp, and realized he had one of those thirsts it feels like you can quench with booze, a fight, mostly any wild pleasure, but you can't even touch it. All you can do is wait it out. He put down the glass, got out his briar and Walter Raleigh, watched the stage, and tried to observe any new gesture of Cynthia's, any change in her manner or voice. When his food arrived, he devoured the steak. If he hadn't minded taking his eyes off the girl, he would've gone into the office and gnawed morsels off the bone.

Cynthia's encore was "Ain't Misbehavin'." She let the final note carry long and high, then cut it off as if she'd suddenly gone mute, and without waiting to revel in the applause as usual, she swept off the stage and down the aisle to the bar, her eyes on Hickey all the way. She stopped a foot in front of him, hands clasped on her waist. Her cheeks were flushed, eyes damp and glinting.

"They love me," she said breathlessly. "They've never seen anybody like me."

"Yeah. Who has?" Hickey stood, took one of her hands. The skin felt at least a hundred degrees. He showed her around the bar to a quieter nook by the office. The rolled manila envelope started to fall from his coat pocket. He rolled it tighter and shoved it back in. "Let's go someplace and talk."

"Sure, get away from this joint," she said tensely. "Around here I feel like the Maharani. Half the men want me to marry them and the others want to pounce on me. You'd think I was Susan Hayward."

He gave the compliment she'd fished for, then stepped into his office and brought back her coat, a long fleecy number in eggshell white, and helped her into it. From a pocket she produced a second red glove, stretched it over her fingers and up her arm, watching all her motions carefully as though glad for the excuse to avoid his eyes. She hadn't worn a hat because it would've crushed the orchid.

They left Rudy's the back way, circled the block, and walked down Fifth, Cynthia keeping slightly in the lead though she held his arm. Twice or so every minute she looked back furtively. A cold, damp wind whooshed around them. It gusted hard straight up Broadway. Black clouds had massed low over the harbor. A few large raindrops splashed down, and crowds at the bus and trolley stops jogged for cover or hoisted umbrellas.

Cynthia whisked Hickey along faster, a block west and across Market Street to the part of town where charred buildings didn't soon get rebuilt and music from rival Negro clubs clashed on the sidewalks. Dodging an occasional hooker, they strode the three blocks down to the Horton Grand Hotel, a place that must've been elegant about the year Hickey was born, with its cut-glass windows, Persian carpets, chandeliers, and doilies on every table in the cocktail lounge. Hickey tossed the doilies from their table onto a nearby Grand Rapids chair. He ordered scotch for himself, ginger ale for the girl, who sat stiffly wearing a petulant scowl, already defending herself against the questions she anticipated Hickey'd ask.

"Where you been?"

"You should know. You broke in to my room, then followed me five hundred goddamned miles."

"Yep. And I learned a couple things. You're going to tell me more."

"The hell I am." She turned toward the lobby and pressed the heels of her red gloved hands to her eyes. After a minute she dropped the hands, slowly peeled off the gloves, folded and crammed them into the pocket of the coat hanging over the back of her chair. She reached out for Hickey's hands. "Sorry. I don't like to swear. See, I didn't want you to know about my family. My mother the swami's whore. My daddy . . ." Her voice choked and faded.

"Hey, you're not the only one with creeps in the family."

She made a hiss with her tongue. "Go on, tell me about yours."

"First, outta curiosity, what were you doing with the gun?"

She tried doeing her eyes their widest, but the innocent look wouldn't hold. Her lips curled as if to spit and she slapped a hand onto the table. "I rode the bus, nitwit. You know what I do to men."

Hickey wagged his head, figuring the more riled she got, the more likely she'd come clean.

"What do you think I had it for, you old crook? See, Pop, I know Rudy's is a front for the mob and that you stink as much as anybody."

At three tables away, the navy high brass and their girls Hickey'd seen working the Playroom, the lovey couple, and four dowagers had turned to listen and stare.

"Swell. We're gonna talk about that anytime you please. After you tell me where you went and why." Hickey sipped his drink and gazed around until the eavesdroppers turned back to gabbing. He leaned over the table close to Cynthia. "You shoot Emma Vidal?"

"Oh God, you're a fool," Cynthia yelled. She lifted her glass as if to throw it, then lowered it slowly, set it on the table, and raised a finger to one of her weepy eyes. "I can't make it with her gone," she blubbered. "She was the only person who cared about Daddy and me. The only one who could've saved us."

"Saved you from who?"

"It doesn't matter anymore. Daddy's dead and so am I." As if to prove her claim, she looked up with dry, vacant eyes and a face so calm it spooked him.

Maybe he could shock her back to life. He reached to his pocket for the manila envelope. He'd only gotten the drawing halfway out of the envelope when she recognized it. She sprang to her feet, knocking over the chair, grabbed the drawing, and bolted for the door.

Hickey tripped over his own chair and hers. By the time he reached the sidewalk, she was turning the corner onto Island. Raindrops the size of hailstones pelted the street. As he ran, he noticed one of Cynthia's red shoes in the gutter. He slid around the corner onto Island and spotted her half a block ahead, running in her stockinged feet, the slit on her tight dress torn almost to her hips so her long legs could stride freely.

He sprinted, weaving like a halfback to dodge pedestrians. They raced and skidded, down and across Island, up Third, across Market, and around two more corners. As he slid onto G Street—having gotten close enough to hear her feet slapping over the noise of wandering crowds and motors—he slammed into a troop of sailors and marines milling in front of the Hollywood Burlesque. About ten feet ahead, Cynthia was busy slapping a guy. Hickey lowered his shoulder and plowed through, bellowing. The instant Cynthia had tugged her arm free from the grip of the man she'd belted, Hickey reached her and snatched the envelope. In one motion, he rolled and stuck it under his belt, then grabbed Cynthia's wrist.

"Get off me! Get him off," she screamed, as if he were a tarantula.

Hickey got broadsided, then a big arm choked him. His knees started buckling. He only saw a blur of arms and legs firing at him,

84

until a wild kick he threw found its mark and one sailor lurched away howling. The others, startled, backstepped to regroup, which gave Hickey the instant he needed to catch his balance. Backing away, he growled, "Come on, boys. A couple more of you this time. See if you can wake me up."

Several voices hollered for cops. Somebody touched his sleeve, then gripped his arm as if they had a date to go strolling. Melinda, a hooker he knew. She gave him a cheery wink. "You like redheads, Tom, I'm yours."

Hickey wheeled a half circle and spotted the girl, running, tailed by a couple sailors. They disappeared around the corner of Second and G while Melinda snuggled against him. He gave her a peck on the cheek, broke off, and walked away, secured the envelope under his belt. His fury transforming to a knockout headache, stiff, sore, drenched, and worried about the girl, he trudged back through the gentler rain toward the Horton Grand, to pay the tab and retrieve Cynthia's white coat.

NINE

♪ ♪ ♪

On Sunday morning Hickey woke to the buzz, whoosh, and splash of the first speedboat out on the bay. A kid ran past his window, trying to launch a kite.

Hickey brushed his teeth, threw on trousers, a shirt, shoes, and a baseball cap so he wouldn't have to bother with his hair, and walked to the bakery, a half mile around the bay and across Mission Boulevard. He bought a pound of strawberry Danish and a mug of coffee, which he drank on the seawall, watching the breakers crash and roll and inspecting the tent city.

San Diego, since Pearl Harbor, had fabricated twice as many jobs as homes. So a dozen camp towns had risen, where a factory worker could set up his family the day they arrived from Indianola, Dubuque, or Tulsa. Most of the tents were new and respectable. Window flaps, state flags atop the center posts, and laundry batted in the offshore breeze.

The place looked to have doubled its size in the past couple weeks since Hickey'd found the time to walk here. Before Rudy's, he and Elizabeth, sometimes Madeline, used to roam Mission Beach three or four evenings each week. Walking ranked fifth, behind driving, in Hickey's hierarchy of pleasure.

He took off his shoes, stuffed the socks in them, bow-tied the laces, and slung them over his shoulder, then sauntered along the shoreline, drawing lines in the damp sand with his toes and heels. Pencil-beaked cormorants zipped across the sky as if shot out of crossbows. Pelicans skimmed the foamy waves as though scratching their bellies. The rumble and slap of the water slowed Hickey's heartbeat and quieted his brain.

On the way home he stopped at Caruso's Market for a quart of fresh orange juice, and he thought about Cynthia. Instinctively, he didn't believe she'd killed Emma Vidal. But his instinct had proved wrong a few thousand times. She might've killed Emma or somebody else. If the townies of Dunsmuir hadn't learned about the avalanche or the funeral, he could deduce no reason they might not be ignorant of any tragedy or crime among the *Nezahs*. Nor, Hickey thought, was there reason to presume that Katherine had told the truth. Emma Vidal might still be alive. For all he knew, Katherine might be Emma with a haircut.

Elizabeth helped her dad scramble eggs, char bacon, and deliver breakfast in bed to Madeline, along with a poinsettia Hickey'd cut and laid on the tray.

He and Madeline collaborated on plans for the afternoon, then he and Elizabeth took the rowboat out. They labored over rough water, against the crisp breeze, the boat lumbering over the swells and splatting into the troughs as if it were a washtub. The fog burnt off suddenly. The sun looked small and dusty white. They rowed to Crown Point, beached the boat, and lay on the bayside grass. Elizabeth gabbed about a Point Loma boy named Tony she'd met at a party, whose family owned tuna clippers. Elizabeth was mad because her La Jolla friends snubbed the boy and his pal. Her La Jolla gang didn't approve of the Portuguese.

Hickey could've given plenty advice, if he'd sensed she wanted any. She didn't. He patted her arm, kissed the top of her head. They rowed across the bay to Quivera Basin. When Hickey's arms and legs started to feel like they used to in the fourth quarter, he and Elizabeth drifted awhile and he told her about the trip to Mount Shasta. He said it looked like somebody'd gotten buried by an avalanche. Elizabeth frowned and, as if she took the news personally, grabbed a rusty fishing weight and slung it into the bay.

"Funny thing is," Hickey said, "Dunsmuir's one of these towns where everybody knows everybody else's shoe size, but the gal I talked to, a waitress who's as much of a gossip as Eva, hadn't heard about any avalanche."

"Whatta you think that means?"

"Means I should've stuck around a couple more days. But I missed my girls."

Elizabeth smiled naughtily. "Which ones?"

Rather than take that remark as a line his daughter got from Madeline, he chose to splash her and grin. They rowed back along the west shore.

Madeline had fixed a lunch for the road and packed their jackets, mittens, snow caps, and toboggan in the car. They caught U.S. 80, a two-lane which followed the trickling San Diego River through Mission Valley, past the gravel pit, the dairy farm, the orphanage at Mission de Alcala. They passed the college, crossed the mesa. In El Cajon, a valley of groves and ranches, they cut north on Highway 67, through Lakeside and up the grade through the Indian reservation, along the narrow cliffside roads past huge mounds of boulders above which hawks and buzzards glided. They ate lunch in Ramona, on a park bench under oak trees. Hickey pushed both his girls on the swings. After Ramona the air started chilling. They rolled up the windows and drove into the pine forest singing dopey songs like one about three liddle fiddies fwimming.

Julian's orchards were packed in snow. Sunshine glistened off the white-capped roofs of gold rush–vintage houses. The only cleared road was the main one through town. Kids sledded down the steep side streets, braked by crashing into barricades. Hickey and family stopped at the café for apple pie and cocoa, then drove a couple miles farther to the meadow they tramped across to get to the toboggan run. For a couple hours they sped down the hill, alone or in tandem, greeted each other's arrival at the bottom with snowballs, chased and tackled each other, hiked up beyond the toboggan run to the crest of the hill because Elizabeth wanted to see the view.

All day Madeline only got off one lousy crack. While Elizabeth trudged up the hill for her last run, Madeline took off her scarf, flicked away snow that had gotten under her collar. As if Hickey had crammed the snow down her shirt, she turned and gave him a wicked smile.

"Did you remember to cancel our reservations at the Beverly Wilshire?"

"Naw," Hickey said. "The social calendar's your job."

"It's a tough job, Tom, scheduling the one night a month you dedicate to me."

"You can handle it." He watched her stoop to pack a snowball. He thought he'd get it in the face, but she heaved it at the sky instead.

On the drive home, Elizabeth bundled herself into a quilt and fell asleep in back. Hickey and Madeline sat quiet and moody. The sky kept brightening with new stars, as if heaven were shooting flares in advance of a battle. The radio picked up nothing in the mountains. Hickey didn't like the silence, but he wasn't going to break it by acting pleasant and phony, and he didn't know how to pierce Madeline's armor anymore. It seemed she'd collected a stone for every time over the years he'd wounded her pride or let her down, and now whenever he stepped into range she chucked one at him. He tried to shoo her out of his mind by thinking about Cynthia Moon.

Tonight he'd ask the girl, suppose Emma Vidal got murdered—what were the chances that Cynthia'd be next? With luck, there'd be enough truth in the notion to frighten her into talking. If that didn't work, he'd grill her until he knew, at least got an idea, about who and where was this person she called the Bitch.

Madeline gazed straight ahead as stiffly as if her neck were in a brace. She was scratching her lips with her teeth, obviously pondering things. Hickey wondered how they could ride so long without speaking, how too many nights they could sleep so close without touching. The silence never got comfortable. But to speak or touch was more dangerous. One wrong move you get stabbed in the heart.

In the foothills Hickey tried the radio again. He picked up "Dreamland" from L.A. Harry James's Orchestra live from the Rendezvous in Balboa. Hickey sat waiting for Madeline to crack, "Gee, Tom, we could've been there."

She fooled him, didn't even chuckle snidely. When Helen Forest crooned, "I've Heard That Song Before," Madeline sang along. Madeline was better. So much that Hickey's eyes misted, a rare occasion. It had been months since Madeline sang for him.

They got home before ten. Elizabeth went straight to bed. Hickey kissed her and switched the light out.

He made himself two nightcaps while Madeline used the bathroom. He was hoping she'd wear the same nightgown as last night. When she stepped into the bedroom, in pajamas, and found him sitting on the floor beside the bed holding a drink out for her, her eyes roamed for a moment, then she yawned. Hickey got the message.

Midnight at Rudy's, the orchestra was on break. Hickey shook a few hands, listened to Daisy, a bleached chatterbox cocktail girl, complain because the chef goosed her. Hickey had started toward the kitchen to bawl out the chef—thinking how LeDuc, a pudgy character who was about as French as Pancho Villa, might've taken the name figuring it gave him a license to paw females—when he spotted Cynthia. In the dimmest corner, she sat at a cramped table across from a guy Hickey'd known professionally in L.A.

Charlie Schwartz. An old-time thug who'd risen from carpenter to union rep and upward. Charlie and his fat twin, Frank, used to bodyguard a bookie and whiskey runner, Arnold Rimmer. A few years ago, when Rimmer moved to Alcatraz, the Schwartz brothers headed south, muscled the takeover of a construction company. They owned about fifty apartment buildings around North Park and a couple mansions in Kensington.

Hickey walked over, pulled a chair up to the table, straddled it backwards, lay his hands flat on the table, and drilled his eyes into Schwartz's forehead.

"So, Charles, should I clarify what I meant the last time, when I told you to beat it?"

Schwartz took a puff off his cigar and popped a few smoke rings. Lean, yellowish pale, balding in the middle, with a tuft of greasy black hair at the crest of his forehead. Dressed in silk, a maroon shirt with yellow tie, a woolen zoot coat, alligator shoes. His voice was thin and glossy. "Yeah, it didn't make sense, so I talked to Paul. He says you got a spike up your ass. When I heard your songbird was back, just couldn't miss her."

"You didn't. Now scram, Charlie, unless you prefer I should walk you back to the dishwater and wash your mouth."

Schwartz puffed once on his cigar, stubbed it out, and rose; he smiled and tipped a hat he wasn't wearing to Cynthia. "Excuse me, dear. Rude fellas give me hives." He strolled toward the rest room.

Hickey took Schwartz's chair, across from the girl. There was red in the corners of her eyes, like tiny blotches of lipstick. Her lips quivered furiously.

"Go squeeze a buck out of somebody, old man."

"You know Charlie's a gangster."

"Sure I do," she hissed. "I know almost everybody who counts in this town."

"They'll tell you he's gone legit. Don't buy it."

"I don't care." Her face began softening into a pout, as though a spell of fatigue had caught her.

"Maybe one of us ought to apologize about last night," Hickey said.

She dropped her gaze to his hands. In a minute she reached over and began petting his index finger with her own. There was a new ring on her next finger over, a silver one with a large stone the same emerald color as her eyes, only duller.

"Look, babe," he said while slowly withdrawing his hand, "I got a wife, and times on that front are rough these days. You know, the world's full of snitches and folks who get their jollies making trouble."

"Sure, Tom. I'm sorry. It's just . . . There are things . . . you can't imagine."

"What things?"

She pantomimed tossing the things away, over her shoulder. "I need a favor. You're the first person I'll ask," she said regally, as though bestowing nobility upon him.

"You didn't already ask Schwartz?"

"Jealous?"

"What you need?"

"Two thousand dollars."

Hickey rubbed his chin and stared, waiting for her to look up at him, but she kept gazing shyly at the fork and spoon.

"What's it for?"

"I can't tell you."

Hickey pondered a moment, then flagged a waiter, Julio, and called for scotch. The orchestra had started to gather on the bandstand. Hickey excused himself, got up and intercepted Clyde, asked him to let Martino thrill the folks with a couple tunes while he finished talking to Cynthia.

Without waiting for his drink, Hickey led Cynthia around the dance floor and through the bar to his office. On the way, most diners and drinkers had turned to watch the girl passing. A navy captain stood and lifted a hand in position to touch her shoulder. Cynthia's look deflected the hand.

The office Hickey and Castillo shared had once been a pantry. It was large enough for a rolltop desk, two straight-backed chairs, a hat rack. With Hickey and Cynthia in there, the space left over might've held a broom or mop handle. They both crossed their legs and sat with knees touching.

"Two thousand dollars," Hickey mused, "and you're not going

92

to say what for. Tell you what. I'll think about getting you the money as soon as you tell me—and make me believe it's the truth—why the trip to Mount Shasta, what that picture means. The one you wanted back so badly. Maybe a couple other things."

Cynthia bolted out of her chair. "The hell with you." She threw the door open, raged out, and slammed it. In a second she reappeared. "Listen, brother," she yelped loud enough to instruct the crowd at the bar, "every man in the club wants me, and they're all willing to pay. I only have to ask. I could get ten thousand, twenty thousand, more, couldn't I?"

Maybe she could, Hickey thought. Even if he didn't believe it, he wouldn't have told her. It wouldn't change her mind about anything, but it would break her heart.

"Couldn't I?" she demanded.

He nodded. She threw her hair back and ran off.

Hickey stayed in the office through most of that set, the last of the night, trying to think but getting distracted by the girl's voice, which carried into the tiny office and surrounded him. Her asking for money had distressed him fiercely. Things looked bad. The odds that she was in quicksand had doubled. Because Cynthia wasn't much fascinated by possessions. He couldn't see her buying a car, a mink coat, a huge diamond. According to her landlady and Clyde, she didn't have close friends who might be in a fix. Almost surely, he thought, the money had something to do with her family—maybe to grab more land in Dunsmuir or on Mount Shasta—and clearly, anything dealing with her family meant trouble.

Still, if he didn't lend her the money—he remembered the line from Cynthia's book, "I promised Daddy I'd stay a virgin until Saint Ophelia brings me the Man."

To watch or imagine the theft of innocence racked Hickey with fury. The girl's virginity didn't concern him. Only the scars that a tumble with somebody like Charlie Schwartz would etch into Cynthia's heart.

He needed to stall her until he ferreted out the truth. Tomorrow he'd go back to see Henry Tucker, push the old man harder. Or maybe Laurel would come clean.

When Hickey stepped out of the office, Cynthia was singing her encore that asked the people to dream about her. She finished in a strange tremolo he'd never heard out of her before, one that implied she was saying nighty-night for good. She took her bows, blew a kiss around the room, sauntered off the stage coolly as ever. As soon as her feet touched the floor, her strides doubled, to the coat check for her wrap, a red Mexican shawl. She turned toward the door and got waylaid. Hickey stood beside her, squeezed her limp, sweaty hand.

"We're in public, dear," she cooed sarcastically.

"Yeah," Hickey said. "Here's the deal. My cash is tied up in the club. Tomorrow I'm gonna talk to Castillo, see what I can get out of the business account. How's that?"

"Thanks, Tom." Her eyes darted around him as she leaned, kissed his cheek, coyly pulled her hand free, and glided outside. "Night night."

At the curb sat a white Chrysler limo Hickey didn't recognize. The driver, a lanky young black fellow in mechanic's clothes and a brown baseball cap, sprang from where he was leaning on the fender. He approached Cynthia and whispered, then he opened the rear door and guided her into the limo. She was alone there.

Hickey dashed through the club and out back to his Chevy. He skidded out of the parking lot on the Fourth Street side, raced up to Broadway and scanned both directions until he spotted the limo waiting at a light a couple blocks toward the harbor.

Past the Santa Fe depot, the limo turned north on Pacific Coast Highway. He stayed a block behind. A white beast like that couldn't disappear quickly on a night as star- and moonlit as this one. It cruised up the highway past Con Air, made a left on Barnett, into a traffic jam. There was a brawl at the main gate to the marine depot. Probably a gang of drunken recruits had jumped the guard. A shore patrol wagon came screeching to the rescue. The limo turned left on Rosecrans, headed alongside the Naval Training Center onto Point Loma. A couple miles down, it turned and sped to Catalina, where it jagged across and started up on Canon Street, then Point Loma Avenue past hillside cottages and the Moorish villas higher up, where the tuna barons lived, where Elizabeth would go for a party next weekend. The crest of the hill overlooked the seacoast. Tonight the Pacific looked flat black and crinkled.

The windward-side homes and cottages were slums compared to those that overlooked the harbor. The hillside appeared dry, mostly barren, except the one garden spot, on the cliff a mile south—the grounds of what used to be Otherworld, with its rows of giant palms, olive and mulberry groves, the mosque's bronze dome, the cliffside amphitheater.

Where Point Loma Avenue met Sunset Cliffs Boulevard, the limo cut south a hundred yards or so and rolled into a vista point. No other cars in the lot.

Hickey pulled to the curb a few blocks up the hill. He watched the chauffeur ease out, saunter around, and help Cynthia from the limo. She walked out of the parking lot and hoisted herself over the guardrail to stand on the very edge of the cliff and stare down into the waves that broke an instant before they battered the cliffside. The chauffeur had gone to his limo, which pulled out of the lot after a minute or so.

Watching the girl alone down there, it took all Hickey's will not to rush after her. It felt as if something evil like a ghost or big wind might heave her off the cliff. He watched the coast road both ways. No cars. Nobody at all. Cynthia paced along the trail, staring down. Five minutes passed.

A man came walking from the south. He wore a dark overcoat and hat. He got within a couple yards before Cynthia jerked around to face him. They were equally tall, given the man's hat, which he tipped and replaced. They didn't touch. Squared off, an arm's length apart, they talked for several minutes, until a taxi approached on the coast road from the north side. As if that were a signal, the man turned and strode off, back the way he'd come. The taxi pulled in to the lot. Before the cabby could get to her door, Cynthia opened it and climbed in.

Hickey let the cab go. The man walked the dirt shoulder, then crossed the road and got into a convertible roadster, top down, half hidden behind a stand of palm trees. Hickey let his car roll down the hill until the roadster, a Buick, pulled onto the coast road.

Hickey fired his engine and timed his descent to reach the intersection just after the roadster and file in behind it. But the roadster inched along, as though its driver were savoring the moonlight. If Hickey'd slowed any more, he figured it would give him away. He made the intersection first and stayed there, fingering his pen, a notepad on his lap, until the roadster crept by. The man had an arm sprawled across the seat as if a woman sat beside him. But he was alone. His sprawled arm rose, the hand dropped and came up with a pint flask. As he put it to his lips he must've caught sight of the Chevy. He turned his face that way, scowling at the Chevy as though it belonged to a traffic cop. When he saw that it didn't, he looked back at the road, took a long pull from the bottle, and cruised on toward Ocean Beach.

Hickey didn't write down the license number. He knew the man. So well that if the guy had sneered, Hickey might've rammed the Buick, plowed it into the sea. If he'd reacted quickly enough—instantly absorbed what that meeting told him about Cynthia Tucker—he might've rammed it anyway.

Donny Katoulis. Hickey'd known him since Donny was a kid, when he started busting heads for Arnold Rimmer. A year later, at seventeen, Donny killed an old Mexican fellow who'd welshed on his bets. He got arrested and walked. A gift to Rimmer from the DA, in appreciation. In 1929 the kid snuffed a pal of Hickey's, a waiter who used to play trombone with Les Butterfield. Everybody knew the shooter was Katoulis. Accuse him to his face, he wouldn't deny it. He walked. Insufficient evidence.

One night at a card game, a foursome of drunken cops drew lots to see who got to waste the punk. Tom Hickey won.

TEN

♩ ♪ ♪

HICKEY WASN'T SLEEPING ANYWAY. THE PAST FEW HOURS HE'D been lying on the hammock on his screened back porch. He watched the moon drop behind the fence of sailboat masts at Santa Clara Point across the bay. The water looked like a dark window. A wandering soul passed by, kicking up splashes and spray along the shoreline. All night, insomniacs or dreamers had walked the beach. Maybe the clarity of the moon and stars, after yesterday's storm, had gotten people thinking too much about heaven, or the crap you had to wade through on the way there.

Hickey rose and walked outside, in pajamas and bare feet, across the sand to his pier, a low one that ran only fifty feet into the bay. Just far enough so the ketch he hoped to buy someday wouldn't plant its keel too deeply when summer's low tides fringed the bay in mud flats. He sat on the end of the pier, his toes flicking the water, shoulders hunched against the chill, his neck hardened with the anger that had rippled through him ever since he'd seen Donny Katoulis.

Eleven years ago he might've iced the guy and earned a commendation, a pay raise, and drinks and cheers from every cop in L.A. If Hickey'd shot when he was supposed to, the way they'd planned, in the alley behind the Chi Chi Club, by now the punk would've been only a smudge in Hickey's memory, and no telling how many fewer people would've died over the past eleven years. Donny wasn't one of your cold-blooded thugs who mostly knocked off welshers and bad guys feuding with other bad guys. He was a gun strutting around. A rookie aiming to lead the league, make the hall of fame. Like John Wesley Hardin, a desperado Hickey'd read about, who blasted a fellow in a bunkhouse because he snored too loudly.

When the phone rang—Hickey assumed it belonged to a neighbor—he was recalling the last line in Cynthia's book: "Evil survives because good people don't have the heart to kill evil ones."

"Tom!"

The second time Madeline yelled, Hickey shouted, "Out here." He got up slowly and started for the house while Madeline stomped across the porch and out onto the sand in her nightgown, hair flying wild, eyes like roadside flares. She skidded to a halt a yard in front of him, far enough so she didn't have to crook her neck back to glare into his eyes.

"Two grand. A little extreme, lover," she snarled. "A hundred bucks'd get you the tastiest whore in town, and she'd treat you better. Miss Moon'll just lie there wanting you to tell her what a dreamboat she is."

"Whoa."

"You got a phone call, baby."

"Cynthia?"

"No. The lucky girl. She calls here at four A.M., I pluck her eyes out and serve them in martinis. Tell her for me, will you?"

Hickey dodged around her and trudged across the porch into the living room, with Madeline stalking him from behind. Flopping onto the sofa, he grabbed the phone. "Yeah."

"Good morning."

"Castillo? What the hell?"

"That's the same I'm asking you. Few minutes ago, I'm having the best dream, I'll tell you when I'm not so damn mad, the Cynthia girl calls. Tells me you say she can have two grand that she'll get from me."

"Swell. What'd you do?"

"Don't you got manners, Tom? How about an apologize?"

"Yeah."

"Okay. I told her I'm giving her nothing until I have a long talk with Mr. Hickey. Then I hang up and call to yell at you."

"Look, call her back—she give you a number?"

"No. She's calling me again."

"Okay, stall her. Make her think you're getting her the cash tomorrow, say midafternoon. She say what she wanted it for?"

"She says you know."

"Yeah, I think I do. I'll tell you someday." Hickey's voice deepened into a growl. "What I'm wondering now is, you call to talk to me, why'd you blab the whole deal to Madeline?"

After a few rough breaths into the phone, Castillo said, "You and me going to talk, this morning, at Rudy's, first thing."

"Sure, boss."

Hickey slammed down the phone, stared at his feet then up at Madeline, who stood over him. If she'd held one hand behind her, he would've bet she was holding something to conk him with. He pushed himself up, mussed his hair, and raked his fingers through it. "You and the Cubano . . . you his confidante?"

"Nice try, Tom, but I'm not letting you wipe dirt on me just to get it off your own mug. Spill it, baby," she hissed. "What's with you and your songbird and two grand?"

Hickey stood, rubbed his brow, kneaded his petrified neck, thinking how strange it was that after fifteen years he understood Madeline less fully than he'd thought he knew her the first week. People are so damned complicated, he thought, a bright fellow could study a lifetime and barely get acquainted with his best companion. Fifteen years, yet Hickey couldn't say whether Madeline, if he told her about Cynthia and Katoulis, would use the knowledge to ruin the girl and get rid of her, out of jealousy.

"Don't give me any confidentiality crap, any lies about you took her on as a client." Madeline grabbed a clump of her hair, on the side, as if she might rip it out and lash him. "One word like that and I'll raise such hell the neighbors'll think Tojo parachuted into my bedroom."

"Remember Donny Katoulis?"

Her right hand let go of her hair, made a fist, and dropped to her side. "Sure."

"Cynthia met him tonight, on Sunset Cliffs. Earlier she was having a drink with Charlie Schwartz. My guess is, she's arranging a hit on somebody."

"Who?"

"That's what I'm trying to figure."

Madeline paced around the table. She started for the kitchen, then turned back and leaned against the archway. "So why get the two grand from you, when she knows you're snooping on her?"

"Let's say there's nobody else she trusts that can deliver two grand."

Madeline slapped the wall hard, two slow bars in four-four time. "Yeah, and let's say why in the hell do you give her the cash so she can pass it along to Donny Katoulis so he'll waste some poor sap you don't even know who it is? You're feeding me a line, Tom."

What Hickey wanted was to grab her neck and squeeze, he felt so betrayed that she wouldn't believe him. The one person besides Elizabeth whose trust he needed leaned against the wall glaring at him as if the sight made her flesh crawl. He rested one knee on the sofa and gripped on top of the backrest with both hands. "If I don't give her the money, she goes to Charlie Schwartz for it. Guess why he gives it to her."

"Oh God. Cynthia loses her virtue. What a tragedy," Madeline wailed. "You'd have to share her with a gangster."

His eyes pinched shut; hands knitted together to keep them inert, Hickey dropped himself onto the sofa. He didn't see Elizabeth walk in. "What's the deal, Madeline?" he said hopelessly. "What is it makes you want so damned bad to think I'm playing house with Cynthia?"

"Go to bed, Lizzie," Madeline snapped.

Hickey jumped up, saw his daughter's fists bunched together covering her chin and mouth. He started around the sofa, to comfort her, but Madeline beat him there. She threw an arm around Elizabeth's waist, pushed her into the hall, guided her to her room and followed her in, slammed the door.

Hickey stood a moment trying to think of some magical word. There wasn't any. All he could do was try to fix this Cynthia business, get it over before Madeline steeled her heart against him. He went to the bedroom and dressed. He shaved, brushed his teeth. As he walked out, he heard his wife and daughter talking in low tones. They sounded like angels singing a two part lullaby.

The moon was gone, the stars paled. It was almost 6:00 A.M. Layered strips of rose and alabaster crossed the horizon. He drove across the Ingraham Street bridge, cut down Frontier and Rosecrans to the Coast Highway, doubled back, and stopped at Milly's for hash, eggs, and enough coffee to make his brain whiz too fast to hold steady on the image of Elizabeth clutching her head so it wouldn't explode, her eyes dripping silver tears and staring at him as if he were a storm trooper.

He walked out into daylight and drove away. Failing to let his Chevy warm up, he sputtered away with the choke out. He sped along the Coast Highway, through Old Town, and up to Kensington, took El Cajon Boulevard past the trolleys and jalopies full of dreamy-eyed welders, riveters, engineers in felt hats on their way to build ships and bombs.

The only signs of life on Wisteria Court were two boys trying to make a football spiral and a young veteran in khaki trousers who limped and used a cane, out walking his dog. Hickey parked across the street from the Tucker house. A maroon DeSoto sat in the driveway. The sign on its door read MURPHY AND ASSOCIATES. Hickey figured waking her up wouldn't be the route to Laurel

Tucker's confidence, especially if she was the hothead Leo claimed. He thought of driving to a pay phone and calling Leo, getting a tail on Cynthia. But Laurel might scat while he was gone.

His mind felt chopped in two, and no matter which way he turned, he got stumped. If he could talk sense to Cynthia, clue her that he knew about Katoulis, it might spook her enough so she'd give up on murder. More likely, though, she'd lie, slap his face, and disappear. He could notify the law, ask his pal Thrapp to lend a gang of cops to swarm around the girl and Katoulis, so at least she'd have to fall back and regroup. Whoever she meant to put to sleep might survive another month or two. Meantime, he could snoop, maybe find the fuse and snatch it away.

In return, he'd probably lose Madeline. The only chance he saw to keep her was to lavish her with time and attention without letting his bank balance decrease noticeably. Which meant he'd keep playing ball with Castillo, and tell Leo—after nine years, when the old guy was scrambling for loot to send Magda, his youngest daughter, to Stanford—to find a new partner, go it alone, or retire.

Either give up Madeline or become a louse. Then a louse he'd become. Losing Madeline would be like siphoning the blood out of his heart and filling it with acid. If she ran off and took Elizabeth, he'd walk around as dead as Henry Tucker.

Once he'd decided, he got anxious to certify the deal. To call Madeline and vow he'd give up the detective business, as soon as he'd taken care of the girl and Donny Katoulis. On impulse his hand reached for the key in the ignition. He might've driven to the phone, except that he saw a curtain rustle in the Tucker house.

Rolling the manila envelope and stuffing it into his coat pocket, he jumped out of the Chevy and crossed the street, climbed the porch steps, and knocked on the door. It flew open so fast his hand was still up and fisted.

"Sock me, mister, your life will be one long regret."

The voice was steady, rich as an orator's. The woman stood almost as tall as Hickey, a couple inches higher than her sister. She had Cynthia's pale but rosy coloring, eyes closer to blue than green, a mouth that looked ready to bite or kiss, depending on your next move. Except for the five or so years between them, she and Cynthia might've been twins raised by different parents, the younger pampered and cultivated while the elder got trained with a belt and a backhand. Laurel had rounder hips than her sister, the same tiny waist. Her hair was darker with only traces of auburn. Her breasts stretched the terry-cloth bathrobe she wore.

"I wasn't going sock anybody, except the door," Hickey said. "You're Laurel Tucker."

"In person. Yourself?"

"Tom Hickey. Friend of Cynthia's."

"Friend, huh?" She backed off a step and looked him over. "You won't find her around here, fella. She doesn't like me. Ha, tell the man true, Laurel. Right now she might be toying with her rosary, praying for an earthquake to swallow me. I'm surprised she hasn't cursed me to you."

"I'm not looking for her. I came to talk to you."

Laurel grinned coyly. "She must've showed you my picture."

"Maybe she did," he mumbled.

"Huh?"

His eyes scanned her while his hand felt for the manila envelope, lifted it out of the pocket, and bent it flat. "I smell coffee. Got an extra cup?"

"Not the timid kind, are you? Aw, c'mon in."

She led him through the edge of the parlor. There was a dusty piano, a window seat stacked with papers the size of deeds and magazines, a white leather sofa and chair, two impressionist seascapes in muted colors. Hickey read the name Joshua Bair in the corner of the one he passed by. The kitchen was small and cluttered. A small table sat in a nook by the porch window, across from the sink, beside a knickknack shelf where Hickey laid the envelope. Laurel motioned to a chair, fetched them each a teacup of black coffee, and sat across from him.

"Here we are."

"You and Sis just got back from a trip, right, two pals out having a good time?"

"Funny man. Cynthia rode the bus there to visit our dear friend Emma, and naturally to torment our mother as she always does. Mother called, though, with the news that Cynthia was converting, becoming a sister in the *Nezah* Society. I had business up there, so I used the opportunity to drive up and attend the ceremony . . . but it was a funeral I attended."

"Emma Vidal's," Hickey said, and waited a respectable time. "I forget how she died."

Wetting her lips with her tongue and leaning closer, as if to unnerve him, catch him off guard, and steal a glimpse into the depths of his eyes, she said mournfully, "Buried in an avalanche, on Mount Shasta, the day of Cynthia's purification. Do you know anything about the *Nezah* Society?"

Hickey shrugged. The less he knew, the more she might enlighten him. "You one of them?"

"Not so much in faith as in loyalty. Mother is fervent, she can't understand disbelief. To keep harmony in our family, it's wiser to join. I believe—don't you?—religions only serve to give us passions we can share, common enemies and objects of worship. Otherwise, we couldn't live in the same house, could we?"

"You worship Master What's-his-name?"

"Pravinshandra." Her eyes had narrowed, the brows furled and darkened while the rest of her held eerily still. "Are we just chatting? I'd rather you tell me exactly what you want to know. A policeman came here the other day looking for Cynthia. I'm a little worried. It's why I let you in."

"Sure. Sorry. Your sister got enemies?"

Laurel gave a chuckle, took a long sip of her coffee, swallowed, and chuckled again. "My sister's always had enemies, and they all live in the same place." She pointed to her head. "Upstairs. I mean, they're real people. You see, Cynthia expects to be adored. If someone doesn't kiss her feet, the only reason she can buy is that the person must be evil, which makes that somebody her mortal enemy."

"Anybody in particular right now?"

"How should I know? I'm the last being on earth she'd confess to. It's one reason Venus and I were delighted that Cynthia would join the society—it might eventually bond the three of us, at least bring the feud to a cease-fire."

"That'd be swell. Take a guess, would you? Let's say she has a particular enemy right now—maybe she let slip a curse or wicked look, or groaned somebody's name in her sleep. If you can't think of anybody, say the first words come to mind."

Laurel drummed her fingers, chewed on her lip, roamed her eyes around the table as though inspecting the spices and place settings. "It could be the master. Because he was leading Emma down the mountain when the avalanche struck, she may blame him. Besides, according to her silly Catholicism, Pravinshandra took her mother to live in sin."

"Yeah, and didn't he swipe Venus away from your father?"

Laurel seemed to enlarge and harden as if a burst of air had pumped into her. She leaned back stiff against her chair. Her nostrils flared, lips dried instantly. She was damned mad at somebody, Hickey thought—at Venus, the master, her father, or him. "In a sense, he did," she said coldly.

Time to knock her over the edge, Hickey decided, and he reached to the shelf beside him for the manila envelope. He rolled it backwards to flatten it better. Laurel folded her arms across her breasts and scowled at the envelope, then at the picture he slipped out and placed on the table in front of her. She studied, closed her eyes for a moment, opened them, and shoved the picture at him. She wet her lips and pressed them tightly together.

"Any idea who drew it, what the note at the bottom means?"

Laurel grabbed her cup and saucer off the table and carried them to the sink. As she rinsed and laid them on the counter, using one hand, her left hand brushed and patted the terry cloth against her hip, about the place where the Tree of Life tattooed on the woman on her back in the drawing would be.

She turned and leaned against the counter, watching him like a boxer who might jab any second. "Mister, Cynthia's crazy.

Without going into any stuff that's nobody's business except my sister's and her conscience's, I'll tell you she has delusions. Here's one—she used to dress in the simplest tunic, cut her hair, hack it off just below the ears, trying to look like Joan of Arc. I can't count the times she's accused me of plotting to kill her. My guess is, your picture's something she drew during one of her spells."

"She draws pretty well."

"We grew up at Otherworld. All of us there learned how to draw. Joshua Bair taught us, the same style as in your picture. Notice the heavy lines and crisscrossed shading, the alternate light and dark blotches."

"Yeah. So maybe any student of Bair's could've drawn it. Why do you figure it's Cynthia's?"

"The writing is hers."

"Ah." Hickey remembered the writing in Cynthia's book, the graceful flowing hand, while the note on the picture was more like block italic. "You sure?"

"Yes. Look, I have an appointment. Think I can sell a duplex today." She glanced at the wall clock. "At nine."

Hickey nodded, replaced the drawing in the envelope, picked up his hat, stood, and followed Laurel across the living room to the front door, which she held open for him. He stepped outside, put his hat on. "Say, I forgot to ask—who's the Bitch?"

Laurel jerked back a couple inches, as though in all her life she'd never been affronted with such profanity. For an instant her upper teeth caught her lower lip, her gaze turned downward, and her shoulders hunched; she looked like a naughty girl. "I don't know what you mean," she muttered savagely.

Hickey lifted his eyebrows, gave her a wink. "Thanks for the coffee."

He could feel her watching him cross the street. By the time he'd settled behind the wheel and looked her way, she'd closed the door. He drove off musing that he'd learned two things. Master Pravinshandra could be the guy Donny Katoulis would kill. And Laurel didn't give a damn about her sister. She'd even failed to ask what kind of trouble Cynthia was in.

ELEVEN

♪ ♪ ♪

ABOUT 9:00 A.M., AT THE BOOTH OUTSIDE THE PIGGLY WIGGLY market, Hickey made phone calls, the first to Leo Weiss. As their office phone rang, Hickey steeled his resolve to tell Leo he was deserting, giving up the detective racket. Leo didn't answer. Relieved, Hickey left a message with their answering service, asking Leo to find Cynthia Moon and shadow her.

If Hickey had a gift, it was steady nerves, yet the phone receiver slipped in his sweaty hand while he dialed his home number. Elizabeth answered.

"Hi, kiddo. You okay?"

"Sure, dad," she muttered somberly.

"Sorry about last night."

"It's okay."

"You want to ask me anything?"

"No."

"Then I'll tell you. The only women for me are you and your mother. She there?"

"No, she went to the club."

"Who with?"

"I'm not sure. I was throwing horseshoes on the beach with Evelyn. Mom left a note and took off."

He could drive to the Del Mar Club, Hickey thought, but suppose he found her with Castillo. Suppose she made light of his solution, and his temper flared, and he punched somebody who got in the way, like Castillo. With everything at stake, working on zero sleep and a gallon of coffee, no telling what might occur.

"Babe, give her a message, would you? Tell her I'm through with the detective game. I'll be working nights, staying home days, taking her to Paris if she gets the whim. Got it?"

He could see Elizabeth's grin over the phone. "Dad, you're a kick in the pants."

"That's me," Hickey said.

Driving east, he swelled with the elation you feel when you burst through a dilemma and discover there's life on the other side. Mornings he could lie in bed with Madeline, running his finger along the ridge of her hip, laying his head on her belly, admiring the smell of her skin, like the blossoms of winter oranges. He could marvel at the rough, adobe-colored flesh of her nipples, a whole little wilderness to explore. He could help paint her toenails, read lots of books, putter on the sailboat he was going to buy soon. When Elizabeth got home from school, they could wander the beaches on the oceanside. A while back she'd asked him to teach her the saxophone. He hadn't played the damned thing in years. If he got the rust out, maybe some nights he could sit in with the band at Rudy's, even talk Madeline into climbing up there with him, to sing. All kinds of happiness might befall them, as soon as he settled this business of Cynthia Moon's and finished with Donny Katoulis.

The bells of the Saint Ambrose Home rang out "Hark the Herald Angels Sing." As though the priest were throwing a party, most parking spots on that side of the block were taken. Hickey found one in front of a barbershop, closed for Sunday. He checked his appearance in the barber's window, took off his hat

108

and used his fingers to neaten his scraggly hair, grimaced, and turned toward the rest home.

A hefty nun stood like a bouncer at the entrance. Hickey asked for Sister Johanna or Father McCullough, got informed they both were at mass, back through the grounds in the chapel. She led Hickey to the rose garden, where he waited on a concrete bench surrounded by gnarly stumps and the rosebushes that must've just gotten pruned, listening to "The First Noël," thinking about the old woman called Donia who'd asked if he were the devil. Sister Johanna had explained that the old gal asked lots of men the same question, as if the devil's primary characteristic was masculinity.

The bells switched from carols to a hymn he didn't know. A procession began, from the chapel a couple hundred feet up the hillside, down the concrete trail between the hedges that fenced off the groves of loquat and mulberry on one side and olive trees on the other. Like a parade of mangled veterans in fifty-dollar suits, the old folks, many held upright by relatives or nuns, inched their way down the hill. Too late to hide, Hickey spotted Donia the accuser. She hobbled past him, concentrating on her tiny steps, chomping her false teeth every couple seconds, then opening wide as if to swallow flies. Sister Johanna was the wrangler at the rear of the herd, until she veered away and hustled around the jacaranda to Hickey, who stood and tipped his hat.

The sister's rabbit nose quivered and she blinked her watery eyes. "You found Cynthia," she said anxiously.

Hickey nodded. "I guess that means she hasn't visited her old man."

"No." The sister bowed her head, crossed herself, looked up with a wan smile. "She's safe."

"Is she?"

"Tell me, please."

"Looks that way," Hickey said. "Any change in Henry?"

"Very little. He still won't eat until he's prodded, and then he only accepts a few bites. Yesterday I found him weeping."

"What about?"

"Over his sins, perhaps?"

109

"Or somebody else's," Hickey muttered.

The nun touched his sleeve with one finger. "Sir, if Cynthia won't visit, I'm certain he'll perish before the New Year."

"Yeah, and he's not the only one."

The sister's hand jerked up and cupped the side of her face. "She's in danger, then."

"You bet. Look, I've got to ask Tucker something, in a hurry."

Sister Johanna wagged her head stiffly. "He's demanded to be left alone. Father promised."

"Go get the father, will you?"

"He's still in the chapel, conferring with Mrs. Gallager's daughter, I believe."

"Five bucks if you'll interrupt, tell him it's urgent."

"Five . . . sir!"

"A joke," Hickey said. "Please?"

Finally she nodded, eyed him dubiously, then walked around the jacaranda, turned up the hill. Every dozen or so steps she looked over her shoulder, checking on him. When she disappeared into the chapel, Hickey jumped up and double-timed across the patio, opened the heavy door to the rear ward. The air seemed to gust at him, dense and foul as if they'd cremated somebody and fumigated by tossing a crate of incense onto the fire. Halfway down the hall, a skeletal woman sat rigidly in a wheelchair, holding a broom, handle forward, like a medieval knight—the broom her lance, the wheelchair her steed—poised to charge.

He ducked into the third room, where Henry Tucker lay still, on his back, his eyes open but dull as if they'd gotten sanded and primered. Hickey watched for a blink, a twitch, any hint of life. At last the man sipped air, enough to fill a thimble.

"Tucker?"

The face stiffened as if suddenly doused with quick-drying glue. It turned a half inch or so, maddening Hickey, whose patience could endure plenty if he'd slept a full dose, gotten some peace and affection lately; otherwise. . . . Harshly, he said, "Before I've gotta tell somebody else, who's sure going to snitch to the cops

110

and get your daughter lots of years in San Quentin—who's she trying to kill?"

The pitiful fellow Hickey'd pity no more lifted one bony arm across his body, the other straight up, reached for the side rail, gripped it in both hands, and pulled himself halfway to sitting with such fierce effort that it made him quake all over as if palsy had joined his afflictions. Through lips so parched they had blisters surrounding each scab, he gasped, "For Christ's sake, let us be." One hand then the other slipping from the rail, Cynthia's daddy collapsed.

He lay sipping and spitting air while Hickey glared down on him and wiped his own brow. He'd known steam baths cooler than this dungeon—the effort of wiping his face made it wetter. "You sound like a preacher," he growled, "asking Christ to help you kill somebody. Christ or nobody's going to back me off, pal. See, I figure you put her up to it, but look, Tucker, Cynthia's got all the tools, she can find her own way to wreck her life." He caught his breath, then softly requested, "Why don't you just tell me who you sent her to kill, then confess, and rest in peace?"

Tucker might have lapsed into a coma, from the way he looked before Hickey kicked the lower bed rail, turned, stomped out of the room. He rushed down the hall, threw the door open, sucked in a gallon of clean, tangy air before he spied Sister Johanna leading the priest down the pathway from the chapel. As they neared, he caught the sister snitching to Father McCullough, ". . . but he disobeyed me." Head pushed forward so her wriggling nose led the way, she marched up to Hickey and hissed, "Shame."

Hickey wheeled on the priest, to fend off a lecture. "We've gotta talk in private."

The father dismissed Sister Johanna, nudged her when she didn't hustle away. With a sour gaze and a wave of his hand, he motioned Hickey to take the lead crossing the patio. They paused at the office door while the priest stepped forward, pulling a large ring of keys from a pocket in his cassock.

111

The heavy door creaked open. Father McCullough threw it shut behind them, harder than he needed. "Urgent, is it?"

"Yeah, but first I'm wondering what's the limit of your confidentiality, Padre? I mean, suppose I tell you something about one of your confessees. Can you make it extend far enough to keep her out of prison?"

"No," the priest answered swiftly, but stood pondering a moment before he led Hickey across the anteroom to the carved mahogany door to the inner office. He slammed it harder than he had the first door, like a guy overwrought by constant intrusions. He motioned Hickey to the wing chair, made straight for his desk, and dug out the Irish whiskey. After pouring them each a half tumbler, he delivered Hickey's, sat down, and leaned heavily on his desk, chin in his hands, then removed the arm he needed to lift his tumbler. He took a drink and rolled it around as though rinsing his mouth. "A confessor's right to confidentiality is circumscribed. But . . . God forgives."

"Which means?"

"In this case, I can break a promise."

"Good for you," Hickey muttered, and tasted the whiskey. "The girl's trying to raise two grand to get somebody snuffed. She's already met with the gunman."

Father McCullough rose off the desk, sank into his chair, and started pounding his forehead with the palm side of his fist.

"See, if you didn't clam up on Thursday, maybe I could've fixed things. What I mean is, don't even sit there thinking what you ought to tell me and what you ought not. Just spill the whole deal."

The priest leaned forward. So did Hickey. They aimed both cannons at each other, like opposing tackles across the scrimmage line. The father gave way first. Eyes dropping, he placed both hands on the desk top as though for push-ups. Finally, he slid the chair back, opened a drawer, and removed three red books. Ledgers, bound in red leather. "She gave me these to hold, one at a time, as she finished them, over the past several months. She asked me not to open them or even allow them out of my safe, unless she were to die."

"But you read 'em."

"I did."

"So who's she want to kill?"

"A number of people," Father McCullough said darkly. "It's a grisly story."

"I got a preview."

The priest skidded the books across the desk as though anxious to rid himself of them. "If you can return them to me, and not let her know you've seen them . . . I'd owe you."

"Who knows?" Hickey said. "First I've gotta find her."

"I thought you had."

"That was yesterday. All right if I use the phone?"

Father McCullough shoved the phone at him, and Hickey dialed his office number, got the answering service, who gave him a message from Leo:

"Picked her up leaving the boarding house at nine A.M. She taxied to Otherworld. Spent an hour there. Next, breakfast in an Ocean Beach coffee shop and back home. Got her digs in sight from the Richfield station."

"News?" the father asked.

"Yeah. My partner's keeping an eye on her."

"You'll go to the police?"

Hickey grimaced, donned and straightened his hat. "It'd be nicer, don't you think, if we could leave her with a future?"

TWELVE

♪ ♪ ♪

At the top of page one, a few lines had been written and then scratched out, blotted over so Hickey couldn't decipher anything. After that, Cynthia wrote in a large, confident hand.

Juliet is a goner the first time a Capulet kicks a Montague in the shins. Oedipus's daddy gives him to the trashman. Hamlet, pushed over the edge by Uncle Claude. Orphan Annie, Saint Joan, Tess Durbeyfield, Cynthia Tucker. All of them doomed from birth. Spare the poor children, Holy Father.

Daddy says our ruin started with two pretty girls tying ribbons into their hair. Venus, the nine-year-old, wore a silver ribbon, a rosy dress, and a round silver pendant studded with a triple cross of tiny chips of ruby. Her sister Ophelia had a red ribbon, a yellow dress, and hair of gold mixed with auburn. People called her the most beautiful child in Dublin. She looked like me. I wish I could have seen pictures, but the day the mailman delivered them after

Grandmother and Grandfather drowned in a shipwreck, she made Daddy build a bonfire, and she cooked them in front of the Bitch and me.

"Give me the silver bow," Ophelia commanded like spoiled children do. "If you will, I'll be good and I'll give you my tart."

"You will give me your tart," Venus said, "because Papa will give you another."

"Yes, he will. Please tie the bow in my hair."

Venus didn't care for ribbons or bows. A girl her age wanted jewelry. Still it was a good deed, she thought. She tied the silver ribbon into Ophelia's hair.

My grandmother stood downstairs welcoming guests to her party, a chance for the Enlightened to meet their prophetess, Madame T. The guests were dizzy with joy and fervor. The nitwits believed Theosophy could save them from poverty and war. The true esoteric faith would unite us because all religions flow from the same spring, the primal revelation given to us at the Golden Dawn of history. The great religions are hardly more than parodies of the ancient Secret Doctrine revealed to Madame B by the Tibetan masters, whose Truth will lead us forward to the golden age when the feminine, nurturing yin again reigns equally, alongside the tempestuous yang, blah blah.

My grandmother had flaxen hair and china skin, Venus told me. She covered her bosoms in lace, so men would look hard, trying to steal a peek at her luscious flesh. She was flirty like Venus and the Bitch, nothing like me, and kissed all the men with their top hats and red noses but only shook hands with the snippy wives. As she beckoned to her daughters, they scampered from their lookout atop the stairs, where they squirmed in starched pantaloons and petticoats, itching for the nasty old madame to show up so they could hurry outside and quit acting civilized. They curtsied and preened for "Dublin's most astute minds," the snooty professors, artists dressed like chimney sweeps, harried Catholic mothers with children dangling from every limb, then they ran upstairs and made ugly faces at each other, while Katy the maid shooed the guests' brats out back to play and Grandmother walked the guests into the parlor where my grandfather offered them dark bread, Danish cheeses, and Spanish wine. Grandfather was a young colonel in the militia, given to black moods, a Celt by ancestry and disposition. The day she got hypnotized, Venus told Miss V that Grandfather looked like somebody who would slice little Nell up the middle with a buzz saw.

Back at their perch overlooking the foyer, with Grandmother gone, Ophelia climbed onto the banister, pushed off, and flew down, holding the rail only with her thighs. Venus stood chafing with jealousy that Ophelia could do with impunity what she was not allowed. When Ophelia ran back onto the landing, Venus commanded, "You shall not exhibit your petticoats and bare legs."

"My petticoats are clean and pretty," Ophelia snapped, "and my legs are not bare above the knees."

As her sister ran back to the landing, Venus thought of later in the day when Grandmother would order her to play piano while Ophelia sang. The guests would rave for the little one. Godmother Callahan would call Ophelia the loveliest, a child for the golden age, like the crones at Otherworld used to call me. Oh, the other girls got so furious they dreamed of watching me bounce down the cliffs and scatter like moon dust into the sea. Still, Father, everywhere I go, jealous females hate me, the men want to devour me, I haven't been out of danger since I left the mission.

Madame T's carriage arrived, and Grandmother, arm in arm with Godmother Callahan, rushed out from the library to meet the great personage at the door. Naughty Ophelia had already climbed the railing, over the knob onto the downgrade, where she giggled and pointed at the doorway, at Grandmother and Mrs. Callahan practicing their poses and rehearsing the lines they'd use to greet their Deva. Looking back at her sister, naughty Ophelia tittered, "I will slide into the madame's fat arms."

"You won't," Venus yelped, and grabbed for her sister,

who ducked just beyond her reach. "Father will give us the whip if you do."

"Not to me. Father will not punish me."

"You would betray me after I gave you the ribbon?"

"Yes," Ophelia cried.

The rest I saw in a dream Saint Ophelia sent me. In Venus's story, the lie she even told when Miss V hypnotized her, she only lunged for the silver ribbon, to pluck it out of her sister's hair. But truly Venus pushed her.

Ophelia threw up her hands to balance herself. Her thighs in the slippery petticoats and pantaloons couldn't hold their tight grip. Swooping down the banister Katy had waxed that very morning, Ophelia hollered for her mama and shrieked as she hit the knob that probably smashed her pubic bone and tipped her forward so that as she sailed off the inclined end of the railing she soared headfirst across the foyer. Her arms shot out. One of them shattered a window. The other socked Mrs. Callahan in the neck, at the very same moment Ophelia's skull bashed against the door molding.

Before she had to gobble any poison fruit and learn to secure the buttons over her heart and hide her pantaloons, lucky Ophelia died.

"Whoa," Hickey muttered, dropping his feet off the desk and slapping the ledger book down on it. So Venus killed her little sister, probably by accident, unless he credited Cynthia's dreams. And he was more convinced now that Emma Vidal was Miss V. A hypnotist who'd at least once used her power to dig out the secrets somebody—Venus, in this case—had buried from herself. The more secrets you know, Hickey mused, the better your chances of getting crushed by an avalanche.

He filled his pipe, torched it, set it in the ashtray, and forgot it was there as soon as he picked up the notebook; he leaned back and propped his feet on the desk again.

I got this out of a pamphlet Madame A sent all over the world.

117

The grounds of Otherworld, inspired by the gardens of Tivoli, Fontainebleau, and shrines in Japan and India, were sculptured to touch the most ravenous heart with peace. There are seven main buildings. A pagoda, used for our rites-of-passage ceremonies. A Greek temple, where our classrooms are located. Two Mediterranean villas overlooking the sea, which provide quarters for our married residents, their infants, and visitors. Our students, of every race and color from all corners of the world, are provided for in the adobe barracks halls.

People of all ages thrive at Otherworld, in a balance achieved by spiritual, intellectual, artistic, and physical pursuits. The gardens sustain us and allow us the blessing of healthy labor. The mulberry orchard feeds our silkworms. The girls weave fabric, the women tailor our garments. In service to each other and all humanity, no one at Otherworld feels useless. Every soul is vital here.

It is the children who sanctify Otherworld. Sent here to be raised in light and goodness, educated in our Raja Yoga school, uniquely dedicated to scholarship, creativity, and discipline, our students will forge the future as creators and governors of the Golden Age.

Hah! If I wrote the pamphlet, I would say, Come to Nitwit World, where everybody thinks she's a star, where the food tastes like grass, the fog makes you sniffle, the abundant flowers make the whole place a beehive, where they work their Raja Yoga slaves from dawn to curfew at both hard labor and their studies, so to outsiders who might contribute they look like Spartan athletes and geniuses. Come to Otherworld, I would write, where Madame A will preach about the Ring Veda, symbolism of the lotus flower, the perfect imperfection of bamboo, or the transmigration of souls until you think you are smarter than Christ, instead of the nitwit you really are.

That is what I would write, Father, but to you I will confess the truth. Since we got banished, having spent two years at the mission, almost three more on the outside, if it were possible I would run back there and take Daddy with me, to live or die. To Daddy and me, Otherworld is still our palace in the stars. Even if she had spared Daddy, I would hate Venus always, for destroying Otherworld.

It began in 1912, when Grandfather exiled Venus from Dublin. Grandfather acted as if Venus were a stranger who'd foully murdered his precious, while she lay in her room weeping, trembling in a fever. Her skin grew rashed and her eyes got bilious yellow. Lucky for Venus, Madame T was there. Because she saw that Grandfather harbored no mercy, Madame T advised Grandmother to send Venus away until he could forgive her. Madame T would arrange everything. It would be like going to heaven, the madame promised, and Grandfather replied, "Heaven is not where she belongs."

No one remembers what Grandmother said, but she let Madame T wire Madame A. She let Grandfather purchase two tickets on a passenger liner. Katy got two weeks to bid good-bye to her sisters and the fellows at the pub around the corner. Then she and the poor girl, wrapped in a quilt, who shivered with each draft and breeze, and stared in fright at everything, got put on a train. The next day they sailed out of London.

As he scanned a few pages about the voyage and the fever that wracked Venus, Hickey wondered where the girl had learned the details that left him sweaty and seasick.

Hooray, hooray, Father, Venus survived, as the wicked most always do. The damned doctor probably still believes he is tops because he saved her, like the doc who cured Herr Hitler's pleurisy. The only clear thinker was Grandfather, who would have buried her alive. When you murder somebody, you simply must die. Ten thousand years of civilization, still they let murderers bear children, and the poor, damned children have to pay. Doesn't anybody read the Bible?

Cursing softly, Hickey threw his feet off the desk, grabbed his pipe out of the ashtray, and lit up. For a minute he watched the smoke rise and curl toward the window, absorbing the knowledge that, if Cynthia was true to her word—and sometimes the looniest people proved the truest—if murderers had to die, it wasn't just a murder he needed to thwart. Also a suicide.

A gal in a million, with brains and a voice that could make the devil pray for an encore, who soon might get fan mail from the king of Sweden, proposals from the Rockefeller boys, apt to stick her head into the oven. Hickey didn't have to strain to imagine the girl hiring Katoulis, making certain the murder was as good as accomplished, before she could go to her reward.

He shuffled to the hat rack where he'd draped his coat, took his notepad out of the breast pocket, and dialed the number for Dolores Ganguish's boarding house.

A breathy voice crooned hello.

"Cynthia Moon, please."

"Who's asking for her?"

"Tom Hickey."

"Sure, I thought so. You're the fellow with the parrot on his tie. This is Brenda, remember me?"

"You bet. Put Cynthia on, would you?"

"Suppose she's indisposed, dreamboat."

"I don't know big words, doll, and let's not play cute right now, huh? Tell her it's about the money."

Brenda made a poof sound and must've let the receiver drop, hanging by the line. It rapped like a metronome against the wall. Hickey sucked on his pipe and blew smoke as if there were dead things piled all around and Walter Raleigh could perfume the place.

"Whoops," Brenda said. "The last thing I knew she was sleeping, but now she's gone. Señora says Miss Moony stepped out a while ago."

Hickey thanked her, hung up, and sat brooding. It's okay, he thought, Leo's got her in sight. Besides, if Cynthia's going to kill herself, she'll wait and play it for utmost drama, use it as an encore.

He reached into the desk, second drawer down, got out a pint bottle that used to be full of Dewar's but now contained a spoonful, enough to wet his mouth and prick a little going down. He phoned the Pier Five Diner, ordered a corned-beef sandwich with two pickles and a pint of Dewar's. The delivery boy, usually Raul, would pick the latter up on the way. Hickey grabbed the ledger book, leaned back, threw his feet onto the desk once more.

THIRTEEN

♪ ♪ ♪

DADDY WAS THIRTY-TWO YEARS OLD WHEN THE *ORPHEUS* docked in San Pedro. He and a Puerto Rican lady were waiting to take Venus from Katy the maid, who told Daddy the story I have written.

Daddy was raised in Silver City, New Mexico by a Baptist father and mother. He left home at sixteen, worked as a ranch hand, and discovered liquor, which swiftly drove Jesus away. In place of loving Jesus, Daddy told me, he chased after barmaids and wild señoritas. He stole about a hundred head of cattle before he got caught and condemned to a year and thirty days in the prison on Skull Mesa, where the brutes whipped and clobbered him with a rifle butt, yet Daddy is so brave he wouldn't have told me except, all these years later, he still has the scars across the small of his back and beneath his right shoulder blade. After New Mexico, Daddy tried Oregon, where he lusted after a fancy Danish girl, robbed a payroll wagon, and got condemned once more.

In prison, Daddy swore off fancy women, began his studies to become a shyster, and launched his quest for the Way. After prison he trekked restlessly from one employment or teacher to the next, down the coast to Oakland, San Luis Obispo, Santa Barbara, L.A., and into the study of scriptures and tracts on subjects from the Apocrypha to necromancy. Prison, his studies, the moral teaching of Madame T, and his devotion to Venus kept Daddy celibate for sixteen years. The day Venus ran off with the Fiend and Daddy got drunk for the first time in three decades, he told the Bitch and me that he should've wrapped a leather thong around his gonads until they dropped off like a steer's.

"The Fiend," Hickey mumbled. He sat up and glared first at the telephone, then at the door. No call from Leo. No corned beef and whiskey. He plucked the manila envelope from underneath ledger volume II, slid the drawing out, and reread the note at the bottom.

"Beloved, you saw through him from the start. He truly is a fiend. . . . Every day the Fiend grows bolder. Soon I may die."

He'd gotten from Sister Johanna and the priest that Venus had run off with this Pravinshandra character they called the master. Unless she'd made a career of ditching one man for another, the master and the Fiend would be the same guy. As he laid the drawing back on the desk and reached for Cynthia's book, Hickey mused that whomever a murderous female calls a fiend becomes a candidate for murder.

The next page was in light blue pen. Hickey rummaged through the top desk drawer for his glasses and read descriptions of Otherworld and its children, an African pygmy, a cossack, Chinese, Hungarians, a Spanish albino, Persians, and a troop of orphans recently delivered from Cuba. Even the children with parents at Otherworld slept in the adobe barracks, chaperoned by a live-in teacher, so parents couldn't sabotage their education. Only Venus got her own quarters, a tiny maid's room in the cliffside two-story Moorish hacienda, the residence and offices of

Madames A and Esmé, and of Madame T on her brief respites from the round-the-world crusades where she hustled the dough to run Otherworld. Venus was princess, and the special ward of Madame A, on account of a psychic message Madame T had received from her Tibetan master—that the girl could become an adept, possibly a mahatma, one day.

Otherworld had three choirs, a small symphony orchestra, a drama company that produced Shakespeare, Goethe, mystery plays, and adaptations from the Vedas. Madame A, a Greek dowager, encouraged particularly the works of Sophocles and myths she contended were allegories of mysteries revealed in the Secret Doctrine. At the sunrise services around the sea-cliff gazebo, in her pup-tent-sized, rainbow-colored silk gown, Madame A interpreted the dramas spiritually, citing Aristotle's *Poetics,* hermeneutic texts, and a source she called the Akashic Record, an ethereal library from which a sensitive could pull anything ever done, written or thought.

Hickey sat gnawing through his pipe stem, grumbling in distaste at the mystical stuff until he skipped ahead to the next mention of Venus.

> While her soul and heart putrefied, Venus's body flourished in the sunny gardens and sea breeze of Otherworld. At twelve years, already taller than puny average women, she compared to most beauties like a swan to a chicken. With her gift for the harp and piano, already the favorite of Madames A and T, she was Otherworld's darling, as I would later be. Yet she made no friends besides the madames and Daddy. The children resented her privileges, her haughty ways, and the meanness that launched her into a fit or pout if another student earned more praise than she did. Besides, guilty people don't ever let strangers get close, do they, Father?
>
> But neither can they bear solitude. All day and evening, Venus dogged Madame A or Daddy. In the Raja Yoga school, where Daddy taught classics, history, and law, she would bring her work from other classes to finish while

sitting beside him—a liberty nobody else got, not even me—then show it to him and bask in his praise.

While Hickey was reading about Venus's sorrow and anger over her mother's brief and ever more infrequent letters, he started to a knock on the door. He tossed the book onto the desk, jumped up, and let in Raul, a freckled busboy who muttered, *"Buenos días,"* shoved a sack at him, and reached into a coat pocket for the Dewar's, which he handed over stealthily, peering over his shoulder as though he were delivering heroin.

Hickey checked his watch: 3:48 P.M. "What goes?" he grumbled. "You stop and take in a show at the Hollywood?"

"Mucho busy. The boss say no rush for you. Maybe he don't like you so much no more."

"Why's that?" Hickey passed him a five, told him to keep the change.

"The boss say, 'Why Señor Hickey's joint's not getting lousy meat like everybody?' "

After shooing Raul away, Hickey stood a minute feeling slimy as always when he got a reminder that a white hat wouldn't fit him anymore. He tucked the sack under his arm, tugged out the Dewar's cork and took a double gulp, then flopped into the chair and reached for the phone. He dialed home, let it ring about twenty times, slapped the receiver down. A sweep of his arm across the desk cleared a space for the food and drink. He chomped the end off a pickle and grabbed the ledger.

One July morning in 1917, just before dawn, Daddy crept into Venus's little room, woke her, beckoned her outside and to follow him across the central lawn where mystics knelt in sunrise prayers, into the sanctuary where Madame A lay on her feather bed underneath its silk netting. The Enlightened who crowded around her parted to let Daddy lead Venus by the shoulders to the bedside. Madame A's giant head was propped on red silk pillows, hair looking just-brushed, skin damp and transparent blue. Her breath,

125

which Daddy says was always minty sweet, smelled like hot tar. Each time the tiny, wrinkled eyelids blinked, a tear or two spilled out. Madame Esmé, standing beside her, wiped her Deva's cheek with a hanky.

Daddy kept steadying Venus's shoulders, even when Madame A motioned with her head for Venus to come nearer, and Venus leaned close to the bed, her ear a few inches from the face of Madame A, who whispered too soft and gravelly for her to understand. Madame Esmé knelt with her ear to Madame A's lips.

Skinny, gaunt Madame Esmé, who had eyes like searchlights and icy fingers long before Venus killed her, whispered, "Yes, dear," over and over. When at last she rose, she proclaimed in a raw monotone, as if she'd been kidnapped and the brutes held a gun to her temple, "The Aryan master whose initials are CCB has spoken through Madame A, confiding in us that our Venus's soul, which once occupied the flesh of Saint Isabella, has been sent here on a mission, to lead us through a coming tribulation. The master requests that we honor Venus accordingly, and. . . ." She turned to Daddy and glared as if he had just yanked her cat's tail. "Henry Tucker is to be her guardian."

As Dr. Fontaine dispersed the crowd, Venus broke free of Daddy's grip. She ran outside and dashed across the lawn to the cliff trail. Of course Daddy followed behind. Venus, wild as the ghost of Heathcliff's Catherine, kept vanishing and appearing out of the fog. Hands out like a blind girl's, she staggered along. About a hundred yards up the trail she gave a raucous laugh, spun around, and collapsed. Father, isn't it obvious that Venus laughed because she had been handed a crown?

There'd been magazine and newspaper articles enough on Otherworld, especially last year while the place suffered bankruptcy, to acquaint Hickey with the Raja Yoga school. Writers had called it revolutionary, Platonic, a glimpse of the future, heathen, brutal, communistic. Whatever it was had done right by Cynthia's brain. She might be loony, but she was one educated seventeen-year-old.

He shut his eyes, leaned back, listened to her crooning "Got a Date with an Angel," the line where she's on her way to heaven. He brooded over the tragedy it would be to let her go to hell. Restlessly, he wondered why Leo hadn't phoned, and he might've gone out searching except that he'd reached the sexy part.

Of course Venus had always been seducing Daddy, but now she turned all three guns on him. With Madames T and A gone, and Daddy the only person who knew her shameful history, Venus would make him her slave.

The first time she visited his room after dark, she asked him to rehearse with her a scene from a Lashlee drama in which she would play Leda. Daddy read the lines of Zeus disguised as the swan. For an hour they sat on the floor, leaning against the bed, praising each other's beauty. In one part, Venus would reach up and pet Daddy's brow. By the time she kissed his cheek farewell and left, Daddy had caught fire so torridly that he lay squeezing his head in both hands and groaning until finally he got up and walked the cliff trail most of the night. He was a lusty man, Father, deprived for nearly twenty years—I bet you know how that feels.

One week Venus would snuggle against Daddy's arm, lay her head on his shoulder, her hair damp and fragrant from bathing, or tiptoe up behind him while he worked at his desk in the school, reach around and caress his face. For days thereafter, on his every approach, she stiffened and talked icily as a good French girl addressing a German. While Daddy racked his brain trying to recall whether he had acted improperly, and reasoned that she was a troubled child who must be treated with utmost patience, she fattened her pride on his agony, and when she observed him regain his balance, she knocked him reeling again, sneaking up behind as he walked toward the pagoda, clasping her arms around him, squashing her tits into the small of his back. "Oh, Mr. Tucker," she exclaimed. "I've grown so fond of the Chinese. I've begun *The Tale of Genji*. Don't you think it's a marvel?"

On foggy nights in May and June, after the winter sea currents had begun warming, Venus would go alone down the cliffs for a swim. Poor obsessed Daddy, from watching her so closely, knew everything she did except in her own little room. One night Daddy stood by the gazebo when he heard a scream. Believe me, Father, you would have to scream loud and shrill to be heard atop the cliff, at least two hundred feet, with the waves bashing the rocks and rumbling out again. I used to stand in that very cove, the water swirling around my hips and thighs, and bellow love songs as if Saint Ophelia had sent the Man but I had to lure him out of hiding.

Daddy sprinted down the trail and up the beach to the cove just below the gazebo, staring frantically into the purplish mist, his heart pounding so fast it felt like a steady whir. When he tripped over something, he discovered her clothes, rolled into a ball. "Venus!" he hollered. "Please, Venus!"

Through the fog he heard the breakers crashing thunderously in hundred-yard walls, the most treacherous kind. The surf frothed around his feet. He called out again. Still she didn't answer. He kicked off his shoes and raced into the mist and waves. Before he reached waist deep she appeared.

She rose straight up as if surfacing from a dive. Her darkened cinnamon hair fell in ringlets over her shoulders. Her purplish flesh sparkled as if flecks of mica in the water had stuck to her. Daddy tried to stare at her eyes, which gazed sternly at him, but he couldn't resist stealing glances at the hard, slim belly, the tits that quivered as though water were rippling over them, at the long legs, muscular from climbing and dancing. Finally, with a glimpse of her golden fleece, Daddy swooned, Father. When he told me so, he wept in shame. He had gone to save her, but all his blood swamped his head and he keeled over, plop, into the water. Venus had to drag him to shore.

She was dressed and standing over him. "Why would you betray me like this, Mr. Tucker?"

"I heard your scream."

"I did *not* scream."

"But . . . even so, I had no idea you were . . ."

"Naked. Oh, truly? *Liar!* I saw how you looked at me, as if we were creatures."

Daddy lay there realizing that he could never look at her chastely again. "We *are* creatures," he groaned.

With a scowl, Venus wheeled and strode away, while Daddy lay already wondering what kind of life he was going to make outside of Otherworld.

The very next day he confessed his transgression to Madame Esmé who, agreeing that he could no longer be trusted, assumed Venus's guardianship. Daddy borrowed Madame's car and scouted San Diego for an office from which he might practice. Days passed without his getting closer than across a room from Venus. Even in school, she sat in the rear, looked his way only rarely and then with a cruelly vacant stare, until the night she boldly entered his quarters.

She wore the rainbow-colored tunic Madame A had given her on her fourteenth birthday, but she had grown and fleshed out so in those months, it was snug as an evening gown, and the hem barely reached her knees. She was barefoot, and her damp hair was scented with lavender. On her way from the showers she had picked a white gardenia and arranged it into her hair.

"Mr. Tucker," she whispered, "I'm going to speak the truth of my heart and hope you can forgive me."

"I can," Daddy said.

"A foul sickness has come over me, since the night. . . . Mr. Tucker, it's horrid. I can't for a moment forget the feeling that possessed me when you saw my . . . as if many hands were clutching my body at once, the fingers invading me with heat and bitter cold. . . . Henry . . . I wish to feel it again." Suddenly she grasped the hem of her gown and flung it upward, tearing a seam and knocking the gardenia from her hair. She stooped to pick up the flower, replaced it, and tiptoed to within a yard of Daddy, her eyes boring into his heart.

Father, imagine me standing before you wearing nothing but a white flower and glowing with the heat that fills a girl when she's adored. Venus was almost as exquisite. Imagine me inching ever closer until my belly is so near that you can see the downy hairs and watch the skin flex every time you breathe on it. Who could help but reach around, cup my rear in his hands, and guide me even closer? If I quivered and fell limp in your hands as though asking you to possess me, uttering little gasps and moans, wouldn't you lift me onto the bed?

Daddy wouldn't tell me the rest, but I know what she did. I know Venus. With arms, hips, legs, and filthy lies she drew him closer and closer until she had lured him inside. Once she got him there, she wept, called him a beast and pounded on his back, but whenever he tried to release her, she wouldn't let go.

Venus slept beside poor Daddy, who lay all night gazing in awe, dedicating his heart and will to her happiness—he might as well have been ordering his coffin.

It is clear, isn't it, Father—Daddy was Venus's guardian angel the same as Ophelia is mine. Daddy came to save her from hell and she killed him, she and her henchwoman the Bitch, because he betrayed her over me. He wouldn't let them kill his true darling.

Hickey caught his breath, kneaded his forehead, got up, and paced. At the window, he stared at the cloudless silver-blue sky above the buses and signs around Horton Plaza. DOCTOR YALE; POSTAL TELEGRAPH, from before Western Union had driven them out of business—and at a B-17's menacing shadow as it crossed Broadway. He kicked the wall lightly, turned back to his desk, chewed the last bite of his sandwich, and sat for a minute envying Henry Tucker. Not because the old fool had got Venus—Hickey'd seen in the rest home what that prize had bought the man. Besides, Hickey wouldn't have traded Madeline for Venus or anybody. What he envied was Cynthia's devotion to her Daddy. He couldn't see Elizabeth writing about him as a paragon, upright and pure. Not unless she ignored a ton of evidence.

He grabbed the phone, dialed his home number, let it ring a dozen times, then hung up, corked the Dewar's, and swallowed a mouthful. After letting his brain spin a minute, he focused on the puzzles.

It looked as if Cynthia believed not only that her sister and mother had plotted to destroy Henry Tucker but that Venus and the Bitch had tried to enlist Tucker to help destroy his own daughter. A few more pages like this, Hickey figured, and he'd know how to keep Cynthia from Donny Katoulis—drag her to a nuthouse.

He'd also found two more candidates for victim. Lots of folks had murdered a brother or sister, and more cold-bloodedly than Venus had killed hers, even if Cynthia'd written the truth. There were only a few crimes older than fratricide. But slaying your mother—Hickey wondered if anybody with a piece of heart left intact could do it. "Yeah," he muttered, "somebody could."

He wadded the butcher paper that had wrapped his sandwich, tossed it at the trash can between the coatrack and file cabinet. Leo could've swished a double bank shot off the wall and cabinet. Hickey's shot bounced halfway back across the room. He wagged his head, adjusted the glasses on his nose, and read about the morning after, how Venus wailed, wept, punched Henry Tucker in the eye, then bolted and wouldn't get near him for weeks. She kept her door padlocked, refused to attend school. From chance meetings on the grounds, she fled as though he were a leper. Tucker, of course, spent those weeks on the edge of leaping from the cliff into the lesser despair of hell.

At last she returned to his classroom. A few days later she sat beside him at dinner. On Christmas she brought him a gift, kissed him thanks for the bracelet he'd given her, invited him to the New Year's dance. By February she was riding along on Tucker's excursions into San Diego and stopping at the windows of jewelry stores. The day she led him into Jessop's on Fifth Avenue and stood admiring the rings, Henry promenaded her down Broadway and, kneeling on a harborside lawn beneath a palm tree, proposed.

If you ever hear of anybody answering a proposal the way Venus did, Father—"I think it's best," she said—stop the poor fool, send him on a mission to Borneo.

As always, the one who can love, who is really the prize, gets demeaned by the one with the rotten heart.

Madame Esmé took charge of the wedding. It was in early June, at sunrise, at the gazebo. Rarely in foggy June is there a brilliant morning like this one. A happy omen? Ha! Daddy got led from the villa they called Majorca across the lawn to the gazebo by Mr. Bair and our poet Will Lashlee. More dread irony, Father, since Mr. Lashlee would become the Bitch's first victim. As they stepped into the gazebo, Miss V began reciting a monologue from a Lashlee drama, a lament in heaven by Helen of Troy in which she grieves for the burden of her beauty that wasted the lives of great men. Ha! Madame Esmé knew the score.

The orchestra struck up the bridal march as Venus and her retinue of Cuban girls stepped from the mosque where they had dressed her. Her hair was plaited with flower buds. Her shoulders were bare. The white silk gown hadn't a frill or pleat. Designed by Madame Esmé, it was loose, unbelted with a tapered waist, and sheer so you could see the jostling of her body beneath, the points of her nipples, the roll of each hip and forward press of her thighs. She looked like a virgin being led to sacrifice. Madame Esmé, who taught by symbols, must have been chortling at the joke she had made—Daddy was the one to be slaughtered.

Hickey laid down the book, walked out and down the hall to the rest room, wondering about the comment that a poet named Lashlee would be the Bitch's first victim. He stood over the toilet, brooding about Emma Vidal, almost surely Miss V. Tonight, he vowed, Cynthia was going to tell him about the "avalanche." Whatever it took, he'd convince her.

He zipped his slacks, splashed water on his tired eyes, decided to run downstairs to the drugstore for coffee. At the landing he met his partner hobbling up the stairs. Leo's iron-colored eyes peeked indignantly out of crinkled sockets. His graying walrus mustache twitched, as though pointing at the swollen crest of his cheekbone, at the bruise that looked like somebody'd pelted him with an overripe plum and it had stuck there. His hat was off, gripped in his right hand. He slapped it angrily against his knee.

"Go ahead, chew me out, punch me in the nose, where the other guy missed. I got it coming." Leo waddled past Hickey into the office, tossed his hat onto the rack as he rounded it, and flopped onto the love seat.

"Where's the girl?"

"Gee, Tom, if I knew, maybe I'd be on her like I'm supposed to. In case you give a fig who slugged me, it was a Negro fella, young enough he oughta been in uniform. Wearing leathers and a Texas sombrero. Drove a limo, big silver Chrysler. I checked it out. Belongs to Charlie Schwartz. See, the limo pulls up in front of the girl's place, she struts out, talks to the driver, and points at me. I don't know we're playing rough, so I leave the thirty-eight in my glove box. I get out and stand by the car. He strolls up, implores me to give the girl some privacy, then suckerpunches me a couple times, and while I'm down he snatches the keys and heaves them into a yard full of watchdogs, three man-eating German shepherds. The wise guy runs off laughing. By the time I hot-wire the Buick, they're way the hell down India Street. I kept them in sight until they crossed Broadway. Last half hour I been driving around the Gaslamp district, looking for them, down into National City. . . . Wouldn't be scotch in that bottle, would it?"

Hickey delivered the pint of Dewar's, walked back to his desk chair, and sat down hard. "Christ," he muttered.

"What do you figure?"

He sighed, made fists, and socked them together. "Either the girl scored the money she wants and she's going to pay Katoulis, or Charlie Schwartz is gonna give her the money." He stared at Leo, hoping the old guy would offer a prettier solution.

"Why would Schwartz give her money?"

Plucking the manila envelope off his desk, he slipped Cynthia's publicity photo out, walked it over to Leo. "There's why."

FOURTEEN

♪ ♪ ♪

AT 5:15 RUDY'S SALAD-AND-DESSERT COOK WAS YELLING AT HIS assistant and the pot washer. From what Hickey made out, *borrachos* was the key word. Waiters and busboys fussed over the table settings. Castillo sat in the office, holding a pen and scrutinizing a stack of receipts. When Hickey stepped in, the Cuban leaned his chair against the wall, pursed his lips, drew his eyebrows together.

Hickey set the ledger books on the file case, draped his overcoat and hat on the rack. "You seen the girl?"

Moving his head sideways an inch, Castillo said, "Only she called me about noon. I say she don't get no money till maybe tomorrow, the bird hangs up on me. I tell you, I don't like how people been treating me today. First she's waking me up, then you don't show this morning like you said to talk with me."

"Damned shame, partner." Hickey was tempted to follow with an inquiry as to just how good pals Castillo and Madeline had become. But that could wait. "I'm here now. You wanta tell me something, or ask?"

Castillo ran two fingers through his slick hair, clasped his hands behind his neck, and stared like a warrior relegated to the bargaining table. "What for the girl needs this money?"

"Family business," Hickey said. "She's got a sick daddy in a Catholic rest home. You know Catholics, if she don't pay up, they're gonna excommunicate him or something."

After a pause to calculate while he gathered the receipts and crammed them into a desk drawer, Castillo leaned forward, leading with his nose. "She wants two grand, okay, we sign her to a contract. We're taking twenty percent, whatever she makes for two, maybe three years. You tell her. I got a dinner engagement."

Hickey watched the man stand, edge around the desk to the door warily as if they were wrestlers and the bell just rang. True to form, Hickey thought. The girl's in a fix, Castillo figures an angle, a way to squeeze her. There was a businessman for you, a guy who slept with his antennae out, scanning the atmosphere for chances to grab the advantage. A gambler who won't play without a stacked deck. The kind Madeline always wanted Hickey to be.

He walked out front, told Phil, the maître d', to look out for Cynthia and fetch him the minute she showed, and returned to the office; he sat on the desk, picked up the phone, and dialed his home number. On the sixth ring, Elizabeth answered, panting into the receiver.

"Who's chasing you?" Hickey asked.

"The Big Bad Wolf." Elizabeth chuckled and caught her breath. "I rode my bike to the plunge, Dad. Swam twenty laps, but I could hardly ride back. I almost stopped and called a tow truck."

"Talk to your mom yet?"

"No, but maybe she's here. I'll go look. I just walked in. Ran, I mean."

As Hickey sat waiting, lighting his pipe, the door got pounded, Hickey shouted, "Yeah," and Romero, the dessert-and-salad chef, strode in. He was a wiry little fellow, hardly five feet including his chef's hat, who lived inside a cloud of smoke that he constantly fed by sucking down and blowing out Lucky Strikes, consuming each one in three or four drags.

"How you like this, boss?" Romero screeched. "That *cochón* Felipe is hacking lettuce, he knocks a big head on the floor, he kicks it around the cutting table like a *fútbol,* he picks it up, he dips it in the dishwasher's greasy water, he throws it back on the cutting board and starts hacking again."

"No sign of her, Dad," Elizabeth said. "Didn't leave a note either."

Hickey sat still a moment, making fists, flexing the muscles of his arms and shoulders, squeezing his eyes shut. Finally he barked at Romero, "So fire him."

As Romero spun and marched out, Elizabeth asked, "You there, Daddy?"

"Yeah."

There came another rap on the door, and Phil shouted in, "The girl just pulled up in a limo."

"Listen, babe," Hickey said. "Soon as you see or hear from her, call me, huh? Promise?"

"Sure. Sorry, Dad."

Hickey said good-bye, jumped up and around the desk to the door, then remembered the ledger books. He turned back, grabbed and stuffed them into a file drawer, and hustled out front. Cynthia leaned on the hatcheck counter. She wore an emerald green sleeveless dress, a white shawl around her shoulders, and white gloves, no hat, only an orchid, ivory white and violet, pinned into her hair above the left ear. In heels that leveled her with Hickey, she glared at him, her pupils dilated.

Her voice sounded twenty years older, racked by smoke and booze. "Why'd you sick the old fat guy on me?"

Hickey grabbed her arm and whisked her across the floor, through the kitchen, out the back way to his car. She only resisted by trying to walk slow, stiffly holding onto her poise.

In the Chevy, she took a compact out of her purse, checked her makeup, dabbed a little powder onto her chin. While Hickey wheeled out of the lot and up Fourth toward Broadway, he was trying to decide where to take her. Someplace deserted, where nobody could hear her scream, where he couldn't get pestered by Good Samaritans or the law.

She kept mute all the way down Broadway and partway up Harbor Drive. Finally she snapped, "Where do you think you're taking me?"

"Someplace we can talk. How about the scene of the crime?"

"What crime?"

"How many you done?"

Cynthia wheeled her face toward her window. On the sidewalk beside the docks, couples strolled, a drunk staggered perilously along the rim of the harbor. A fisherman standing beside a pile of nets shoved another man, who coiled up and flew at the guy, throwing a roundhouse. Just beyond the county offices, as Hickey slowed for a stop sign, the girl flung the door open and lunged that way, but he caught her arm and yanked her back, squeezing cruelly.

She yowled, but Hickey wouldn't let go or ease off until she got righted in her seat and had closed and locked the door.

"Bastard," she hissed. "Get this—I'm not talking, and you better cut me loose. Drop me at the Pacific Ballroom or else. I know guys lots tougher than you."

Hickey straightened his hat and tie. "Bring 'em on."

FIFTEEN

♪ ♪ ♪

THE FOG ROLLED IN, DARKENING FROM GRAY TO BLACK AS THEY crossed Point Loma. Hickey pulled in to the lot at the same Sunset Cliffs vista point where last night Cynthia had met Donny Katoulis. The only other car, a Hudson that looked like a submarine surfacing out of the fog, had steamed windows. Its radio crooned a smarmy love song.

Cynthia stared at her persecutor in bewilderment, as though he were a medium who'd just gleaned from God-knows-where the exact number of ounces she'd gained since Thanksgiving. As she recovered she gave him a sneer and a wink. "You gonna try to kiss me?" She tossed her cigarette at the ashtray. It hit the radio knob and dropped onto the floorboard. Hickey retrieved it, stubbed it out. The girl rarely smoked, yet she'd sucked two Pall Malls on the drive, rapaciously as though she'd become Romero, the chef. She lit another while Hickey walked around the car and opened her door.

"Familiar?" he asked.

She stepped out slowly, warily, checking around as if cops might spring from behind the century plants.

"What'd you think of Donny Katoulis? An old pal of mine." Hickey ushered her ahead of him onto the narrow, slippery trail that led down the cliffside. At his mention of Katoulis, the girl's shoulders locked, and her hair rustled as though from a shudder.

Quickly, she recovered and growled, "I can't walk here. If I take off these stupid shoes, I'll run my hose."

"Want me to carry you?"

"Don't touch me, rat," she commanded, and walked on, teetering. The trail was a switchback, about two hundred yards bordered by ice plant and cholla cactus, that brought them to a small sandy beach at the base of the fifty-foot cliff. The waves crashed the rocks to their north and south. Cynthia paced back and forth in the sand, stumbling and snorting until finally she kicked the shoes off. One shot like a missile at the cliff. The other sailed, hovered, and plopped about thirty yards out to sea.

Hickey leaned against a boulder while the girl did a one-legged bounce, hoisting her dress to unhitch her stockings from the garters. "Now's your chance, you old lech. Get yourself an eyeful?"

She bounced and wiggled out of the stockings, rolled them and stuffed them into her handbag, and withdrew her Pall Malls and lighter. She lit up, took a couple steps toward Hickey to see clearly into where he stood in shadow, out of the moon-brightened fog. The mist had beaded on her makeup, and it hung there like tear-shaped crystals dotting her face.

"You trying to scare me, old man? That why you brought me here?"

"Naw. Scaring won't do any good, if playing ball with the Schwartzes and Donny Katoulis doesn't scare you. And reasoning with you—hell, somebody pays a killer, I don't figure they're reasonable. Naw, those things won't work. Guess I'm gonna have to hurt you."

She scampered backward with tiny steps. "You won't hurt me. It'd cost you too dear. You wouldn't get another peep out of me,

139

then you and Clyde might as well start peddling encyclopedias."

"Seems I remember Clyde having an orchestra and me owning a restaurant before you flounced in. Who you trying to kill, babe?"

She paced a few steps toward the water, her heels drawing grooves in the damp sand; then she wheeled and flung her cigarette at Hickey. "Let's see you hit me, tough guy, I dare you."

"Maybe it's Laurel, the Bitch? Pravinshandra? Venus? You paying Mister Katoulis to eliminate your mother?"

Cynthia had frozen with hands on her hips, her head cocked, nose wrinkled, perplexed once again by his mind reading. She strode closer, until the next step would've bumped him, and peered into his eyes. "What'd they tell you up there?"

Work her into a fury, Hickey thought, and she'll drop her guard like an Italian boxer. "Ladies I talked to both said you're nuts."

"Ha!" She spun around, 360 degrees like a ballerina, and slung her handbag down. It hit her in the foot and she kicked it away, into the ebb tide. "And you're stupid enough to believe the sluts. That's what they are, the whole lousy brood. He didn't have to rape *them.*"

Hickey rolled his shoulders, wagged his head slowly, posing his most earnest bedside manner. "Meaning he did have to rape somebody, right?"

"Good one, Sherlock." She backed a couple steps, slowly as if she were going to run, then lunged forward again. "You saw the picture, moron. If you couldn't see that was a rape, who'd you figure was lying at Mary's feet in the pietà, her milkman?"

"And the one getting raped was?"

"The Bitch. The Bitch," Cynthia growled exasperatedly as a snooty professor lecturing freshmen. Suddenly her eyes flashed like gems in a sunlit whirlpool, and a sly crack of smile appeared before she wiped it away with her arm. "You wanta hear the truth, I'll tell you. Where do I start?" she asked, cockily, as though certain that once he'd gotten her story, he'd see that justice deemed the murder her right and duty, so he'd quit nagging her about it.

Hickey reached for his pipe and tobacco. "How about you start with the picture. So it's Laurel getting raped, who's doing it?"

"Him," she snapped. "You read the note."

"Him being the master?"

"Yes."

"So who drew the picture, Emma Vidal?"

"Yes, yes, yes. Give me your coat."

After moving his glasses from the coat to his shirt pocket, he tossed it to her. She laid it on a flat, footstool-high rock a few feet toward the sea from the boulder Hickey leaned against, and sat with her ankles crossed, chin in her hands, elbows on her knees, lip in such a pout that her snapshot might've resembled the negative of a Watusi.

"Why'd Miss V send you the picture?"

The girl sighed as though resigning herself to his stupidity. "She sent it to Daddy, not me. But Laurel had already killed Daddy. Dead people can only do their work through the living, right? He gave the picture to me and begged me to stop the Fiend."

"Your father asked you to kill a guy," Hickey muttered.

"The hell he did. Daddy wouldn't kill anybody. He wanted me to give the picture to Venus. He knew what she'd do."

"What's that?"

"I don't know," the girl snapped. "Lash him to a redwood, squirt cat piss up his nose, slice off his eyelids, and cover his head with a fishbowl full of red ants. Something like that." For a minute she stood still, breathing deliberately. Finally she kicked the sand. "But it wasn't so easy, Tom," she howled. "There are more damned people than one in the world. Why do I have to save everybody, smart guy? What about Miss V, when Venus found out she was a traitor, a spy, that she knew everything? What would Venus do then?" She clutched both sides of her hair, yanked them together in front of her face. "What *did* she do?"

141

Parting the hair, she glared at Hickey, her bottom lip and cheeks sucked tight against teeth and bones.

"Venus started an avalanche?"

"Avalanche," Cynthia groaned. She stared at the ground a minute, probably looking for a rock to heave. When she didn't spot one, she yanked off her silver cone earrings and flung them into the sea. She whipped back around. "I was the only one who could save them. I bought the gun and went there to kill Pravinshandra, for Daddy and to save Miss V, and to stop him before he could breed a whole tribe of baby fiends like him."

"Whoa. You're saying all those pregnant women . . ." Listening to the girl's bizarre tale, Hickey's brain was beginning to feel like soap bubbles. A ruthless, homicidal mother teamed with a preacher who rapes, or otherwise diddles, every cutie who steps through his portals, apparently withholding the fact from said ruthless mother—or getting her permission—while the cuties, big with child, become sheep in his loyal flock.

"Naw," Hickey droned, though he was remembering some improbable loyalties, like his mother's to Mary Baker Eddy. No question, if Ma had been Abraham, Hickey Isaac and Mary Baker Eddy Jehovah, the old woman would've had the boy gutted before the Almighty got a chance to announce the reprieve. He recalled 1923 or so, the ecstatic hordes outside Aimée Semple McPherson's Angelus Temple. Driving by there one Sunday, he saw a multitude, some dancing frantically, arms flailing the air, others crawling toward the doorway on their knees.

Cynthia kept reaching behind herself as if to scratch or unsnap something. It looked as though any second the girl might leap out of her clothes and go bounding, screaming, into the sea.

"Even I don't know which ones he raped," Cynthia wailed. "It was the only letter from Miss V Daddy showed me, and up there she wouldn't say much. She was trying to protect me. With Laurel and Venus already trying to kill me, I didn't need *him* after me, too." She caught a deep breath, blew it out, and slumped, as though settling into an easy chair, and her voice began to shift from a lunatic's whine to a storyteller's introspective drawl.

"If she would've trusted me. . . . Oh, Lord—she'd be alive, he'd be dead, and I . . . I would've proved I must be the world's greatest actress, the way they fell for my pose when anybody ought to know I'd marry Hermann Göring before I'd join their nitwit gang, embrace their vile religion, but nobody caught on—Venus, Laurel, not even Miss V. Nobody had a clue I was only taking him up that mountain to shoot him in the head. You see, my plan was brilliant. I'd pretend to join their coven—"

"Whoa. Why call it a coven?"

"I'll call it what I want. Let me talk, for Christ's sake." She flashed him a glare as indignant as though he'd stopped her in the middle of a song and asked her to repeat the previous verse. "To join, you have to first take communion, meaning you sit on their Holy Mountain as long as it takes until their phony masters contact you, with a message."

The girl sighed and let her shoulders sag, as if mentioning the "communion" had cost half her blood. She stared listlessly at Hickey until he asked, "Which masters?"

"The Aryan masters," she said dreamily. "Venus preaches that the Aryan masters, more ancient than the Tibetan masters, have been holed up around Mount Shasta since the age of the primal revelation, when the Aryans set out from their homeland in the Urals to spread the faith. This band crossed the land bridge from Siberia. They got chased ever south by hostile Indians until they finally dug into the mountain, where they still live, in a cave the size of Monaco."

"Cave," Hickey mumbled.

"Look, the Aryans won't appear in the flesh, but they give signs and messages, which is what you wait for on the mountain. Get it? The gimmick is, nobody receives any lousy message, but they're so damned tired and cold on the mountain that finally they lie just to get out of there. They make up a line of nonsense and say they received it from the masters, something like 'Her heart had not yet opened for the one ray to enter, thence to fall as three into four in the lap of Maya.' Then, you see, they feel so guilty and spiritually bereft—with everybody lying, and wearing her stinking lie like a silver badge, and each of them thinking she's the only liar—they need to follow our good Master P to save their rotten souls.

"It's a perfect setup for me to get Pravinshandra alone. All I have to do is ask to join up, agree to commune with the Aryans of Holy Mountain. It's always three people who go up, always *him,* of course, and a woman when it's a woman communer—or is that communicant? Or communist? Aw, why ask you? You don't know anything." The girl was smiling faintly now, as if she'd extricated herself from the weird story to enjoy the telling of it. "The way they do this ritual, there are three stations, little huts on the north trail, about a mile apart. He goes to the high station, the pilgrim to the middle one, the helper to the lowest. The helper and Pravinshandra are supposed to funnel the spirits toward the middle. This way. That way. Ha! Wait, oh, the helper, the one at the lowest station—really stationed there to chase back the communer if she tries to escape—has to be an apostle. That's anybody who's been around since the beginning, almost five years ago, who stuck by Venus when she stole the money."

"Which money?"

"Don't you read the news?" Cynthia snapped. "Venus embezzled seventy thousand dollars from Otherworld. That's why—well, one reason—she killed Madame Esmé. How do you think she's bought the Black Forest? Where was I—ah, the only women apostles still living at Black Forest are Venus, the Bitch when she's there, and Miss V. Oh God . . . Miss V." Cynthia covered her face with both hands; her fingers spread as though she were peeking, then one hand reached up and clutched her hair and raked through it, scattering the orchid and hairpins onto the sand.

The tide was rolling in closer, trickling around the rock where she sat, and the waves boomed louder against the cliffs on both sides of them. Cynthia's voice carried over the noise, getting stronger, as though the story shot juice to her batteries.

"Of course I wasn't going up any mountain with Venus or Laurel, so that left Miss V. Perfect. Pravinshandra up there alone with me, Miss V the only other soul on the damned mountain, except the Aryan spooks. Ha! Miss V's not capable of violence, you see—she's a sensitive. Madame Esmé used to call her a lotus flower. It's why she had stuck beside Venus—a week or so on the outside, away from the insulation of Otherworld or Black Forest, she panics, runs for cover. So I don't tell her my plan, but after it's done, I know, she'll help me drag him to some crevasse where they won't find him until next summer, long after the wolves have chawed his flesh and spit out the bullets. Or they might never find him. Some ravines up there, you wouldn't hit bottom until you landed in hell. You think the locals are going to search for *him?* Oh no. They can't abide a man who throws blue fire."

Hickey scribbled a note in his mind, to ask the girl later about the fire-throwing trick, but he wouldn't stop her now, risk diverting her story.

"Naturally Miss V's horrified that I'm going to communion. She tried to talk me into running, offers to steal me away and drive us back to Daddy, and when I won't listen, at last she tells me what he may do. What he's already done to the sluts. You ready, Tom?" she growled. "First he's going to hypnotize me, the way he learned from Miss V and she learned from Doctor Murten, a student of Mister Freud. He'll knock me out, probably using the excuse that he's guiding me into a receptive state, which will allow the Aryan spooks to visit. He's going to knock me out, she says, with his voice, a touch of blue fire, and our Prana Yama breathing, then he'll give me a potion. Dope! Something that blots out memories, and finally he'll . . ." Cynthia raked her hair again. "Miss V knows how desperately he wants me. Like Faust wanted Helen, he'll bet the whole wad on me. Not like the sluts—them, he probably just snaps a finger, one blue spark, and, hocus-pocus, they're on their backs, oozing."

Cynthia grasped her temples with both palms and pressed hard. Her eyes bulged. "I'm the grand prize," she wailed. "For me he'll risk the whole Venus deal.

"Oh, Miss V. God, I laughed at her like I think she's crazy, which breaks my heart, Tom—she loves me dearly, but I can't let on or she's liable to botch things. Miss V's too tender to . . ."

145

Gripping both cheeks with her fingernails, she screeched, "I killed her. I killed her. . . ." Her voice kept fading. By the fifth repetition, it got so low that Hickey couldn't hear over the waves. Finally she clasped her hands on her belly, pushed as though helping herself breathe, and found her voice again.

"It was still dark when we set out for the mountain in the long black car. We started climbing at sunrise, each of us with a canteen and a bedroll hanging off our backs—in case I didn't receive any message the first day, there's a mountaineer's hut where we could stay the night. I carried the pistol in my bedroll. Pravinshandra had all his stuff in an army pack. Fruit, matches, a can of Sterno, his potion," she snarled at Hickey as though pinning him, or every man, with the blame. "He led the way. I could've killed him before we got ten feet. You see what a coward I am?" She leaped up and paced in a sharp circle around the rock, peering frantically in all directions as though just discovering that she was lost, then lunged toward Hickey, threw herself at his feet, and gazed up beseechingly. He touched her hair. She spat between his shoes. Finally she turned and crawled back to her rock, straightened Hickey's coat, sat as before, and docilely resumed her story.

"We hiked a million miles through knee-deep snow—I had to wear army boots, imagine—to the low station. We left Miss V there. As I tromped off behind Pravinshandra, to march the last mile, Miss V saw me watching her over my shoulder, waiting for her sign. She pointed to herself, then motioned up the trail, meaning she'd follow and protect me, oh God save us, she loved me so.

"A hundred yards ahead, we walked into the cloud that always shrouds the damned mountain. It's thick as drool and icy. My brain had started to freeze and my legs felt like splinters. I kept trying to rest, but *he* wouldn't allow it. At first he tried to beguile me with cow eyes and that gushy voice, like Martino's. When I snubbed him, he started nagging like Cinderella's stepmother. God, he despised me, the way brutes always do, since I've got them overpowered. By the middle station I was three or four steps

146

from death by exhaustion, but I had worked out my final plan. I'd send him ahead to the high station, then rest until I spotted Miss V, on her way up to watch over me, then I'd take off, motioning her to follow but keeping ahead, a hundred yards at least, so she wouldn't get in my way. At the high station I'd sneak up and blast him. Once it was done, Miss V would thank me and say a prayer for me and help drag the body a little farther up the mountain. The higher up, the better to stash a corpse, the more crevasses and ghastly cliffs with craggy rocks and snowdrifts."

Cynthia fell silent and stared blankly at Hickey. Her face had turned so pale that even through the fog the scratches she'd made with her fingernails stood out like bloody welts. For a minute or two she sat motionless.

"Then what?" Hickey asked.

She muttered something he couldn't make out over the waves.

"Louder."

"He fucked me!"

Hickey watched the girl walk her index and second fingers up and down her forehead. "You mean . . ."

"I mean he fucked me!" she screamed. "He took out his goddamned Sterno. He made me cider. I was freezing to death, wasn't I? I gulped it down. Who wouldn't? Then I got woozy. The next thing I know, I'd gotten fucked and there was a needle welt in my arm."

"Whew," Hickey said, and shook his head to clear it. But Cynthia must've thought he was calling her a liar.

"Don't I know if I got fucked?" she howled. "With blood in my panties and a stench like—he lubed me with some kind of stinking goo. You still don't believe me, look! Get your jollies out of this."

She sprang up, flung the hem of her dress high like a Tijuana hooker showing her wares, and caught it between her teeth. She grappled with her girdle and panties until she had them on the sand. Then she slapped the side of her butt, yelped, and pointed to the same spot. In the wedge of the dimple was a piece of raw skin the size of a silver dollar, surrounded by stitches. Hickey had to bend close to make it out in the foggy dark.

"You've seen enough," she hissed, and let the dress fall.

"A tattoo?"

"No! Jesus! A brand, like a cow," she wailed. "The *Nezah* Tree of Life. I had the vile thing cut off!" A second later she gazed around and finally started gathering her underclothes, the soggy handbag, the orchid that had garnished her hair.

"Let's get you someplace warm," Hickey said.

She allowed him to wrap the coat around her shoulders, and she walked steadily against him when he took her by the arm. To get out of the inlet and reach the trail, since the tide had risen, they had to wade through icy knee-high surf, which startled her into violent, teeth-clacking shivers, as if the dunking were a baptism that transformed her from a fierce, murderous woman to a deathly sick little girl with her pride smashed. Now she looked admissible to heaven—pallid, her jaw and forehead wrinkled with fear, eyes fluttering.

Hickey wrapped her in his arm, guided her along the trail. In the Chevy she drew her knees up, leaned her cheek on them, and turned her face toward the passenger door. Hickey smoothed his coat over her back and shoulders, switched the heater on, and adjusted the wind-wing to defrost the windshield. The girl made a few little peeps, like a woeful bird; besides those and the chattering of her teeth, she offered no sounds, even when Hickey started musing out loud.

"Miss Vidal must've caught him in the act, huh? I guess he whacked her, heaved her into a snowfield. Might've even climbed up above and kicked loose an avalanche."

"Sure," the girl whispered.

Maybe they could get Pravinshandra fried for killing Emma Vidal, Hickey thought. If he convinced Cynthia of that, maybe she'd nix the murder. He tried to imagine a jury believing all this lunacy. The only chance would be if they could get a few of those pregnant women to testify about their own trips to Holy Mountain. Except Hickey didn't for a second believe that the master had gotten away with raping one of them after another. In an hour, after he'd disposed of the girl and unraveled his mind, he wasn't apt to believe a tenth of her story.

"Talk a little more," he coaxed. "What'd he say when you came to? How'd he try to cover up?"

"Blamed it on the Aryan masters," she muttered. "Look, he knocked me out with the dope. Later he claims everybody gets knocked out by the masters. You have to reach zero consciousness of this plane before you can perceive the next higher one. If you don't get knocked out, he says, he knows the message you bring is a lie. But whoever gets knocked out, she's got a message to bring him, even if she doesn't remember, *and* she's become a novice adept. That's why he brands you, to commemorate, to seal your destiny. He does it while you're knocked out so it won't hurt." Her voice reaching high with amazement, she exclaimed, "And the nitwits believe him. At first I half believed him, while he stood over me an hour or more, begging to hear what profound morsel the masters had granted me. Besides, you expect me to think right after I'd got knocked out and fucked and suffered the death of Miss V? It took me three days to figure what happened, with every chance him grilling me about the message. I damn near made up a story just so he'd leave me alone." She threw herself back against the seat, her face constricted as if there were no windshield and they were speeding into a gale, and shouted, "How do you know what's a dream and what isn't?"

He reached his arm across the backrest, and she fell into it, let him draw her close, laid her cheek on his shoulder. "Evidence, that's how you know," she said softly. "Did I tell you about the blood and goo?"

"Yeah. You told me."

"Evidence," she murmured.

"On the mountain, after you came to, you try to kill him?"

"He took my gun," she groaned. "It was in my bedroll. He'd already hitched it onto his pack. All the way down he kept me ahead of him, and I was weeping so—it was all I could do to stagger along, worrying where Miss V could've gone. He only said she'd vanished—nothing about an avalanche until we'd got to Black Forest and Venus and the Bitch held me down while he shot me full of poison. A sedative, he called it. They could've killed me. You know why they didn't? The Bitch wouldn't because *he* had her believing I was going to spill the secrets I'd gotten told on the mountain. And he wouldn't kill me because he hopes to fuck me again." For a moment she quit shivering and cackled, as if realizing that the master wouldn't be fucking anybody. Katoulis would fix that.

"Two days he kept stabbing me with the needle. I couldn't get to my bedroll. They hardly left me alone until the service for Miss V. When I woke up, nobody was guarding me. I got the pistol. My right leg wouldn't move; still I dragged myself across the compound, before Saint Ophelia came to help me. I couldn't see her—I could hardly see the ground—but I felt her hand on my shoulder, like before. Miraculously my legs got strong as Tarzan's. I marched into the chapel and ran at the altar, aiming the gun between his eyes. 'Here's your message!' I yelled. I didn't hit *anybody,"* she wailed, and fell to weeping, with spasms crossing her shoulders and deep, eerie moans.

As a cop and musician, Hickey'd known his share of loonies. To make any sense of their tales, he'd finally deduced, you had to remember that part was always true, another part delusion. A tough job, because often the craziest stuff was true and the reasonable things were delusion.

Luckily he didn't have to pass judgment. What he needed to know was if she'd already paid Katoulis. Not a chance she'd confess if he asked her straight out.

Two miles along Rosecrans past the marine and naval bases, up Barnett Avenue, Hickey used his free hand to rub her back and shoulders. While he waited for an opening to cross the Coast Highway, he bent and pecked a kiss on her shoulder. "It's okay, babe. Pravinshandra's a goner," he promised. "First we go with the law. If they don't fix him, I will."

"Too late," she whispered. "Too late. We're all dead, all dead. Dead."

Meaning Donny was paid and on his mission, Hickey knew, but hoping against the obvious, he asked, "You still need the two grand?"

Though he couldn't see her head wag, he felt it, and it sparked a shudder that began at the base of his cowlick and zinged down to his tailbone. It was one of those moments when the news comes, clear and strong, that the muck you've just stepped into might be quicksand.

The girl was still shivering. He patted her head. "Hey, I'm with you. A guy like that, you do what you've got to."

"Thanks, Tom," she murmured. "You're okay."

He'd count on Cynthia's stupendous pride convincing her she had him collared, that he wouldn't go after Katoulis or snitch to the law, that a man to whom she'd bared her soul would remain her slave eternally.

As they turned onto her street, she braced herself up in the seat. "Give me a minute to powder my nose, then we'll go to Rudy's. I want to sing."

"Some trooper," Hickey said, and pulled to the curb in front of the boardinghouse. Cynthia had gotten her strength back. She didn't need help up the steps to the porch where Dolores Ganguish, in a daisy housecoat, met them at the door, her face shining from a dousing of Pond's cream. *"Madre de Dios,"* the woman gasped. "What this man did to you?" She clutched Cynthia's arm and tugged her out of harm's way, wedging herself between the girl and Hickey.

"It's okay, Mama," Cynthia cooed; she wrenched herself free and headed for the stairs, while Mrs. Ganguish rotated to glower at one of them and then the other. Hickey fished his brain for a story to keep the woman from pestering Cynthia but got no bites. Anyway, the girl was plenty able to tell stories of her own. He flashed Mrs. Ganguish a disarming smile and asked if she had a phone he could use in private. Warily she led him to the phone in the downstairs hallway, on the way to the kitchen. She turned back toward the parlor, casting a glance over her shoulder every step or two.

151

From up the stairs came tiptoeing footsteps and girlish whis-
pers. Hickey dialed Leo's number, got an answer on the second
ring.

"You rested?"

"Naw. Give me till February," Leo grumbled.

"I need you to meet me at Rudy's, quick as you can get there."

"For a nightcap only, I trust."

"Need you to watch the girl for a day or two," Hickey said
quietly.

"Speak up, will you?"

"Nope."

SIXTEEN

♪ ♪ ♪

HICKEY LEFT THE GIRL AT RUDY'S, HAVING CHARGED LEO TO KEEP her away from any silver limos. He left his Chevy in the lot behind Rudy's, hustled the four blocks to his and Leo's office. Amid the litter on his desk was the itinerary for Venus and the master, which he'd gotten from Katherine at the Black Forest.

Tonight they were due to arrive in Denver. Tomorrow evening they'd lecture. Hickey made a few calls, learned that commercial flights to Denver left at 6:50 every morning. Tomorrow's was booked full, as was every other flight through January 5. No Katoulis or any other Greek name appeared on tomorrow's boarding list.

Hickey phoned Rudy's, asked Phil if Castillo'd come in yet. Phil said no. Hickey asked him to page an army colonel named Creaser, a regular, who by this time of night was merry enough so he might've loaned out an airplane if anybody'd asked. All Hickey sought was a lift to Denver. Creaser told him the fellow to call, said to drop his name. Ten minutes later Hickey was booked on a military hop to Lowry Army Air Force Base, departing at 2:30 A.M.

He stuffed the change of clothes he kept at the office into an overnight bag, along with shaving gear, Cynthia's ledgers, and two guns, a Browning .45 automatic revolver and a Smith & Wesson .38. Finally, at 11:25—with hands sweating like those of a fat guy drinking beer at noon, in August, in the Sahara—he called Madeline.

If she answered, he didn't know whether he'd bawl her out or sigh and murmur how he loved her. After seven rings Elizabeth picked up the phone and yawned into it. " 'Lo?"

"Sorry to wake you, babe."

"Hi, dad."

"Your mom ever come home?"

"No, I guess she's still at the club." She yawned again. "Why don't you call her there?"

Swell, Hickey thought. If he caught her there, fearing she was with Castillo, he probably couldn't smother his anger any longer. He'd snarl the wrong words, and she'd snap. He'd yell. Then she'd march back to Castillo with another excuse to ignore her conscience, if she still had one. If all she'd done with Castillo so far was flirt and pal around, now, in spite, she'd lead him to the honeymoon suite. Or so Hickey would imagine and fret over, squandering his concentration, while he took off after Donny Katoulis, a mission about as safe as trying to infiltrate the Gestapo.

"Babe," he said, "I'm going somewhere, probably won't be able to call until late tomorrow night." If ever, he mused. "When I get back, this job's gonna be over. Ask your mom to make reservations at the Cedar Cove Lodge in Arrowhead. See if she can get one of the cabins with a fireplace, two bedrooms, no phone. Tell her . . ." His throat felt clogged with a thick, steamy vapor, on account of the thought that had gripped him—he might be speaking his last words to his daughter, giving his last message to Madeline.

"Dad? You there?"

154

"Sure. Tell her I see what went wrong." It was a lie but an honorable one.

"Went wrong with what?"

"Aw, you know, don't you? We used to be happier, didn't we?"

"Sure, before you had to work every night. We miss you, Daddy, that's all."

"Yeah, well, that's almost over. Because I love you and her more than all the rest of everybody, combined."

"Aw, Daddy," Elizabeth yawned. He let her go.

Ten minutes he stared at the first line in the next page of Cynthia's book and brooded. What if, right this minute, Madeline were sitting by the sea-view window listening to Paul exclaim her beauty more over one drink than Hickey'd done in years? What if, this instant, she were deciding to leave him and all that could persuade her to hold off a few days was hearing his promise in person? To leave without seeing her might amount to strike three.

He grabbed up his suitcase, doused the lights, hustled out, and downstairs. As he jogged up the sidewalk toward Rudy's, his suitcase bowled over a sailor who'd staggered into his right-of-way. It was one of those trips when happenings seem to warn you to run back home. The block before Rudy's, the catch on his suitcase sprang. His shaving kit and Cynthia's ledgers flew out and skidded a couple yards, then got stomped by a troop of giddy salesgirls returning to their lodgings at the YWCA. When he reached his car, the trunk key wouldn't turn. He slung the suitcase onto the front passenger's seat, sped sans headlights out of the lot and straight down A Street past the courthouse and the visiting team's side of Lane Field, across the Santa Fe tracks and onto Pacific Coast Highway.

The four miles before he turned on Garnet then started up Mount Soledad, he drove crouched forward like a jockey, squinting into the dark and chewing on the pipe he would've lit except that he was too agitated to bother. There'd been a wreck on the highway next to Milly's. A truck backing out must've whacked a lights-out Buick. The cops and ambulance had already arrived.

Hickey drove by, made a left on Garnet. He turned right on Ingraham, spinning tires on the gravel, and started up the dirt road that wound around the coastal side of Mount Soledad. He flicked on his headlights. The odds of getting stalled by a cop on rich folk's turf were slight, as long as you drove a respectable car. When they didn't know what bigshot or bigshot's kid they might offend, most cops chose tolerance.

Hickey sped along, gazing down at the moon-white foamy waves, glancing in his mirror at the two dark bays and beyond them at the harbor full of warships. Above them the sky was flecked with lights. He spotted a squadron of fighter planes—probably headed toward some carrier to replace the ones blown to splinters last week in the China Sea—lifting off from North Island where, in a couple hours, he'd depart to wage a battle, maybe the decisive one, in his private war.

Madeline wanted to live on Soledad, where the houses were as big as mausoleums, with sprawling lawns surrounding the tennis courts. It was some people's idea of a sanctuary, built for those who chose to watch all the commotion down below from a safe distance. Hickey remembered a story of an uncle in Kansas who'd bought atop the tallest hill in his county and started bragging. Soon enough, the mayor, a banker, and some other chumps came bidding for it. Hickey's uncle turned a 1,000 percent profit.

Soledad didn't charm Hickey. It reminded him of Beverly Hills. Sure, the mansions were elegant, the company refined, the garden parties catered, the wall hangings chosen by tasteful designers. But why up here, where you viewed so much of the damned, stormy world? Doesn't it keep them awake nights? Hickey wondered.

The pinkish crescent moon seemed to bounce off the cliffs beyond La Jolla Shores where the Del Mar Club sprawled like the headquarters of some military dictator in the tropics. Hickey coasted down the mountain, making wishes. That he wouldn't find Castillo with Madeline, but Madeline would be there alone, so he could promise to give up investigating and watch the spark in her eyes.

He skidded up to the gate. In one motion he jumped out, tossed the valet his keys, and said, "Guest of Ada Litton." She was a La Jolla socialite who'd lavished Hickey and family with privileges ever since he'd rescued her son from the clutches of a showgirl by taking him for a ride to a tavern where they caught her playing two-timer.

The Chinese guard saluted, and Hickey strode up the path between the front garden and tennis courts seven through ten. He rounded the fish pond and one of the fountains, then cut into a garden trail lined with a dozen varieties of stubby palms and shrubs that looked like peacocks, with bird of paradise plants, and ferns on trellises around the fish pond. A piano melody cut through the whoosh and boom of the surf. He stepped out of the garden a few yards from the window of the cocktail lounge overlooking a mile-long sandy beach that dead-ended at the sheer cliffs that rose to meet Camp Callan.

Madeline wasn't sitting at the window. She was on a stool, leaning on the teakwood bar, her shoulders bare, the fox stole Hickey'd bought her to celebrate the opening of Rudy's draped across her lap. Smoking one of her Pall Malls, she cocked her head just enough to turn the smoke she blew away from Paul Castillo's face.

Hickey shuffled on the path along the building to the steps of the dining porch that led off the lounge. Nobody drank or smooched on the porch tonight, on account of the chill. He flopped into a wicker chair and sat awhile, letting his stomach grow accustomed to a new feeling, as though he'd just swallowed a cannonball. Finally heaving himself up, he crossed the porch, opened the French door, and entered a part of the lounge hidden from Madeline's view by an oak hutch. A curly-haired Mexican waiter he knew grinned sheepishly and waved him in. Hickey wagged his head and motioned the guy over, then put a finger to his lips. The waiter trudged that way, arms to his sides, his chin down so far that the bald dome faced forward.

"Aren't we chums, Paco?" Hickey said low. "I mean if your girl was drinking with some stooge at Rudy's, I'd give you a call."

"I been watching," Paco whispered. "They don' kiss or holding hands or nothing."

"Ask her to step out on the porch, huh?"

Hickey turned to the French door, walked out, and stood facing the sea, paralyzed as he listened to the door swish open and the footsteps approach him. By the time he felt her near, his plan was to open his arms and draw her into them, kiss her until—and long after—he felt her anger dissolve, and give her his promise.

He hadn't heard Castillo's footsteps behind Madeline's. The second he turned and saw the man's head peering over Madeline's shoulder, a primitive groan issued out of him. His teeth had clamped together so tightly that he could hardly push sound through, yet his chin quivered, vibrating his words. "You didn't need to bring him out here."

"I didn't *bring* him." Her drawl was the one that always arrived after three or four drinks. She was chewing her upper lip. The stole hung over her right shoulder and one of the breasts that her red gown, Hickey knew, left exposed to within an eyelash of the areola.

He flung his gaze at Castillo, crucified the man with his eyes. "You wanta disappear, partner?"

"Maybe not." The Cuban's nose and bared teeth hung directly over Madeline's shoulder, the flip of her hair tickling his chin.

"No, see," Hickey rasped, "you figuring you oughta be out here while I'm talking with my wife—it's a bad sign."

"You gonna make a scene, Tom?" Madeline hissed. "Why the hell come tailing me—tired of your songbird already?"

Fiercely, she wrapped the stole around her shoulders, grabbed its ends in her fists, and tugged them down to her sides. On her chest hung the sapphire Hickey'd bought her last year at Bullock's Westwood, the one she'd fitted with a chain that would place it exactly at the cleft between her breasts as they dived beneath the scarlet gown.

"You wanta get rid of him, or do I?" Hickey snarled.

With a dispirited chuckle followed by a sigh, Madeline turned toward the door, leaving Castillo in the open holding the burgundy purse Madeline had bought four summers past in San Francisco. If the Cuban had followed her, maybe Hickey would've written a note, gotten Paco to deliver his promise to become first a husband, second a father, third a businessman, fourth nothing. But Castillo had to get the last word, play Lancelot, chase off Hickey's remnant of sense.

A crowd had gathered at the window and French door. Pale old fellows in dinner jackets; a couple drowsy females with sculptured hair and face powder deeper than a mortician would dare to apply; a trio of draft-age tennis bums whom a critical eye might've guessed Uncle Sam had booted out of his army when they flirted with him. None seemed willing to step beyond the glass. They'd rather stand back and pass judgment. Probably thinking that whoever allowed a Latin into their club was the first to blame.

"You got problems with me," Castillo droned, his voice a key lower than real, "you talk to me. How about that?"

"Yeah," Hickey muttered. "Good idea. Listen to this."

With an uppercut that started at his hip pocket, Hickey knocked Castillo onto his toes, from where the Cuban backpedaled a few feet before he tripped and collapsed onto a Mexican strawberry pot beside the French door. He fell forward onto his hands and knees. Hickey followed and set to kick the man if he tried to rise, but the Cuban held still like a boxer waiting for the eight count, until Hickey couldn't wait anymore. He was like a grenade with the pin loosed. He let fly a kick over Castillo's back. It shattered the strawberry pot, spraying Castillo and the French door with loam.

The Cuban had dropped to crawl position, and Hickey'd retreated to the center of the porch, when the first ashtray streaked past his ear. The second one nicked him in the shoulder, just as he caught sight of Madeline standing beside the French door.

"That's it, Tom," she screamed. Her arm whipped up and forward. The corner of a silver-and-rhinestone cigarette case, the one Elizabeth had given her last Christmas, stabbed Hickey in the chest.

He would've grabbed Madeline and carried her out of there, except that she'd fled inside. He'd have to chase her all over the club, and by then the police would be swarming. Either in the air or his mind, he could already hear the sirens. Days it might take him to talk his way free, after disturbing the peace of the Bigshot Club. So he wheeled and charged straight up the walk toward the Chinese valet, who dodged as though from a fearsome tackler, and tossed Hickey the Chevy keys.

SEVENTEEN

♪ ♪ ♪

HICKEY LEFT HIS CAR BEHIND RUDY'S AND CAUGHT A CHECKER cab, which dropped him, at 1:40 A.M., as close to the ferry landing as traffic allowed. The ferry was a shortcut across the harbor to Coronado Island, actually part of an isthmus that met the coastline twenty miles south, almost to Mexico. The ferry saved the sailors and civilian workers commuting to the air base at North Island half an hour each trip and a couple gas stamps a month.

Long after the graveyard rush, a troop of cars still backed up into Harbor Drive, and gangs of stevedores and mechanics bunched at the pedestrian turnstile. The ferry creaked and moaned as if each machine that rattled on were the last it could bear and every swell caused a pang of woe. Finally the horn bellowed. The ferry pitched into the harbor with implausible speed, heading straight for the destroyer *Alabama* as though on a ramming mission. It bounded over the wakes of patrol boats, landing craft on training maneuvers, pilot boats racing to deliver a captain or admiral who'd closed Rudy's or the Playroom, back

161

to his quarters on one of the dark ships that lined North Island or anchored in midharbor. When the ferry cut north to round the *Alabama,* Hickey watched Point Loma. Low on the cliffs, there were flashes like brief signal lights from where antiaircraft guns sentineled the harbor. Above them, a couple miles from Otherworld, the lighthouse glowed.

Hickey'd made his way along the rail—lined with pedestrians and drivers who relished the splash of fresh, salty, oily air—to the bow. As they turned south and passed beneath one of the barrage balloons, Hickey scanned the mile-long shoreline of dry docks and gazed around the south bay at condemned barges, homemade rafts, sailboats with rotted side planks and broken masts, skiffs tiny enough for a kid to row yet outfitted with tarps or tents—the floating squatter city of laborers from Consolidated, National Shipbuilding, or North Island.

"Hell of a mess, ain't it?" the tremendously wide fellow beside Hickey philosophized. "We got a harbor fulla Okies. I coulda got crew chief last week hadn't been a Okie whines to the super he's got eleven brats, needs the six extra bucks a week, gets the job."

His pal beside him attempted a laugh, which ended in a mighty wheeze. "You was crew chief, Gordo, Howie and me'd be snoozing all night long."

The fat guy snatched the asthmatic's cap and whacked him a few times as they ambled toward an old Ford, while the ferry bumped, repelled, finally righted against the dock. The asthmatic climbed into the driver's seat.

Hickey approached and asked for a lift to North Island. He rounded the car, got into the back, and sat beside the fat guy behind a stately Negro fellow, about fifty, tall enough so the drooping headliner grazed his hair, quiet as though he were the white men's prisoner.

They rattled off the ferry and up Fourth Street, the fat guy alternately gobbling pork rinds and peanuts and grumbling about Okies while the asthmatic wheezed and chortled at his pal's vehemence, and Hickey sat as still and ponderous as the Negro, staring with his eyes closed at the bodice of Madeline's red dress and the sapphire hanging there. Whenever his gaze started rising toward her face, he flinched and looked back down.

The stevedores dropped him at the main gate, showed their passes, and drove on. Hickey's passage was about as easy as gaining admission to Betty Grable's dressing room. He showed his guns, the permits, and the copy of his investigator's license to the Shore Patrol guard, a boy who looked fourteen or so and seemed to move in slow motion. He called for reinforcements, a chief whose cowboy boots with three-inch heels and hair poofed higher than Billy Martino's still brought him only up to Hickey's chin. Barking like a terrier, the chief made Hickey repeat the whole routine before he phoned somebody who phoned Colonel Creaser's aide, who woke the colonel, who grabbed the phone and raged at the chief, commanding him to get Hickey to runway seven on the double.

The chief gave Hickey a one-fingered salute, wheeled, and stomped away. "You got five minutes, is all," the guard said. A minute later, a jeep came speeding that way.

Hickey bounded into the jeep beside a stocky Wave who wore goggles as though to blaze through the night in a biplane or race car, but who drove like Grandma, leapfrogging and grinding every gear, swerving timidly around the B-17 Flying Fortresses, the Mustang fighters, the biplane trainers, and a Consolidated Catalina flying boat to the Douglas DC-3 Hickey was booked on, which looked more like a dirigible with wings and had the inscription DUMB DUCK lettered beneath the pilot's window.

The passenger seats had been gutted, all but a dozen removed to make way for cargo. Every space except a single aisle was stuffed head-high with crates marked LOWRY beside a collage of numbers and the symbol of Consolidated Air. Hickey commandeered a double seat in the rear, hidden by the crates and half the length of the craft from the other passengers. They were a trio of marine privates who'd smuggled aboard a bottle of something that pleased them enormously. Every few seconds one of them would guffaw. There were a few empty seats up by the marines, but Hickey chose solitude. He had reading to do, except that there was no light. He had sleep to catch up on, if allowed by the accommodations and turbulence—both of the sky and of his mind. And there were several matters of life and death to consider.

The plane taxied, then lurched and seesawed up and out to sea. After climbing through the fog, it swung a wide turn and headed northeast. From what Hickey could see—the crest of Mount Soledad and a few glimpses of coastline through breaks in the fog—they passed over La Jolla, where Madeline might still be with Paul Castillo. Licking his wounds.

He bounced up, grabbed a crate for balance, and staggered forward past the marines into the cockpit, where he asked the copilot—a hairy civilian with a gray-flecked beard and the gaze of a football coach looking for an excuse to launch into sarcasm—if he could borrow a flashlight. The copilot rummaged through a cardboard box and found one. On the way back Hickey nodded to the marines. They scowled as if he'd threatened to impound their bottle.

Cold was already seeping through the metal of the fuselage when Hickey put on his glasses, arranged himself crosswise on the seats, drew his knees up close, and opened the last of Cynthia's books.

Over several pages, she described how Venus had stolen the reins to Otherworld, using her sex magnetism and reminding the Enlightened in blatant and subtle ways that Madame A had received from the master whose initials are CCB the message that she was destined to lead them. Where Madame T had been the snake charmer and lawgiver, Madame A the benevolent despot, the matriarch, Madame Esmé was a simple mystic. The previous madames had gathered a following of wealthy patrons who funded the community and its many publications and crusades. Mild, honest Madame Esmé couldn't charm new money to the society or bully old money into staying, the way the others had. In 1925, the year Cynthia was born, Madame Esmé turned all fiscal matters over to her attorney, Henry Tucker, and to Venus.

The Bitch was almost seven, a mean one already. From birth

she'd been colicky, demanding, the kind who'd tug people's earrings or hair, gouge their eyes or bite rather than let them pet her. More and more, Venus avoided her, leaving Henry in charge. When he couldn't stand the brat, he'd drop her at the orphans' nursery.

Naturally, when the world got blessed with Cynthia, she was the other extreme. A lovable baby who slept through the night from her second day, such a beauty that all the women of Otherworld begged for time with her, and even Venus cherished her company. But nobody loved her the way Henry did. For hours he'd ride her around Otherworld and along the beach, on his shoulders and in his arms. At dinner she'd sit on his lap while he spooned each bite for her. If she got a mild fever, he'd stay up all night, swabbing her with cool washcloths.

The Bitch learned to hate me because Daddy loved me so. The year I was born, she'd gone to live in the Raja Yoga school. It was only two hundred yards from our cottage, but under Madame T's system, with studies all day, arts in the evening, garden and kitchen chores in between, and since all students—except Venus when she was a girl—lived in the barracks, the Bitch only stayed with us on Sundays. At every chance she would slap or scratch me, tear my clothes. If Daddy gave me a doll, the Bitch would steal it and throw it into the incinerator.

Once she realized Daddy loved me more than her, Venus hated us both—she can't abide sharing love, so just by existing, I turned her against me and Daddy. Before my first birthday she weaned me, though the Bitch had gotten to nurse for three years. The first time Venus slapped me for trying to suckle, Daddy says, was the same day she hung the curtain between her side of the bedroom and Daddy's. It was heavy, like canvas, only bright royal blue. She'd always insisted on separate beds, and now she denied him the sight of her, knowing her beauty inspired him. She commanded that nobody should budge the curtain. There were doors on each side of the room, allowing her to sneak out whenever she pleased. He never caught her roaming. He never knew she'd been visiting Will Lashlee until she boasted of her whoring, that summer after Saint Ophelia first saved me.

If Ophelia had only stayed invisible like other guardian angels, who knows how different our lives could be?

The vision appeared at twilight, in August. I was splashing in the shore break below the cliffs. The Bitch swam out to deep water and waved and called to lure me out there like she always did, so she could laugh at the surf knocking me down while she pranced over it like a dolphin.

Between each wave I would splash out a little farther. I didn't frighten as long as I could touch bottom, but I crossed a ledge, and while three swells tossed me, even my toes couldn't reach the sand, and the ebb of each wave dragged me farther out. I screamed. With every roll and heave, I bobbed down and gulped water. Then a towering breaker whacked me squarely. I tumbled head over heels and swirled, until my back crashed on the sand in only a couple feet of water.

Venus stood at the water's edge, gaping in horror, as if my face had gotten shredded by the sand. I leaped up, bawling, my knees slapping together.

"Who are you?" Venus yelled, then fell to her knees, head in her arms, and wept hysterically. When I touched her shoulder, she threw her head back, glaring at me, and demanded, "Did you see her?"

"Who?" I asked.

Venus sprang up, bolted to the cliff trail and ran away. I never knew why until years later when Daddy told me about the vision, how Venus had seen her dead sister Ophelia standing behind me, aglow, her fingers caressing my hair. How all that night Venus had wept and confessed to Daddy that Ophelia had returned from the dead to destroy her.

You see, Father, she believes Ophelia and I are the same spirit.

Over and over, I've asked Saint Ophelia why she had to appear to Venus. Nobody but me has her guardian angel materialize. Nobody else has to watch her mother run away from her in terror, to hide out in her room behind a blue curtain and hear her mother yell at Daddy, "Keep that devil away from me!"

It was fear of Ophelia that punished her with the searing headaches and fevers that had started the day of the vision and kept growing worse, so bad at the end that she'd run out at night just to wander the grounds, cursing and howling like a harpy. Two years she lived in torment, until Miss V returned from studying psychology and hermeneutics in Salzburg and hypnotized her. Only then Venus remembered how Ophelia died, and the demon headaches and fevers left her. Like Miss V taught us, demons only thrive in our unconscious. Once we raise them to consciousness, their banishment can begin. Venus banished hers by vowing that she or the Bitch would kill me.

Hickey slammed the ledger closed, slapped it down on the seat beside him. He sprang to his feet, grabbing into a pocket for the golf tee he carried, and crushed the fire in his pipe, then hurdled his suitcase and staggered down the aisle, hoping to God the pilot would let him radio a message to Leo.

EIGHTEEN

♪ ♪ ♪

AT THE PASSAGE TO THE COCKPIT HE STOPPED ABRUPTLY AND anchored himself to the curtain rod, to keep from teetering while he thought through the quandary that gripped him.

Even certain that Cynthia'd paid off Katoulis and sent him on his mission, Hickey'd only guessed that the mark was Pravinshandra. Almost as likely, it could be the Bitch. So he ought to send Leo to shadow Laurel. Except that he might as well ask the old guy to swim the English Channel and sink a few U-boats on the way. His partner, at times, could be shrewd enough to compensate for age and slow hands. But Donny was a genius.

Hickey staggered back along the corridor to his seat, stared at the black universe, and thought how this show could end like one of those operas Madeline dragged him to, with bodies flopped all over the stage—the Bitch and Leo murdered, Cynthia a suicide, himself gone berserk with rage in pursuit of Katoulis, guaranteeing his own swift demise.

If he could orchestrate things so that only one person had to die, besides Katoulis, Hickey's choice would be the master. He could only think of three humans who might deserve extinction more than a murdering rapist charlatan. He could forget Denver, leave the master to his deserts, make a U-turn, go home, and cover the Bitch himself. Not likely, from a mile in the air, with a pilot who surely wouldn't disobey orders, risking court-martial, for the sake of one girl, when there were whole continents dying. Maybe at Lowry he could phone Colonel Creaser, arrange for return passage, but it would cost him most of today.

The best he could do was give the Bitch up to fate, hope that if she took the five-millimeter slug—Donny's favorite ammunition—between the eyebrows, he could salvage a little of Cynthia's future by getting her to cut a deal that allowed them to fry Katoulis. Meanwhile, he'd fill and light his pipe, open red ledger number three, and lose himself reading.

Over twenty pages Cynthia relived Laurel's attempts to kill her. By spooking the pony Henry had given her, while Cynthia rode along the cliff trail. By shoving a radio off a bathroom shelf into Cynthia's bathwater. Each time, Ophelia saved her.

During summer, 1932, as Otherworld suffered fiscal woes and shortages after their patrons' generosity had waned, Venus began challenging Madame Esmé's leadership. She questioned the madame's dogma, the curriculum of the Raja Yoga School, the expenditures for philanthropy.

Over a year of skirmishes, gentle Madame Esmé realized that to save Otherworld, she would have to silence Venus, the reason she finally called Daddy into her quarters and gave him the truth of Ophelia's death, as she had heard it from Madame T.

"I beg your forgiveness, Henry. I should've told you before the marriage. Charge my failure, if you will, to concern for poor Venus. She desperately needs the stability I hoped she could find with you."

"Venus pushed her sister?" Daddy moaned. "But under hypnosis she revealed that when her sister thrust herself off to slide, Venus lunged to stop her but missed her altogether. She was only blamed because her mother and godmother, even Madame T, mistook her lunge to save Ophelia."

"There are men who become women under hypnosis, Henry," wise Madame Esmé replied, "and women who believe they are elephants or onions. Ask yourself, if Venus was innocent, why did her mother and father send her away?"

There's the evidence, Father McCullough. How many more of us will she kill, besides Ophelia, Will Lashlee, Mr. Murphy, Daddy, Madame Esmé? Look at the old photos of Daddy, then look at him now. How much evidence do they need? Why isn't she on death row?

The day Madame Esmé told him the story, Daddy started searching for Katy the maid. You see, he is the one of a thousand people who seeks the truth no matter if it profits or ruins him. Of course, he hoped to bring Madame Esmé proof that Venus's hypnotic recollection was true and learn that the woman he cherished wasn't a born murderer, so the day an attorney Daddy knew located Katy in Seattle, Daddy rushed up there on the train and learned the truth.

He never told Venus or Madame Esmé, or anybody except me, and that almost nine years later. Last summer, after the Bitch killed him, he confided in me, when he couldn't protect me any longer and he saw I would have to fight her on my own, to the death. Even Saint Ophelia never told me that Venus had murdered her. She never meant Venus harm. Her mission is to bless and protect me.

Knowing the truth only deepened poor Daddy's love for Venus. In a fit of passion, anyone can murder, he maintains, and he believes that Venus had already paid far too dearly. He kept seeking a route to peace between Venus and Madame Esmé, which earned him Venus's hatred.

The war escalated with Venus's claims that the madame was losing her sense, entering her second childhood. Meanwhile, Venus would order the Bitch to take me swimming in the ocean after reports of a fierce riptide or dare us to scale the most treacherous cliffs, and each attempt I survived left

170

Venus more terrified of me. By my ninth year she rarely touched me except by grasping my shoulders, holding me at arm's length. While she used to gaze tenderly at me or, after the vision, stare distressed and bewildered, as though I carried the black plague, now she couldn't look at me without her eyes blinking twice as often as they should and her mouth constricting, wormlike. Only the Bitch got her tender glances.

Hickey had filled the rear of the cabin with smoke from his pipe, attempting to counter his sleepiness with nicotine. Once he'd staggered up front and bummed a mug of lukewarm coffee from the copilot. The marines, having killed their bottle, performed a cacophony of snores as though rehearsing for the din of battle. Besides all that to keep him awake, he'd got jolted by teasers from Cynthia's story, like her listing of Venus's victims—Will Lashlee, Otherworld's semifamous poet, and Mr. Murphy, who could be the realtor, Laurel's boss. The plane clattered and sent eerie, quivering sounds coursing around its shell, like the music people got out of a saw, and Hickey's mind kept flashing images from eleven years ago when he should've killed Donny Katoulis. Except he'd been a—what? A sap. Coward. On top of the rest, there was a feeling like his guts had got knotted in barbed wire from worrying about Madeline. Still, two mostly sleepless nights had caught up. His eyes kept snapping closed, his chin whacking his breastbone.

He skimmed the next few pages, on the lookout for stuff that mattered, especially the kind that might convince him that the master, or Venus, anyway not the Bitch, had to be Donny's target. Or stuff that would help him choose between the two plans that had started congealing—basically the same except that plan X had him exterminating Katoulis *before* the murder. Plan Y incorporated a slight delay.

He read more accounts of attempted murder. The Bitch had an MO of conspiring with wildlife in her wicked deeds. She tugged little Cynthia by the arm through waist-high water to where she couldn't miss stepping on a stingray, whose tail shot up and jabbed its tail spike into her butt, at about the same location where she'd gotten branded nine years later. The Bitch led her to a similar assault by a jellyfish. Another time she almost got Cynthia to pet a rabid wild dog that lived in the cemetery. The night of Cynthia's first bloody flow, she was home alone with the Bitch, who ordered her to lie down, tore the panties off her and stuffed her with a dishrag, so deep it ripped her flesh and infected her, causing weeks of a high-grade fever. Enough, Hickey thought. He'd earned a respite. He staggered up front past the marines—two of whom had forsaken their seats for the floor in between and lay with arms and legs sprawled over each other— and asked the copilot for one of the blankets he'd noticed earlier piled behind the seat. The blanket was wool, from a sheep that ate brambles and thumbtacks, Hickey mused. Between scratching and analyzing Cynthia's tale, he drifted into sleep.

He couldn't exactly remember the dreams, but when he woke to the plane falling like a bomb through an air pocket, the dread and shame stayed with him, like before whenever his dreams recalled that he should've killed Donny Katoulis.

Eleven years ago. Four cops—Mouse, Smollet, Arturo, and Hickey—were playing poker at Mouse's place, Hickey for the first time that year. Mouse answered the phone. A minute later he slammed it down, then furiously guzzled his beer and wrenched open another. The call had been from a fag bartender at Moonglow, a jazz club on La Cienaga. From a swishy but otherwise decent guy they'd nicknamed Myrtle, who snitched now and then, usually to Mouse and Hickey. Myrtle had a sister, a black-haired, lavender-eyed doll with knockers that landed a job every time a studio cast harem-girl types. Not often enough, though, to keep the wolves from her door. The latest wolf had been Donny Katoulis. Myrtle, like most everybody, hated the guy. After a month or so, he'd talked his sister into skipping town, to ditch Katoulis. Which brought Donny to Moonglow the night of Mouse's poker game.

Katoulis backhanded Myrtle a couple times, pounded his head

against the wall, and requested the sister's whereabouts. At which point Myrtle got in a lucky kick, gaining time to draw the stiletto he carried. When Katoulis blindly flew at him, Myrtle, going for the kill, missing by a foot, sliced a lamb-chop-sized hunk off Donny's left bicep. For half a minute the shooter glared at his arm, then checked to see nobody stood close by—the club's entire population, bouncers included, had migrated to cower against the far wall, rather than cross Katoulis. Myrtle stood clutching the knife in one hand, steadying that hand with the other, but even so trembling like a bush leaguer pinch-hitting against Walter Johnson, while Donny leaned a little closer and flashed his toothy grin.

"You got an hour to live, big brother," he drawled.

Myrtle used the first five minutes calling Mouse, who wasted the next few minutes relaying the story. By the time Hickey and his drunken pals had decided this was the chance of a lifetime to exterminate Katoulis, a half hour had passed. Finally Mouse phoned Myrtle and told him the plan. All he had to do was let Donny find him a mile down La Cienaga in the Chi Chi Club and run out the back door into the alley, hoping to God Katoulis wouldn't kill him inside, in front of witnesses.

Hickey and the others took positions along the alley and waited there most of two hours. They had cut cards and Hickey'd won the honor, a spot behind a stack of milk and vegetable crates directly across the alley from the back door of the Chi Chi Club. Mouse was twenty or so feet down the alley on Hickey's right, Arturo about the same distance up the alley to Hickey's left, behind a broken section of slat fence. Smollet crouched at the corner of the building, hidden by what looked like half a bus bench somebody had leaned there. According to the plan, whichever of them had a clear shot when Katoulis first showed his piece was to aerate the boy's head, preferably with one or two shots, making it look more professional, less like a gang of premeditating drunks. If the first cop missed or Donny didn't fall, the others would finish him.

A suitable plan, except that when Katoulis ran out he didn't show his gun. In the doorway he'd made a lunge for Myrtle and caught him by the neck. Myrtle had tripped over something and fallen into the alley. Katoulis kicked him in the face and the belly but wouldn't draw his damned piece. Hickey should've blasted him anyway—what'd it matter if they had to lift the gun out from under Donny's jacket?—but he wasn't thinking fast enough, he couldn't adjust. Something froze him. Instead of blasting the punk, he bounded out of hiding and barked like a rookie at Katoulis.

Donny tossed up his arms like a lazy fellow stretching. He got ninety days' probation for assault, and Myrtle got to live until that summer when a hit-and-run driver interrupted his holiday in Santa Barbara, where he'd gone to visit his little sister.

Over the next five or so years in L.A., until he quit and moved south, every murder that looked like a pro job Hickey pinned, in his heart, on Katoulis. Therefore on Tom Hickey, for his sin of omission.

About when Hickey and family landed in San Diego, Katoulis vanished. Rumor had him living on the Costa Brava and in Athens until, in 1939, displaced by the war, he returned to L.A. and followed the Schwartz brothers to San Diego, where he became their ace property manager. Nobody stiffed him on rent more than once.

Hickey lit his pipe and sat watching the smoke. When the rising sun flashed against his window, he stared outside. The only clouds were small wispy ones that dimmed but didn't block the view. Below them lay nothing but endless Rocky Mountains, blinding white cut by lines made of angles and shadows, like a miraculous jigsaw puzzle Hickey had pieced together. Dawn over the Rockies made everything below seem trivial and everything past feel as if it happened in another age that didn't matter anymore because you were starting a new one. The same old lie that dawn always tells, Hickey thought, as he picked up the ledger book to finish Cynthia's story.

NINETEEN

♩ ♩ ♩

MEN ARE NITWITS. EVEN THE BEST, LIKE DADDY AND YOU, Father, are pushovers to an evil woman. She will find hordes of you eager to massacre for her. Even the Fiend—it took Venus's claw in him before he got rabid. Once he has made her fortune, she will suck the last of his blood and spit it into his dead eye.

She must have seen in his pictures and in the letters he wrote seeking a teaching residence at Otherworld that he was a huckster, with his claims of a breathing method that could release us from ego and open our third eye. Besides, the rumors had preceded him, about the blue fire he could throw out of his fingertips, and he was pretty. Not handsome. With the wavy locks and petulant eyes under the bushy dark brows, his coppery skin, high squarish cheekbones, protuberant chin, and cupid lips, he could have passed for a Persian princess. The sexiest person alive, before Venus started bleeding him.

The Fiend claimed mastery of hatha-yoga, on which he

lectured and drilled us daily—only in yoga postures could you breathe correctly, so he twisted us into shapes you can't imagine, with our butts in the air and legs spread rudely. Most all the Enlightened attended his sessions, because only those who completed his month-long training would be allowed to watch him throw blue fire or to learn how we could do the same. He commanded us to focus on parts of our body that, you know the parts I mean, Father. He was trying to drive us wild, but it wasn't the half of what he did to Venus.

At the very southwest corner of Otherworld, next to the cliffs and the graveyard, there was a sanctuary built of stones Madame T had gathered from around the world, as gifts and during her travels. The stones made the place holy, she believed. Hardly bigger than a chicken coop, it was surrounded by lilacs and roses. While the children and teachers were in school and Venus was supposed to be managing the books and correspondence, the Fiend took her up there, for private instruction in hatha-yoga and tantric yoga. You must have heard of the Tantrics, Father, who believe sex is one of the four paths that can open the doors of perception and show us the infinite.

Venus wasn't his only disciple. Among others, from the start, he bewitched Miss V. Though I have no evidence and she never confessed to me, I think for that month she was one of his concubines. Whenever she caught him unoccupied, she followed him like a caboose, and every evening she spent an hour or more teaching him hypnotism.

One afternoon the Bitch pulled me out of school and dragged me to the sanctuary. I was almost twelve. The Bitch was seventeen and familiar with the place. I knew three boys, besides Mr. Murphy, who had already poked her there.

Mr. Murphy was an Otherworld orphan who had gone to study at the University of Oregon and returned to stay with us while he sought a career. Having been a wrestler, he could walk on his hands all the way from his quarters to the cliff. He didn't use the trail to the beach but scooted spider-

like down the cliff. Every day he ran along the beach. Half
the females of Otherworld, and Mr. Lashlee, would find
cause to walk the trail from where they could admire him.
Mr. Murphy loved Miss V. She cherished Daddy. The
Bitch, who loves nobody, wanted to possess Mr. Murphy.

As Hickey paused to refill his briar, he recalled how Murphy the
realtor had looked, spoken, moved, and shaken hands as if his cup
overflowed with woe.

The sanctuary was bolted closed, but there were portholes
we could reach by climbing. The Bitch was panting with
outrage and jealousy.

Venus sat naked, in lotus, her hair down and wild as if
she'd fought a tornado except that there were flower petals
strewn all through it. She glistened like a statue freshly
shellacked. Her arms were lifted, the heels of her hands
together, her fingers stretching upward to absorb the atmo-
spheric fire. She sat perfectly still while the Fiend paced
circles around her, naked except for his phony turban, his
shoulders hunched, head down, eyes on Venus like a sergeant making his inspection, his pride and joy erect and
swishing like a horse's tail.

Nausea washed through me, my heart got fluttery, and I
fell. The Bitch cackled. As soon as I could get up, I ran off
to weep and scream.

I couldn't tell Daddy and expect him to comfort me. In
fact, I would have clawed the tongue out of anybody who
tried to tell him. All afternoon and evening I wandered,
through the graveyard, up to the lighthouse, back to Ocean
Beach, until my feet were scorched and bloody. Even after
dark I kept wandering, muttering vows of chastity or death,
to the crest of Point Loma and down toward the harbor,
because no matter the pain in my legs and feet, whenever I
stopped, the pain that seared my stomach worsened and my
head throbbed with rage. If I had been a man or the Bitch,
I would have found something to kill.

Far more than the knowledge of Venus's wantonness,

more than disgust, what afflicted me was terror of what would come. I knew she would cast Daddy off for the Fiend.

As I trudged back through the foggy night, over the point to Otherworld, Saint Ophelia spoke to me. Perhaps she had spoken before, but it was the first time I heard her. Her voice was sweet like woodwinds. "I'm here," she promised many times. Gradually my heart calmed enough to understand her message. "You're our savior, Cynthia Tucker, Henry's girl."

Imagine the burden, Father. *"La niña triste,"* Sister Guadalupe used to call me, remember? Now you know why I strive so, why I devoured all the books you gave me and treasured every word of advice, why I must excel and outmatch any rival. It is only I who can repair the damage. Only I can save our family. No one else has the grace to amend Venus's sin.

Hickey rested his eyes for a minute, then looked out the window. Between the blotches of clouds, there was glimmering in the distance that looked like the capital of heaven. Probably Denver. He leaned back, listened to the mutters and groans of the marines, filled his pipe, and wondered if there was any hope for the girl. Besides that, she might be a pure-blooded loon; he'd watched lots of people with fervor like hers, rushing out to save somebody who hadn't asked to be saved. She'd have been safer as a marine landing on Corregidor. If, as he could easily imagine, she yearned to rid the earth of every seed her mother had planted, the Bitch would surely be a target, maybe followed by any number of Venus's disciples. One murder could be the first drop of a bloodbath.

So, Tom, he mused, you gonna tail her till everybody dies of natural causes? Maybe he ought to back off, forget what he'd seen, quit risking his family and everything for the girl. Except that no matter how screwy she was, Cynthia had a gift. The way she could release an audience from their minds and bodies by inviting them into hers. Besides, if the girl destroyed herself when he could've saved her, she'd haunt him. From an asset and a joy—somebody who made his heart swell even though he was prudent and faithful enough not to touch her—she'd metamorphose into a nightmare.

Not many guys had steadier nerves than Hickey. Yet a few things startled him into terror, made him quake dizzily, and sweat like a fat lineman running sprints in full gear. One of them was nightmares. He'd been fighting them for twenty-seven years, since his father ditched, ran off to the war, leaving him to wake up at midnight with the saint's fingers on his belly, her gray shadow covering him.

The *Dumb Duck* was already nosing downward with metallic screeches and violent quakes when he picked up Cynthia's book for the last time and read that Cynthia, on her way back to Otherworld, heard Laurel wailing. At the edge of the cliff by the gazebo, a hundred people stood waiting for Laurel to dive from a ledge about halfway down the cliff. For a minute she stared below at the waves battering the rocks, then she wailed again and stopped short to wheel and yell up at Madame Esmé, "Get him away from Venus!"

Venus sat on the edge, her knees up and face in her hands, Pravinshandra kneeled behind her, gripping her shoulders.

Henry Tucker, Will Lashlee, and Mr. Murphy had already secured a rope to the gazebo and were measuring it out and tying it around their waists, hitching themselves to each other, Murphy on the end, then Will Lashlee, with Tucker closest to the gazebo. Murphy started down first and to the left of Laurel, groping for foot- and handholds on the jagged rocks. Lashlee, about fifty feet along the rope, climbed down to Laurel's right. She must have glimpsed or heard them, but she gave no sign.

They were going to encircle her, the first two heading for ledges below, Tucker climbing last, straight down toward her. When she finally turned his way, she threw her hands up as if to push him off, then skittered back so close to the edge that Lashlee made a leap to his side, trying to reach the outcrop directly beneath her. The loose rock gave way. He tumbled into the sky. For an instant the rope held taut, until the knot slipped. He fell silently. Landed on his back, on the largest, flat boulder, beside a tide pool, just as a wave rolled out. Blood sprayed like mist from his head.

Tucker slid past Laurel before he grabbed the root of a scrub tree. He got a broken ankle, while Murphy swung out and back on the rope, bashing the rocks. By the time some men reeled him in, he was ruined.

While the plane circled Denver, Hickey skimmed a few pages that told how Venus, exposed by rumor, in danger of banishment from Otherworld, sold two parcels nearest the Fort Rosecrans Cemetery. According to Cynthia, she had to forge Madame Esmé's signature on several documents, since all papers had to be countersigned.

Eleven days after Will Lashlee got crushed on the rocks, when Venus was already gone, Madame Esmé had the Bitch consigned to the mental ward at a hospital called Riverview, near the Sweetwater River, about ten miles inland. The Bitch had been raving and threatening whoever restrained her. Henry Tucker was in Mercy Hospital. Miss V helped him decide to place Cynthia somewhere the ghosts wouldn't haunt her. For most of a year—while Tucker's bones healed and he bought a car and traveled alone to visit the graves of his family and sacred Indian places in New Mexico, where he hoped to find peace or inspiration, a reason to stay alive in a world without Venus—all that time Cynthia lived a few miles up the San Diego River from Otherworld, in the children's home of the Mission de Alcala.

The final scene in the third ledger was of Cynthia's first encounter with Father McCullough. The priest had come to sit beside her in the garden. For an hour or more he observed her and said nothing except to field her queries about the orphanage's food, its library, the uniforms they had to wear, and if there was a piano she could play. He listened to her pleas to be given a room of her own and consoled her when she wept because that wasn't possible.

Finally he asked her what was the meaning of life, a question so blunt it left her speechless, Cynthia claimed. Hickey tried to imagine Cynthia speechless, as he turned to the last page, where

Father McCullough answered his own question. What the priest said, Cynthia had transcribed in letters that filled the page.

THE MEANING OF LIFE IS TO KNOW LOVE AND SERVE GOD.

The plane bumped, sailed, bumped, skidded to a stop. Hickey looked out the window and shivered. He sat for a minute, hoping that it was only because the air looked damned cold and thinking that he should hurry to call Leo and then track down Venus and the master. Yet he gathered his things slowly, folded the blanket, and delivered it and the coffee cup to the cockpit from which the pilot and copilot had already fled. The marines were long gone. Finally he stepped off the plane; he glared around at the hangars and Quonsets, and over them at snowdrifts up the side of craggy mountains capped with black clouds that looked too heavy not to be falling right now. Suddenly he missed Madeline, and Elizabeth, voraciously as though in another few minutes without them he'd starve. All he wished for at that moment was to get home alive. Denver looked like a hell of a place to die.

TWENTY

♪ ♪ ♪

THE SUN LOOKED PALE AND TIMID RISING INTO THE ICE-BLUE SKY, like a tourist from the north on her first tiptoe into the ocean. Either the temperature hovered around zero, or Hickey'd caught a deadly case of the jitters, or both. Quaking spasmodically, he hitched a ride in a jeep whose driver hunched bundled so deeply in coats and scarves that you could hardly guess the race or gender. They skidded and swerved through a legion of biplane trainers toward the front gate, Hickey's teeth clacking together so hard that he began to wonder if they could shatter.

The gate guard leaned out of his booth and muttered a few words that froze to death in the air. Hickey managed to stammer that Colonel Creaser had arranged his passage, that he was in Denver on the colonel's business. He dug out his billfold, passed it to the fellow, who glanced inside, jotted something on a note-pad, tossed the billfold back, and waved Hickey away as he retreated into the deepest corner of his booth.

A half dozen soldiers paced outside the gate, wearing scarves and earmuffs, hands beating against their sides or stuffed into the pockets of their long coats. The wind seemed to gust from both east and west, as though it had raced across the Great Plains, driven by some evil purpose, and had gotten thwarted by the Rockies and sent flurrying back toward its home. Hickey kicked snow off one end of the bench and sat, his butt numbing, all of him stupefied by the cold, until the trolley bus arrived like an angel of mercy, its overhead cable sparking.

As he began to thaw, Hickey quizzed the private sitting across from him, a red-nosed, snuffling kid. He learned that the Brown Palace Hotel—where the master and Venus's itinerary placed them—was downtown, a few blocks from the mint and the state capitol. The bus turned right at a city park where children pulled each other on sleds and kicked balls around on hard-packed snow. It passed a row of brick mansions surrounded by trees gray and gnarly as a witch's hand, made a left on Colfax, fell in behind a convoy of olive-drab flatbed trucks, their loads covered with tarpaulins. The stubble of last summer's wheat and corn blemished a half mile of snowy fields, across the road from a suburb of flat-roofed brick houses cramped beside each other as if land were scarce, as though nobody'd yet discovered the billion acres of plains.

The trolley bus stopped every half mile or so, letting on school kids and workers until they jammed the aisles and warmed the car with their body heat. By now Hickey's shivering had quieted a little. His teeth only clacked in momentary spasms. The road had widened into two lanes each way, bordered by brick shops which stirred Hickey to remember hearing that Mayor Stapleton owned a brickyard, which he obliged local builders to patronize. Eastside Ford's showroom was boarded up, and the gravel lot, at least an acre, displayed fewer than a dozen cars. The newest was a '36 Chrysler. The picture window at Weckerly's Tire and Brake was blackened and lettered VISIT OUR REOPENING SALE—AFTER THE WAR. Over the door hung a sign: U.S. ARMY RECRUITERS. Oscar's Grocery, Wholesale and Retail, had a half-block line outside. Word must've leaked that a stash of some rarity like coffee had appeared. Vince's Café was next door to Eldorado Dry Cleaners.

Hickey grabbed his bag and wedged his way between seats and bodies to the door. He leaped off the bus, hit the icy sidewalk, skidded, and braked by grabbing onto a light pole that had nearly whacked his skull. His feet catching hold about every third step, the wind pushing him from behind, he walked back to the dry cleaners. A sign on the door promised the place would open at 9:00 A.M., twenty minutes away unless Hickey'd turned the hour hand too far when he'd set his watch to mountain time. He stepped into Vince's Café, checked the wall clock, and flopped into a booth with chilly clear-plastic seat covers over checkerboard fabric. A hairy Italian fellow delivered a menu and coffee that smelled as rich as Judy Garland might've to a lonely boy stationed a hundred desert miles out of Tripoli. Hickey guzzled it, got a refill, and ordered a Denver omelet. A furnace near the booth, the coffee, and finally an omelet soaked in Tabasco warmed him everyplace except the heart, which remained gripped by the mightiest chill, the one you're not likely to shake while staring at your own mortality.

He reasoned that the odds were on his side, no matter if Katoulis were ten times the gunfighter. Unless Cynthia had gotten suspicious and made contact with Donny, or with Charlie Schwartz, who might pass word along, Katoulis wouldn't be looking over his shoulder for Hickey or anybody. Not in Denver. Besides, they hadn't met face-to-face in nine years. Unless he walked up and said howdy, chances were slight that Donny'd recognize him. The man would be concentrating on his business. Hickey held all the best cards, except one. Katoulis had the ace of spades—he was a pro, while Hickey barely qualified as a novice killer. It had been years since he'd shot anybody; only once had he gone out intending to kill. Then he had frozen, watching Donny Katoulis's grin.

Next door at the dry cleaners, after greeting a stub-nosed older man as cheery as a blizzard, Hickey cast his eyes down. "See, pal, I been working out on the coast. Last year, day after Pearl Harbor, my mother calls and says I oughta join up. I promised her

I was gonna. Damn proud, it made her, and I tried, but the louses wouldn't take me—on account of I'm a borderline diabetic. I was too shamed to tell her. Now, with her bragging to the neighbors and all . . . I bet you've got a uniform about my size somebody's forgot to pick up." He plucked a couple twenties from his billfold. "Seventeen neck. Thirty-four waist, thirty-four inseam. A cap and tie, if you've got 'em, and the heaviest coat you can rustle up."

The old guy sneezed, wiped his nose, and turned to the back room. A few sneezes later, he returned with an outfit all pressed and starched, on a single hanger. He led Hickey past the machines, racks of dresses and suits, a Chinese girl washing linens in a tub, to the storeroom and flicked on an overhead light.

The uniform fitted Hickey a little snugly around the waist and neck but loosely enough through the shoulders. He crammed the civilian clothes into his suitcase, except his hat, which he carried so it wouldn't get squashed. He crossed the street and walked down to the bus stop, filled his pipe, and concentrated on lighting and sheltering it from the wind until the trolley bus came. There was standing room only. Riders pitched and swayed unconsciously, reading their dime novels or morning papers. Hickey gazed over their heads and hats, between newspapers. Other than that the trees appeared dead and the Victory gardens frozen, and that Stapleton's bricks prevailed, Denver looked like home. The same flat-tired cars waiting for the price of rubber to go down, the blackout curtains people had failed to lift after daylight, the same resolute expression on most every face. They'd known worse times. They might be harried or plagued with nightmares about their brother fighting in Algeria or New Guinea. Still, they had work and purpose. They didn't go hungry anymore.

A copper-skinned woman whose elbow had been jabbing Hickey the last couple miles showed him his stop, a block past the frozen slope leading to the state capitol.

The last mile or so he'd gotten lost in a glorious dream, about the Christmas gift he desired. A walk around the bay at twilight, tomorrow evening, with Madeline squeezing his right hand, Elizabeth clutching his left. He jumped off the bus and landed in another realm, wherein every shadow to his side or rustle behind him could be Donny Katoulis, and where he felt as conspicuous as if he wore signboards advertising his name and his mission. The wind snatched his hat, which bounced and flew up Broadway. He ran, slipped, skidded, finally cornered it against a newsstand.

You couldn't miss the Brown Palace, it was so tall, brown, and triangular, like a Hollywood studio mountain that covered the block between Tremont, Seventeenth Street, and Broadway. At the Seventeenth Street entrance, the doorman wore a braided cap, earmuffs, and a long blue coat with epaulets. Hickey nodded and stepped into the lobby. Before he noticed the decor, he scanned the room for any face like the master, Venus, or Donny K. He'd never seen Venus or the master, in person or photo, but he'd know them. Already they seemed like familiars.

Finally he stared in awe at the lobby, a grand atrium with pillars and arches of onyx on the ground floor and mezzanine, the six upper floors railed in tarnished copper. Hickey would've bet that there were more palms here than alongside San Diego's harbor, only these were in pots beside the potted red-, green-, and white-lit cedars. The floors were polished tile decked with Oriental rugs, velvet- and leather-covered stuffed chairs and sofas, white mahogany and cherry wood dining and coffee tables. Yet the rest looked drab compared to the chandelier, a Christmas tree about fifty feet high, made of a thousand tiny crystal starlights. Beneath it, beside a grand piano, a woman in a floor-length white tunic fingered a harp, making tunes that drifted through the atrium sounding as if they came from beyond the moon.

Hickey dropped his suitcase and hat on the tile. The desk clerk had sleek hair combed back without a part and a lipless mouth concealed behind a bushy, drooping mustache that looked stolen from a cowboy.

"Single, one night," Hickey said.

"We're sorry," the man said primly. "You know how it is, with the war and all."

"Yeah, I know how it is. What'll it cost?" Hickey grumbled, flashing the contents of his billfold.

After Hickey'd checked in and sent a bellhop carrying his bag to room 306, he asked to use the telephone and got ushered into an alcove with two chairs, each beside a wall phone. Hickey dialed the operator and gave her Leo Weiss's home number.

"Vi, it's Tom. In Denver. The old man keeping out of trouble?"

"Hi, Tom. He seems to be. He figured you might call. Left a message that the girl sang like her angel self last night, went right home afterward, and hit the sack. Leo dozed a few hours, got back to shadowing her not long past dawn. That's the last I know. Now, what're you up to in Denver?"

"I ran away to join the rodeo. Do me a favor, huh? Call Madeline, tell her I love her."

"You two still fussing?"

"Yep."

"Call her yourself, Tom, if you want her to believe it."

"There's things I gotta do today that require I don't get preoccupied brooding about Madeline, which is what'll happen if we talk."

"What things?"

"Can't hear you, Vi. Bad connection. Tell him I'm at the Brown Palace." He placed the receiver on the hook as softly as if someone were sleeping beside him, got up, and walked outside. The doorman was scraping ice off the steps with a shovel that, compared to his bulk, looked the size of a tablespoon. Hickey asked him for directions to the Trinity Methodist Church, where Venus and the master would perform that evening. The doorman suggested he go to the corner and look to his right, up Treemont.

The church was brick with a conical spire, topped by a cross, the tallest thing in sight. The brickwork looked old as the Brown Palace, too ancient to blame on Mayor Stapleton.

Hickey walked past the church, continued around the hotel, scouting for entrances and exits. Only one on each side led directly into the Palace. You could also enter through the Ship

187

Lounge. At Broadway and Treemont he crossed the intersection to get a longer view, check if you could spy through upstairs windows. On the far corner a woman in a Salvation Army uniform played "Greensleeves" on an oboe. As Hickey passed, her keying hand shot out and brushed his sleeve. Her face was the color and shape of a peeled potato, but Hickey fell for her meek smile, tossed a dollar into her kettle. A few steps farther he stepped on ice, ran in place, then crashed, and bruised his tailbone. He sat awhile, cussing and puzzling why anybody lived here—back in antiquity when tribes were migrating across the earth, why didn't they keep moving until they reached the tropics? If nothing else, the walking might've helped keep them warm. A man in a bank guard's outfit offered him a hand. He used it, thanked the fellow, and hobbled back to the hotel.

Three-oh-six was a corner room, diamond-shaped but vast compared to most old hotels where only the public rooms were elegant and spacious. Hickey's room had a private bath, a fireplace with three logs, and a bundle of kindling. He tried out the bed. Firm, with no lumps. He lay staring at a floral design in the ceiling plaster; he groped for a scheme that would let Katoulis do his job, make sure he'd get hung for it, and guarantee that Cynthia wouldn't. For a minute or so, his overcharged mind blanked. Then it flicked to a new preoccupation—wondering, if he survived Denver, could he make good his promise, give up Hickey and Weiss, to hold onto Madeline? Yeah, he thought. People live without arms and legs.

When his temples began to throb, he rose, kicked off his shoes, replaced his socks with two clean woolen pairs, tightened his shoelaces. He got the Smith & Wesson .38 service revolver and shoulder holster out of his suitcase, strapped them on, and laid his rumpled suit coat and slacks on the bed. After slipping into his long coat and soldier's cap, he checked himself in the mirror above the dark oak vanity, tugged the cap down lower to hide most of his graying hair. You saw plenty of middle-aged corporals, but gray ones were still an oddity.

He walked out, passed the elevator, wanting to keep space

around him, and trekked down the three flights of stairs. In the lobby he picked a love seat near a couple high-backed chairs he could duck behind should he wish to become invisible. The harpist must've taken lunch early. Between Hickey and the piano, three old dames in mink wraps sat arranging each other's hats and brooches at the most flattering angles. On a coffee table lay a picture book about Denver and the hotel. He picked it up and started to browse but gave up. Knowing the quirks of his mind, he feared getting engrossed in some stupid article while the master and Venus passed him by. Or while Donny K spotted him, strolled over, and popped him between the eyes. So he sat gazing around at the guests as they entered from the streets or one of the several cafés and saloons around the atrium's perimeter, at the bellhops, and at the cabbies who carried in luggage. He got up and made a turn past the elevator to assure himself that the ancient Negro operator wasn't Katoulis disguised, and returned to his chair wondering how long it would take before the desk clerk or the cigarette girl got suspicious and sent a house dick to grill him.

Every twenty minutes or so he wandered outside, made a turn around the hotel or crossed the street and glanced through the window of the drugstore or scanned the newsstand racks with one eye while he fired up his pipe and smoked a half bowl. The third trip he bought a deck of playing cards at the newsstand.

Back in the lobby, the harpist was playing. Surrounded by celestial music, a decor he would've bet the pope's house couldn't match, and the fragrance of thirty or so cut cedars, Hickey kept snapping to attention in shock to remember he was waiting here to kill a guy.

He dealt five games of solitaire, slow ones, on account of his looking up and around between every card while he thought about his own life and death and those of Pravinshandra and Katoulis. There was some truth, he mused, to Cynthia's observation that evil people thrive because good people don't have the heart to kill them. Try to act righteous and peaceful—you and a continent full of innocents get skinned by Nazis. Choke when you should've wasted Donny Katoulis, the man returns to haunt you. Likewise, if you save a freak like Master Pravinshandra . . .

There might be a way to exterminate them both, Hickey thought. If he let Donny snuff the master first, before he silenced Donny, the girl might go free. Maybe he could cover for her, pitch a tale about the contract on the master being the work of Henry Tucker, who'd probably die before the New Year anyway. Not likely Cynthia's daddy would deny the story. He might glory in saving his daughter's neck and depart counting on a martyr's reward. Only Charlie Schwartz and his chauffeur had the knowledge to botch things. What would Charlie do? Hickey sat wondering as Venus entered the lobby.

If she'd been surrounded by a dozen beauties her age, all with cinnamon hair, Hickey could've instantly picked her out. First, even in the flat pumps, she stood taller than most men, erect as though she marched in a drill team. She wore a tan business suit, but the hems of the jacket, the sleeves, and the skirt, as well as the collar, had been trimmed in rainbow fabric of red, orange, and blue. There were gems hanging off her ears and a big one, mounted in silver, pinned to the little hat that rested on the back of her head. From across the room he could see that her eyes were like Cynthia's, emeralds in sunlit water. When she stopped just inside the door to let the man beside her remove her wrap, and she surveyed the room, Hickey caught himself ducking away from her eyes, as if he feared she had the power to recognize even somebody she'd never seen. It was Venus all right.

Her escort wore a turban. A slender man in his prime, built remarkably like Venus only without curves. Their chins, shoulders, hips, and knees all at the same altitudes. He wore a banker's suit, gray with pinstripes, double-breasted, a cream-colored shirt, and a red tie. The only peculiarity except the turban was his footwear, beaded sheepskin moccasins. His skin appeared soft and dark as caramel, the trim, angular face serene as if he'd either faced every trial and vanquished all the demons or had his feelings gutted. His eyes were deep and steady, pale brown. He walked gracefully, arms swinging loosely at his sides.

Two bellhops followed the pair. The Negro labored with a steamer trunk across his shoulders; the white fellow juggled three large suitcases. As they followed the master and Venus to the elevator, Hickey gathered his cards, pocketed them as he got up, and walked to the stairway. When the elevator door shut, he double-timed up the stairs, peered around a corner and down the hallway while the elevator passed, then hustled up the next flight, and so on, until the elevator clanked to a stop on the fourth floor. He stayed out of sight behind a wall while the elevator door opened and shut and footsteps drummed softly along the hallway. Peeking around the corner, he watched one of the bellhops usher Venus and the master into their room. When the door closed behind them all, Hickey entered the hallway and ambled slowly toward the room. In a minute the bellhops stepped out and passed him by with hardly a glance, too busy laughing at something. Hickey sauntered past the room—409, wide as a suite—listening for a shot or a scream, just in case Donny had threatened to boil the desk clerk's mother in oil, gotten the room key, and gone to wait in a closet, to greet them. Hickey circled the landing and turned down the stairs.

Venus and her pretty-boy would be freshening up, unpacking, for at least long enough to give Hickey the chance to use his toilet. After making that stop, he climbed back to the fourth floor, encountered nobody suspicious in the hallway, returned to the lobby. He scanned the place for newcomers, then wandered outside, stopping for a minute to chat with the doorman, who'd bought his nine-year-old a rusted bicycle and spent all last weekend at a cousin's place sanding the thing, making ready for Christmas. His kid wanted to be a paperboy. Hickey admitted he hadn't yet bought his daughter a gift.

He crossed the street considering what might happen if he took an hour off—he could buy Elizabeth a sheepskin coat, Madeline a silver fox stole—and returned to find Venus wailing over the master, who lay missing the back of his head. There'd be one less monster on earth, was all, and a slight chance they'd trace the murder to Cynthia. Hadn't Donny been executing folks since

1929 and going free? It was almost enough to make you admire the guy.

Hickey returned to the hotel lobby, to the love seat from where he could watch three entrances and the doorway to room 409. He flagged a cocktail girl, ordered coffee, lit his pipe, and sat trying to anchor his mind on the business of watching while it kept floating off toward visions of a party dress, a swimsuit, a set of paintbrushes he could buy Elizabeth. Here in Denver he could probably find her a swell pair of cowboy boots that she'd love to wear in a couple months when the mountains warmed and they drove up to ride stable horses in the Lagunas.

Over two cups of coffee, he fought so hard to keep his mind on the job that an illegitimate fury brewed inside him. Not over Katoulis's crimes or the master's. Rather because it was on account of them that he couldn't do what he wanted—go Christmas shopping. He was acting childish but didn't give a damn. If Katoulis had entered the café, Hickey would've been tempted to exterminate the monster immediately and then run out and see if he could buy something special for Elizabeth before the cops tracked him down. Otherwise, he thought, he might go to hell and leave his daughter nothing but grief and a bitter taste on Christmas morning.

TWENTY-ONE

♪ ♪ ♪

THAT FAR NORTH, DUSK CAME TOO EARLY. IT WASN'T EVEN 4:00 P.M. in the Brown Palace when the bellhops started lowering blackout curtains.

Hickey used the last daylight to run an errand, to go out and cross Treemont, hustle to the drugstore at the corner of Seventeenth, and buy a tin of Walter Raleigh. Through the drugstore window and from the curb outside, he could watch both the Seventeenth Street and Treemont entrances to the hotel.

Down on the corner of Broadway, the Salvation Army woman still tooted her oboe. Only the highest notes carried over the wind. Traffic had multiplied. Merchants, clerks, secretaries, and tailors fled their shops, the U.S. Mint, the federal, local, and state offices clustered around. The eastbound streetcar rattled up Seventeenth, blocking Hickey's view. He tapped out his pipe on a lamppost, jaywalked, nodded to the doorman.

For tea and cocktail hour, the lobby had filled with guests who jabbered rudely as though the harpist were a lounge hack. Hickey found a stuffed chair near the front desk and tried not to let his mind drift too far skyward with the music. When the harpist curtsied, packed up, and fled, Hickey thought all the lights and colors dulled a little. Soon a fellow wearing tails and a black upturned mustache approached the grand piano, sat, and loosened his fingers. Hickey didn't get to watch him play.

A strange pair had entered from Treemont. They wore long belted robes and Arab headgear, like towels cinched on top with headbands and draping down their shoulders. Their cowboy boots clip-clopped on the floor. The taller one laughed and slapped the other fellow's shoulder. The shorter man was too flabby, pale, and hairless to be Katoulis. The other might've been Donny on stilts twenty years hence, except that the laugh was high-pitched and gay. Hickey remembered Katoulis's laugh. Like the bark of a sea lion.

As the pair approached the desk, gabbing, Hickey decided that they must be costumed as biblical shepherds. The taller, louder one instructed the desk clerk to ask Master Pravinshandra and party to join Randolf Drew in the Ship Lounge. The desk clerk turned to his switchboard. The shepherds crossed the lobby to the lounge entrance. Hickey began rotating like a periscope, scanning all around, every floor, staring into shadows where Donny might stand with his sights on the door to room 409, if these shepherds had set the master up. Or Donny might be waiting in the Ship Lounge. Hickey felt for his gun, straightened his army cap, adjusted his glasses, and continued scanning the atrium. Finally Venus and the master stepped out of their room.

She wore a long ermine coat, a dark fur hat. The master wore a double-breasted suit, light brown and pin-striped, a maroon tie and turban, a woolen coat thrown over his shoulder. They walked arm in arm to the elevator and waited. When the elevator door shut behind them, Hickey stood and made a final sweeping check of the mezzanine and ground floor, then followed the shepherds' lead.

The Ship Lounge reminded Hickey too much of home. Porthole windows. Around every table sat captain's chairs. Wall shelves held model square-riggers, frigates, clipper ships. Above one end of the bar hung a painting of a sultan in a rowboat so crowded with naked dolls that they barely could hang on. At the bar sat a cowboy, an air force captain, three prosperous civilians, none as swarthy as Katoulis. Only two tables were occupied. One by a gang of secretaries and the boss. The other was a long banquet table that paralleled the bar, where the shepherds sat flanked by a third of their kind, three men in frilly shirts with bloused sleeves and caps with peacock feathers, and several uncostumed, stylish women.

Hickey declined to check his hat and coat. The maître d', large and wary as a bouncer, scrutinized Hickey's uniform and frowned. Corporals weren't legendary tippers. A dollar got him the table he wanted, a small one beyond the bar, next to the Seventeenth Street door. He seated himself, folded and piled his overcoat and hat on the floor behind him, just as Venus stepped in.

She gazed around serenely, awarded Randolf Drew and party a delicate wave. They stood to welcome her and the master. Though Pravinshandra might be the guest of honor, everybody watched Venus. At least as tall as Cynthia. Full rosy lips. Darkly shaded emerald eyes so large they implied omniscience. The green stones of her earrings glimmered as though electrified. As she passed Hickey, her dress rustled loudly.

She and the master got seated at the head of the table, facing away from Hickey. He tried to eavesdrop but caught nothing except compliments and pleasantries above the piped-in orchestra tunes. A waiter who sported a hearing aid and a towel over his arm brought him a Dewar's and a menu which he waved off and ordered a small dinner salad with Roquefort and a pile of soda crackers. He smoked, sipped, and nibbled, trying to keep one eye on the doors while the other admired Venus's bare shoulders and loosely coifed cinnamon hair. He thought about a refill of scotch but settled on coffee. Another drink might lift the curtain behind which he'd been hiding visions of what could happen in the next few hours. Or he'd start missing Elizabeth, worrying about Madeline, loathing Paul Castillo. Coffee might sharpen his claws, make him a closer match to Donny Katoulis. Or it might give him the jitters, a terminal case. Whatever drug he used, waiting was hell when he couldn't even guess how long or know if Katoulis might be stalking somebody a thousand and some miles away, or catching a nap, or swimming in a hotel bathtub with a hooker while Hickey sat wasting his finite pool of energy, sinking into a funk that could soon drive him back to room 306, where he'd probably curl up in bed and suck his thumb. He nibbled cheesy lettuce and Nabiscos, scrutinizing each man who stood up from a table or stepped into the room. He tried to think about nothing, imagine nothing. Above all, he coached himself, don't think about Castillo and Madeline or about what it'd feel like to die with Katoulis grinning at you. Lose your head, he mused, and your ass goes with it.

About 6:30 Randolf Drew and his fellow shepherds led Venus, the master, and the rest across Treemont to the Trinity Methodist Church. The sky and the city had gone so dark that Hickey was forced to wedge himself among the dinner guests to keep the master in sight. The shepherds led Venus and Pravinshandra through a side entrance.

Hickey lined up with the public, "donated" five dollars. Stepping inside, he decided he'd get his money's worth as long as somebody played the organ. There must've been forty pipes, the shortest about twenty feet tall, others rising twice that high to the vaulted ceiling. At floor level were a couple dozen rows of polished wooden pews separated by two wide aisles. About half the seats were filled. Eyeing the people as he passed, Hickey gravitated toward the front. He took an aisle seat in the second row. From there he could look back and see faces, watch the first row closely, peer into the opera boxes that recalled pictures of John Wilkes Booth firing on Mr. Lincoln, and watch the dimly lighted balconies. Most of the lighting was toward the front, over the altar. The chorus benches ascended to the right and left of the altar and the podium which was flanked on each side by a pair of red upholstered seats as big as thrones. The altar's red carpet tinted the light all around.

Hickey began studying the people up front. Out of twelve in the first row, eight were women. One of the four men was stone bald. The man straight in front of Hickey showed a ruddy, heavy-jowled profile. Of the two men farthest away, he couldn't certify that either wasn't Katoulis. The best he could hope for, Hickey figured, was to eliminate most of the crowd and keep watch over the remainder.

People kept filing in, a curious assortment. A tycoon rancher in shiny, tooled boots. A flock of dowagers so old and stuffy Hickey wondered if they might've got lost and mistaken this place for a meeting of the DAR. Others looked like factory workers. Laborers. Housewives. Young widows. Retired teachers. Three cripples escorted by nurses and a guy whose face was a tapestry of burn scars and scabs. Maybe they'd come to get healed. Several could've been protestant ministers. There was a trio of Salvation Army officers, and a few sets of parents with children hanging off them, others pushing surly boys along, hoping the holy man would inspire their brat to change his hoodlum ways. A couple about Hickey's age with a golden-haired daughter of thirteen or so sat directly behind him.

A section on the opposite side from Hickey, from the sixth row back to the eleventh, an usher had been holding in reserve until a pack of lost souls got led in by a fellow in a railroad porter's outfit. The men looked frozen stiff and filthy, as though they'd ridden across the Rockies on a flatcar and gotten dumped in the railyard. Their presence must've dismayed the audience. After the usher seated and silenced the hoboes, the hall lay tensely quiet.

Finally, led by the tall shepherd, Master Pravinshandra and Venus entered by the door behind the altar. Venus had left her ermine coat, her gloves, and her hat backstage. Before taking her seat on one of the thrones left of the podium, she made a subtle turn, giving the audience a chance to gaze. The master had stripped off his turban and let down his wavy dark brown shoulder-length hair. He lowered himself into the chair beside Venus, his eyes sweeping the audience slowly as if he meant to hypnotize them all.

Randolf Drew gave a brief introduction and took his seat on the right side. Pravinshandra stood and approached the podium, where he seemed taller, stronger. The bones of his face looked straight and sharp, chiseled in wood. The whites of his eyes appeared gigantic, the irises tiny black dots. His hands lifted gracefully into the air and stopped level with his shoulders. When he finally spoke, the deep, calming voice filled the room. The girl behind Hickey whispered too loudly, "God, he's sexy." Her mother gave her a slap on the knee.

While Hickey'd sat loathing the man, Venus had joined him at the podium, gotten introduced as the better half of his soul. Resting a hand on her shoulder, the master explained that Venus would translate the message he'd receive from an ascended master whose initials were TLS. In this way, he could channel without distraction.

He stepped aside, folded his hands, let his chin drop to his breastbone. At last a soft, high-pitched voice issued out of him in a language of mostly vowels. After each phrase or so he paused, and Venus translated.

"It is written, 'The Jews appear to have ascended no higher than to worship the immediate artificer of the universe. Moses introduces a darkness on the face of the deep, without even insinuating that there was any cause of its existence. Yet never have the Jews in their Bible—a purely esoteric, symbolical work—degraded so profoundly their metaphorical deity as have the Christians, by accepting Jehovah as their one living yet personal God.'

"In truth, the spirit world is like a tree that grows outward in concentric layers. The middle layer of a physical tree identifies the year of its creation. The eternal tree has no years, knows no middle. The layers reach inward and outward endlessly. Call the layers spirit realms.

"The angels inhabit six realms. The Aryan and Tibetan masters each claim a realm of their own, as do humans, a race no less spiritual than angels. The distinction between gods and other spirit beings is that gods can travel at will between realms. . . ."

Hickey's brain shorted, his vision pulsed, and his ears rang, he loathed preachers so deeply. When the crowd murmured, nodded, sighed, Hickey supposed the master had tossed them something that made them feel like bigshots. Pravinshandra turned his hands palms upward and graced Venus, and the audience, with a beatific smile. Venus tenderly ran a finger down his cheek. Turning to the mike, giving her voice a tremolo on the first few syllables, she translated, "Who then is Jehovah but a god artist, the builder of the human realm? Not its architect. Not its conceiver. Not the source of the urge to conceive. Each of these is a god all his own."

Hickey's throat burned as if the sermon had activated a toxic secretion. He closed his ears, wondering if Cynthia might've fallen for this quack, flirted, gotten seduced, and made up the rest of her story out of shame. Maybe Emma Vidal had climbed the mountain and plunged into a chasm in despair, because she too adored the master. Half of the females present, Hickey thought, looked plagued right now with fluttery hearts and damp panties.

In the second seat from the far aisle, third row, a Santa Claus had appeared. He must've slipped in while Hickey's brain was misfiring. The beard covered all but the man's dark eyes and a couple inches of swarthy forehead. Hickey's arms tingled. He reached into his coat and adjusted his gun. He shifted in his chair, trying to keep one eye on Santa, while scanning the audience and watching the podium.

The way Pravinshandra stood with head bowed and the high, watery voice he was using tweaked Hickey with a dose of sympathy. A guy that pretty, bright, and smooth—the way people fawned on him could've been his ruination. In L.A. Hickey'd known a few women who'd gotten so choked with vanity that they devoted their lives to snagging and devouring men. Like Pravinshandra, they'd dangled a vision of salvation in front of their hungry prey.

The master's eyes closed, his voice dropped and quieted into

199

a low monotone while Venus translated a spiel about the Aryans and Semites being the sources of all the great religions. The Semites, she claimed, infected the world with their dualistic monotheism, while the Aryan-inspired Eastern truths held closer to the wisdom of the primal revelation which was being recaptured piece by piece by seers such as Madame B and the pilgrims to Mount Shasta.

The master lifted out of his trance, raised his hand, held it for a moment over Venus's hair. In turn she gave the audience a brief and humble smile, bowed, and floated to her chair. The master stepped forward, rested his hands on the podium.

The girl behind Hickey muttered, "I wish he'd shut up and throw fire." Her mother jabbed with an elbow and the girl yelped in a low voice. Santa squirmed, scratched the back of his neck, replaced his hands on his lap, while Pravinshandra's voice, a little hoarse, with an accent that sounded more Minnesotan than British or Indian, seemed to echo through the church.

"On my last journey to the mountain . . ."

"You raped Cynthia and killed Emma Vidal," Hickey mumbled.

". . . the Aryan master whose initials are YOS appeared as a ball of light, dense as the sun, small as an orange. To my inner ear, he revealed that the origin, the spark of creation, lies in the darkness Christians call hell."

Hickey's brain throbbed with anger and disgust while the master spouted off about the current war being a blood sacrifice by which some gods had to be appeased. Hickey wanted to spit, but Santa and the rest applauded heartily.

As Randolf Drew replaced Pravinshandra at the podium and proclaimed that now they would witness an achievement only reached by the highest caste of yogis, Hickey's wandering eyes found their mark. Seven rows back, halfway across, one man over from the front right corner of the pack of hoboes, Donny Katoulis sat paring his fingernails.

Hickey'd only caught the briefest glimpse of the man when

suddenly the overhead lights flickered out, all except a very dim one above the altar.

The man had a two- or three-day stubble and a tattered hat pulled so low you couldn't see if the hairline, like Donny's, ran a couple inches above his bushy eyebrows. He'd been slouched in the seat. Not like Donny. But any second now, while every stare was fixed on the fire-throwing act, the man would probably stand up and force Hickey to choose between risking the life of whoever might dodge in front of a deflected bullet and letting Katoulis drop the master.

As he squinted through the dark at the hobo, Hickey only caught sidewise glances of the blue fire. He saw Pravinshandra raise his arms above and outside his shoulders as though to flex his biceps for the ladies. He curled his fingers inward and they started to glow, first yellow, then orange, which instantly transformed to blue. The fire, or whatever it was, lengthened steadily out of the fingers of each hand, until it formed a straight, quavering line. For his next trick, he sent the fire upward, about ten feet high, fading as it climbed.

All around Hickey, people issued groans, sighs, impulsive bursts of applause, and when Venus stood, several men whooped as if the rodeo'd just hit town. Venus and the master faced off in front of the podium, about five feet apart. He slowly lifted his arms straight in front and pointed the fingers, already glowing, at a slight angle down from his shoulders, as if to make a lunge at her tits. He bowed his head, switched on his magic fingers. The fire jumped between them. For about two seconds, before it poofed away, it haloed all of Venus in blue.

A ninety-yard touchdown pass at the Rose Bowl could hardly have gotten such devoted applause. Venus and the master bowed sedately three or four times, and Hickey perched on the edge of his seat, watching the hobo and thinking, *He's got to move now.*

The lights flashed on. Venus stepped to the podium. She gave a little sigh and whistle that implied the blue fire had humbled and thrilled her.

Melodically, as though asking for a kiss, she launched into a pitch about the Black Forest and their plans for expansion. Though she failed to plead for donations, any dunce would've inferred that the *Nezahs* needed benefactors if they were to carry on the great Theosophical work interrupted by Judas elements blind to the fact that spiritual matters had to precede the battle against social injustice, because everything on earth must begin with the spiritual.

Hickey kept watching the hobo, again hidden behind the bushy wino next to him. But the man sat still.

The longer Hickey tailed them, the greater chance he'd get recognized. Maybe Donny'd already spotted him. If so, he'd be sure to reason that Hickey can't stand by the master through the entire reception. All he's got to have is patience. Until Hickey starts to piss his trousers or gets a violent urge for peanuts, or some Theosophist doll asks him to polka. Then Donny steps in, invites the master to bend over, listen to a secret. He places a small, silenced gun between the master's eyebrows and wishes him a pleasant trip back to Hell.

Or, if Hickey could maintain perfect vigilance, always stay by the master's side without Pravinshandra getting suspicious of his attentions and siccing a gang of shepherds on him—eventually Donny would creep around behind Hickey, splatter his guts, then pop the master. He could do it all in about three seconds. If a spectator rubbed his eyes, he'd miss the whole scene. Donny was that good. He'd shag out one of the doors in an instant. If Hickey was still alive, not a chance he'd catch Katoulis running. Hickey'd been fast enough to play fullback but not because he could outrun the defense. Because it took both tackles and a guard to bring him down.

Hickey got a vision of tomorrow's *Denver Post*. "RELIGIOUS NUT MURDERED BY ZEALOT—. . . the perpetrator, claims Sheriff Beauregard, was undoubtedly a Christian offended by "Master" Pravinshandra's heretical doctrines, which include his reverence for the Aryan race, his pantheism, his reference to the global war as 'a blood sacrifice.' The gunman appeared to be a transient.

'He's probably long gone by now,' Sheriff Beauregard speculated."

Randolf Drew was inviting everyone to the Raja Yoga schoolhouse on the corner of Thirteenth and Logan to witness their Nativity play and imbibe their food and libations. By the time he'd finished his invitation, the hoboes were already on their feet, migrating toward the door. While Hickey rushed around to the front of the seats, he lost sight of his quarry. He shouldered a path through the crowd and out to the sidewalk, caught up with the pack of hoboes, and sidled in among them. Finally he spied the man, about five yards ahead. Several hoboes walked between them. The man's hair wasn't as shaggy as the others'. It looked like a barber's work. The olive skin of his high cheeks and forehead didn't appear raw or windblown.

At Seventeenth and Broadway the Salvation Army woman was tooting "O Come All Ye Faithful." Hickey caught himself muttering the words. As he glanced her way, the woman's appearance whacked him like a short dose of lightning. A white, violet-tinted glow surrounded her. Her doughy potato-shaped face looked glorious. He slapped his head and jumped to catch up with the hoboes. Following the railroad porter, who took strides like a gazelle, they crossed Sixteenth and Colfax, then turned east along a row of bus benches beside the capitol lawn. Up the hill, across some acres of dead grass and snow, the dome of the capitol looked like a black puddle in the iron-gray sky.

The man was Donny's height and build, for sure, but he didn't strut like Katoulis, which might only indicate that Katoulis was a consummate actor. A burly hobo staggering beside Hickey tripped over his feet or a rut in the sidewalk and jostled Hickey so that he slammed into the guy on his other side. He wheeled back, with an urge to sock the fellow who'd bumped him. Only the voice in his head stopped him. It commanded, "Take the punk out now, Tom, or you're a goner."

Hickey loosed a button on each of his two coats, plucked the .38 from the holster, and lunged between the two men who separated him and the guy he felt certain was Donny. The hobo had sensed the action behind him and started to turn just as Hickey clutched his left arm, twisted it behind his back, lodged the gun in his kidneys, and yanked the man out of the pack, onto the capitol lawn.

"What the hell?" the hobo screeched. "Lemme go, bub."

It wasn't Katoulis's voice. It rasped like a veteran wino's. Hickey almost dropped the arm. But he stepped on ice, skidded. Clutching the hobo tighter, he toppled them both. He fell across the man's legs. He'd lost his grip, needing one arm to break his fall, another to hold his gun. The hobo slid out from under him, sprang up, and bolted toward the capitol. A native of snow country would've gotten away. Donny was another Californian. While his slick shoes grabbed for traction, Hickey clipped him in the spine. Knocked him chest-first into the snow. He wrenched the hobo to his feet, spun him around, bent the arm behind his back, and jerked the man's wrist nearly up to his shoulder. The hobo yowled.

"You've got one hand," Hickey snarled. "Use the gun."

The man tucked his chin around his shoulder, rolled his eyes sideways, caught a glimpse of his tormentor. "Hey, save it for the Krauts, why don'tcha, pal. Lemme go now or I'll . . ."

"Go on, Donny. You'll . . . ?"

"Hell! Donny ain't my name. Lemme go. Lemme turn around. Take a look at me, will you?"

Suddenly the world got bright. Hickey inched around, turning the hobo with him, just enough to see the glare of a cruiser or taxi's spotlight at the curb. "Turn the damn thing off!" he shouted.

"No, I ain't," a man yelled back. "Not till the police comes."

"Lemme go, pal," the hobo rasped. "You got things all bungled up here. You and me both gonna land in jail, for nothing."

Hickey pondered a moment, then released the hobo, who whipped around and faced him, eyed the gun pointing at his middle. "See, now. I ain't who you think. I ain't no Donny. Name's Lester Coolidge, swear to God." Each couple words he gained a step backward toward a monument the size of a walk-in tomb, topped by the statue of a horseman. Though Hickey still believed the guy was Katoulis, he knew he was fatigued, confused, capable of error. The man could've gotten away. Except that just as he tipped his left shoulder and crooked it an inch toward the monument—the second he'd gotten set to bolt for cover—he flashed Hickey a grin.

Hickey didn't feel himself squeezing the trigger either time. But the noise thundered in his ears and the man flew backward as though an invisible tackler had caught him gut high. A woman began wailing. She sounded like Hickey's damned mother.

TWENTY-TWO

THE DETECTIVE NAMED GEORGE GROUND HIS ELBOW INTO THE desk and yawned. "How is it the cabbie tells us Stavros didn't show his gun? First anybody saw his piece was when you lifted it out of his belt."

They sat in the lieutenant's office, Hickey in a hard straight-backed chair by the window that overlooked Thirteenth Street, a vacant lot, gray trees along a creek. George, in the leather-quilted swivel chair behind the desk, had slick dark hair from which a scar angled down to his eyebrow. Sickly pale. A big fellow, yet his clothes fit like a kid's who'd borrowed from his older brother.

The lieutenant sprawled on the love seat squeezed between two wooden file cabinets. Past retirement age, he might've been hacking at golf balls in Phoenix if not for the war. He was paunchy, with buzz-cut hair and puffy, reddened eyes. He kept kneading both sides of his neck, underneath the ears, as though trying to fix his swollen glands. Every couple minutes he'd sneeze heartily.

"What'd I tell you?" Hickey droned. "I didn't say he got to his gun. I said he was reaching for it."

"How'd you know he had one?"

"Twenty years I've known the punk. When has he not had a gun?"

"Michael Stavros?"

"Donald Katoulis. Anybody call San Diego yet?"

"Sure. And your pal Captain Thrapp's out on the town. We even told him to call collect. Generous, huh? How about you reciprocate, partner? Tell us the awful truth so the lieutenant can go home and snooze. If he comes down with pneumonia, we're gonna see that you fry."

"Uh-huh." Hickey gazed out the window, through the space between the window frame and the blackout curtain, at the headlights of three airplanes flying toward him side by side. Every word he uttered or breath he exhaled seemed to waste valuable air, as if Denver weren't just one mile high but four or five, and his lungs were like divers' tanks—once they ran out, he was through.

"Make him run through it again, George," the lieutenant grumbled. "Tell him, watch out every detail's the same, no slip-ups, or his ass is charcoal."

"Take it from the top, will you, Tommy?"

"I got a phone call," Hickey muttered. "Some guy, squeaky voice, says Donny K's gonna knock off this swami. He wants me to stop him."

"Why?"

"Beats me."

"Why don't he call the law?"

"He says cops've been after Katoulis a long time. They had their chance. Anyway, Charlie Schwartz owns cops. This guy isn't taking any chances."

"How's he know so much about the kike mob?"

"Maybe they go to the same temple," Hickey snapped. "He wants me to take a few guys along, grab Katoulis in the act. I tell him I'll think it over. Next I know, a messenger drops off two grand for me at the nightclub."

"Ruby's."

"Rudy's. I'm supposed to get five grand more when Donny's in the joint."

"Or dead?"

"Wasn't supposed to happen. I messed up. This guy didn't want anybody done in. That's the point of why he called, George. I think the fellow hired Katoulis, then had a nightmare or something. All of a sudden his feet get cold. That's my surmise."

"Fuck your surmise. I'm asking what'd he say."

"Not so much. I'm telling you what I got from his tone of voice."

"Hey, Lieutenant," George called over his shoulder, "Ol' Tom's not lying about one thing. I'm damned sure he used to be a Tinseltown cop, the way he thinks he's Sigmund Freud." He cocked a big finger, gazed down the crest of it at Hickey's right eye. "So how many sidekicks you bring along?"

"Nobody. I only had a few hours."

George rubbed his eyes, scowled disgustedly. "Tom, if you're gonna lie, make it good, will you? I'll give you an easy straight line here, see what you can do with it. Why'd you drag Stavros out onto the tundra? Invite him to a picnic, did you?"

"I got spooked. I figured, once we got to the reception, it'd be too easy for Katoulis. Too crowded, might've turned into a bloodbath."

"Try this angle, George," the lieutenant offered. "Tommy's not a liar, he's a retard."

"I like it." George slapped the desk, leaned closer, craned his neck. "Mystery man's paying you to take some guys, grab this shooter in the act, turn him in. So you go it alone, drag him onto capitol lawn when as yet he hasn't so much as tickled the swami. Then, like maybe you don't want him to talk about something, you pop him twice, dead center. Make a hole you can already see daylight through, then widen it a little."

Hickey was staring out the window, trying to follow the line that silhouetted the Rockies against the obsidian sky, using his vision to blur the movie that played on the backs of his eyelids, of Donny's fall onto the snow. Every few seconds a shiver zinged across his back, between the shoulder blades. A numb spot at the base of his skull felt like an ice pack rested on it.

"What's he gonna come up with next?" The weary lieutenant raised the pitch of his voice, gave it a tremor, like an actor trying to sound appalled. "He figured to hold the bum until we showed to bust Stavros for trespassing on the capitol lawn? Ask him, George."

"I messed up," Hickey mumbled. "I lost my head and messed up bad, all right?"

"Yeah." George leaned back in his swivel chair, clasped his hands behind his neck for a second, then lunged forward and grabbed a cigarette out of the tray on his desk. "Want a smoke, Tom?"

"Naw."

"Shot of bourbon?"

"Not unless you're planning to cut me loose directly, give me a lift back to the hotel."

"Why's that?"

"A drink and I'd probably nod off."

"Or mouth off, right?"

"I'm tired, is all."

"Take it lightly, don't you, this murder routine?"

Hickey glared silently, pinning George's eyes until the cop wagged his head and rubbed the bridge of his nose. "Maybe we'll cut you loose before long. Soon as you spill your guts. About your mystery man. He tell you how he knew your buddy Katoulis was gonna hit the swami?"

"Way I figure," Hickey droned as if repeating for the fiftieth time, "he's some religious quack, maybe a rival Theosophist, didn't like the swami's game. So he buys a hit on the swami, then gets this nightmare—or, hell, maybe an angel visits him, he thinks—something tells him to repent. That's a common MO of religious fanatics—sin big, repent, sin big."

"Can't fault you there, Tommy," the lieutenant grumbled. "I got a son-in-law's that way."

George chuckled quietly, crushed out his cigarette. "Suppose we're gonna buy the mystery-man story. Not that we're about to, but suppose. Here's what I think. It was like you say, except he wasn't paying you to get Stavros busted. He was paying you to hit the guy. What I mean, Tom, Stavros gets nailed, he rats on the chump that hired him, next thing you know the mystery man's busting rocks. How do you figure?"

Hickey kneaded the back of his neck, giving himself a moment. "Could be he knows Donny wouldn't rat on anybody. He'd wait thirty years if he needed, then pop the guy that set him up. Maybe the guy that called me figured on getting lost. Or he's the kind of nut that wants to get punished."

"Oh Lord," George moaned. "Freud again."

The lieutenant sneezed, sat up, and gave Hickey a wry smile. "You're a lotta laughs, Tommy."

For another half hour the detectives fired the same questions in different disguises, until a sergeant rapped on the door. George let him in. He looked like a rookie, promoted every couple weeks since all the able-bodied cops had run off to the war. He wore a fuzzy mustache, a mop of blond hair. "I got what we needed outta L.A.," he said, "and outta the morgue. The stiff's name's Katoulis, an old-timer with that kike mob that runs Hollywood."

"Who says?"

"Not much doubt, Lieutenant. He's got the same tattoo, says *Irene,* on the upper right bicep. Same appendectomy scar. Name on the driver's license, Michael Stavros, is one of the guy's aka's. The prints are on their way, special D."

The lieutenant sneezed, wiped his nose with his sleeve. "Get Tommy outta here, will you, son? I'm allergic to him. Give him the honeymoon suite."

The sergeant motioned Hickey to his feet, held the door for him, followed behind giving Hickey directions down two flights of stairs. He chatted a minute with the jailer about some local basketball team, then used a giant key to open the cell block and waved Hickey in.

The jail looked like a kennel. No interior walls, only bars, small cages with iron bunks. Some Mexicans who'd clustered around

210

the junction of four cages—shooting dice or playing cards by flashlight—fired commands at the cop. The Spanish all mixed together. *"Venga cabrón su madre dame una mota."* Beyond the Mexicans were the whites. Orientals next. Negroes, Hickey guessed, were at the far end. He couldn't see that far in the dark. An old fellow with gray skin pushed his face between the bars. "Boy mussed hisself. Ain't nobody goin' clean him?"

"I sure ain't," the sergeant said.

Hickey got shoved into the fourth cell on the right. There was a seatless toilet alongside a one-tap basin, beneath the small, high window. In the adjoining cells, everybody looked asleep except a wild man who shot piercing glances around as he paced from the cage door to his wall and back. Hickey's cellmate, a bald white fellow wearing khaki work clothes, lay facedown on the upper bunk, snoring like a V-8 with corroded spark plugs.

Hickey flopped onto the lower bunk, wrapped the fetid, scratchy blanket around him, cussed the police for taking his army coat. Bone-cold and sore, his stomach painfully tender, his head throbbing, muscles taut as guitar strings, he lay sideways, his knees tugged against his chest for warmth, wondering if there could be any relief or if he'd always feel this way. He'd amazed himself by holding his desolation in check the two or three hours those detectives had made him sit there lying until they saw there wasn't going to be any wearing him down beyond where the hunt for Katoulis had dragged him. They'd recognized that, like a prisoner of war, Hickey'd steeled his will, locked the truth so deeply inside him he might choose to have his nuts removed before he'd tell. It might be less painful. If he gave up now, turned on Cynthia, every time he looked in a mirror or reflecting window, he wouldn't only see a murderer. He'd see a weakling, a forlorn clown.

What he couldn't figure, what tormented him most, was—why couldn't he rationalize it, take a little pity on himself? No matter what he'd done, somebody had to die. If he'd backed off, minded his own affairs, and let everything else run its course, then Pravinshandra would've got it between the eyes. If he'd called in the law—with no solid evidence against Donny, and the girl knowing who'd betrayed her—wouldn't Katoulis have been waiting behind the oleanders at the end of Fanuel Street when Hickey stepped out of his car one night? Sure, he would. And the girl, after a few years in jail for conspiracy, comes out with a felony record, dropping the odds to one in a million any bandleader's going to take her on. Even if somebody did, likely she'd be so filled with venom, who's going to fall for her love songs?

Somebody had to die. Who better than Donny Katoulis? In the past week or so, Hickey'd been too preoccupied to read the news or keep up with the headlines on the radio, yet just in passing he'd heard of a few hundred thousand soldiers and innocents shot, bombed, stabbed, cremated. There was no logic Hickey could find that wouldn't excuse him for killing one of Earth's viler creatures. He couldn't find a single reason to grieve for Donny Katoulis or to blame himself for killing the man. But logic didn't rule the heart. From the moment after Donny's last spasm, his muscles felt colder and his blood flowed thickly, on account of the knowledge that he was going to pay forever. A day might not pass that he didn't watch the man writhe and stiffen, didn't feel himself standing there, playing God with his .38. What you don't know about playing God until you've tried it, he thought, was that there's no place lonelier. His mind pulsated with the noise of gunshots, the kick of the discharge against his hand and arm, and visions of Donny's eyes dilating as if they filled with dark blood. For a couple hours, every time he'd accepted the sounds and visions, made them take on a rhythm that began lulling him into a dazed slumber, as close as he was likely to get to sleep, some Mexican would howl a curse or demand.

The jailer woke Hickey. The blond sergeant led him up the stairs to a counter where a pock-faced matron returned his wallet, coat, everything they'd appropriated except the gun that had finished Katoulis, while uniform and plainclothes cops sat on their desks swilling coffee and giving him a variety of stares. Cold. Amused. Analytical. The blond sergeant told Hickey to call him

Mitch. Leading the way, he bobbed up and down, walking as if there were springs in his shoes.

The streets were icy, the sidewalks bunkered with ridges of snow. A near-empty streetcar rattled past while they waited at Broadway and Colfax, from where Hickey chose not to look at the scene of his crime. Otherwise the streets were deserted as though an air raid had driven the citizenry underground. A garbage truck crossed a distant intersection. A valiant newsboy skidded his bike along the icy street, saluted as they passed him.

"Seems your pal in San Diego made a deal," Mitch commented. "Promised to conk you on the head and ship you back here if the DA won't fall for your self-defense crap."

"Swell," Hickey said. "Where we going?"

"The Palace, pick up your gear. Next stop Denver Municipal Airport. Lieutenant wants you long gone. I guess you bored him."

"You're gonna break my heart, talking like that," Hickey muttered.

"I wonder what kind of deal your chum made. He must've swore you was next in line to Christ, getting Lieutenant Pluim to let you go home when they got a solid witness against you."

"Who's that?"

"Why you wanta know? Maybe you figure to ice him?"

"Tell you what, Sergeant," Hickey growled. "Let's you and me practice keeping our mouths shut."

Mitch slid the patrol car around the corner of Broadway and Seventeenth, where the Salvation Army woman had played her oboe. The thought of her and the sight of the Brown Palace, as they parked in its loading zone, touched Hickey with a violent nostalgia, as though one age had concluded last night, the moment he'd spotted Katoulis, replaced by a new and sinister one. The doorman, the desk clerk, the elevator boy all had new faces. The onyx looked duller, the copper more tarnished. On the chandelier and Christmas trees, he noticed all the darkened bulbs.

He didn't bother to change out of his uniform, just collected his gear, crammed it into his suitcase, and retraced his steps, leading the sergeant out of there. As the elevator descended, Hickey wondered briefly if Venus and the master were still asleep, and if they even knew what might've hit them last night.

On the drive to the airport, the sergeant pointed to a tract of shoe-box houses. "Used to be wheat fields." Hickey pulled the watch cap over his eyes, trying to concentrate on simple things. The inside of his eyelids, how they kept looking redder. Whether he should eat cereal or eggs. The pain and weakness in his right ankle. "Over here, used to be a ranch of longhorns, now it's some damned outfit makes runners for tanks."

"The nerve," Hickey grumbled.

In the airport he bought a sandwich and milk, devoured them, tried futilely to relax with his head on the table. Somebody'd left behind a *Denver Post*. Hickey's eyes watered, couldn't focus on the headlines. He got up, left two dollars, and walked to the phone booths. Two or three people waited at each one. He bribed an ensign and a Mexican woman to cut in front of them. He would've called home except that he couldn't bear the thought of Elizabeth's voice. Just as he'd given the operator Leo's number, the loudspeaker announced his flight. In the middle of a ring, the line clicked and Leo grumbled, "It better be good."

"Collect call for Mister or Missus Weiss, from Tom Hickey."

"Yeah. Sure. You there, cheapskate?"

"I'm here. Tell Madeline, will you? I'll get back sometime today."

"Where's Katoulis?"

"Same place we're all gonna be, one of these days."

The line buzzed a while. Finally Leo said, "You okay, Tom?"

"Sure. Top of the world."

On the DC-3 to L.A., Hickey slept without nightmares, at least ones he could remember. He woke a few times in turbulence, his heart pounding as though it had prophesied the plane was about to nose-dive. He fell back into a reluctant sleep, trying to obliterate a weird idea he'd caught, that if the plane did crash, the blame for splattering a hundred and some people all over the desert would land on him.

At Los Angeles Airport the soldiers and sailors looked more battered and weary. It seemed half of them wore bandages, used crutches, lugged duffel bags with their solitary arm, or weaved through the crowds in agonized stupor. Hickey made a stop at the rest room, changed to his civilian clothes and left the uniform with the washroom attendant. Everything, including the long coat with his watch cap and gloves tucked into the pockets. The old Chinaman could make a few bucks. Hickey wouldn't have to look at the costume again.

He walked outside, stood in the sunlight, caught a scent of ocean breeze through the sooty air. He pictured Madeline and Elizabeth. They stood blocking the doorway, underneath his carport. Madeline glared with contempt, her lips dry and twisted. Behind her stood a shadowy form, maybe Castillo. Elizabeth leaned against the doorjamb, watching her father with mournful, forsaken eyes.

TWENTY-THREE

♪ ♪ ♪

THE SHINY THING IN THE CARPORT WASN'T PAUL CASTILLO'S
Cadillac, like Hickey'd feared at first glance, when he was still half
blinded from watching the sunset while the taxi brought him the
final lap, down Pacific Beach Drive. It was his own Chevy. Madeline must've picked it up from the lot behind Rudy's. Though he
hadn't washed it in too long, it glittered as if it ought to hang from
a Christmas tree.

Hickey got out of the cab, empty-handed except for the suitcase that had ridden on the seat beside him. He'd dropped the
suitcase and reached for his billfold when the driver's door of his
Chevy flew open and Elizabeth came running, her smile so wide
it looked dangerous, as if it could tear her face. She squeezed him,
rubbing her head and cheek into his chest.

"I've been waiting for you, Daddy."

"I see, babe. How'd you know when I'd get here?"

"Didn't. I've been waiting a couple hours. Did you see I
washed and waxed your car?"

"You bet. Never looked so shiny."

Most kids, Hickey thought, would've asked him straight off about the guy he killed. Elizabeth had more sense than most kids. Or she didn't know. He fished for his billfold and, behind her back, while she still held on, paid off the cabbie.

"Mom's cooking a feast. She said you get steaks every day at Rudy's, and tomorrow we'll have turkey. So tonight she's making chicken stuffed with ham."

"Cordon bleu?"

"Yep. I guess. And she's got us a cabin reserved at the Pine Hills Lodge, for tomorrow. There's brand-new snow up there, it fell again last night. Did you get me a Christmas present yet?"

Hickey wagged his head. "Been waiting till tonight."

"How about a bigger sled? One we could ride together."

He tickled her ribs, gave her a smile and a kiss on the forehead. She stepped back, picked up his suitcase, clutched his hand, and pulled him toward the house. "Close your eyes, Dad."

Hickey followed her orders, got led past his car, inside and across the tile to where the hardwood began, at the entry to the living room.

"You can look now."

When he opened his eyes, he might as well have been standing on top of a mountain gazing across a moonlit ocean at a city built of gold and jewels. Elizabeth's face streamed with happy tears. Behind her, on his sleeping porch, a Christmas tree glowed, and beyond that, a bright orange boat with a silvery sail glided through the foggy dusk across the bay toward Crown Point. He heard the rustle of fabric, smelled lilac, and turned to face Madeline. Her damp hair and satiny face looked haloed in the light from the fixture in the kitchen. Her lips moved, then her chin began to quiver, as though she felt as shy and clumsy as Hickey did, like a boy and girl discovering love.

"I feel so awful, Tom," she said breathlessly. For a moment she quietly watched his eyes, as if inspecting them for secrets, then reached a finger up to his lips, inviting him to kiss it. "I heard what you told me," she said, "about Cynthia wanting to hire

217

Katoulis, but I didn't stop to think what it meant, I was so busy with poor little Madeline. Honest to God, it never occurred to me that you were going to take on Donny Katoulis. I know," she whispered, "it should've been obvious."

Hickey didn't care to speak. Instead he squeezed her until he had to loosen up so she could breathe, and still he kept hold, losing himself in the pressure of her body and the touch and smell of her hair.

"You know how it is, Tom, being a cop's wife. You teach yourself not to go around fretting, or you turn into a hag from worrying all the time. After a while, you start to ignore things. Even so . . ."

"Hush." He kissed her lusciously, then drew back. "Forgive me for socking Castillo?"

"Dad," Elizabeth gasped. "You socked Mr. Castillo?"

"All in fun, babe," Hickey said.

Madeline gave him a neutral smile. "I bet it wasn't the first time he's got socked, or the last." Laying the side of her head on his chest, she stood quietly awhile, then eased away. "I better get back to cooking before I scorch the whole mess. You want to lie down, or get a bath?"

"Naw. Not yet."

"Lizzie's got a party she'd like to go to, with that La Jolla crowd. You guys want to gab awhile? There's about an hour before she ought to start getting ready."

"I don't have to go, Dad," Elizabeth said.

"It's okay, babe. Your mom and I need to do some things." She made a wry face, and Hickey winked at her. "Like Christmas shopping. How about you and me go look at the bay? Make sure nobody swiped it, while your mom slaves over dinner?"

"Let's go."

They exited through the sleeping porch, past the Christmas tree, a bushy Douglas fir trimmed with the soft-colored round lights they'd bought last year and the angels, trees, stars, and such that Elizabeth had been making out of dough since she was a baby. "Where'd all those presents come from?" Hickey asked.

"You'll find out. It's getting dark. We should drop the curtains."

"Naw. Japs aren't gonna bomb us on Christmas Eve."

"They're pretty mean, Dad."

"Well, some of 'em are Catholics who'd probably tell the other guys that God'll smite anybody that pulls such a lousy trick."

They scuffed through the sand, west and around the turn of the bay. Hickey asked what else, besides a new sled, she wanted for Christmas. She listed an angora sweater, Coty's Emeraude perfume, pastel drawing pencils, a few shades of lip rouge.

Along that side of the bay, a sidewalk ran between the sand and the dwellings, small wood-frame or stucco cottages on narrow lots. They passed fifty or so houses. At least half were decorated, with bulbs hanging in oleander, bougainvillea, from a loquat or magnolia tree; with a wooden Santa on the roof, creeping through the mist toward the chimney; with glittery stars in the windows or atop a flagpole. While the sky's last gray faded into dark, they passed three Nativity scenes and walked onto Santa Clara Point. Hickey stopped and turned, facing the bay. A speedboat thumped by, circling over its own wake. The driver whooped something at them. Elizabeth slipped her arm around his elbow and leaned against him.

"Want me to tell you what happened in Denver?"

"Sure, if you want."

"How much your mom say?"

"I think she didn't know too much, but she figured you must've gotten hired to protect somebody."

"Yeah, that's how it was. A couple of religious nuts were on a tour, giving speeches, trying to shuck people into giving them dough. I got wind of a plan to kill one of them."

"Which one?"

"Probably the man."

"Why'd somebody hate him that bad?"

Hickey rocked onto his heels then forward and back, deciding he should go no deeper unless he wanted to spill the whole truth. "Couldn't keep his hands off women, for one thing. Anyway, I tailed this pair around Denver until I spotted the shooter, and I figured the best way to keep the most people safe was to get him alone somewhere."

Now the story got tricky, Hickey thought. Either he lied, another crime to answer for, or he gave her the truth and risked everything, hoping she'd understand what he didn't—why killing somebody just because you're scared and furious could be right.

"I walked him a little way onto this lawn below the state capitol, and he started trying to throw me with lies, backing away. . . ." The shape of an unlighted sailboat motoring slowly around Santa Clara Point reminded him of Katoulis's grin, which he'd already seen a dozen times, in a slice of orange at the Denver airport, in the crescent moon when it passed a break in the fog, and in the unpainted half of a headlight beam. He loosed his right arm from Elizabeth's and laid it around her shoulders, pressed her closer against him, keeping her eyes off his face.

She reached up and patted his hand. "You're cold, Daddy."

"Not hardly. I just got back from Denver. You wanta hear about cold?"

"Uh-huh." She reached her arm around his waist, held it firmly, and turned him back toward home. They'd walked about ten yards when Hickey got walloped by the news that a daughter can feel for her dad as much as the dad feels for her. It would take a hundred times more than his murdering Donny Katoulis to wrest him and Elizabeth apart.

"Look." She swept her free arm across the length of the bay. The lights on Christmas trees glimmered in a dozen or so houses atop the low cliff of the west shore, as if the people had taken their cue from the Hickeys and declared that for tonight the Japs or nobody was going to dim their pleasure. They walked holding hands, arms swinging, admiring the airy lights diffused and brightened by the fog.

At home Madeline was chopping a cucumber. Elizabeth checked the clock and ran for the bathroom, hollering, "Uh-oh, Keeny's gonna pick me up in twenty-five minutes."

Hickey stepped into the kitchen, kissed Madeline's neck. "Who's Keeny?"

"Short for Joaquin. Portuguese. Heir to a million tuna boats. I called the kid, made him swear on the pope's toupee that he'll get her back by eleven, and no drinking."

"You're a tough customer," Hickey said.

"You bet. Get out of the kitchen."

Hickey laughed for the first time in so long that it felt awkward. He grabbed his suitcase from where Elizabeth had dropped it by the door, carried it into the bedroom, and discharged its contents, all but the bathroom gear and his .45, into the laundry hamper. He walked back out to the living room, used the phone directory, and called Marston's to ask how late they'd stay open for Christmas shoppers. Ten o'clock, the girl answered.

A few minutes later, lounging in the bathtub with his briar and a tumbler of Dewar's, Hickey marveled at how the world could change from hell to paradise so fast it left you dizzy.

The Portuguese kid arrived in his flashy red coupe while Hickey stood shaving, wrapped in a towel. Elizabeth ran in and kissed her dad good-bye. After he'd splashed on cologne and fixed his hair as well as the scraggly mess allowed, he called out to Madeline, "How we dressing?"

"Formal."

In the bedroom he shed the towel and slipped into his best gabardine slacks and silk dress shirt. No underwear. He left the shirttail out and strolled through the kitchen to the dining area where Madeline waited, sipping red wine, wearing only the blue silk dress she'd bought for their third anniversary. No bracelets or earrings, nothing on her hands but the wedding band. She was barefoot like Hickey. When she leaned toward him to light the candle, the silk bodice clung to her roughened nipples.

They'd finished their salads and a glass of wine each, and had started on the chicken when Madeline finally said, "I think Thrapp's a little tweaked at you."

"How's that? He call you?"

"Yeah. He's not sure you didn't just venture up there to get

Katoulis. You might have to convince him. Own up about the girl and all." Hickey shrugged, filled their wineglasses. "Thrapp let something drop about a gang war, like I was supposed to know what he was talking about. Can you give me a clue?"

"All I know is—the girl hired Donny to knock off a guy that raped her. I shadowed the rapist, spotted Donny, and got him first. That's not the official story, which I'm going to tell you later, and which is the one I'm gonna have to give Thrapp. He's not likely to buy it any better than the Denver bunch did, but maybe he'll look sideways for a pal."

"He's mad, Tom."

Hickey nodded. "Anyway, the toughest part's over. You wanta know what the toughest part was?"

"Sure."

"Leaving you guys."

She reached out and caressed his fingers. Her other hand forked a bite of chicken and delivered it to her mouth without looking away from his eyes.

For dessert they had kisses, short ones at first, while Madeline sat on his lap in the easy chair, before she led him to the sleeping porch. On the way she peeled the dress over her head, shook out her hair, bent to unplug the Christmas tree lights. She made a half pirouette and toppled gently onto the hammock, where Hickey joined her. He'd kissed around her belly only for a minute before she invited him inside her. They rocked for a while, giggling and cooing, then for a long time they lay sideways where each could see the other and at the same time gaze across the bay, at the quavering water and foggy rainbow of lights. They lay coupled, sideways, then with Hickey mounted, then with Madeline riding him, for the longest time in almost sixteen years, since the week before their honeymoon, in Little Bear Hotel overlooking Lake Arrowhead, the night Hickey lay awake until dawn staring at her mouth, her eyelids, the flesh of her neck and shoulders, like a blind guy who'd only that minute got healed.

Madeline whispered, "Now make me scream, Tom."

222

The hammock swayed. Once it nearly reached the ceiling. The porch creaked and Madeline screamed.

Twenty minutes later Hickey raced down Pacific Coast Highway, believing he might've discovered a natural law. It could be, he mused, that you can't forgive yourself alone. First, you need somebody precious to forgive you.

TWENTY-FOUR

♪ ♪ ♪

HICKEY'S WATCH READ 10:15 WHEN HE GOT BACK TO HIS CAR IN the lot behind Rudy's and crammed a small fortune's worth of parcels, all labeled MARSTON'S, into the trunk. The girl ought to be in the middle of her second set, he calculated as he walked to meet Skeeter. He tipped the boy three dollars. "Watch my car extra close tonight, huh?"

"Sure, boss." The kid gave him a dopey smile. "How come everybody's riled at you?"

"Who's everybody?"

"Miss Moon. Mr. Castillo, and that bald guy that has the big Chrysler."

"Charlie Schwartz. What'd they say?"

"All I heard was them cussing you while they came out the door. Then I had to run for Mr. Castillo's car. It was just a while ago."

"They all leave together?"

"Only Mr. Castillo. Miss Moon and the bald guy went back in."

Hickey nodded, told Skeeter happy Christmas, and walked through the kitchen door. Over the clatter of pans and the steaks hissing, the girl sang a promise to work and slave for her man. Hickey dashed through the kitchen to avoid Chef LeDuc, Phil, and the waiters who, after his two days gone, would sure have disputes or petitions to throw at him.

Rudy's was so packed it didn't leave people enough room to sweat. Castillo must've gathered more tables, squeezed everything together, pinched the dance floor down so small that Hickey figured they ought to post a sign—NO FAT DANCERS OR PET-TICOATS. He made his way to the dimmest corner, where the bar ended near the door to his office. From there he watched Cynthia. The Santa cap she wore was white. A red one would've clashed with her hair. Christmas lights above the stage—green, blue, red, orange—reflected off her shoulderless knee-length pearl-colored gown. The shoes and gloves matched. A ruby brooch adorned her chest, dead center.

She'd talked to Charlie Schwartz, must know about Katoulis and realize that any second a cop might stroll in and drag her away, yet no agitation appeared in her voice or demeanor. Lost in the song, she radiated passion, and afterward she stood coolly as Venus in Denver, basking in the applause. As though each of them believed she'd caught fate in a headlock.

Again Hickey scanned the dining booths and tables, searching for Leo or Charlie Schwartz. He spotted the gangster at a table along the wall near the kitchen and made his way there through the bustle of waiters, busboys, wandering customers. Schwartz faced the stage, sitting across from a Latin doll who looked as if she'd spent three sleepless nights and days perfecting her makeup. There were no empty chairs to pull up. Hickey squatted beside the gangster, who turned just far enough to shoot a murderous scowl.

"Go on," Hickey said. "Tell me I'm a goner or something, before I boot you out of here."

Scooting his chair around, the man faced Hickey. His right eye squinted while the rest of his face looked mild, perplexed, as though he couldn't comprehend anybody wasting such a kind soul as Donny K. "All I'm gonna do is wreck your life, Tom. Buy you a ticket to the gutter."

"How's that?"

"First, the girl's mine. You can have her till New Year's. Don't want her to land in L.A. with a bum reputation, for leaving you cold. Two weeks, she'll be headlining at the Doubloon, Santa Monica pier. Me and my brother are buying the place, branching out. Real estate's a bust these days."

The orchestra kicked into a bouncy number, "Don't Sit under the Apple Tree." Clyde had snatched Harry James's arrangement from the film *Private Buckaroo*. When Cynthia cut in, she energized the lyric more than had all three Andrews Sisters. Charlie Schwartz offered Hickey a predatory smile.

"Drink up and scram, before I've gotta embarrass you in front of the lady." Hickey stood, ambled away.

"Watch out for Donny's ghost," the gangster called after him.

Hickey weaved his way back to the bar, where he found Leo straddling his own favorite stool, next to the olives and cherries. Offering a handshake and troubled frown, Leo said, "Hell, I figured you'd take the night off or else crawl in looking like what's-his-name when he climbed out of the whale's belly."

"Jonah?"

"Sure. And you come strutting—makes me wonder if Denver was a lie and you been hiding out at Warner Springs, soaking up mineral waters, leaving your old partner to drive himself loco following this jailbait around, watching her shimmy and croon. Meanwhile, Mrs. Dortmeyer's in a tizzy on account of I haven't had an hour to deduce which one of the Okies is pilfering chocolate cream pies outta her bakery, and Vi's badgering me just as bad as the Dortmeyer dame. The girl beds down, I sneak home, figuring to snooze a couple hours, but first I gotta whisper sweetheart stuff to Vi, else in the morning she'll pout and accuse me of planning to run off with some piece of young fluff, on account of she's gone droopy. I gotta tell her droopy's pretty as anything. It wears a guy out, lying at four A.M."

"That was a mouthful," Hickey said.

"You try mixing bourbon and coffee," Leo grumbled, "see if you can shut up. You feeling as good as you look?"

"Better. Charlie Schwartz threatens to ruin me, first by stealing the girl. Oughta bother me, but no—see, after tonight it looks like Madeline and I are okay."

"Swell news. You drinking the usual?"

"Yep."

Leo hailed the bartender, motioned toward Hickey. "Bring my pal a Dewar's, on the house."

"How's she doing?" Hickey asked.

"Who's that?"

"The girl?"

"Looks mighty fine to me. Tom, next time she puts a hit on the guy, if there is a next time, Schwartz'll take care of the deal. You could follow her till doomsday, all the good it'll do. You and me oughta get some rest, forget the girl."

"Soon as I talk to her," Hickey said. "Wait around a few minutes, would you?"

Leo nodded. Hickey took a sip of Dewar's, then set down the glass and walked through the crowd to where he could watch the girl more closely, from the street-side corner of the stage. He stood against the wall. The girl leaned toward the microphone.

"Takin' a chance on love," she crooned.

Clyde waved the horn section to a crescendo, then lowered them into the melody, while Cynthia announced that she heard the trumpets.

Hands behind her back, she swayed a little, side to side, as if the delight she sang about had loosed her body to move as it pleased. Her head bobbed. The ball on the end of her Santa cap swung like a metronome. When Ben Sykes soloed on trumpet she stepped back, holding her wistful smile, and gazed across the room, from the kitchen wall where Charlie Schwartz still sat to the opposite side, where her eyes caught Hickey's. Her lips shrank inward, her body stiffened, and the hands jerked around from behind her to grip and press against her thighs. For the last two bars of the solo, she stood like that, before stepping forward to sing about rainbows and happy endings.

The first couple words had strained, then her hands unpeeled, swung at her sides. A blissful smile broke free and carried her through the last few lines. An instant after the final note, her knees folded slightly, her shoulders seemed to drop a foot. It looked like she'd faint. She held herself up. Tried to bow. Her head jerked so fiercely that the Santa cap flew off. For a hideous moment, before the eyes of Rudy's all-time biggest crowd, Cynthia wept into the microphone, with guttural sobs and her face streaming as if her tears were the last drops of hope leaking out.

She started to bolt toward Hickey, then halted and groped on the stage for the Santa cap. She clutched it to her breast and leaped off the stage. When she hit the floor, one of her heels snapped. She kicked the other one free and ran, shouldering her way through the crowd, jarring a couple tables, clipping a waiter so that his tray slipped and steaks got delivered plateless onto a booth. Cynthia plowed and staggered her way past the coat check and out the front door.

Hickey found her perched on the green rim of the sidewalk, waving her arms as though hailing a cab or any other car that might stop and whisk her away.

When he touched her shoulder, the girl wheeled and socked him in the belly, hard as some men had walloped him there. "Judas," she screamed, and tried to kick him in the groin. Hickey sidestepped, only got a glancing blow to his thigh. It must've sprained her bare toes. She hopped on the other foot and bellowed, "Bastard, you killed my daddy," then whipped around toward the street and yelled it again.

Leo, who'd been watching from the doorway, edged close to Hickey. "Schwartz just beat it. See him running?"

Hickey looked in time to watch the gangster jump the curb and disappear behind the office building across A Street. The girl must've believed she saw a cop or her guardian angel up the block because she'd started hollering in that direction, "Help me. Get me out of here."

Charlie Schwartz's silver limousine nosed around the corner off Fourth onto A, drove halfway up the block, then swung a U-turn that included both curbs and prompted squealing brakes and a medley of horns all along A Street up past Sixth. It skidded to the curb's green zone. The rear door flew open. Cynthia dived in, and the Chrysler sped away.

Clutching Leo's shirtsleeve, Hickey yelped, "Keep it in sight." He darted into Rudy's, dodged like a swivel-hipped halfback through the kitchen, and sprinted out to his Chevy; he sped out of the lot and up Fourth to where Leo waited beside the stop sign. The old guy jumped in. "They made a right on Broadway, Tom."

The Chrysler had only gotten a few blocks head start. Hickey caught sight of it as it passed the Santa Fe depot. The girl, Schwartz, and probably the driver, all knew Hickey's car. But in traffic with all the lights dimmed, you couldn't tell a Chevy from a houseboat as long as it kept more than fifty feet away. The silver limousine—a beast like that you couldn't miss. It crossed Pacific Coast Highway, swung north on Harbor Drive, and cruised at a polite speed passing the Municipal Pier. Over the harbor the sky was sooty black. The barrage balloons gyrated in an erratic off-shore wind. Where Harbor Drive veered left following the bay, the limo made a right, then cut into the parking lot beside the Pacific Ballroom, bullied its way through a gang of sailors trying their moves on the jailbait who gathered there, scheming to get inside. Hickey'd pulled into the public spaces out front of the civic center, across Harbor, flicked off his lights. He and Leo watched the ballroom's valet open the girl's door, then sling it shut and run to the driver's side rear, where he ushered Charlie Schwartz out of the Chrysler. Schwartz tipped the valet, enough to keep the guy stuck to his elbow while the gangster knocked on the girl's window, spoke to her, then turned toward the entrance. His limousine pulled out. It made a right, then another, and headed south on Pacific Coast Highway.

Near the city jail, across from the ferry landing, the Coast Highway and Harbor Drive merged, snaked right, then right again and left, became Main Street in National City. The limo and

Chevy rolled past the shipyards, trailer courts, junkyards masquerading as used car lots, Okie saloons, Mex cantinas. The wind had risen, gotten wet and steady. It blew handbills, rags, newspapers across the road. Mist shimmied on the windshield.

"What the hell?" Leo grumbled. "They sneaking the girl over the border?"

"Could be. Got any ideas why?"

"Suppose Charlie got word the cops are on to Cynthia—about the hit, I mean."

"Somebody clued the cops to Cynthia?" Hickey snarled.

"How should I know?"

"Not you?"

Leo angrily snuffed his cigarette in the ashtray. "Only cop I saw was Thrapp, and he did all the talking."

"About what?"

"I been waiting to tell you after we got some rest, when we had a while to jaw, but I'm getting doubtful such a time'll ever come. I'll tell you now. Thrapp's losing his wits, Tom. He's got this notion of how Castillo was sent out here from New Jersey by some mob bossman—that old fool with the big red nose, gets his mug in the paper a lot, what's his name?"

"Santa Claus?"

"Yuk yuk. Anyhow, Thrapp figures the Jersey Italians and the Hollywood Jew gang are both drooling over the loot that's gonna fall on whoever slips the noose around what used to be our sleepy little border town. You've heard talk, right?"

Hickey nodded. "Had to happen. Soon as the hordes came migrating. Somebody's gotta steal their paychecks."

"So Thrapp says the Italians figure if they work both sides of the line, they can launch this international gambling mecca. Beach and bay resorts here, casinos in TJ, gambling ships out past the three mile. Big time. Now, it may be no coincidence, says the captain, that you got hooked up with Castillo, that Katoulis is Schwartz's best boy, that you got a grudge against Donny going back to the Dark Ages. Thrapp can't feature you in on the mob action, but he thinks maybe Castillo knew what he was doing when he partnered with you, and he's got hooks in you some way."

"Christ," Hickey muttered. He fished in his coat pocket for his pipe and tobacco. "Thrapp figures I knocked off Katoulis for the Jersey mob?"

"Not intentionally. He figures you're a dupe."

Hickey lit up, squinted at his partner. "And maybe you slipped him something about the girl, trying to save my neck."

"Hell, I did."

"Who did, then? Thrapp talk to Madeline?"

"How do I know? Nobody's saying anybody snitched on the girl."

"Why else are they taking her over the border?"

"Ask me in about a half hour."

National City had fallen behind them. Hickey rolled down his window to clear the smoke away, got his nose bitten by the chill, misty air and acrid whiffs of fertilizer rising off lettuce, tomato, and strawberry fields. The limousine cruised a half mile ahead, one car between them. The fog kept thickening. When he could barely make out taillights, he hit the throttle until he closed the gap. On the northbound side of the highway, a few jalopies crammed full of soldiers and sailors passed, weaving back from the dives of Tijuana, where the boys had drunk away Christmas Eve singing carols to the hookers on their laps. One convertible, a '38 Chevy, had soldiers spilling out of the rumble seat.

The dark mesas of Tijuana were camouflaged by the fog. While Hickey stared at the scattered lights flickering as if they hung in the sky, his eyes scratchy and raw from three nights with maybe nine hours' sleep between them, the foulest notion pierced his brain. It coursed through his body like poison, settled in his stomach, churned like a puny but lethal storm. What if Castillo was what Thrapp figured? The girl might've cried on Paul's shoulder about Pravinshandra, and he'd set her up, through Charlie Schwartz, with Katoulis. Castillo might be more shrewd than he seemed. Instincts could've told him that Hickey would make like the girl's invisible chaperon, stumble upon Katoulis, get

231

in a beef. Whichever one of them lost, Castillo'd be the winner. Either he and the Jersey mob would lose the threat of Schwartz's top gun, or Madeline would become a widow.

Hickey leaned out the window, let the mist shock his face until the squall in his stomach quieted. Whoever Castillo was, he thought, whatever role the Cuban played, not much had changed. Katoulis had still been gunning for the master, the girl had still bought a hit. It still looked like Schwartz was delivering her over the border. Donny was still dead. The most that could've changed was—in Thrapp's version, Hickey becomes a world-class chump.

Leo dug into several pockets, finally produced a handkerchief, and buffed the windshield clear. "What're you thinking, Tom?"

"I'm not. I'm having a nightmare."

"Spill it. Keep me awake."

"Never mind. What I can't figure, Charlie told me he was gonna steal the girl away, book her at a Santa Monica club he bought. How's that match with them taking her over the border?"

"They might be going to meet somebody. Or, hell, maybe they signed the girl up for a tango lesson."

As they neared the border, Hickey pulled over and coasted along the shoulder so they wouldn't approach too closely while the Chrysler was stalled at the gate. The Chrysler got passed through in no time. Hickey sped to the line, where the Mexican officer, tall and stern, with eyebrows like Adolf's mustache, yawned and circled the car, then poked his head in through Hickey's window, peered at Leo and into the backseat. He gave Hickey a caustic smile. "You wanna open the trunk, Señor?"

Hickey rushed around and raised the lid. A wrapped and ribboned shoe box fell out. The Mexican displayed his teeth and gums. "I bet you got radios, maybe a rifle in there? You gonna pull over to the office. We take a look."

"Whoa," Hickey said. "I gotta catch up with that limousine."

"*Compadres* of yours, no?"

"Yeah."

"*El negro* or the *muchacha?*"

"Both. What's the duty on this stuff? Thirty dollars? Forty?"

After Hickey'd dealt the Mexican two twenties and was pulling away, Leo muttered, "Smooth. You should've slipped him a ten before he opened his yap."

"You got any more advice, let's hear it now," Hickey snapped.

"Respect the speed laws, unless you got a pocket full of Jacksons. We'll catch up. Only way to hide that battleship is cut it in half, scrape off the paint, sink it in the ocean."

The Mexican road pained Hickey deeply, the way it crashed and battered his Chevy's undercarriage and springs. He tried swerving around the ruts but only found bigger ones. They banged across the bridge over the riverbed shantytown, rattled through a black cloud of diesel exhaust that gushed from the pipes of two buses at the depot near the main intersection. The smoke mixed with fog made a vaporous mud that clung to their skin and eyes. They swung left onto Tijuana's one paved road, Calle Revolución. Four narrow lanes that looked endless in the dark, as if they ran straight to oblivion. The sidewalks were busy with hawkers, pimps, Indian beggars, and refugees. Barren of streetlights, headlamps tinted, and most curtains down, the place looked like a sanctuary for ghosts and shadows. As many people out now—at twenty minutes before 1:00 A.M., Christmas morning—as there would be on a Saturday noon, they appeared in the flashlight beams of nightclub doormen, vanished, reappeared in a different-colored flashlight beam thirty feet closer.

The whole second block on the left was a cantina called the Long Bar, out of which servicemen careened in a flow as steady as if the building had gotten tipped sideways. Two cops stood on the corner looking puzzled. Probably trying to choose the richest soldier, the best to shake down, Hickey thought. He braked for the stop sign and whistled, motioned a bony, hump-shouldered cop over.

"*Muy grande auto*," Hickey stammered, and groped for the word that meant silver. "*Plata. Dónde va?*"

"He turn leff on Six Street. Calle Seis," the cop repeated, in case Hickey's English and Spanish were equally stupid. He waved a skeletal hand in the direction.

After four more stop signs—at each of which Hickey paused a few seconds and nodded to the officer on the corner, to avoid the bite for a rolling stop—Hickey spied the Chrysler a block down the hill, parked with two wheels on the gravel sidewalk. He made the turn, coasted down past a nightclub, a gated outdoor *mercado,* a tiny café where four marines squeezed around each of two miniature tables beside a pit grill mesquite-broiling pork.

The Chrysler was parked before a storefront from which a sign jutted out like a flagpole. Leo had the better eyes. He noticed first that the sign displayed a caduceus. Hickey pulled over just down-hill from the café, about twenty yards above the limousine. Both men climbed out. They met on the sidewalk and started down carefully, Hickey slightly in the lead, wishing he carried a weapon. He'd left his automatic at home, and the Denver police had his .38. Leo's pistol was back in San Diego, in the glove box of his Packard in the lot behind Rudy's.

They crept to the high side of the storefront and squinted at the block lettering on the blackened window. DOCTORES HINAJOSA Y VILLAREAL, EMERGENCIAS, 24 HORAS.

"Some kinda clinic," Hickey whispered. "What you figure?"

"Getting her nose fixed prettier? Or say there's a dentist in the outfit and she's got this throbbing toothache. Maybe that's why she was bawling at the club. Or maybe Schwartz belted her, sent her down here to get her face sewed up. Could be she's got outta hand, *muy loco.* I bet they're loading her up with dope, sedatives. They're gonna put her in a Mexican nut farm, keep her from pulling any more stunts that'll tarnish her reputation. Teach her how to act before they whisk her off to Santa Monica."

"I think we oughta take her."

"Then what?"

"Hard to know that till we find out what's up. At least we get her away from Schwartz."

"Tom, far as we can prove, she's down here on her own and Charlie's not pulling anything illegal. Think we should risk it?"

"She's seventeen."

"Oh yeah." Leo stuck his hand into a coat pocket, then yanked it out, as though reaching for a cigarette before remembering he didn't have the leisure to smoke it now. "Schwartz's boy—did I tell you he's the same gentleman that chucked my car keys in the dog pen? Big, long baboon arms. You'll have to crowd him. I caught a glimpse of steel underneath his coat, first time we met."

"We just gotta do it fast. Carrying your old badge, right?"

"Yeah."

"We run in, you wave it around, I'll go right for the big guy. Anytime you're ready."

Leo straightened his hat, caught a deep breath, and socked his fists together. "Let's go."

Hickey stepped to the door, paused a couple seconds. Slammed it open. Behind the desk on the left side sat a sleepy dark female in white. In the middle of the back wall, a doorway led into a hall. On the right, on a flowered couch, Cynthia Tucker lay sprawled, both arms under her head, her body pinched into the corner, as far as she could get from the big Negro whose eyes were just blinking open. His arms, across his chest, started unfolding while Leo waved his souvenir L.A. badge and shouted, *"Policía del Norte."*

Hickey rushed the chauffeur, who'd just pushed off the couch and begun straightening his legs when Hickey's fist with two hundred pounds of old fullback behind it drove into his jaw. His skull dented the plaster wall, cracked it all the way to the concrete block. The man slumped and collapsed sideways. His head flopped over the couch arm.

Cynthia was on her feet, howling and battering Hickey with her fists and arms, while Leo stood by the desk warning back the nurse and the pudgy doctor who'd appeared at the hall doorway. One arm shielding his head from the girl's attack, Hickey lifted the lapel of the Negro's leather coat and found a holstered automatic. He snatched it, tried to dodge the girl. Before he got to Leo and passed him the gun, she landed a right jab on his ear. She flew at him, her claws out in front, groping for his eyes. He stooped and jammed his head into her belly, drove her across the room, where she slammed the wall and toppled forward, groaning and panting rapidly. He got her heaved over his shoulder but as he started for the door, she commenced to thrash and kick, pounding him on both sides.

"Don't let anybody outta here," Hickey yelled. "Give me a couple minutes, then run for the car. You're driving."

Outside, the first ten yards, the girl kicked and flailed, cussing him so loudly that he knew he couldn't get her into the car before a squad of marines heard the battle cry and ran out of the café to massacre him and save the damsel. Suddenly she fell limply against him. The next moment she gave a roaring laugh.

"You killed it, Tom." She laughed again as he lurched the last few feet, slung open the door, knocked the front seat's backrest forward, and crammed her into the rear. "You're gonna kill everything, aren't you?" She howled a grand laugh, the kind comedians must dream about, and slapped both hands over her eyes.

Hickey fished the car keys out of his pocket, tossed them onto the driver's seat, slipped in beside Cynthia. "What're you talking about?"

Her head cocked, a sneer on her lips, the girl peered into Hickey's eyes as though gauging whether he could truly be so ignorant. Finally her gaze drifted, down over her wrinkled clothes. She rubbed at a stain on her knee, then tugged the dress snugly around her legs. "I'm cold. Let me wear your coat."

He was slipping the coat off when Leo dashed out of the clinic and hustled up the hill, rounded the front of the car, and pounced into the driver's seat. "Give me the keys."

"You sat on them."

His partner dug for the keys, crammed them into the ignition, and tromped on the starter. "I was hoping the big fella would wake up, give me an excuse to thump him. But no. You sure fixed his insomnia."

"Probably killed him," the girl muttered.

"Naw," Leo said. "Which way, Tom? It's faster if I cut down here to the river road, except it'll bang your car all to hell."

"Take the fastest way."

The girl was raking her hair with her fingers. "Where're you taking me?"

"Hadn't thought about it," Hickey said. "Depends on what you've got in mind, who you're gonna hire to knock off who, things like that."

Fast as a champion welterweight, the girl backhanded him squarely in the nose. He grabbed her arm, pinned it to the seat, and used his free hand to feel for the handkerchief in his pocket and wipe the first gush of blood off his lip. "Next time I bind and gag you, sweetheart."

"Sure," the girl snarled. "You might as well, as long as I'm your prisoner. Maybe you think you can lock me up, let me out every night to sing. Is that how you figure?"

"What's with you and Schwartz?"

"He thinks I'm great. Four hundred a week he's gonna pay me, and that's not including the record deal. Next year this time, I'll be in movies."

"Goody."

Cynthia wriggled to the corner, stretched her legs against the floorboard, pushing herself into the wedge of the seat. After a minute she relaxed and gazed smugly at him. "Aren't you gonna try to keep me around?"

Hickey wagged his head slowly. The Chevy skidded to a stop. They'd reached the border, with four cars lined up ahead. Because the girl flashed him a wicked grin, Hickey said, "Make a fuss, we all spend Christmas morning at the police station, till they get the whole story, starting in Dunsmuir."

"You wouldn't dare."

"Don't bet four hundred a week and the movies on it."

"You'd go to prison. Longer than I will. It was you killed a guy, Tom, not me."

"Nope. I'd be in the same fix I am now. Everybody knows I

237

killed him, babe. Either it's self-defense or no. What happens to you's got nothing to do with the fix I'm in."

"If you got me busted, Charlie'd have you killed."

"He's probably gonna try anyway. As long as I'm around, somebody's got the goods on his favorite songbird. He'll figure when you're not singing for me, I got no reason to cover for you anymore."

"Besides, you shot down his pal."

"Yeah. There's that."

"Hush." Leo pulled alongside the civilian gate guard, whose cheeks pooched as though he had mumps, and a young MP who leaned against the post, staring at something in Mexico. The guard asked for their citizenship. While quizzing Cynthia, he craned his head in and stared at the ruby brooch between her breasts as though it were the object in a hypnotism. Finally he retreated and asked what they were bringing from Mexico. Hickey swallowed a groan, remembering his load of gifts in the trunk. No doubt the guard would order them to pull over by the office shack where some fool would make him unwrap every package. Before they got loose, the phone would ring. A query from the Tijuana cops, about a kidnapping.

"Not a damn thing," Leo grumbled. "How we gonna buy anything after we lost every dime, even hocked the girl's mink, at that crooked casino in Rosarita?"

"Learned your lesson, huh?" the guard gloated, and waved them through.

The second their front tires spun off the gravel, onto the highway, Cynthia wheeled on Hickey. "So that's how it is," she hissed. "I get it. You think you can blackmail me into singing at your dump forever."

"Naw. Matter of fact, you're fired."

The girl stared at him in bewilderment, her eyelids quivering, as though never before had she been rejected or even imagined such a thing. Finally she chuckled. "Yeah, sure." She straightened her dress and sat primly, now and then scratching her lower lip with her teeth or fidgeting with her earrings.

They weren't a mile into the States when the girl yelped and clutched her belly. She'd fallen forward, her head dropping onto the front seat behind Leo's. She held that posture until Hickey touched her shoulder blade; then she squealed piercingly, fell straight backward, and began quaking. A moment later she launched herself against the front seat and back again, her head flying loosely in convulsions.

"Pin her, Tom," Leo hollered. "Cram something in her mouth. Must be she's an epileptic."

By this time Hickey had her in his arms, squashing her against him, letting her arms flail and claw his back. She alternated howls with gagging noises, a few inches from his ear, and finally she screamed, "It's still there. I hear it. God, I feel it squirming."

"Take the next crossroad. Right," Hickey snapped. "You know Riverview Hospital?"

"Yeah, Tom. Hold on, I'll get you there."

The girl resumed thrashing, cursing Hickey because he wouldn't let go. She dug her fingernails into his back. When that didn't free her, she worked her head loose enough to chomp his throat. If he hadn't grabbed her hair and nearly yanked it out, she might've severed his jugular. Furiously he shoved her off the seat, onto the narrow rear floor, and rolled her over so her face pushed into the floorboard and her hips jutted upward on the drive shaft tunnel. He secured her legs with his feet and pinned her arms behind her. She could move neither sideways nor up.

For a minute or so she lay there spent, butt up as though she'd volunteered for a spanking. Then she thrashed and raged, screaming things that got muffled and skewed because her mouth was shoved against the floorboard. Hickey caught only words and phrases. Charlie. Ophelia. A devil baby. Over the last mile before Leo turned into the driveway of Riverview Hospital, Hickey pieced those morsels together with the phrase she yelped several times: "They were going to flush me out."

"I got it," Hickey said. "Charlie sent her down there for an abortion. When I head-butted her, she thought I killed it. Now she thinks different."

"Okay. Fits so far. You got a guess who's the daddy?"

"Yep."

"Out with it."

"Pravinshandra. Her mother's pal."

"Him again," Leo growled. "Somebody oughta fix that boy."

The hospital was blacked out. Only one dim light glinted, on the side of a curtain in a room off the lobby behind the main doors. The curtain shimmied as if somebody'd disturbed it, peeking out.

Leo ran to check the main door and found it unlocked. He came back to help Hickey with the girl. She lay corpselike, didn't squirm even when her arms got twisted weirdly, until she was out of the car. As though she'd recovered and lost the motive of her tantrum, she stood a moment looking around calmly. Then she bolted.

Hickey tackled her around the ribs and held on, pinning her arms there. Leo got hold of her legs. She went stiff and only whimpered while they carried her inside.

A pale nurse with long gray hair tugged harshly back and plaited into a single braid stepped out of the lighted room and ushered them ahead of her, serenely as though a whimpering, board-stiff lunatic got dragged in every hour or so. Before requesting names or details, she used an intercom to ask someone named José to join them, then to inform a Dr. Carroll they had a potential intake.

While Hickey tried to coax the girl into a chair, two Mexican orderlies appeared at an interior doorway, glanced at Cynthia, and jumped to hover eagerly around her. She was leaning on the chair, her eyes closed. When the Mexicans each took one of her arms and half dragged, half walked her into the hallway, she didn't resist. Didn't even open her eyes.

The door shut. Hickey got a wave of nausea, then a rush of intense foreboding, as if the girl had just entered a place like Hades from where only a few blessed souls could return.

While Leo helped the nurse with her forms and all, Hickey sat in a corner dialing first information and then the Saint Ambrose

240

Home. On his third demand, a grouchy nun rousted Father McCullough. The priest must've stayed up drinking in the holiday, Hickey deduced from the voice, too cheerful to belong to anybody whose sleep had just got arrested.

"Sorry to disturb you, Father. It's about the girl. Henry Tucker dead or alive?"

"Alive."

"Okay. Well, Cynthia cracked up. I've got her at Riverview Hospital. They're gonna ask for a release from one of the parents, before they'll keep her. I'm sure not going to call Venus, if I can help it. Tomorrow I'll come out and get Tucker to sign papers, if she's still loony. Meantime, I need you to convince the doctor here you've got Henry's okay. He'll go for it. The doctor, I mean. You know, who's gonna call a priest a liar?"

Father McCullough withheld his reply long enough for Hickey to wonder if he was jotting down a list of disbelievers. "I doubt Henry will give me his okay, even if I can rouse him."

"Fine," Hickey said. "No sense even bothering the poor guy, is there? I'll have the doctor call you back. Sit tight. Merry Christmas."

TWENTY-FIVE

♪ ♪ ♪

BY THE TIME HICKEY HAD NEGOTIATED WITH THE DOCTOR, GOT-
ten Leo back to his car, driven himself home, played Santa Claus,
fed Madeline a brief version of his adventures, and managed to
find the OFF switch in his brain, he didn't log much sleep before
Elizabeth pranced into the room delivering coffee she'd made,
singing, "Fa la la la la . . ."

A little shy of 6:00 A.M. Hickey creaked out of bed feeling as
if he'd spent the night crashing into immovable, sadistic tacklers.
He sipped his coffee and looked out the window. A trio of sea
gulls tap-danced on the silver bay. A pelican leaped off the water
as if its feet were burning.

He brushed his teeth, eyed the bruise on his neck on which a
couple tooth marks remained, splashed his face, and wiped the
last traces of blood from his nose and lip.

Madeline was cooking bacon and waffles. Elizabeth had
plugged the tree lights in, lifted all the window shades, put a
record of Christmas carols on the Motorola. They ate sitting on

cushions around the tree, then started tearing the wrapping off gifts.

Elizabeth had gotten Hickey three ties with hand-painted tropical birds, a new briar pipe, and a pair of swim fins. Madeline had bought him cuff links, lapis lazuli set in silver, a tie bar to match, and a bottle of cologne. She'd got Elizabeth a party dress, a couple frilly slips, and a set of long underwear decorated with hearts. When Madeline modeled for them the sheer, scanty nightgown Elizabeth had bought her, Hickey crossed his legs and wondered what had passed through his daughter's mind when she'd bought that—if at fourteen she glimpsed the dreadful power of sex, the way it could bind people or rip them apart.

He'd requested that they wait until last to open the gifts he'd bought. In less than an hour at Marston's, including wrapping time, he'd not found the leisure to discriminate much. On the run, he'd purchased a selection of fragrances the perfume girl chose, gotten two cashmere sweaters, blue and green for Elizabeth, burgundy for Madeline. He'd bought the toboggan Elizabeth wanted. Velvet gloves, a new pair of mittens, and a hand-knitted snow cap for his wife. For each of them, he'd picked out a pair of fleece-lined boots. His last stop had been the jewelry counter. The gold rings, Madeline's set with one large and four tiny diamonds, Elizabeth's a single ruby, had set him back a week or two of packed houses at Rudy's.

He got repaid double in hugs and kisses. The rings fitted, though Hickey'd only guessed, knowing their middle fingers were about the size of his little one above the knuckle. Elizabeth called it her best Christmas ever. Hickey shivered and his heart swelled even though it was her standard line, which she'd said about every Christmas since she'd grown old enough to remember past ones.

A few minutes before nine, the spell got broken when Madeline examined the bruise on his neck and noticed the tooth marks. Elizabeth was in the bathroom. Hickey started to explain. With a hand on his cheek, Madeline stopped him. A second later she disappeared, to straighten things and pack for their trip to the mountains.

243

Hickey went into the bedroom for the notepad he kept in his coat pocket. Returning to the living room, he flopped onto the couch and picked up the phone on the end table. He looked in his notepad, called Laurel Tucker, let the phone ring a dozen times. Nobody home. He dialed information, got the number for Dunsmuir's sheriff. Same results.

His third call connected. To the Castle Crag Motor Hotel. A man answered. When Hickey asked for Fay Giles, the man sounded peevish but called her.

"Fay here."

"Tom Hickey. We met about a week ago, on my way to the Black Forest."

"I remember." She muffled the phone and spoke to somebody. "What can I do for you?"

"A couple things," Hickey said. "At the Black Forest I heard a tale about an avalanche. Would've been on Saturday. The twelfth? A lady got killed."

"No," she said breathlessly, then repeated the word, drawing out the *o*. "I'm sure we'd have heard."

"They were climbing Mount Shasta," Hickey said. "A couple *Nezahs*—the dead woman, Emma Vidal. The guy they call the master. And Venus's daughter Cynthia. You heard nothing like that?"

"No. When the *Nezahs* first arrived, we watched them closely but no longer. Except their real estate transactions. I . . ."

"Whoa. Let me finish, please. I tried to call the sheriff. He must be out shooting a turkey. I wonder if you'll tell him what I said, soon as you can? Ask him to call me. In San Diego, Belmont 63459. Avalanche or no, it looks like there was a murder."

Fay Giles muffled the phone and spoke to the man Hickey guessed stood over her. "You mean Venus's daughter and the man conspired . . ."

"Not the daughter." Unless, Hickey thought, Cynthia was loco enough to have dreamed up the rape and believed it. Unless Cynthia had been in cahoots, maybe in love, with Pravinshandra and had finally gotten jilted. "I've been snooping ever since I left Dunsmuir. If I get my way, the master's gonna take a fall."

"Are you a policeman?"

"A friend of the girl's, like I told you before. And a private investigator."

"I see. . . . Mister Hickey, do you think this will stop the Venus woman?"

"Stop her from what?"

"From buying up our town. I don't want to sound like an opportunist, but . . . a few days ago she found someone to sell her two hundred acres near Black Butte. Mrs. Barbato, a widow who plans to move to Arizona."

"Maybe," Hickey said, and he paused to let an idea grow. "Let's try something. Get your checkbook ready. When she starts selling, buy up a foresty parcel or two and sell me ten acres, with a pond or near a trout stream. Give me a rock-bottom price."

She muffled the phone while Hickey crossed the room, picked up his pipe, looked around for the Walter Raleigh. "Mister Hickey?"

"Yeah."

"If you can stop her from grabbing Dunsmuir, we'll *give* you ten acres."

"Deal."

"Is there anything I should do, besides talk to the sheriff?"

"Just keep your eyes peeled. Any news about the *Nezahs,* call me."

"Well, you might be interested that Venus and her friend have arrived back in town. At least, I believe so, in their big car. It passed about an hour ago."

Hickey calculated, decided that was some hasty driving from Denver. Maybe they chose to flee before the cops pried into their affairs, speculated who'd have a motive to gun the master, and started asking why. "Thanks, Fay. Give my best to the nosy guy."

Hickey cradled the phone on his lap, stared at the wakes of motorboats splashing against his pier. Ten acres, he thought. Maybe he'd end up with something to show for a couple weeks' trouble, a dead man who might rise to sting his conscience now and then or cause Charlie Schwartz to finger him, and a few hundred in expenses. Maybe ten acres would serve as some small justification for the whole lousy business. It seemed clear he wasn't going to get any personal satisfaction out of what he'd done for, or to, Cynthia Tucker. Not when it looked like the girl was bound for hell by one route or the other. Ten acres might also help console Madeline when she learned about their gold mine caving in.

Rudy's was a goner. If losing Cynthia Moon didn't break the place, his next chat with the Cuban would, unless Thrapp's story about Castillo and the Jersey mob proved a fairy tale. And unless Castillo vowed not to get within ogling distance of Madeline. Fat chance, Hickey thought.

He scanned the room, spotted his tobacco on the window ledge. He lit up, listened to Madeline instructing Elizabeth on what should go into her suitcase. After a minute he checked the directory for the numbers of Western Union and Riverview Hospital. He called in a telegram, to Venus Tucker, Black Forest, Dunsmuir, California:

CYNTHIA'S HAD A BREAKDOWN. HOSPITALIZED. MAYBE PREG-
NANT. ASK YOUR MASTER. THEN YOU AND I NEED TO TALK. IN
SAN DIEGO. ARRIVE IN 48 HOURS OR I START NORTH, SEVERELY
OUT OF PATIENCE. TOM HICKEY. B63459.

He dialed Riverview Hospital and asked for Dr. Carroll. The nurse, whose squeaky voice sounded like an old dame imitating her great-granddaughter, told him the doctor was unavailable until 4:00 P.M. Hickey gave his name.

"Oh, *yes.* The man who promised to deliver the *signed* intake forms this morning."

"How's the girl?"

"Not well. When Doctor left her alone, though she *was* sedated, she tried to hurt herself. She broke a chair and gouged the sharp end of a piece into her abdomen. If the orderlies hadn't caught her . . ."

"Where's she now?"

"Sedated more heavily, in a safer room."

"The padded kind."

"Yes. I'd like you to tell me more about her, if you will, when you deliver the intake forms. When can I expect you?"

"Tomorrow," Hickey said. "Not on Christmas. I've got a family."

"So do I," the nurse snapped. "I'm meeting *all* my responsibilities."

"Good. I hope you're paid accordingly. Tell me something— you think she's carrying a baby?"

"That's certainly what she believes. By and large, women seem to know those things."

"She's a girl," Hickey said. "A crazy one."

"True. Doesn't she sing beautifully, though? I heard her as I passed the room this morning."

When he got off the phone, he sat a moment picturing Cynthia Moon on stage. Her body turned sideways, swaying lithely, she sang "Boo-hoo," looking over her shoulder, wearing a coy little smirk. The vision clobbered him the way Charlie Schwartz's big chauffeur would try to one of these days, if he didn't choose to run Hickey down or bound from behind the oleander hedge at the dead end of Fanuel Street, holding the twin of his automatic that Leo now possessed.

Hickey dragged himself into the bedroom. When he landed on the bed, it seemed that every worry and grief he'd dodged or outrun in the past nine days joined forces, tackled him, and piled on. It felt as if the bed were one hard, spiny boulder and the air were another. Yet he wasn't inclined to move. If not for Madeline and Elizabeth, he might've lain there halfway through the New Year.

An hour later he was driving through Mission Valley past the dairy farm and the orphanage at Mission de Alcala, where Cynthia had lived, where she'd met Father McCullough, while her daddy roamed the West trying futilely to kick Venus out of his heart.

As they climbed the mesa, Hickey started yawning. Over the next five miles, past the college, the chicken ranches, the citrus groves, and the trout pond at Grossmont summit, his eyelids slammed shut ever more frequently. He strained, using every muscle in his head to winch them open. They kept banging down. Elizabeth rubbed his shoulders and cooed, "Poor daddy." Finally he turned the wheel over to Madeline and crawled in back. In the wedge of the seat, he caught a whiff of Cynthia.

Elizabeth woke him in Pine Hills, after they'd checked into the lodge. Her mother led him by the shoulders through a misty snowfall into their cabin, aimed him at the bed, and shoved gently. The feather mattress seemed bottomless. He kept sinking the whole time Madeline helped him out of the street clothes and into his flannel pajamas.

When he woke, the fireplace was crackling. Madeline sat beside it in a chair made of planks and cushions. Her elbows on the chair arms, hands folded at her chin, she appeared to have been watching him sleep. She sat pensively still as a painter's model. Iron gray streaks in the sky out the window clued him that the sun had dipped behind the mountains, giving him less than an hour to catch a toboggan ride down the hill with Elizabeth.

"Wanta go sledding?" he asked Madeline.

She finally moved her head, wagging it slowly. "I've been out with Lizzie, got my fill. Your turn."

Hickey dressed and stepped outside, found the path that led between the rear cabins to the base of the hill, where a dozen half-frozen humans hopped and flapped around to guarantee they'd survive. Every few seconds a sled, toboggan, or chunk of wood or thick cardboard came zooming down the hill with one or more bodies atop it, howling.

Elizabeth's new toboggan nosed out from behind a cedar. It was past Hickey's clear vision—he hadn't worn his glasses, since they would've frosted anyway. He couldn't be sure if the figure riding behind Elizabeth was a huge person or a bear. They swerved off the trail and back, picked up speed, and finally careened past Hickey as though bound for Indianapolis. When the toboggan crashed into a snow mound, Elizabeth lurched forward but didn't sail off. Apparently the big fellow's knees had her cinched there.

While they brushed off, Hickey wandered over, eyeing Elizabeth's partner, inches taller than himself, dressed in lumberjack clothes. He was blond, round-featured, pale as a snowman. About eighteen. Elizabeth held his giant mittened paw. "Howdy, sleepyhead. The toboggan works great. Wanta try it?"

"Tomorrow," Hickey said.

"Okay. This is Olaf—he lives in Ramona." The kid bobbed his head and gave a hillbilly smile.

"Nice place. Babe, you'll be back at the cabin by dark, right?"

"Sure, Dad."

Hickey strolled toward the lodge between rows of pine not much older than Christmas trees, figuring that if the big kid gave Elizabeth any heartache, he'd phone the Selective Service board, tell them Uncle Sam badly needed this palooka.

He found Madeline waiting for him, the fire burned to coals beside her. Her elbows still on the chair arms, knees slightly parted, it looked as if she'd only moved six inches while he was gone, dropping the hands from her chin and leaning forward. Her eyes slanted inward, as if she'd been grieving.

"Sit down, please, Tom."

On a corner of the bed, he sank until he was almost squatting. Madeline slid to the edge of her chair.

"Look, baby, I don't enjoy being played for a stooge. If you've been frolicking with Miss Moon, I wanta know about it."

"Christ," Hickey snapped. "Maybe if she stays locked up, after a year you won't ask anymore. Why're we starting this again? You figure I'm liable to grill you about Castillo, so you're gonna attack me first, that it?"

"Go look at your back in the mirror, and try telling me anything smaller than a Bengal tiger gouged you like that through a shirt and coat."

"Look at the shirt I was wearing, Madeline."

"I did. It's not torn. There's some blood, but that might've got on it afterward."

"You know," Hickey said wearily, "I could've got killed easy in Denver, the way I couldn't stick to business from thinking about you. You figure I was lying about giving up PI work? Elizabeth gave you my messages, right?"

"Of course."

"Why the hell would I quit the work I do best, forsake old Leo, and spend my time glad-handing at Rudy's, unless I was doing it so I could finally buy the stars for you, like I promised?"

Madeline swallowed hard. Her eyes roamed his face, then cast themselves down. "It could be a lot of jive."

"Yeah, and Mrs. Roosevelt could be a chorus girl."

"Are you really gonna let the day job go?"

"Depends," Hickey said.

"Right, here it comes."

"Depends if what Captain Thrapp has to say about your Cuban pal checks out."

Her face shot up. "What about him?"

"Thrapp's saying the Cuban's a mobster. Maybe he comes from Havana, but he got here by way of New Jersey. One of the families sent him to squeeze out the Schwartzes, see who gets to corner the border action." Hickey watched his wife's eyes narrow, her flesh harden. "How's that look to you?"

"Ridiculous," Madeline snarled. "My God, I've spent . . . a good deal of time with Paul. At the club. And he's said nothing, associated with nobody that'd make me believe such crap for a second."

"Maybe it's just your average gangster isn't snooty enough to hang out at the Bigshot Club."

"I've heard his life story, Tom. Want me to give it to you?"

"Nope. Not even part of it." Hickey felt his lip curling, tried to flatten it down. "All I want's your opinion."

"You got it. Now . . . look me in the eye. . . . Have you made love with Cynthia Moon?"

250

"No, baby. How about you and Castillo?"

"No." It was the closest he'd ever seen Madeline come to a whimper.

The door rattled. He looked that way, decided it must've been a gust of wind or a kid heaving a snowball. He leaned toward Madeline, pried her hands off the chair arms, squeezed them for a minute. Scooting farther back on the bed, he pulled her toward him. When she landed atop him, he grabbed her behind, pressed her hard against him, and kissed her neck ravenously.

Outside, snow crunched, the steps creaked. The door flew open. "Who let the fire go out?" Elizabeth hollered. "Oops."

They ate turkey, succotash, yams, and rhubarb pie in a drafty lodge hall with a sopped wooden floor and sprigs of holly and mistletoe tacked on most every bare-log rafter. Later, around the fireplace in their cabin, they talked about fifteen years of Christmases.

TWENTY-SIX

♪ ♪ ♪

DIRECTLY AFTER BREAKFAST HICKEY ITCHED TO GET BACK ON FLAT land. Check on the girl. Make a date with Captain Thrapp and learn what dope the police had on Castillo.

His girls thought differently. So Hickey and his daughter crashed down the sled run a dozen times, and after checking out they stopped in Julian for cider and apple pies to carry home. The back road through the high meadows and the pine forest was icy, and most every time they rounded a blind turn, a coyote, a doe and a couple fawns, or a cow would step into the road. It was noon before, in Alpine, they passed the sign that boasted THE BEST CLIMATE IN THE UNITED STATES, just as a cleft in the hills offered a view of the coastal plain. Soon they rolled down the windows. There was a balmy onshore breeze. The bay, while they rounded it, looked jammed with an armada of sailboats.

Hickey let the girls unpack. He walked inside, straight to the phone, and dialed Riverview Hospital. When he asked for Dr. Carroll, the nurse squeaked, "Intake papers, Mr. Hickey?"

"Darn. How'd you recognize my voice? I was trying to sound like Jack Benny."

"You were expected this morning."

"Patience, dear. I'm on my way to see old Tucker, soon as you let me talk to the boss." She made a *pfff* sound and deserted the phone. A minute later Dr. Carroll announced himself. He sounded like a Texan auditioning to play Hamlet.

"How's the Tucker girl?" Hickey asked.

"I'm afraid that an adequate response, sir, would require volumes. The young lady's quite an enigma."

"Yeah, but is she pregnant?"

"She places the conception only two weeks ago today. It's not yet productive to test her. Nowhere near."

"She tell you who's the lucky fellow?"

"I'm not free to repeat what she's told me."

"How about what I tell you? That confidential, too? Meaning you don't blab anything I give you about her. Scout's honor?"

"I suppose."

"Yeah. Then see how this stacks up with what she's professing. I'm going to spill only the stuff that, far as I can see, is what's eating her. You got a notepad?"

"Always."

"Tops has gotta be this baby. See, other than the one time, which she labels a rape, she's either a virgin or was till a certain mobster got to her. The rapist—'fiend,' she calls him—is her mama's lover boy and partner in crime. He's quite a character, by the way. You ever seen anybody throw blue fire outta their fingers?"

"The *Nezah* master," Dr. Carroll said, pronouncing each *a* like a Brit. "The *Los Angeles Times* ran an article, last year, I'd say."

"I missed it. So, on top of the rape, and her daddy sinking fast of a broken heart, and a dear friend getting snuffed by an avalanche the same day this fiend sowed his seed in her—besides all that, she's gotten hooked up with one, maybe two mobsters. And"—Hickey tried to phrase this last tidbit in a way that

253

wouldn't send Carroll squealing for a cop—"earlier in the week she set out to kill a guy and just got lucky, that she couldn't pull if off. . . . That mesh with the line she fed you?"

"Fairly well."

"How's she acting?"

"Decently now, though it's a pose. She's quite a dramatist and has convinced herself that if she behaves, exhibits superior manners, charms us with her intellect, we'll release her at any moment."

"You're not buying it?"

"Certainly not, though my mind could change rapidly if the *signed* intake forms are not delivered posthaste."

"A couple hours, I promise. Thanks, Doc."

Hickey pushed the hang-up button, sat a minute with the receiver in his hand, considering that if Cynthia were actually pregnant and half the story she'd told him on the beach were true, Pravinshandra ought to be exiled to a stud farm in some underpopulated land. It had taken Hickey months to start Elizabeth percolating. The master appeared to hit the bull's-eye every shot.

Hickey dialed the police. Their operator switched him through to Captain Thrapp. "Damn, Tom. I came close to sending a man out to chase you in here. You get my messages?"

"Sure. Merry Christmas, Rusty."

"That was yesterday. Good riddance. Now, get down here, would you?"

"When a porpoise pitches for the Yankees, I'll go down there. Your place has got lousy atmosphere, and I'm tired of cops. When's your shift up? Meet me at Rudy's."

"Six-thirty." Thrapp dropped the phone into its cradle from a foot or so high.

Hickey finished nibbling his sandwich, stood up to carry his lunch plate to the kitchen. The phone rang. His answering service switched through a call from Dunsmuir.

The sheriff sounded old, touchy, and displeased. Without introductions, he asked if Hickey had a murder to report. The shortened version of Cynthia's story of her trip to the mountain lasted several minutes, while the sheriff never uttered a sound. At the end of his story, Hickey asked if he were still on the line.

The man snorted and finally said, "This Cynthia see the swami whack the lady, shove her into the crevasse?"

"I told you, she was back in the hut, doped. Knocked out."

"Doped. Look, ain't a whole lot I'm gonna do till the girl contacts me directly, least about any murder. Far as the rape goes, I'll bring the swami in, all right, providing she promises to get herself up here and testify."

"She'll testify, but it's gonna have to wait. At the moment she's in the nuthouse."

"Swell," the sheriff droned. "Ain't no problem with her credibility. Look, I'll run the boy in, have us a talk."

Hickey gathered some things, kissed Madeline, walked out back, and waved good-bye to Elizabeth, who sat gabbing with a neighbor girl on their pier. He took the Mission Valley route east to Palm Avenue, swung left on La Mesa Boulevard, and coasted down the hill to the Saint Ambrose.

His preference was to sneak in, confront Henry Tucker, convince the old man to scribble on the forms, and flee the tomblike joint before he got cornered by Sister Johanna or the priest. But the sun was out. A pack of old folks lolled around in the garden patio through which he had to cross from the lobby to Tucker's room in the rear east wing. A stalwart, toothless old fellow, a baritone, stood before two ladies seated on a bench, crooning a slurred melody. The chaperon nun attended to a rosebush, pinching off buds or aphids. She didn't look up to catch Hickey sneaking by. He would've gotten away clean if not for Donia, the old gal who suspected he might be the devil. She stood clinging to a stake among the bougainvillea against the chapel wall, peering around through her frizzed ropes of hair, intently as if the old folks were under siege by armies of malevolent spirits. Spotting her there, Hickey tripped along the path's far perimeter. Just as he thought he'd evaded her gaze, she spied him and issued a shriek. Her call to alarm startled a tall fellow whose cane flew up as though to conk somebody, which skewed his balance and toppled him backward into the baritone, who tipped like a domino and landed on the lap of one of his frail admirers.

Hickey was double-timing toward the rear east wing when the nun who'd been tending roses hollered, "Sir. Sir, come back here."

All he could do was retreat and surrender. He mustered his best innocent smile and strode over to the hefty, pug-nosed nun whose attention was split between watching him and caressing Donia's arm. The old gal's eyes wandered vaguely across the sky and she hooted, ever lower as if her battery needed a charge.

"Father McCullough available?" Hickey said cordially.

The nun gave him a scowl and a jerk of her head toward the arched doorway beneath the jacaranda. Hickey let himself in to the parlor, crossed the Turkish carpet, and rapped on the office door. Footsteps came trudging, the heavy door creaked slowly open, and the priest appeared. His eyelids looked puffy as if they'd swollen shut, had to be slit open. The father's voice was raw, gravelly. "How is she?"

"Loco," Hickey said. "Vicious. Came at me like a vampire. You got a cold?"

"A doozy."

"Sorry. Look, when—if—she calms down enough so they'll spring her, she's got herself mixed up with a mobster, Charlie Schwartz. You heard of him?"

"No."

"Well, he's making like her sugar daddy. I expect if it wasn't him, it'd be somebody else—the girl needs a dad, I guess, and now that Henry resigned . . . Schwartz plans to launch her career in L.A. But there's a catch. She's got this little fiend growing inside her that's gonna raise hell with her hourglass figure. That's what she says anyway. Could be hysterics, but I'm betting it's real."

The priest groaned, raised his hand as though to cross himself but left it in the starting position, arm across his chest. "A fiend?"

Hickey nodded. Once more, he recounted the story Cynthia'd

told him on the beach. The priest blew his nose into a handkerchief as large as a bath towel.

"Venus's lover is the father?" he moaned.

"That's the one. You oughta see him throw fire someday. Quite a trick. Any idea how he does it?"

With a cock of his head, as though perplexed that anyone would ask such an obvious question, he muttered, "Demons."

"Right. Glad you cleared that up."

"Then it *was* him Cynthia plotted to kill. And you . . . ?"

"Postponed it," Hickey said icily. "Caught up with Venus and her boyfriend. Got sight of the gunman, called him out, and shot him dead."

With cupped hands hiding his mouth and nose, the priest gazed studiously at Hickey, long enough so that Hickey got the idea he was waiting to see if the killer showed any trace of remorse. Hickey dug for his pipe and lit up.

At last the father offered him a drink. Hickey declined—two sips or another minute of silence, he'd commence spilling his guts. He was that close to making his confession, asking the priest how his God would judge somebody who knocked off a guy who hadn't even reached for his gun.

"Tell you what I think, Padre—see, when I hijacked the girl, she was in TJ to get her womb scraped. Maybe I did wrong. This baby's gonna mean nothing but danger and misery to all concerned, including itself."

"You're suggesting an abortion."

"You bet. There's a chiropractor across the hall from my office. You wouldn't accuse him of being honest, but he's clean and he knows if something goes awry, he's on his way to Alcatraz, not just to the bank for a couple hundred pesos *mordida* like those TJ croakers. Think about it, Father, what this kid'll mean to Cynthia. . . . Meanwhile, what we've gotta do is keep her locked up at least until Schwartz gets tired of waiting or she has a massive change of heart, decides to be a good little Catholic girl."

Father McCullough nodded, rubbed his puffy eyes. "I'd feel

most secure about her if Venus also agreed to her confinement. Otherwise . . . You see, they never settled custody—I find that peculiar, Henry being an attorney."

"Makes sense if you buy Cynthia's tale. Venus could've asked Henry to hack off his arm, feed it to the dog—Henry would've rolled up his sleeve."

"True, and it still applies, doesn't it? She could easily have Henry ruled incompetent. Suppose this Schwartz approaches her, convinces her with prophecies of fame and fortune to have the girl released, turned over to him."

"Which Venus might jump at," Hickey said. "A little piece of Cynthia's contract might buy her a ton of loot." Hickey pulled the hospital intake forms from his pocket, displayed them. "Let's go get Henry's *X* on here. I'll see about keeping Venus outta the way."

Father McCullough trudged in front, having used all his weight, grabbing the doors by the handles and leaning backward, to tug them open. He seemed to have aged a decade in the past week, and he wasn't the only casualty. When Hickey asked about Sister Johanna, the father told him she was laid up with a high fever. There'd been an epidemic, the priest said. On the way to Tucker's room, they passed three more nuns, each one appearing fatigued and downhearted.

"What's the deal?" Hickey asked. "You and the sisters go on a Christmas bender?"

The priest chuckled wanly, lay a hand on Hickey's shoulder, used it to balance himself as they entered the rear wing, and walked down the hall.

It was the first time Hickey'd seen Tucker sitting up and looking human. His thick hair was combed, almost glossy. The light beside his bed flickered and a Knights of Columbus tract lay closed on his lap. He stared at the wall as though pondering what he'd just read. Either, Hickey thought, the man was recovering, or he'd already made his appointment with death and resigned himself.

Tucker murmured hello to the priest, gazed blankly at Hickey for a second, then angled his head toward the window.

Hickey leaned in close. "Mr. Tucker, you got a beef against me, that's fine. You can't imagine how many people do. But you're gonna listen, because I'll stand here till you do, and then you're gonna sign some things for me. Otherwise, your daughter's sunk. By the next time you see her, she'll be the moll of a mobster a couple years older than you, or locked up for conspiracy to commit murder. Or worse. You listening?"

Without shifting his head, Tucker gave a stiff nod. "Okay," Hickey said, "Here's the deal. I'm gonna do my damnedest to see that nobody, including and especially Venus, Laurel, or Pravinshandra—who's still alive, by the way—will get near enough to Cynthia to meddle in her life. I'm gonna keep your darling out of jail and away from the mob. To make it work, she's gonna have to spend a while at Riverview, the same place, I believe, Laurel visited after you all ditched Otherworld."

Tucker yanked his head around, pinned Hickey's eyes, coughed from the effort. "What's your name?"

"Tom Hickey."

"Cynthia's told you our history?"

"A whole lot of it."

"Then you must be an arrogant son of a bitch . . . to think you can pacify either of Venus's daughters." Tucker spewed his words, between coughing fits, holding one bloodshot eye on Hickey. "They're addicted to turmoil, shackled by vanity. And they're foes to the death. You might as well try to negotiate a truce between Lucifer and Gabriel. One will kill the other. The only question: Who will it be?" He lurched forward, began to cough and gasp in spasms. When the worst had passed, he reached out for the papers, skimmed each one for a moment, then scribbled his name on the line.

A nun entered, carrying medicine. Hickey and the priest slipped away and down the pungent hall, double-timing until they escaped and tasted fresh air. As they walked side by side through the patio toward the lobby, Hickey said, "I figured the old guy didn't need to know about his grandbaby."

259

TWENTY-SEVEN

♪ ♪ ♪

THERE WAS STILL A SIGN MARKING THE PLACE IN WHICH VENUS and Henry Tucker had conceived all this madness Hickey'd gotten tangled in. The sign read OTHERWORLD in flowing calligraphy. The gate was locked. A newish chain fence skirted the olive groves, just beyond which lay the foundations of several enormous houses whose completion awaited the end of the war. Between the foundations and the sea cliff, the low sun flashed so brilliantly off the bronze dome of the mosque that Hickey couldn't look straight at it.

A few hundred yards up the road, across the street from where the last olive grove met the cemetery, Hickey made a U-turn and pulled up in front of Joshua Bair's home. During his brief stop at Riverview—where he'd only dropped off the papers, learned that the doctor was out on a call and the girl was sleeping—he'd phoned the Hillcrest Plen Aire Gallery, claimed to be an L.A. reporter, and gotten the painter's number. He called, said he had questions about the Tuckers.

The painter's house was a low-slung sidehill place. The front was all redwood siding and windows. A redwood stairway led up from the road to a wide deck, furnished with lounges and umbrella tables. Hickey crossed it and met the painter, who waited beside the door. A tall, gangling fellow like Henry Tucker used to be. Hickey figured his age, probably from something he'd read, as close to seventy-five, yet he stood erect, shook hands vigorously, walked in large strides. His skin looked sun-parched, flecked with dark blemishes. He wore a clipped goatee and a sporty driving cap, which he left on, though Hickey removed his hat the moment he crossed the threshold. His sainted mother had demanded such impeccable manners. If he'd worn his hat indoors, in a minute it would've pressed on his skull like an anvil. He gave his name and occupation. "You knew all the Tuckers, right? Henry, Venus . . ."

"Very well." The painter's voice was deep, touchingly gentle.

"Good, because Cynthia's neck-deep in hot tar. I've got an idea what landed her there, but could be I'm missing something."

Mr. Bair showed him to a den beside the entryway, seated him on a couch facing a picture window. The view was immense: the crystalline Pacific and most of Point Loma from the lighthouse, across Fort Rosecrans Cemetery, over the grounds of what used to be Otherworld, miles northeast along Sunset Cliffs. The section of Otherworld straight ahead was checkered with mounds of dirt that must've once been flower or vegetable gardens, and a shed-sized building made of rocks about twenty yards in from the cliff. The sanctuary, Hickey surmised. Where Cynthia and Laurel watched their mother frolic with Pravinshandra the day Will Lashlee fell to his death, Murphy the realtor mangled his legs, and Henry Tucker's life exploded.

The painter asked what drink he could serve, retreated to the kitchen, brought his juice and Hickey's scotch, set them on a scarred plank coffee table between the couch and his tattered easy chair. He sat down, wriggled until he got comfortable. "So, tell me what's become of the Tuckers?"

"Well, Venus is thriving. She and Master Pravinshandra have

261

got a swell racket, doing their magic show, bilking their followers, and investing the loot in Shasta real estate. Laurel is prospering, maybe in cahoots with Mama. Henry's got TB, appears to be heading for the last roundup, and Cynthia—she's standing one foot in hell." He gave the painter her whereabouts, told him about her singing career and plans to hit the big time under the wing of Charlie Schwartz. He left out Donny Katoulis and lied about his acquisition of Cynthia's ledgers, said he found them in Cynthia's room at the boardinghouse when he'd gone searching for her. Then he started from the beginning, from the death of Ophelia.

Several times Mr. Bair stopped him to ask for a repeat or elaboration, or to reminisce. About the beauty of Venus as a child. The charismatic presence of Madame T. The inspired life of people at Otherworld during the years when they still believed in their utopian dreams. Listening to Hickey describe Pravin-shandra's pregnant disciples, Mr. Bair had nodded credulously. Even the rape, though it induced a woeful frown, didn't appear to surprise him.

But when Hickey said Emma Vidal was dead, the painter tottered to his feet as though age, which had been in hot pursuit, suddenly caught up and thumped him. He staggered to the picture window, leaned against it, both palms flat on the glass, muttering sounds too low and slurred to make out. Hickey let him grieve. After minutes of silence the painter returned to his chair. He sat breathing deeply, laboriously. He cleared his throat. His voice seemed to echo out of a distant room. "My wife died twelve years ago. She'd gone to India with Madame Torrey and con-tracted malaria there. Since then . . . Emma is thirty-four years younger than me, Mr. Hickey. Aren't I a foolish old man?"

"Naw."

"She would've married me, regardless, except . . . she was one of those who keeps her purity by prizing her dreams more than her life, and consequently choosing to love from afar, people she could never have."

"Henry Tucker," Hickey offered.

262

"And Pravinshandra."

Mr. Bair rolled his hands palms up on his lap and stared as if he blamed them for something.

Hickey said, "Maybe you could tell me what you think about Cynthia's story?" The old man looked up perplexedly, as though stumped by a riddle. "Cynthia's story," Hickey repeated. "Any truth in it?"

Crooking his head stiffly toward the picture window, Mr. Bair shaded his eyes. The window flickered like a kaleidoscope. In its center, the half of the sun that remained above the Pacific threw violet streaks that started brilliant and gradually dulled until they blended with the gray-blue sky.

"Oh, yes. The story's quite accurate. Factually. I only question her interpretations. Did Venus truly kill her sister, intentionally? I've always believed it was an accident. Because Venus . . . though she may at times have a murderous heart, wouldn't foul her own hands. She's too . . . refined."

Mr. Bair fell into silence, gazing thoughtfully at the window as though analyzing colors of the sunset, deciding how to match them in oils. He picked his glass off the table and sipped.

"Care for something stronger?" Hickey asked.

Mr. Bair nodded, told him where to find the liquor, what to pour. When Hickey served the drinks, the old man lifted his as though in a toast to someone invisible. "Cynthia, you said, believes Venus seduced Henry, but I'm not convinced it wasn't the other way. Tucker was a vital, experienced man. Venus was a girl. No doubt she took charge later and treated him with disregard. Still, her withdrawal and remoteness, even her disloyalty, might never have flourished if it weren't for Henry's jealousy. I suspect he tried to constrain her, fearing that if she rose too high, she'd leave him behind."

The sky had faded, dusk settled in. Hickey had to squint to catch the old man's expression. He'd expected Mr. Bair to get up and turn on a light, but the old man had slipped into a dimension where you could see just as well in darkness. "Let's review the murders Cynthia charges. Ophelia, very likely an accident. Will

263

Lashlee—certainly you could lay the blame on Venus, if it's true that Laurel ran to the cliff in response to watching her mother fornicate, but that doesn't strike me as consistent with Laurel's character.

"About Madame Esmé . . . although clearly she died of grief over the demise of Otherworld, the doctors called it pneumonia. I think, under our jurisprudence, that's hardly a punishable murder. If, Mr. Hickey, any of us looked back and saw each tragedy one of our actions played a role in, we might all hold hands and plunge into the sea." Mr. Bair reclined his head. His eyelids dropped. For long enough to startle Hickey into wondering if he'd lapse into a faint or coma, the old man kept perfectly still except that his nostrils flared with each breath. Then he sat up, struggled to his feet. "Have you noticed the portraits?" He gestured toward the wall opposite the picture window, crossed the room, and flicked on lights. More than a dozen portraits appeared.

The first portrait on the left was a beauty with long black hair, eyes so humble, mouth so broad and kind, it made you want to thank her for living.

"Emma?" Hickey asked.

Mr. Bair nodded stiffly and turned to the portrait of a naked girl, about thirteen, walking out of the ocean in knee-high shore break. Her right hand flipped the cinnamon-colored hair out of her eyes while the other hand poised in front of her hip as though reaching to cover a private part, but unable to decide which. Her emerald eyes gleamed as if the painter had secreted a light bulb behind them.

"Venus," Mr. Bair said reverently. "Her power is subtle, elemental, tremendous. It's almost as if she only has to wish and someone appears to do her bidding. Madame Torrey. Henry. Laurel. Pravinshandra." His hand lifted to chin level. He stood a moment, pondering. "If Venus were to stand trial, even if she'd ordered those people killed, for each death she'd plead self-defense and believe it. Ophelia was killing her spirit, stealing her father's love. Madame Esmé tried to keep her from inheriting the kingdom, Otherworld. Henry Tucker had stolen the best years of her life and would *not* let go. Emma . . ."

He waved his hand in front of his face and turned to the next portrait. A brazenly handsome fellow about forty with a shy, lovable tilt to his head, a comic seriousness to his mouth. Eyes that just missed looking straight at you, no matter from what angle you watched them. "Poor Henry. He broke the first rule of manhood. He let go the reins on his heart. Those are his words, by the way."

Laurel was next. A young beauty, nineteen or so, full of zest and gaiety. But Hickey noticed something that repelled him, made him want to look away. He studied until he saw that the eyes were out-of-round and had tiny sparks of flame orange behind the green.

"In torment," Mr. Bair said. "As if she inherited her mother's guilt, and it lives like a devil inside her. She's the one who frightens me."

The last portrait in the row was of Cynthia, a few years younger but the same girl Hickey'd watched dozens of times while the audience threw her kisses and flowers. The smile looked like she'd just bought the deed to heaven.

Hickey stood for minutes admiring the paintings, until Mr. Bair said, "May I ask a favor of you?"

"You bet."

"If you would see to the punishment of the man who killed Emma, I'd be more than indebted. I'd give you Emma's half of everything I own."

"Don't worry about it," Hickey muttered. He shook the painter's hand, walked out, and hustled across the deck with Mr. Bair's last words echoing inside him. From the top of the stairs, he glanced south, at the sky over Sunset Cliffs where he'd watched the girl meet Katoulis. He stopped and stood a moment, realizing how perfectly he'd botched things. He should've let Pravinshandra die.

* * *

265

There would be no orchestra at Rudy's tonight. The few parties of early diners clustered in and near the booths. Hickey took a corner table, ordered his usual sirloin, vegetable, bread, no potatoes, a glass of cabernet.

A cacophony of thoughts bombarded him. About Cynthia's family, the master, Donny Katoulis. The loudest concerned Joshua Bair's conception of Venus as a far less evil being than Cynthia made her. Things could be like the painter saw them or, Hickey mused, Bair might've pardoned her on account of he'd fallen for her charms.

Thrapp arrived a few minutes early. He was a broad, hard-packed fellow with reddish gray hair Hickey suspected he got cut at the navy base. He had ruddy skin, a smashed nose, and a neck that appeared wide enough to tunnel out and drive cars through. Before the club had cornered Hickey's time, he and the captain had met for a drink and an hour of gab every week or so. The last time had been around September.

Thrapp looked sour, purely unthrilled about their reunion.

After forking his last piece of steak, Hickey chewed it on his way to meet the captain. They shook hands coolly and Hickey led toward the office. As they passed the bar, he ordered a Dewar's, a manhattan for Thrapp, told the bartender to send them in. He rapped once and threw open the office door.

Castillo must've been startled, the way his hands lay fisted on the desk and his face craned forward, accenting his big liquid eyes.

"We got some talking to do, partner," Hickey said flatly. "Soon as I get done with the law here. Go out and have a drink, why don't you? Make it a stiff one."

Castillo sat still long enough to pretend he was choosing to leave. He got up, sidled around the desk, nodded chummily at Thrapp, wedged past, and made his exit. Hickey rounded the desk. The captain hung his overcoat on the rack. As they sat and eyed each other across the desk, before either of them spoke, the drinks arrived. Hickey lit his pipe, watched the smoke rising toward the vent. He asked about Thrapp's family and a couple mutual pals.

"So you gonna send me back to Denver?"

"Depends if Donny had his gun out, Tom. They're still interviewing tattletales—you know how things move a little slow around Christmas, what with relatives and all. Lousy time of year."

"Thanks for getting me outta there."

"Sure. I had to argue like that guy Socrates. I'll tell you, if you'd shot anybody else but Mr. K, Houdini couldn't of got you loose. The guy in Denver called L.A., and somebody up there told him you oughta get a congressional medal. How about it, Tom? The boy have his gun out when you popped him? Or'd he keep it stashed, like that night in the alley, back a few years?"

"Not losing your memory quite yet, are you, Rusty?" Eleven years, Hickey thought, and he'd only told four people about that night. Madeline, Leo, an old pal from his USC days, and Thrapp. If you land in the hot seat, he mused, that'll teach you to get tipsy and run off at the mouth.

"How about it?"

"Some fella in Denver took it all down shorthand, made me sign the paper. I think they call it a statement. Remember those things? Why don't you get them to send you a copy, save me some breath?"

Thrapp shrugged, sipped his manhattan, nibbled the cherry. "I did that, Tom. Got it over the wire, read it three or four times. Still sounds fishy."

"Aw well. Next item, Leo's been telling me you guys don't make my business partner for a respectable type. Something about a mob from Jersey."

The captain repeated what Leo'd passed on. "See, Castillo's just a pretty-boy that got his start dealing cards in Havana. One day he lands in Jersey, finds his way to a back room establishment. A few years, he's managing the joint, for Angelo Paoli. That's all we got from the Jersey police. The FBI's not cooperating. Pissants."

267

"Paul got a record?" The captain shook his head. "Maybe he decided to go legit," Hickey speculated, "put a few thousand miles between him and the bad company he was keeping."

"Yeah, except out here he ain't only fraternizing with tennis bums and your wife."

"Who else?"

"A few other dames and Vic Sozzani. Know him?"

"Fill me in."

"He's an old codger, spent about half his golden years in Leavenworth, bookmaking, conspiracy to murder. Came out here to retire, in Leucadia. He and Angelo Paoli's daddy grew up together, insofar as their kind grows up."

"Maybe Paul and him just swap stories about old times."

"Okay. Then where's Jaime Montenegro fit in?"

"Who's that?"

"See, Montenegro runs the Las Olas Casino down in Rosarito Beach. A couple of our guys, off duty, saw Jaime, Vic and Castillo—them and a few senoritas—yapping, making toasts, having a grand old time. My guys've seen this little party more than once. What you gotta understand, Tom, this ain't Chicago. It's a border town. TJ's wide open. You want dope, nooky, roulette, horses, where do you go? You need muscle, a shooter—why not hire some pachuco? He works cheap. It's a gesture for international brotherhood. He can disappear faster than your paycheck. What I'm saying is, whoever's gonna run San Diego is gonna run both sides of the line. Castillo—he's the perfect liaison. A charmer. He's clean. Talks Spanish, English, a little Guinea lingo."

Hickey sucked the last of his scotch off an ice cube. "I hear you. Tell me something else. You've gotta know, everybody else does, about we're getting ten times our share of prime beef, all we can use. How you figure Paul managed that one?"

The captain snorted as though the simple question insulted his intelligence. "Vic Sozzani's cousin, guy name of William Martino, Senior, owns Broadway Meat Packers, your suppliers, no? Ain't that why you turn Billy Boy loose on the bandstand, when he's been booed out of clubs from here to Nome? You gotta ask me this, you're losing your touch, Tom."

"Touch has got nothing to do with it," Hickey muttered. The Cuban must've put a squeeze on Clyde. Why else would a classy bandleader settle for a hound like Martino? "It's just you don't learn much you don't wanta know."

"Uh-huh."

"See, Madeline's dying for a bigger place, a car for herself, enough loot to keep our kid in that fancy school and still take a second honeymoon to Paris, after they kick the Germans out."

"Sure. I get it." Thrapp leaned across the desk, squinting, curling his lip. "I mean why you tossed in with Castillo and took care of Charlie Schwartz's best boy."

Hickey stiffened, pressed against the back of his chair. He clutched his glass, his arm itching to fire it at the wall. "You and your mouth better get outta here."

"Not a bad idea." In one move Thrapp rose, grabbed his coat, slung it over his shoulder, and opened the door. "Been swell knowing you, Tom."

Hickey sat a minute, relit his pipe, felt the meal he'd eaten churn in his stomach. Long before he was ready for the next round, Castillo stepped in, looking drawn and petulant as a jilted lover. He turned the chair, sat down hard, dug his elbows into the armrests, folded his hands. "I make you the deal of a life. I make you a bigshot. Now you got so much dough you think you can knock me down, I don' do nothing?"

"First thing, Pablo, you even say the word *Madeline* I'm gonna jump over the desk."

"Oh boy, you making things tough on yourself. Maybe so tough you don' survive."

"Yeah, I hear you got some muscle behind you. Who you gonna sic on me, partner? Vic Sozzani or Montenegro? Maybe Angelo Paoli?"

The Cuban strained to hold Hickey's gaze. His eyes watered. He sighed, crooked his chair around, opened the door, and whistled for the bartender. Held up two fingers, slung the door shut, and turned back to Hickey. "You wanting me to say I don' know those fellows? I know many people. I having dinner with two or three doctors, you gonna come to me when you got a fever?"

"I get it. Sozzani, Montenegro—you guys are chums, is all. Which is why you stuck Clyde and us with Billy Martino, on account of he's Vic's nephew."

The Cuban raised his hands and bowed his head in mock tribute to Hickey's astuteness. The bartender knocked, new drinks got delivered. Castillo sipped. "He don' sing so bad. We know he's going to show up, anyway."

"You bet, and his uncle's gonna keep those sides of prime beef coming. Army doesn't know how to cook the good stuff anyway. They probably serve it well done. I gotta hand something to you, Paul. I figured you for a rich kid. Spanish aristocrat type. Then my pal Captain Thrapp, he says you started off a poor boy. You've done pretty well. What's the secret? How'd you get the dough to open this place? Paoli help you out?"

Castillo smiled wryly, then cleared his throat, leaned over the wastebasket, and spit. "The difference, you and me? That's a good question. Maybe we both make some money, but I keep mine, I invest, I watch it get bigger. What do you do with your money? Maybe give it away, huh?"

"Who told you that? Madeline?"

Hickey waited for a nod, a pronoun, any excuse to slam Castillo against the wall, rattle his head like a speedbag instead of sitting here playing patty cake. The Cuban didn't bite. "Nobody tol' me. A guess, it's all."

Hickey cleaned his pipe with the golf tee he carried, tapped the briar on the ashtray, finished his drink. He stood and donned his hat. "Clyde and I are gonna audition singers, hire a new one, and get rid of Martino. If that means we get no more beef at all, what the hell, we'll specialize in tuna salad. And I'm gonna start nosing around, talking to folks about Sozzani, Montenegro, their associates."

"You and this cop got it wrong, Tom. You go asking around,

you see. Tell me something, huh? If I'm a gangster, why I need you for my partner?"

"Maybe it looked like good cover, working with an old cop, a guy who's mostly upright, but he's hungry for loot. Or maybe it's just you're stupid. Or how about this—it'd give you an excuse to come knocking on my door, visiting the family." He rounded the desk, patted Castillo's shoulder, and grasped the doorknob. "While I'm nosing around, keep yourself a good, safe distance from . . . what's her name? My wife?"

The Cuban sneered. Hickey walked out, told Phil to run things, call him at home if a problem arose. The maître d' gave a nod and patient smile.

"Yeah," Hickey said. "I know. If this keeps up, I'm gonna have to promote you to manager and double your pay."

There were lots of bonfires around the bay. From Santa Clara Point and across Mission Boulevard between the ballroom and the tent city, skyrockets whizzed up a couple hundred feet and fizzled. Hickey reached home before nine, in time for dessert with Madeline and Elizabeth, one of the pies they'd bought in Julian. His girls both looked flushed and dreamy, as if they'd gotten too much sun that day. After dessert Elizabeth returned to designing pastel swimsuits on a drawing pad. Hickey phoned Clyde McGraw at his apartment, asked him to pass the word they were auditioning singers tomorrow afternoon.

For an hour or so Hickey sat on the sofa, Madeline leaning against him, Elizabeth on the floor, while they listened to the radio. To "Dreamland," which tonight featured an anthology of the Dorsey brothers' orchestras, and the ten o'clock news. The Nazis, in their push toward Stalingrad, had gotten driven back fifteen miles. Fourteen thousand, five hundred Germans were reported slain. The recent murder of a tycoon in Chicago had been attributed to gangsters. Sugar Ray Robinson was named boxer of the year. Finally Elizabeth staggered off to bed.

Hickey stroked his wife's hair. "Let's take a stroll. Out to the pier?"

271

"Naw, Tom. I'm ready for the sheets." She crooked her neck to look at him, noticed the resolve in his eyes. "Our pier, right?"

"Yeah."

She got up and went for her slippers and housecoat. Hickey took her hand, opened the door. They crossed the beach and shuffled to the end of the pier. The tide was low, the water glassy with hardly a ripple. Tiny swells whispered against the pilings. Sitting with his feet on the bench of his rowboat, Hickey said, "Thrapp's not buying my story. It's a chance they might haul me back to Denver. The cops up there are still interrogating witnesses."

Madeline squeezed his hand tighter. She kept kicking her foot as though splashing water, brushing his ankle. "What're the witnesses gonna say, Tom?"

He reached his free hand across and patted her hair. "I doubt anybody but me saw Donny's gun." The last couple words had quavered from a shudder that passed through him. He sat waiting for Madeline to let go of his hand, get up, and walk away, to go off by herself and sort through things. Instead, she rested her head on his shoulder. He stroked her hair. "Remember when I came back you said Thrapp mentioned something about a gang war?"

"Uh-huh."

"Here's what he suspects—that Castillo's part of a New Jersey gang, working for Angelo Paoli. So, on account of Donny and I go back a long ways, and the Cuban knows Donny's Schwartz's toughest boy, and Schwartz answers to the Hollywood mob that's got its eyes on the same territory Paoli wants, he offers me a bundle to pop Katoulis."

"Who does?"

"Castillo."

"Paul Castillo paid you to kill Donny Katoulis. That's what the captain thinks?"

"It's what he's saying."

"Jesus, Tom, that's insane." Her arm and shoulder lay rigid against him. She pinched his fingers.

"Will you do something for me, babe?"

"Uh-huh."

"Stay away from Castillo—don't even play tennis with the guy."

Her hand went limp. She lifted her head, looked across the bay, started kicking her foot in the air again. "You got anything on Paul, Tom? Anything but rumors?"

"Not so far, but I'm looking. How about it?"

For a minute or so, nothing in the world made as much racket as the thud of Hickey's heart against his rib cage. "All right," she whispered. "Let's go in now." She let go of his hand, got up, and walked a step ahead of him, taking long, slow strides as if her destination were a place she hated to go, but she'd vowed to go anyway.

In bed Hickey fitted himself against her backside, and she wriggled to make the fit snug as could be. Her skin felt dry and cool. He wrapped his arms around her waist. She folded her arms over his. He listened to her breathing grow soft and regular. Every minute or so he kissed her somewhere. The neck. Her ear. Her cheek. Finally he rolled away from her, lay on his back, and watched the moon shadow on the curtain, thinking of all the ruined lives. Henry Tucker. Mr. Murphy. Will Lashlee. Emma Vidal. Cynthia, barring a miracle. They made him feel queasy, vulnerable as a bicyclist crossing the highway at rush hour. Everything you'd worked a lifetime for could instantly flash away.

He rolled onto his back, felt as if he were sinking through dark water, groping for a hand to redeem him. His chest tightened, the room began to whirl, and suddenly he remembered Mr. Bair's offer—Emma's half of everything he owned.

TWENTY-EIGHT

♪ ♪ ♪

Nine singers had been waiting in front of Rudy's at 3:00 P.M. Over the next half hour while the band members straggled in, a few more arrived. All flouncy, restless girls.

Clyde McGraw sat in a booth with Hickey, twisting the ends of his mustache, tapping his fingers in 6/8 time. He'd appointed Swede the clarinetist to conduct the orchestra. The singers ranged around the room, each performing her nervous routine. One stared at her image in a compact and dabbed on rouge. Another hitched up her nylons. A stump-legged, buxom girl paced like a stilt artist on her six-inch heels. The oldest of them, dressed in tight pants and sweater, leaned against a wall chewing on a clump of her hair.

Two perky sisters auditioned first. They'd come prepared to sing duets, but Clyde wanted soloists, so each did a number of her own. One sang "Sunny Side of the Street" dolefully. The other crooned "Deep Purple," wiggling as if she'd stepped on an anthill. Of the next few auditioners, one had a cute but trilly voice that probably would enchant young sailors while reminding the admirals and bankers who frequented Rudy's of their daughters and send them running home; another looked as if her cheeks were stuffed with cookies; the prettiest, a slinky brunette, sounded operatic.

Number nine was Carline Biggs, a mulatto with soft, wavy hair, somebody Hickey'd watched a few months before in the Blue Note on Market Street. She'd been singing with Earl Watson's group, a Negro quartet. Hickey remembered thinking how she'd fit better fronting a big band. She looked too proud and domineering for the quartet, like she ought to have a brigade of musicians behind her, more concerned with showing her off than with taking their solos.

Clyde gave Hickey a dubious glance. "Who invited her?"

"Beats me," Hickey said. "Word gets around."

She led off with "Mood Indigo." Her voice was silky, tinted with gloom. One of the girls still waiting gave up and left. She might've noticed Hickey fold his arms behind his head, lean back, and give Clyde a nod. This one had the range, the tone, the poise and beauty. A couple bars and it didn't matter if she were a mix of Negro, Siamese, and polar bear—she could draw in the fellows, get them longing, make them want to drown in booze. All she lacked was the magic that convinced every man she was singing to him. She wasn't Cynthia Moon.

Clyde called out to Swede and rolled his hand. Swede conferred with Carline, got the key she wanted, then cued the orchestra to "Moonglow."

Hickey leaned over to McGraw. "If you rehearse her every afternoon, maybe one day off, think you could lose Martino by Monday?"

Clyde crooked his lips and nose sideways, wagged his chin. "I don't know about this one, Tom."

"What's the problem?"

"You don't have to ask, man, 'less you're color-blind."

"No offense, pal, but she's a shade lighter than you."

275

Clyde looked her over once more. "About the same, but she can't hardly pass with those lips and that behind."

"You think when you and Johnny tell folks you come from Saint Croix, half of them don't figure that's a street in Harlem?"

"Long as they hire us. Tom, maybe if I was Count this or Duke that, all the ritzy joints would do us the honor. But my name's Clyde, and I got a white band."

The cigarette girl, who'd just come in, still wearing the coat over her tutu, appeared and tapped Hickey's shoulder. "There's a guy wants to see you, boss."

Hickey nodded, turned back to Clyde. "Fine. When you leave Rudy's, dump her. Meantime, give her a bunch of Cynthia's numbers." He got up, rounded the booth, spotted the man at the bar. He was leaning backward, both elbows on the rail. He hadn't checked his hat or coat. A cop, judging from the impudent frown. Hickey's fists clenched, eyes blurred. He felt the plane lifting off, carrying him to Denver.

The man straightened up and stepped forward. Another young fellow who'd sidestepped the military and was hustling up the abandoned ladder. Already made detective. Medium build. Cool, dark, heavy-browed eyes. He didn't offer his hand. "You Tom Hickey?"

"Yeah. You?"

"Detective Sergeant Ripperger."

"What town?"

The cop scowled as though Hickey were toying with him. "What do you think? Tokyo?"

Hickey caught his breath, let his shoulders drop from where they'd been squashing his ears. "Thrapp send you?"

"You determined to ask all the questions, or do I get a chance?"

"Sorry. Habit," Hickey said.

The cop plucked a notebook from inside his overcoat, browsed a page to refresh his memory. "Seems a couple weeks ago . . . That'd be December seventeenth, Thursday. A guy that looks about like you was driving a 1941 Chevrolet happens to be

276

registered to you, harassed and threatened a motorist, couple blocks from here. Out on Broadway."

Hickey tried not to snicker, couldn't manage.

"Think it's pretty cute, do you?"

Waving a hand toward the office, Hickey led the way. Inside, he shut the door, sat on the desk, left the cop standing beside the coatrack. "I gotta tell you, pal. In the last couple weeks—first my singer disappeared, I tailed her up north. Then a fellow sends me to Denver on a bodyguard job. A louse gets shot and I spend the night in jail. Come home, I lose my singer *and* meat supplier. My wife and I are squabbling. Now you stroll in, remind me I yelled at this horn-blowing fool. Come on, Sergeant. Laugh."

The detective barked a couple times. "Okay, now we got that out of our systems, I'd suggest you devise a way to get the horn blower to drop charges."

"I'll apologize. Give me his number."

"Naw. Suppose you go over there and sock him? My pretty ass gets burned."

"Okay. I drop a letter by your office, you pass it on. Who do I address it to? Dear horn blower?"

"That'll do."

Hickey walked Ripperger out, shook his hand at the door. "Come back off duty, Sergeant. I'll set you up with dinner and drinks, for two, for your trouble."

The cop wagged his head. "I don't hang around any mob joint. Bring me the letter tomorrow."

Hickey sat staring out the door long after the sergeant had vanished, sorting through the mix of dismay and fury that was gnawing at him. Finally he wheeled and grabbed the phone. Dialed the Playroom. The Pacific Ballroom. The Del Mar Club. Castillo didn't answer the pages, and nobody'd seen him. Hickey'd started out to the bar for a scotch when the phone rang.

"Person to person for Mr. Tom Hickey."

"Yeah, that's me."

Fay Giles's voice rasped urgently. "Have I got news."

"I'm listening."

"Sheriff Poole suggested I call you, but I would've anyway. Mr. Hickey, a forestry man was driving up Black Forest Road when he met the swami. Their master. You know. He was staggering down the mountain, Joe Kraft said. At first he didn't recognize him, almost passed by thinking it was a drunken hobo. Oh God, this is horrid. . . . The man was delirious."

"The forestry guy?"

"No. The master. They'd bound his hands behind him. That's how Joe knew something was wrong." She muffled the phone.

"Who'd bound his hands? You there?"

"I'm here. I don't know. There was blood on his trousers. Joe got him into the bed of his truck and rushed him to Doctor O'Day. Oh Christ, Mister Hickey, I knew those people were devils, but . . ."

Hickey rapped on the desk a dozen times. "Yeah. But what?"

". . . There were wounds on his thighs and his torso as if they'd beaten him and . . . someone had tied off his . . . scrotum, with a band of rawhide. Of course Doctor O'Day tore it off. But not in time." She muffled the phone once again, returned with a groan. "Mister Hickey. They castrated him."

"Whoa," Hickey muttered. He squirmed from a cramp in the pit of his stomach.

"Do you believe anybody could . . ."

"You don't know who did it?"

"No, how could we? The sheriff's on his way to the Black Forest now. I'll call you later."

Hickey let her go, resumed his walk to the bar, knocked down two shots of Dewar's. He thought of phoning Mr. Bair with the news, but to gloat over somebody losing his nuts seemed too foul. Even when the nuts were Pravinshandra's.

Just after eight, when Billy Martino took the stage, Hickey turned the place over to Phil, promised him twenty dollars more each week.

On the drive home, until he was rounding the bay, he noticed nothing. Not his speed, or whether he ran any stop signs, or whether he almost careened off the Ingraham Street bridge into the bay. All he saw were visions of hands with painted fingernails tying a rawhide thong around the master's scrotum. He even heard the man screaming, clearly as though it were broadcast over his radio.

Dark mist had erased the moon and stars. Tonight the bay looked miles deep and blue-black, treacherous. He didn't expect his house to be dark, for Madeline to have gone out, at least without calling him at Rudy's. She'd left a note on the kitchen counter:

> Tom, in case you get home early, I'll be back about 11:00. Mrs. Thorndike phoned and invited me to meet with the Relief Society about their charity ball. She wants me to be on the committee, and that's not all. She asked if I'd be willing to sing. Maybe, I said. It's been so damned long. They may ask me to give them a sample. Cross your fingers. Oh, and Lizzie's staying over with her pal Clementine.
>
> Love, M.

He felt mildly annoyed with Madeline but vicious toward whatever chance or fate had snatched her away at this moment when he ached to hold her, hear a gentle voice, find a little assurance that life contained at least a trace of normalcy. He changed to old dungarees, a sweater, and a USC baseball cap. He sprawled on the living room sofa beside the bay-view window, propped himself on a pillow and the armrest so he could look out, reached over his head for the *Tribune* on the end table, and glanced at headlines.

REDS CLAIM 22 NAZI DIVISIONS PENNED IN TRAP—German toll 116,000 dead in 11 days
OFFICIALS HINT EARLY RATIONING OF CANNED FOOD

That afternoon in the Pro Bowl, the Redskins had gotten trounced by the National Football League's all-stars. Dagwood was sleeping on the couch, dreaming of wood nymphs, and because Mickey had called his home a castle, Goofy built a moat around his house to discourage his creditors. Gene Krupa would be at the Pacific for New Year's Eve. As soon as Madeline got home, Hickey'd promise to call in a favor, hustle them up front seats.

He rose and grabbed a pair of oars from where he stored them in the corner of the sleeping porch. He crossed the beach to his pier, unleashed the rowboat, and climbed in. The first quarter mile he rowed strong, straight out; then he angled toward Crown Point, following a track of moonlight. The water looked dark and thick as motor oil. He passed not a single bird or fish jumping. Not a single shoreline house had left the curtain open to its Christmas tree. He rowed in bursts and drifted between, again picturing the mutilation of Pravinshandra, but also worrying, pondering matters from the odds of his being summoned back to Denver to the dumping of sewage in the bay. Anything to fend off doubts about Madeline. He kept looking up, spotting his house, waiting for a light to flick on.

The house was still dark when he tied up the boat. He went inside, to the bookshelf in the dining area, chose a history of China from the books he'd been collecting since his reading time got swallowed by obligations at Rudy's. He lay in the hammock, read the first page several times, and listened to cars on Pacific Beach Drive, waiting for the one that would deliver Madeline. About half past ten, a car pulled onto the gravel of Parker Place. Hickey sat up and listened, recognized the voice of his neighbors, a pair of sisters who both taught at Pacific Beach School. He lay back down, read for another hour. Three pages.

He was in the bathroom when the next car turned onto the gravel. It stopped beside their carport. A loud man said, "Three and a quarter." A minute later the cab backed away. Madeline's heels clicked across the concrete.

Hickey met her in the kitchen. She looked radiant, young enough to be Elizabeth's girlfriend, wearing the burgundy sweater and the diamond ring he'd given her for Christmas, a white, snug-fitting skirt and pumps with medium heels.

"Been home long?" she asked.

"Yeah. You gonna sing for the old dames?"

"They want me to. Mrs. Thorndike had her son play that new Johnny Mercer tune, 'Tangerine.' It's kind of cute. I gave it this sultry mood, like I was this jealous broad. Tom, you look a little peaked."

As he told her about the phone call from Dunsmuir, Madeline staggered toward the living room and flopped onto the sofa. Hickey sat beside her. When the story was done, she reached over and fondled him, extra gently. Her hands felt steaming.

"Imagine," she whispered.

"Naw," Hickey said. "I don't want to."

TWENTY-NINE

♪ ♪ ♪

THE CLOUDLESS SKY WAS STILL SILVER-BLUE WHEN EVA'S COCKERS' yapping got so loud they sounded directly beneath Hickey and Madeline's window. He dragged himself up, pulled on his trousers, a pair of slippers, and a sweater, and walked through the house and out back to the beach. Eva was standing beside the pier, dressed in her usual khakis and jacket, deck shoes, fishing hat. She was petting one of the monsters.

"Hey, you," Hickey growled. "Hand over the mutt. I'm gonna make his paws into key chains."

"Keep your distance, brute." Eva strode toward him swinging the handle end of a leash as if preparing to box his ears with it. They faced off nose to nose and scowled.

"Where you been, Tom?"

"Up north. Denver. The Pine Hills Lodge for Christmas. You miss me?"

"Not too bad. There's more than one man in my life, you know. What's in Denver?"

"Ice. Windstorms. Italian food."

"What brought you there?"

"Never mind."

She reprimanded him with a pout. The cockers tugged at their leashes. Eva started walking and Hickey followed along, past a stone ring filled with ashes and charred cans, an overturned rowboat, a sand castle with dripped spires. By the turn in the bay, he'd asked her twice for the latest gossip, but all he'd gotten back was a curiously sympathetic punch on the arm, until she muttered, "This is gonna pain me, Tom."

She squatted and unsnapped the dogs from their leashes, shooed them off to run, then took his sleeve and led him over to the wall that bordered the bayside walk. "Sit down here." She waited until he obeyed, then joined him. "Last evening I was casting for perch, out at the end of Crystal Pier. Your wife comes walking. What's her name?"

"Madeline."

To avoid looking at him, Eva removed her hat, slapped it on her leg a couple times, put it on again. "She's smooching with a fellow."

"Oh, no. She was out with some ritzy old buzzards. What time?"

"Sunset. She comes walking right past me, arm in arm with a tall guy, black greasy hair, all snuggled up. Every so often they'll stop and kiss."

"What was she wearing?"

"Pants, I think. Maybe a dress. She has the fellow's overcoat on. I sure don't want to distress you, Tom, but I expect you oughta know."

"Sure," Hickey mumbled. "I'll go ask her about it."

He wheeled and took about fifty long strides toward home, stopped still a moment, then shuffled to the bonfire pit and sat on a log seat. Elbows on his knees, he covered his eyes, pictured himself stomping onto his porch, through the living room, finding Madeline in the kitchen. He saw himself grab her by the chin, lift it up, pinch it hard. He got up, left the beach, cut through a vacant lot and down the alley to Mission Boulevard, going for coffee, hoping to clear his brain a little. In the bakery he remembered he wasn't carrying money. The frosty-haired baker's wife poured him a cupful, said pay when he brought the cup back. He returned to the log by the fire pit, sat, and drank the coffee, staring at the glassy water and telling himself it wasn't Madeline. Old Eva hardly knew Madeline. Besides, a night out smooching didn't concur with Madeline's demeanor, the brightness with which she'd told him about Mrs. Thorndike and her piano-playing son, the way she'd described just how she'd sung "Tangerine."

"You got the wrong gal, Eva," he muttered, as he got up and started home.

Or, he thought, if it was Madeline, if she'd gone to Castillo after the way she'd talked when he came home from Denver and in spite of Hickey's promises, after he'd warned her about the Cuban's mob pals and she'd agreed not to step into the same room with the guy—if Madeline was that far gone, if he knew that little about who she'd become, Hickey'd already lost the game.

He left her sleeping, took a shower, then dressed and kissed her good-bye without waking her. Before he reached the kitchen door, the phone rang. His answering service with a message. A lady named Venus would meet him at the Grant Grille at nine this morning.

With an hour to kill, he crossed Pacific Beach Drive, drove the dirt road up to Grand Avenue, took it east across the Coast Highway to Milly's Texaco Beanery.

He ordered a couple eggs over medium, no potatoes, a bowl of cornflakes with half-and-half. The straw-haired waitress, a girl Milly had rescued when a long-haul trucker dumped her, kept refilling his coffee every time he drank it down an inch. He nibbled, sipped, wondered if Venus knew that the Grant Grille was restricted, no females. Thinking of the fuss she might raise, he chuckled and started planning his attack. Not a chance she was the kind you just waltzed in on, bossed around, overwhelmed with your manliness. He sipped, smoked, and rehearsed a few lines. At 8:30 he tossed two dollars onto the table and walked out, aiming to arrive at the Grille before Venus showed, to lead her across the street where ladies were welcome. Open the meeting with him in charge.

He cut east on Sassafras Street, took India, then Ash, and pulled into the lot behind Rudy's. He crossed Fourth and walked fast, dodging around the postal employees and secretaries timing themselves to arrive at work about twenty seconds before nine.

The U. S. Grant lobby appeared built for giants. Marble pillars in rows like the Acropolis. Chandeliers the size and shape of bells whose tolling would've started earthquakes. Niches in the walls held large Grecian urns.

The hostess at the Grille was a girl who usually worked in another wing, at the Rendezvous. He remembered her because she walked as if her hips were in a cast and she had a set of invisible encyclopedias balanced on her head. "This way, Mister Hickey," she beamed.

"Naw," he said. "I'm going to meet a lady here, take her somewhere besides the boys' club."

"But she's waiting for you. Mister Jack let her in." The girl drew closer, lowered her voice. "He does that for special people, only before lunchtime, though."

He followed her through the dim room of dark mahogany, dark carpeting, dark maroon leather booths, sketches of hunting dogs on the walls. The place could be a replica of a billiard hall for the British Parliament. It even stank like half-smoked cigars.

The hostess led him to a booth on the Fourth Street side. Venus had stood to greet him. She wore a snug tailored suit of deep aquamarine, a white silk blouse with hat and gloves to match. In heels she stood level with Hickey. Her lipstick was dark, her smile ingenuous. Her eyebrows looked natural, thick but trim and shapely, slightly darker than her cinnamon hair, which was folded up into layers and held in place with the hat. Her eyes were like Cynthia's, an emerald color so deep it made the white seem especially pure. There were sapphire and silver clips on her ears and an emerald ring on the third finger of each hand.

She offered her hand. He took and pressed it, nodded, pulled out her chair, and watched her graceful descent, a dancer's balance and poise. He sat across from her. "Pleasant trip?"

"No. We weren't able to leave as early as we'd planned. Something came up." She narrowed her eyes and studied him. "We didn't arrive until after midnight. It was a tedious drive."

What a voice, Hickey thought. From deep in her chest yet mild and soothing. Even sexier up close than at the meeting in Denver. A couple words from Venus in the right ear, whole armies charge to their death.

"Mr. Hickey, who sent you to Denver?"

"Never mind."

Her gaze pinned him, as if focused on a tiny dot in the middle of each of his eyes. "At least tell me if the dead man was really there to kill Pravinshandra."

"You bet."

"And who was the instigator?"

"Forget it, lady. You bring the master along?"

"A brother drove me down. I don't drive. Pravinshandra, as I expect you know, is under suspicion of a crime. The sheriff of Dunsmuir advised him not to leave. So, tell me, are you the one who accused him of raping my daughter?"

Okay, Hickey thought, here we go. "Your daughter accused him. I passed it along."

The waiter showed up. A balding, stooped fellow who muttered a string of indecipherable words. Hickey ordered juice. Venus asked for tea and the fruit plate.

"I wonder if you truly believe my daughter." Venus waited, raised her eyes to summon his reply. "You must know she's been affected terribly by our family troubles. Are you two close?"

"Yeah, too close," Hickey said.

The woman's lip rose, almost into a sneer except that she caught and softened it. "I suppose she told you I was to blame for the demise of Otherworld, and that I treated her father wickedly."

"Yeah. All that and plenty more."

"Such as?"

"About how Laurel and you lined up on one side, she and Henry on the other, a long time ago. She says you've been trying to kill her ever since."

Venus gave a bitter sigh, took a sip of her tea, and looked up calmly. "Do you have children?" Hickey nodded. She turned to the window. Her lips pursed and sucked in, fishlike. "The difficulty with raising children is, every flaw in your character, every mistake in your life, is apt to be reflected, even magnified, in them. I certainly haven't been a perfect mother. I'm impatient, exacting, and worst of all, I follow my own star."

"Where's Laurel, by the way? I called to tell her Cynthia's in Riverview. Nobody home."

"She's in Dunsmuir, taking care of the master. He's very distraught."

"He's worse than that."

"What?"

"I'm not sure it was Laurel took care of him, but somebody certainly did."

"Don't toy with me," Venus demanded.

"Laurel give him sedatives, maybe?"

"Why are you asking these questions?"

"I got a call from Fay Giles, runs the Castle Crag Motor Hotel. Last evening. She phoned a while after your boyfriend wandered down the road from Black Forest, doped, beaten, and with a string of rawhide tied just so around his private parts. I'm afraid you have a eunuch on your hands, Mrs. Tucker."

Her expression had frozen, her chin dropped a little. Her eyes brightened and quavered as though something volcanic churned behind their emerald sheen. She stared at the silver sugar bowl in front of her, panting through her nose. Her hands lifted, fingers touching like a spider on a mirror.

"Please don't call me Mrs. Tucker," she said flatly.

Hickey thought, Whoa, she's tough. You wouldn't catch her whining. She reached for her cup, sipped her tea. "You think Laurel did that to him?"

"Yeah. Shouldn't you be stunned or something, lady?"

Her face stiffened momentarily and relaxed into a wan smile. "What happens, Mr. Hickey, when you live by the sword?" The way her exquisite lips had set, he thought it might be a smirk, an innuendo about his fate.

"Look, what I heard, Cynthia isn't the first gal Pravinshandra raped. Seems he liked to dope up, hypnotize, service, and brand his disciples while he had them cornered on the mountain."

Venus rubbed her temples, gazed studiously at him. "I'm afraid you don't know women. Whomever Pravinshandra wanted, he merely had to ask. If she resisted, a little talk would persuade her. In rare cases he might have to touch her hand."

"You're telling me Cynthia didn't get raped?"

Her lips had gone drier and flared. "The easiest conquest on earth. She would give herself to a beggar if she believed it would torment me."

"How about Laurel?"

"What about her?"

"You think it was Laurel who fixed him?"

"Of course not."

"You wanta know why I think she did?" he asked. Venus nodded curtly. "Wait here, then, while I run next door for something."

She picked up a strawberry and bit delicately as though trying not to hurt it. Hickey didn't bother to stop for his hat or button his coat. He scampered out as though fleeing from a packed elevator. When he got outside and waited at the stoplight, he felt reprieved. Somewhere he'd read that beauty was truth, truth beauty, and considered the statement reasonably accurate, even about people. He'd known plenty gorgeous, wicked humans— they had looks but not beauty, which was a feeling that sometimes leaped between the hearts of the observed and the observer. After sitting with Venus, the idea that beauty was truth seemed preposterous. No gesture, tone of voice, nothing hinted she could be a vicious liar. In her presence, Hickey thought, most any man couldn't help but want to win her favor. Each unkind word, he'd felt like a rat.

When the light changed, he hustled across, strode past the display window of the Owl Drugstore, turned in to the entrance of his building, and loped up the stairs past a curly blonde who walked stiffly, wrapped tightly in a coat, clutching her arms across her stomach.

A thumping noise issued from his office. He checked the doorknob, shoved the door open, and found Leo inside, feet on the desk, tossing a tennis ball. Without glancing Hickey's way, while the ball rebounded off the wall beneath the photos, Leo flipped him a salute.

"Way I understood, you were a busy man," Hickey said.

"We're no hod carriers, Tom. Our kinda work requires meditation."

"So that's what I've been doing wrong. Say, you oughta see the doll I left up at the Grant."

"Let me guess. You found a new singer."

"Yeah, but she's not the one. This one's Venus."

Leo caught the tennis ball, set it on the desk while he swiveled the chair around. "What're you doing with Venus?"

"Negotiating, about the girl. I'll give you the whole story later. Maybe tonight, over a couple steaks at Rudy's. Tomorrow we might be serving tuna instead."

"Huh?"

"Later. Now I gotta run. Came to get something out of the desk." Leo rolled the chair back, let his feet drop, allowing Hickey to open the top drawer and remove the manila envelope with Emma Vidal's drawing. "Six or so. I've got a story that'll make you keep your fly buttoned." Hickey gave a wink and turned to the door.

He hustled downstairs, caught a green light, double-timed across and into the Grant, where he found Venus nibbling papaya. Laying the envelope between them, he sat down, reached for his water glass. Venus only squared her shoulders, dabbed at her lips with a napkin, raised her eyebrows, and peered at him. Finally he slipped the picture out of the envelope, adjusted it to lie straight beneath her eyes, and watched her eyes dull as they moved across the picture and down to the note at the bottom. She slid the picture under the envelope and folded her hands on the table.

"It's Laurel," Hickey said.

"I know."

"The way I figure, making the guy a eunuch sounds like the work of a betrayed lover. Meaning it could be any one of who knows how many. But I'm betting on Laurel."

"Did Henry give this to you?"

"Nope. Gave it to Cynthia."

"I see." She leaned back, stared overhead around the room. At last she nodded, returned her gaze to his eyes, intently as though to spook him or fracture his will. "Cynthia hired the killer."

"Forget the killer. Here's the deal. I want you to pay for Cynthia's stay in Riverview, as long as it takes. I want you to leave her alone, for good. You, Laurel, the *Nezahs.*"

She flashed a delighted smile, as though she found his gall fascinating. "Is that all?"

"Nope. You've gotta sell back all the Dunsmuir property. Keep the Black Forest if you want."

Her smile crimped, then re-formed into one as patronizing as a bishop might give to a heathen, or a scientist to a monkey. "Anything else?"

"That's all."

"What leverage do you intend to use to make me accept this proposal? You've already done all you could to see Pravinshandra arrested. You say Laurel perpetrated this castration, but don't delude yourself that the citizenry of Dunsmuir will convict her of punishing the man who raped her. The less if he's a dark-skinned man who threatens their feeble religion."

"None of that," Hickey said. "I'm thinking about the seventy grand of Otherworld's loot you had in your mitts when you skipped town."

She picked the napkin off her lap and began folding it restlessly. "I'm truly amazed at how thoroughly you've fallen for Cynthia's lies, considering she's now committed to the sanitarium where she obviously belongs."

"Look," Hickey said. "If you're clean, don't make the deal."

"Don't you think if I'd embezzled from Otherworld, they would've pursued me?"

"Naw. Madame Esmé was sick. The place was going to collapse, no matter. From what I read in the paper, plus Cynthia's story and what I got out of Joshua Bair and Mr. Murphy, looks like people just ran, on account of they were heartbroken over losing their home. Losing faith. They ditched, cut their losses."

"Mr. Bair." She sighed languidly. "I'm innocent, you know, but I'm sure you could stir a caldron of trouble. You certainly know how to pry."

"Yeah. How about it?"

She placed her hands on the arms of her chair, gracefully pushed herself up, glanced out the window, then gazed down at him coolly as if she'd just granted him knighthood. "Of course I'll pay for the hospital, and if she believes we're dangerous, you're right, we should stay out of her life. The property—that's just business. Business is everywhere. I'll sell, if you insist. I'll buy elsewhere."

Hickey stood, admired the way her face had paled, her eyes and lips became deathly still. One of those people who with a glance could make you ashamed to have bettered her. She offered her hand, pressed his warmly. The damned woman didn't know how to act any way but gracious. If she were slitting your throat, Hickey thought, she'd do it politely, with elegance.

"Thank you for looking after my daughter. Please ask the waiter to bill my room. Two-seventeen." With a pallid smile, she turned and walked off, left Hickey to marvel at her. From behind she could've passed for the queen of heaven. Her voice lingered in the air.

While Hickey sat recovering from the strain, a vision appeared in which he was the master, lying on a cot with trousers bunched around his ankles and a leather thong hitched in a stranglehold around the topmost edge of his scrotum. Kneeling beside him, the Bitch whispered viciously, "It's okay, baby."

He tossed a five onto the table and walked out, his gut constricting, his pulse on double time. Breaths came hard. He stood on the curb through two green lights, telling himself he'd beaten the woman, made the deal, seen the last of Venus. It was no use. Thirty-seven years had taught him to recognize people who wouldn't stay beaten.

As he crossed the street, he allowed himself to think about Madeline for the first time since he'd left home, and he still couldn't believe it was her on Crystal Pier. He leaned against the wall of the Owl Drugstore and reviewed everything Madeline had said and done last night after she'd come home. He recalled her tone of voice, her expressions. Not a damned thing seemed amiss. "Hell," he muttered, "old Eva's jealous, thinks she can land me for her own."

There was a message on the office desk, to phone Thrapp. The switchboard rang about ten times, Thrapp's extension another dozen, before the captain grumbled his name.

"What's up?" Hickey asked.

"Your lieutenant called from Denver. Seems a couple days after the fact, this old woman shows up and swears she saw Donny go for his gun. Swears she saw his hand on it. Lieutenant says why the hell didn't you come in sooner? She pleads too much to do at Christmas. He described her as a churchy-looking dame. Anybody you know?"

"Yeah, Rusty. It's my mother-in-law. We rehearsed a couple days, then I sent her up there."

"I figured. Lucky that lieutenant's not smart as me. You're off the hook, Tom," he said glumly.

"He say what makes this witness the one they're gonna believe?"

"I'd guess, when you got a sweet old dame saying she saw something, and a Negro fella saying he didn't see it—you know. Besides, if one person saw it, a hundred of them that didn't don't mean a damn. Only way they could convict you is break the old lady down. Who's gonna want to risk a lightning bolt in memory of Katoulis?"

Hickey was trying to remember a woman near the railroad yard. He only recalled the taxi and Katoulis, the men swarming after he tossed the guns away. "Swell news, Rusty. I owe you a big one. Look, about the other—believe me or don't, but if Paul's fronting for anybody, I'm in your corner. Doesn't matter if I land in the poorhouse. I'll find my way out."

"Yeah, okay," Thrapp said flatly. "See you around."

It was becoming a glorious day. He'd backed Venus into a corner, made her deal. Some anonymous angel had lifted the noose off his shoulders. At this rate, the clouds would make way for rainbows, soon an old client might show up and give him a fifty-foot ketch. This afternoon the war would end. By tomorrow he, Elizabeth, and Madeline could sail away.

He called the Saint Ambrose Home. Father McCullough answered the first ring, loudly as if he'd been dozing by the phone.

"Good news," Hickey said. "I had a chat with Venus this morning. She's gonna pay the Riverview bill, leave the girl alone, and keep Laurel away. Looks like Henry and you are Cynthia's mama and daddy now. You better try and keep the old boy alive."

"He's breathing better."

"I've got a tidbit you can pass along, might have him up chasing sisters around the garden."

"Oh?"

"The *Nezahs* got tired of their master acting like a bull. They made a steer out of him."

"Oh, aw, uhn," the priest groaned.

"Yeah. I'll say. When you tell Henry, bring a nurse along so he won't die laughing."

* * *

Hickey sat parked out front of Riverview Hospital, debating whether, if he even got the chance, he should tell Cynthia about Laurel's revenge. Still undecided, he walked in, holding the door for a hunched, drooling kid in a wheelchair pushed by a stalwart-looking army corporal, probably his brother. Hickey turned in to the reception area. The receptionist was plump, Indian-looking. On Hickey's request, she paged Dr. Carroll. Hickey took a seat and listened to a volley of shrill cries that sounded blocks away, but probably were close, behind a couple walls. In apparent response to the cries, a howl rose. Like a caveman giving orders to the moon.

The doctor appeared and led Hickey down a short corridor to an office almost as cramped as the one at Rudy's. A dozen or so frameless diplomas looked glued onto the walls. The doctor was sallow-faced, long-necked, about Hickey's age. He had a mop of frizzy blond hair, shoulders so thin that coat hangers must've stretched his shirts.

They shook hands. Hickey asked how Cynthia was acting. The doctor gave a shrug, said he was hopeful.

"Still think she's carrying a baby?"

The doctor raised his eyebrows. "When did I say I thought she was?"

"I don't know. My mistake. What do you think?"

"She may well be."

"Look, I know I'm acting hasty, but I figure it's best we get prepared. So we can act fast if the time comes. You know where she was when I grabbed her?"

"Tijuana."

"Yep. You've probably heard her yelling about the devil baby and the Fiend. As far as I can see, it's a fact she got raped. I'm not suggesting we take her back to TJ, but I know a fellow, a doctor—well, a chiropractor—that'll do it safe and clean."

The doctor wrinkled his nose. "You know this person, what he's doing, and you allow him to go unpunished?"

"You bet. The ones that don't go to him, it isn't like the kid lives happily ever after. Mama gets the job done by some after-

294

hours grease monkey, or she goes to TJ, and you don't know who's doing what down there. A girl dies, a cop takes a third of the fee, undertaker another third, leaving the doc a little short that evening, no big deal."

"I see your position," Dr. Carroll said. "It's rather callous, and fortunately it doesn't apply here. Father McCullough called me. If there is a child, as long as Miss Tucker and her parents assent, the church will see to adoption."

Hickey pondered the idea, decided he liked it. They'd need to hold Cynthia until the child was born, to keep her from ripping it out. Eight months at least. Long before then, Charlie Schwartz would discover another doll.

"Miss Tucker won't agree," Hickey said. "I'll help you get a court order if you need. And somebody better make damn sure they get that baby far enough away so he never comes looking for his mama. I'm no prophet. But I'll give mighty odds on this one—there won't be a moment of peace in that family until they're extinct."

The doctor nodded as though humoring Hickey and began doodling on a file folder. "In all probability, there is no baby."

"Sure. You gonna let me see the girl?"

A few minutes later Hickey followed a sour young nurse down a hallway that led off the reception room. They passed a line of closed doors. One of them rattled as something powerful crashed into it, from inside. The hall opened into a wider area, where a nurse stood beside a counter chatting with a Negro orderly while she filled syringes.

Hickey's nurse peered through a window in a set of double doors. She reached for a key ring from a hook on the wall and used one of the keys.

The brightness of the room behind the doors shocked Hickey's eyes. At first he couldn't see where the music came from, the piano intro to a melody he knew. The nurse ushered him through, then backed out and shut the doors. The lock clicked.

As his vision adjusted, Hickey stared around the long, wide room, one side of it walled in plate glass looking out at a dead vegetable garden. Brown tomato plants. Wilted beet greens. A row of sunflowers stooped almost to the ground. The room held about thirty occupants, a few of them orderlies dressed in green, the others white-garbed patients. Along the right wall several men and a skeletal woman slouched on low stools. Two men stood leaning against the window, one thumping his head on the plate glass. A giant fellow with silver teeth and a nose about an inch off center strode toward Hickey, his eyes flaming. He veered left, circled behind Hickey, and strode back the other way. A gray-skinned woman squatted, stood, squatted again as if that were her style of dancing.

Hickey guessed the oldest person, except a couple of the orderlies, was a few years younger than he. They made him think of massacre victims in a common grave, dead on their feet, mutely staring back at the treacherous world.

The piano, an old upright, sat at the far end of the room. The pianist was a Negro orderly. Another, darker orderly stood nearby, scowling like a tyrant's palace guard, his arms tensed and ready to snap the neck off anybody who might harm the girl standing beside him, her elbow leaning on the piano, the spread fingers of her other hand pressing her abdomen.

She gazed vaguely around, scratched her face nervously, pinched the bridge of her nose, then darted the hand back to cover her belly. The pianist stopped once, tapped the girl's arm. As he ran through the intro a second time, she stood straight, slightly bent her knees. A wistful smile appeared. Her eyes flickered on like a searchlight. All at once she looked at everyone, welcomed each of them into her heart, and sang.

> *"I don't know why, but I'm feeling so sad.*
> *I long to try something I've never had.*
> *Never had no kissing, oh, what I've been missing.*
> *Lover man, oh, where can you be?"*